THE DEMON

THE DEMON

Hubert Selby Jr.
a novel

MARION BOYARS
LONDON · NEW YORK

Reprinted in the United States and Great Britain in 2002 by
MARION BOYARS PUBLISHERS LTD
24 Lacy Road, London SW15 1NL

www.marionboyars.co.uk

Distributed in Australia and New Zealand by Peribo Pty Ltd
58 Beaumont Road, Kuring-gai, NSW 2080

First published in the United States in 1976 by Playboy Press
First published in Great Britain in 1977 by Marion Boyars Publishers Ltd
Republished in the United States and Great Britain in 1989
by Marion Boyars Publishers Ltd

Reprinted in 1994, 1998, 2000, 2002, 2003 by Marion Boyars Publishers Ltd

Reprinted 2003
10 9 8 7 6 5 4 3

A CIP catalogue record for this book is available from the British Library.
A CIP catalog record for this book is available from the Library of Congress.

ISBN 0-7145-2599-5

Printed and bound in Great Britain by Bookmarque, London.

This book is dedicated
to Bill,
who helped me learn
I must surrender to win

A man obsessed
is a man possessed
by a demon

Blessed is the man that endureth temptation: for when he is tried, he shall receive the crown of life, which the Lord hath promised to them that love him.

Let no man say when he is tempted, I am tempted of God: for God cannot be tempted with evil, neither tempteth he any man:

But every man is tempted when he is drawn away of his own lust, and enticed.

Then when lust hath conceived, it bringeth forth sin: and sin, when it is finished, bringeth forth death.

JAMES 1:12–15

I sought the Lord, and he heard me, and delivered me from all my fears.

They all looked unto him, and were lightened; and their faces were not ashamed.

This poor man cried, and the Lord heard him, and saved him out of all his troubles.

PSALMS 34:4–6

THE DEMON

Harry the Lover. But Harry would not screw just anyone. It had to be a woman . . . a married woman.

They were less trouble. When they were with Harry, they knew what they were there for. No wining or dining. No romancing. If they expected this, they were sadly mistaken; and if they started asking questions about his life or indicated in any way that they wanted to start an "affair," he went his merry way. Harry did not want any involvements or encumbrances, no hassles. He wanted what he wanted when he wanted it, then leave with a smile on his face and a wave of the hand.

Taking a married woman to bed provided an additional thrill. Not the thrill of stealing another mans woman, Harry was not interested in that, but the thrill of having to take certain precautions so you would not be discovered. Never knowing exactly what might happen increased the excitement of apprehension.

From time to time Harry White would stretch out in his minds eye and reflect upon the many relationships jeopardized because of confused or poor sexual relations. Why, there must be millions of women living on tranquilizers because of sexual frustrations. And how about the thousands, or hundreds of thousands, who are in mental institutions because of emotional breakdowns due directly to an unsatisfying or nonexistent love life? Think of those broken homes and motherless children struggling in an unhappy world simply for want of an orgasm.

Harry was not what one would call a womans libber, but he did think the double standard grossly unfair. After all, it is a known, and accepted, fact that most men cheat, as they say, on their wives, that they like to go out with the boys and get a "strange piece." Yet, the wife is supposed to stay home at night and take care of the children and beg her night-out-with-the-boys husband to make love to her occasionally. And if she should choose not to wait for his occasional and inept and mostly unsatisfying favors, but should find an occasional, shall we say, replacement, she is vilified, denounced, beaten, divorced or even, sad to say, killed. No, Harry was not a womans libber, but he was aware of the injustice of such situations.

And, in his small and humble way, he did what he could to rectify the situation, or at least, in some measure, ameliorate it. Actually, Harry felt he provided a very valuable service. Who knows how many marriages he may have helped with his ministrations? He may have saved more than just marriages, he may have saved lives too. Who knows how many women are alive and well because the pent-up tensions, anxieties and frustrations were not allowed to build to the point of insanity or death, but were punctured by Harry White in hot pursuit of his avocation?

Although Harry worked in midtown Manhattan, and had to spend almost two hours a day traveling to and from work, he continued to live in Brooklyn with his parents. Many times, especially on an eye cloudy Monday after an exceptionally active weekend, he thought of moving, of getting a place nearer work where he might be only a short, leisurely bus ride from the office, but by the time he had gotten the rest needed to give him the energy to go through the hassle of looking, the urgency was gone. He would think about the pros and cons and study the situation studiously and analytically and then decide against it. As he saw it there were basically two possibilities to be considered in looking for an apartment of his own:

1. to have a roommate; or
2. to live alone.

Now, with the first there are obviously two considerations:
  a. Male
  b. Female

Actually, this does not have to be considered at all. A female roommate is out of the question. If she were merely a friend, it would not remain platonic for long.

And, if she were more than just a friend, which in time she would be, it would definitely complicate Harrys life style. Obviously, no thought was needed in dismissing this possibility.

So we are left with the possibility of sharing an apartment with another guy. What are the advantages? Well, actually there is only one: You split the rent and so can get a nicer apartment.

Actually, thats not much of an advantage. Harry earned an excellent salary, and so that consideration was unimportant.

What are the disadvantages? Many. You would have to depend on him to pay his share of the bills. He might have a girlfriend who will eventually come on to you, and that will create countless problems. . . . . And numerous other reasons.

But *the* one reason that obviates evaluating the others was that Harry definitely did not want to have his life governed, or inconvenienced, in any way by the desires or needs of others.

So, that leaves the second consideration, as obviously Harry would have to live alone. What are the advantages of that?

None, except for the shorter ride to and from work. He certainly could not bring any women home with him. The last thing in the world he wanted would be to have some woman know where he lived. My God, they would never leave him alone. He could just see it: they would be calling him day and night or knocking on his door when those ants invaded their pants. Or after an argument with their husband they would tell him that they were leaving, that they found a wonderful man who will take care of them and the children and— O, no. No. No thank you.

So, where does that leave you? It leaves you exactly where you are now, except you have the additional expense, and the various concerns, of an apartment. You would still be going to their house, or one of their friends, or a hotel, and using your apartment for sleep and an occasional rest. No, tactically it did not make sense.

And pragmatically it did not make any sense either. Living with his parents he did not have to cook, clean, shop, worry about what he might have to pick up on the way home for this or that, all of which dissipated energy, and he wanted to conserve his energy for the more important things in life.

And, in addition to all the other considerations, there was the fact that he was an only child and it made his folks happy to have him living at home.

Harry had analyzed the situation, and looked at it from every conceivable angle often enough to realize that it did not make any sense to move.

And underneath all of Harry Whites logic and careful analysis, and beyond his conscious awareness, was a little germ that tugged and pushed and ultimately had more influence on his decision than any other factor. Indeed, it was the only *real* reason for his decision: security. Not the security of the umbilical cord, but security from himself. Although Harry did not want to accept it consciously, that little germ knew that temptation had a way of swooping down on you when you were the least prepared for it, when you were unable to cope with it or reject it, and who knows what horrendous situation he might get himself into . . .

but that little germ knew that no matter what the circumstances, or temptations, he would not take a woman home to his folks house, in the middle of the night, and explain to them how he was protecting her from a husband who did not understand her and who refused, along with the children, to give her the love she so desperately needed.

No, that was something Harry would not do. It would be far too embarrassing.

So, all things considered, a couple of hours a day to and from work is not so bad. It has its advantages. Some very definite advantages.

Saturday was a softball game. Some of the guys who hung out in Caseys, a bar on Third Avenue, were going to play the guys from Swensons, a bar on Fifth Avenue. Harry was not a drinker, but the guys in the neighborhood, the guys he grew up with, hung out there and so Harry spent some time in Caseys and played ball with them when he was around on Saturday.

Todays game was something a little special as it was going to prove the superiority of one bar over the other; one neighborhood over the other; the Irish over the squareheads. In addition to the display of chauvinism, there were a few hundred dollars being bet on the game.

The game was scheduled to start at 11:00 A.M., in the playground on Sixty-fifth street, and both teams were there by ten-thirty, complete with equipment, friends and cases of beer.

It was a beautiful day, and more and more people drifted into the playground to watch the game. Kids on bikes and roller skates screamed at each other to come on and watch some big guys play softball; and people walking by would stop and watch through the wire fence surrounding the playground.

The teams finished warming up and were ready to play, but the game had to be delayed a few minutes to allow the two guys holding the money to get things straight. When they finally had everything in order, the game was ready to start.

Although Harry no longer played regularly, he was still one of the better ballplayers in the neighborhood. For one thing he did not drink as much as the other guys, on both teams, and so was better coordinated during the latter part of the game, when it really counted. He was as good as anyone in right field, and was an exceptional hitter, especially in the clutch. And Harry figured to be pretty good today as he felt exceptionally relaxed and was in a good mood, a ball playing mood.

Caseys won the toss of the coin and elected to bat last, so they left their beers in the safekeeping of friends and trotted onto the field with a hoot and a holler—Lets go, lets go. Come on, lets toss it around, toss it around . . .

and their pitcher, Steve, warmed up and a few balls were tossed around the infield and the outfield. An off-duty bartender waddled out behind the pitcher while the two other umpires strolled to first and third base and the game began.

Caseys got into trouble in the first inning as Steve had a hard time finding the plate, and it looked like it was going to be a major disaster. He walked the first three men he faced, throwing ten balls before throwing a strike. The only ray of hope in Steves performance was the fact that he went to 3 and 2 on the third batter before walking him. The rest of the Caseys were yelling encouragement and telling him to slow down and take it easy. Where whitchya Stevie baby, we/re whitchya. Just chuck it in there Stevie baby boy. He cant see Steve. Letim hitit, his a crip . . .

and Steve looked down at his catcher as Boiler Head, a huge, redheaded Norwegian came up to the plate swinging a fistful of bats.

The Swenson team was yelling and screaming as beer dribbled down their chins. They sensed the kill and were jubilant as they anticipated winning the game in the first inning. Shove it down his throat Boiler. Comeon Boiler baby, over the fence, over the fence. Lets go, lets go! We all score. We all score. Boiler Head let his brown teeth hang out as he grinned at Steve, swinging the toothpicklike bat, defying him to let him hit the ball. Steve took a slow windup and let a high floater come down and Boiler Head waited and leaned into the ball with a Neanderthal swing, and as the bat splat into the ball it sounded as if it would split it into a hundred pieces, and the ball shot quickly and rapidly up into the air and out toward the left-field fence. Everyone watched, beer bottles stopping suddenly as they approached a mouth, as the ball slowly curved foul and went out of the playground, a dozen kids running after it. Boiler Head snapped his bat as the ball turned foul, then grinned at the pitcher and stepped back in the batters box, his face suddenly becoming gruesomely defiant. Just straighten it out Boiler baby. Chuck it in there Steve, hes nothin. O, pitcher, O pitcher, we gotya now. Throw it past the big baboon. . . .

Steve and Boiler Head stared at each other for a few moments and then Steve spit and went into his slow windup again, then snapped the ball toward the plate with almost invisible speed. Boiler Head swung and hit the ball squarely and solidly, but just a fraction of a second too late to hit it over the left-field fence. The ball went sailing down the right-field line toward the fence and the spectators *ooood* and *aaahhhhd*, and the Swensons jumped and screamed and hollered and the runners took off like thieves and Harry, who had been playing in right center for the pull hitter, ran with the thud of the bat toward the right field fence. The Swenson coaches were waving their arms and screaming at their teammates to run, run ya son of a bitch, and the man from third had already crossed the plate and the man from second was halfway home when Harry leaped in the air, his glove hand high over his head, and crashed into the fence just a fraction of a second before the ball, the ball thumping into his glove. Harry bounced off the fence holding the ball with both hands and cradling it in his gut as he rolled over on the concrete, unwound and stood and threw the ball to the first baseman, who easily doubled the man off first but was unable to throw to any of the other bases as there was a sudden confusion of players all running back to their former bases and the man trying to get back to first knocked Boiler Head into the first baseman and so there was no chance for any other play. Harry stood watching the action, his mind quickly decoding what he had seen and heard as he crashed into the fence as a woman, a woman on the other side of the fence . . . yeah, and she had blonde hair and was wearing a pair of shorts and a halter, and, it seemed to Harry from what he could remember from the brief flash out of the farthest corner of his eye, that she had a nice pair of boobs, too. Harry turned and she was still there. He looked a little closer and he noticed a stroller with a young child in it. Harry walked back to the fence and stood half facing the playing field. The confusion had ended and the next batter was standing in the batters box as Harry smiled at the woman. Hi.

Hi, smiling and shaking her head slightly, I thought you were going to come right through the fence.

Harry raised his eyebrows and his smile broadened. If I had known you were there, I would have.

The game had started again, but everyone was still so excited over the last play that no one, on either side, noticed that Harry was still over on the right-field line with a right-handed pull hitter up.

Sally, she nodded toward the little girl in the stroller, seemed to think it was some sort of joke. She just giggled. I guess it doesnt take much to amuse her.

They both laughed and the count was o and 2 on the batter when Steve steamed one right down the middle and the batter swung an hour too late and the Caseys started hootin and hollerin and spritzin a little beer on each other.

As the teams started to change places, with the Caseys yelling and pounding Steve on the back, the woman nodded toward the field and asked what was happening. Harry turned and smiled. I guess they got the third out. Its our turn to bat. She started to turn as if to leave and Harry told her to stay. Its just the first inning. You have a lot of good softball left in the day.

Im afraid I don't know very much about the game, smiling softly.

Harry leaned against the fence and stared at her for a moment, then told her he could teach her everything she needed to know. You just wait here and I/ll be back in a few minutes. We never hit this guy early in the game. She smiled and Harry went trotting off toward the sidelines as his teammates and friends patted him on the back and cheered.

Harry batted fifth in the lineup and as he waited along the sidelines he kept glancing, from the corner of his eye, at the woman behind the fence. She wasnt bad. Not bad at all. Nice pair of boobs and a nice round ass. And not a kid either. Probably a few years older than Harry, maybe around thirty. He wished they would hurry up and get their three outs so he could go back and see what was happening. Harry remained oblivious to the action of the game until he heard a loud roar and some cursing around him and he realized that the third man had struck out and it was time for them to go back in the field. He joyfully trotted out along the right-field line.

Hi there, leaning against the fence and smiling at her.

You werent gone very long, standing close to the fence, smiling.

Yeah, well . . . actually, shrugging, his mouth opening in a broad smile, it was all planned so that I could get out here faster.

Why would you want to do that?

To see you. After—

Hey, Harry, move over, eh? Comeon for kris sake.

Yeah, yeah, O.K. Dont go away now, and he sprinted over to right center, looking back in her direction, and continuing to look there from time to time during the inning.

Steve was really inspired now and he put the Swensons down in a matter of minutes with three pop flies to the infield. The Caseys trotted noisily from the field and Harry trotted back to the fence.

Why dont you come on in? You can sit on the bench over there.

O, I dont think so. There are some things I have to do and—

On a beautiful day like this? Come on, smiling gently, you can be our good-luck charm.

Her smile opened into a happy chuckle. No one has ever called me that before.

There, you see, it will—

Hey, Harry, youre on deck. Comeon, eh? Get your ass over here.

Yeah, yeah, Im coming. The gates right down there, trotting toward home plate and looking back in her direction and smiling as he noticed her walking toward the entrance. Steve poked Harry on the arm. Screw the broad, eh?

If you insist.

Comeon, knock it off, eh? Lets beat these bastards. I got twenty-five bucks riding on the game.

Dont worry about it, slapping Steve on the back, we cant lose. I feel good.

The first guy up struck out and as Harry walked toward the batters box he looked around and noticed a blonde head just barely visible over the top of the hedges along the path to the ball field. Harry felt nice and loose as he swung his bat and looked at the pitcher. He always did hit this guy pretty good and just stepped back as the first pitch sailed in high. He looked around before stepping back into the batters box and saw the woman as she turned the corner and entered the ball field. Both teams were yelling, and Harry stepped back in and ripped the next pitch to left center and only a great play by the center fielder held Harry to a double. Harry stood on second base listening to the yelling from his teammates and friends and watched the woman as she pushed the stroller to the last bench on the right-field side, and sat. The next batter struck out, but the next man up got a hit to right center, not too deep, and Harry thrust his way around third and flew toward home as the ball reached the catcher and Harry slid around him, scraping his ankle on the concrete. The Caseys yelled and screamed and Harry hopped around, sucking air between his teeth and swinging the burning ankle back and forth, as his friends slapped him on the back. Harry sat on the bench as the next batter struck out, then trotted back onto the field, favoring his right foot. He waved at the blonde, and she smiled, as he took his position in right field.

That inning Steve mowed them down again and when the Caseys left the field, Harry sat with the blonde. By the way, my name is Harry, smiling and leaning close to her.

She smiled and told him her name was Louise, and this is my daughter, Sally, bending over and adjusting her hat to protect her from the sun.

Harry showed her his scraped ankle and joked about it and they continued to chat until it was time for Harry to go back to the field, and as he raised himself from the bench he put his open hand on the inside of her thigh, just at the edge of her shorts, and exerted just the slightest of pressure with the palm of his hand and finger tips, and looked into her eyes for a brief second, then trotted off.

Harry sat with her between innings, and when he got to the bench during the fifth inning, she told him she had to leave. He immediately got a hurt and forlorn look on his face. You cant leave now, youre our good-luck charm. You wouldnt want us to lose the game, would you?

She smiled and looked him full in the face, her eyes closing slightly. My husband will be home in a few hours and there are some things I have to do.

Harry returned her look and was about to speak when Steve yelled at him. Comeon, Harry, you lead off. Harry waved at Steve, O.K., O.K., then pressed his hand against her thigh again, wait just a minute. Harry trotted over to the plate and stepped in the box and didn't move as three strikes went flying by. He dropped the bat and went back to the bench. Then you really have to go?

Yes, I do. We/re going out tonight and there are some things I have to get done.

Harry looked at her for a moment. Maybe I should walk you home.

But what about your game?

O, they dont need me. And anyway, the way Steves pitching that run we got will be enough.

She shrugged slightly and smiled. Well, if you want to.

Sure I do. Harry stood. You start and I/ll meet you by the gate. Louise started to leave, pushing the stroller, and Harry went over to Steve and told him he had to go.

What do you mean you have to go? You cant leave now.

Im sorry Steve, but I have to go. Theres something I got to do—and anyway, my leg is killing me.

O, bullshit, you son of a bitch. There aint nothin wrong with your leg.

Comeon Steve, get off my back, eh? Im tellin you I got to go.

Yeah, you got to go. You know somethin Harry, youre a big prick. A first-class prick with ears.

Lighten up Steve, its not—

You know fuckin well right how much money we got on the game and you dont give a shit about blowin our dough just so you can sniff some broads crotch. Up yours, man!

Im tellin you I have to go and thats all. It aint got nothing to do with no broad and I can hardly stand on this ankle. Im not—

Aaaahhhh bullshit, waving at Harry with disgust and walking away. Your ass sucks wind. Hey Vinnie! VINNIE!

Yeah?

Comere.

Harry started to limp away as the teams started to change places and Steve told Vinnie to play right field.

Whats with Harry?

That son of a bitch? He/d take a fuckin murder rap for a piece of ass.

Harry heard Steves remark, distantly but clearly, and twisted his glove violently as he limped as fast as possible from the field, pushing Steves words from his head by concentrating on Louise and the distance between himself, the teams and the hedge, trying to decrease the distance to the hedge by concentrating on it and bringing to the foremost part of his consciousness the fact that as soon as he got to the hedge there was a corner to turn and he would be out of sight of the teams, the game and Steve, and the noise from the game would soon be a dull din and everything about the game would be out of sight and behind him.

Harry rushed around the hedge, bumping into it, a small branch brushing his face, and his limp subsided and his pace quickened as his ears filled with the sound of children playing and the traffic on the streets, and he saw Louise slowly walking along the path in front of him. He started trotting and quickly caught up with her.

Your friend sounded angry.

Who, Steve? Naw. He just likes to yell, is all. But I/ll tell you one thing, though.

Whats that?

I sure could go for a cup of coffee.

She looked at him for a moment, then smiled. That shouldnt be any problem. I always keep a pot on the stove.

Good, smiling and gently rubbing the back of her hand with the tips of his fingers. Where do you live?

Seventh Avenue. Not too far.

When they got to the corner, she stopped and told him the address and the apartment number. It might be best if we didnt go there together, if you waited a few minutes.

He returned her smile and nodded. Sure. I understand.

As Louise continued walking up the street, Harry walked to the left, up and around the block, to be sure he got there at least five minutes after her. Harry could not remember how many times he had done this, enjoying it more and more each

the anticipation, the expectation, the grinding excitement in his gut and that vague feeling of fear and apprehension
that came from the unknown element that existed in each
and every one of these situations, the fact that she might not
live where she said she did, or the fact that the situation might
be different than anticipated, and also the fact that perhaps
her husband might be there waiting, or suddenly come home,
and it might be all part of some weird joke. There were
endless possibilities, but they had never happened, but the fact
that they could and might added to the excitement. There
was a buoyancy in his step as he walked along Seventh Avenue.

Harry was going to a neighborhood movie that night with
a couple of friends. After dinner he stretched out on his bed,
waiting for it to be time to leave. He had a vague uneasiness
in him that he could not understand or explain. It wasnt the
food he had just eaten—he did not have an upset stomach or
indigestion. Actually he did not know what he had. He just
felt uneasy. And it could not have anything to do with whats-
her-name—Lois—uh . . . Louise. That was as routine as the
meal he just ate. She put the kid down for a nap and they went
to bed, Harry declining the coffee, wanting to be sure to take
care of business properly and to leave before there were any
embarrassing encounters with her husband. And she was as
good as any other broad—kind of frisky and hungry. As a
matter of fact it was fairly long, and frantic enough, for an
afternoon.

No, it wasnt that. As a matter of fact there werent even
any of those embarrassing scenes where the kid wakes up and
comes stumbling into the room asking Mommy for a hug.
Everything went smooth and simple. And he did not think it
had anything to do with the game. There was no big deal
about that. It was just another game, though he did wish he
knew how it had turned out. He had thought, briefly, of
calling someone and finding out, but he felt conspicuous somehow and he just could not get around to it. He could always

find out later . . . and anyway, he did not want to make a thing out of it. It really was not a big deal. And even if they did lose, it was not his fault. He had gotten his hit. You cant expect to get more than that off that guy. And anyway, it was more than most guys got. There really wasnt any reason for him to hang around and finish the game. O well, screw it. Whatevers wrong will go away. Go to the flicks and forget all about it.

After the show they stopped in at Caseys to see what was happening. Harry had already learned that they had won the game, and because the second movie was an incredibly funny one, he was in a good mood. They joined the others and Harry slapped Steve on the back. I hear you clobbered the bums.

One nothin aint exactly slaughterin them.

Whats the difference, you beat them, didn't you?

Yeah. No thanks to you.

Come on Steve, dont start that again.

If I wasnt the best softball pitcher in Brooklyn, we might not have won the game.

Then what you bitchin about?

Steve smiled at Harry and patted him on the back. I aint bitchin. I understand, Harry. A stiff dick aint got no conscience, right?—laughing—any port in a storm. But you know your trouble? Taking his hand off Harrys shoulder. Your trouble is you aint got no loyalty.

What do you mean I aint got any loyalty?

Just what I said. We/re all friends. Grown up together in the same neighborhood and all that shit, but you aint got no feelings about it.

Get off it. I have as much loyalty as you or anyone else— Harry knew that was true. He thought about it many times, and he knew his feelings about his friends—and maybe more.

Yeah, that may be, smiling, but you sure dont show it. You may be a brain, an all that, but youre a son of a bitch— Anyway, you going to buy one or be one?

Harry smiled, tossed a bill on the bar and bought Steve a drink.

Harry liked his job and enjoyed his work. The corporation he worked for was just the right size for his needs and ambitions: large but not mammoth; large enough to offer unlimited opportunity for growth and advancement, yet not so huge as to swallow him up and leave just a number on an IBM card. And, too, because the corporation had such diversified interests, his job was never boring, but, rather, it was exciting and challenging, each new problem being different than the last.

Harry joined the Lancet Corporation immediately upon graduating from Brooklyn College. He finished college on the GI bill, majoring in business administration, with a background in accounting, and when he was interviewed in his senior year by a representative of the Lancet Corporation, it was realized almost at once that they fulfilled a mutual need and so Harry reported for their Orientation Program the day after commencement.

Harry was amiable and fit in very well with his work and his fellow employees on all levels, and was liked by those who worked with him. He advanced rapidly in the couple of years he had been with the firm and was definitely one of the more promising junior executives. One of the first things Harry did upon completion of the Lancet Corporation's Orientation Program was to enroll in a night school and study economics. He thought that it would not only help him in his work, but would make a good impression on those he had to impress, and he was correct in both instances.

The future looked bright, and the path smooth, and Harry White would reflect on these things occasionally, and briefly, not with a sense of gratitude or humility, but with a sense of impatience, wanting the promotions and the money, property and prestige now.

By the time Harry graduated from Brooklyn College he was just barely getting enough sleep to get by, not because he had to spend an extraordinarily long time studying, but because of his love life, which was extremely active. When he first started working at Lancet Corporation, he went on the wagon, so to speak, as he did when he first started college, but as time passed and he became more comfortable and more secure, and the novelty wore off, he gradually drifted back to being Harry the Lover. But other than coming in occasionally on Monday with eyes a little red and hazy, his "outside interests" did not create any problems for him. And he always kept a bottle of eye drops in his desk drawer and would occasionally, and offhandedly, tell his fellow employees about a congenital eye condition he had that was responsible for his eyes' redness at times. He did not really wonder if anyone believed him, but it made him feel good to tell the story anyway.

Harry had been on his good behavior for a year or so, confining his amorous activities to the weekends, when he started finding himself being distracted at work. Not by the women in the office, but by a disquieting feeling within, and he found himself looking up at the clock earlier and earlier in the day, waiting for five o'clock, a tension building up in his body. Then his weekends gradually extended themselves into Monday, then started on Friday, and inevitably it was no longer possible to confine his activities to particular evenings, but he was forced to follow his inner urge.

Eventually this urge led Harry to eating his lunch as rapidly as possible and then walking around the streets. He never associated this new habit with the antsy feelings he would get occasionally, or even considered that it had become a habit. It was simply something he liked to do, especially during the nice weather, and he was unaware that he inevitably would stroll behind this broad or that one until it was time to go back to the office.

Soon Harry stopped eating in the coffee shop in the building and called down ahead of time and ordered a sandwich to go, and then picked it up and walked over to Central Park and sat by the lake and ate his lunch. It certainly was far more relaxing than standing on line in the crowded restaurant and then gulping down a sandwich with all the noise and smoke, and so he strolled the few blocks to the park and watched the ducks ripple the reflections of the skyscrapers.

Harry dearly loved the first warm days of spring when the heavy coats could be left at home and only a sweater or light jacket need be worn. And the colors! O, yes, Harry loved the colors of spring. Not so much the trees and flowers, though Harry did like to look at them, and the birds too, but Harry never was exactly what is referred to as a "nature lover," though he was quick to emphasize that he did love natural things . . . *au naturel*. The springtime colors that Harry loved were the colors of the womens dresses as they bounced along the street unemcumbered or hidden by the heavy winter garments, their legs curved down to their ankles, their filmy dresses clinging to the roundness of their flesh, their eyes shining and faces flushed with a smile as the breeze fluffed their hair and pressed their dress against the soft, gentle slope of their tummy and the inside of their thighs as they met at the mound of Venus. Aaaaahhhhh, springtime, springtime, when the earth and all thereon are reborn and a young mans fancy lightly turns.

And today was as fine a spring day as ever any man could wish to see. There was a blue sky, a cloud or two, birds winging and swooping their way across the lake and through the trees, and a lovely young lady sitting on a bench just a few feet from the lake. Harry finished his lunch, dropped the paper, etc., into a litter can and walked to the edge of the lake directly in front of the young lady. He twirled the water with his fingers for a moment, then slowly turned and looked at her crossed legs, concentrating on the area where the leg flows into the roundness of the ass. He was as open about his staring, and the direction, as possible, and after a few moments she uncrossed her legs, not looking at him directly, and smoothed down her skirt, which reached almost halfway to her knees. Harry continued to stare until she fidgeted, and then he arose and walked over to the bench, smiling widely and warmly, and staring into her eyes. He had read somewhere that Wyatt

Earps greatest weapons were his eyes, which were light blue and seemed to stare right through people and immobilize them. That is what Harry did. He just stared at women and thrust all his lust at them with his eyes. She tried to look straight ahead but was forced to follow his approach. He sat next to her and she girded herself for the usual opening line of, Its a lovely day, or do you have the time, or some such thing, but Harry threw her one of his curves: Your husband sure is a lucky man.

She turned her head and looked at him, startled, a smile softening her face. I don't understand.

Well, staring into her eyes, his lust tangible for a moment, then smiling and gesturing with his hand, what I mean is he has you to come home to. Her eyes questioned him, but her mouth relaxed slightly. Harrys face opened in a sparkling smile. With you to go home to he must just whistle through the day.

She jerked her head back slightly with a: Huh, fat chance.

O, comeon, now, I know he does.

You must be kidding, raising her eyebrows and smirking.

No, Im not. Im serious. I just know it must make his whole day worthwhile knowing that youll be waiting for him when he gets home.

She relaxed a little more and chuckled, and Harry could see the tension slowly drain from her body as he smiled at her. Youre really something else, shaking her head and smiling, a real joker.

O, you shouldnt say that, putting his hand on his breast dramatically, you hurt me to the quick. She suddenly started laughing out loud, and as Harry watched her laugh he noticed a few pigeons from the corner of his eye as they swooped around and above them and wondered what she would do, and what she would look like, if one of them suddenly shit on her head, or right on her nose . . . but then he realized, almost simultaneously, that it might shit on him, so he quickly replaced the image with the obvious thought that she and her husband had a problem or two. He smiled and gestured, See what I mean? With that laugh you just made my life worth-while.

She smiled and shook her head, Youre really something else, then stood, looking at her watch.

Youre not going, are you?

Thats right, time to get back to work.

O, what a pity, looking sad and forlorn.

Sorry, smiling warmly, but a jobs a job. Youre more fun than a barrel of monkeys, but I got to go.

Well, at least allow me to call my coach so you dont have to walk through these sordid streets.

Youre too much, smiling and starting to walk up the path to Fifth Avenue.

Please dont mock me, you might be accosted by ruffians. She continued laughing, and he bowed low and gestured with his hands. At least allow me to protect you, me lady.

Now youre calling me names, laughing out loud.

Well, with a hurt expression on his face, if you wont allow me to call the coach, how about a rickshaw—looking into her eyes with an expression of mock seriousness on his face—a bicycle—she nodding her head and chuckling—a skateboard—both smiling, Harry spreading his arms—how about a piggyback?

Thanks, but no thanks. I think it would be safer if I crossed the street on my own two legs.

O.K., laughing. Do you usually sit by the lake at lunch time?

Uhhhmmmm, shrugging, it all depends.

Well, why dont we make it tomorrow, the same time, same bench?

You never can tell, shrugging, smiling, if the weathers nice.

O, it will be, I guarantee it.

I have to go, smiling and joining the crowd crossing the street.

Harry watched and as she turned before going into her building, he waved, returning her smile, then started back to the office.

He was much more animated, and felt looser, on the way back to the office than he had been just an hour before. He got back to the office ten minutes late, but did not notice the time and got involved with his work and did not give another thought to whatever-her-name-is for the remainder of the day.

The following day Harry strolled over to the park and saw whats-her-name sitting on the bench. Krist, she must really be bugged with her old man. Harry smiled to himself and strolled down the path to the bench. Excuse me, madam, but would you be so kind as to allow a weary proletarian to share this bench with you? She looked up, annoyed, then suddenly broke into a huge smile, shook her head and laughed. Whats so funny?

She shook her head and continued to laugh for another moment. You just dont look like a proletarian.

He adopted an attitude and expression of mock injury and pouted, You hurt me to the quick. After all, while she giggled, its better to be a proletarian than a codfish. She continued giggling and waved at him and shook her head, and his face cracked into a smile and he laughed as he sat down next to her.

By the way, my name is Tom, whats yours, laughing girl? smiling and looking into her eyes.

Laughing girl? Now isnt that something? I havent been accused of that in a long time, but I guess I have been laughing.

Yep, you sure have. Just like a proletarian. Before Harry finished the word she was laughing and fumbling around in her pocketbook to get a handkerchief, Harry watching her and laughing. Eventually she sat up straight and took a few deep breaths, dabbing at her eyes and nose with her handkerchief. She blinked a few times then turned to Harry, O, my God, I laughed so hard Im in pain. My muscles are killing me.

You must be out of practice.

Yeah, I guess so, wiping her eyes and nose, then putting her handkerchief back in her pocketbook, then smiling, carefully, at Harry. No more, O.K.? I don't think I can stand it.

O.K., smiling, but you still havent told me your name. I guess I/ll just have to go on guessing.

No, no. Please, Harry chuckling, my name is Mary.

Well, thats better. I/d feel funny calling you buddy or Mack or—

She started chuckling and put her hands up in front of him. You promised. No more.

O.K., raising his right hand, no more. So, youre Mary and you work across the street.

Thats right, nodding, I'm a secretary. And your name is Tom and you work—

Down the street. Armstrong and Davis. A small engineering firm. Mostly consultants in highly specialized areas.

O, that sounds exciting. . . .

They continued to chat until Mary suddenly looked at her watch and said it was ten after, I have to get back to the office.

That late, eh? I/d better get going too.

They walked up the path to the street, and Harry waited until Mary had crossed the street and entered the building before he started to walk back to the office, not wanting her to see the direction in which he was walking.

He rushed back to the office, realizing he was late, and got back to his desk about twenty minutes late, but for the most part it went unnoticed and he attacked his work with vigor.

The following day was Thursday, and Harry decided he would cool it for the remainder of the week. For one thing he did not want to be late again. And for another, he wanted to let Mary dangle for a while. His evenings were when the real work was done, and he got an additional thrill out of just letting her dangle, knowing she was frustrated, that she and her husband werent making it and that she was chomping at the bit for a little action, any kind of action, even if it was just sitting on a park bench in the middle of the afternoon and have someone show a little attention. Krist, the more he thought about it, the more it excited him.

But, he did have some time to kill, so he thought he would walk over to the park and make sure she was there. He was smiling and glowing inside as he walked toward the park, and then a slight feeling of apprehension started to sneak in behind and under the glow and he started to quicken his pace slightly, anxious to see if she was really there. He had planned to be extremely circumspect, to be absolutely certain that she did not see him, but when he vaguely thought that she might not be there, he lost track of his perspective and instead of walking along Fifth Avenue and peering over the hedges, he walked down the path, unable to see the bench because of the people strolling and standing around, and he was only a few feet from her when the crowd suddenly thinned, but she was looking across the lake and he managed to regain control of himself in time to turn and leave the park before she saw him.

When he was out of sight of the park, he stopped for a moment and became aware of the quickness of his pulse and how he could feel it in his ears. He looked in a store window, took a deep, slow breath, looked at his reflection and smiled at the thought of whatser-name sitting there, waiting for him. He chuckled, then spent the remainder of his lunch hour strolling along Fifth Avenue, looking in store windows and at the women, enjoying his feeling of power.

2

Harry sat at the table, his mother serving, his father carving the roast and putting meat on the plates. Harrys parents were especially happy this evening. They were going to the fiftieth anniversary party of a couple who were friends of his mothers parents, and whom she had known all her life. It was going to be a truly gala celebration, with family and friends of a lifetime, most of whom they only saw on special occasions such as this. But the one thing in particular that was the cause of their happiness was the fact that Harry was going to go with them. Harry was a good boy, and always had been, and because he was an only child he was the apple of their eye and the center and focus of so much of their hopes and dreams, but now that he was a man he spent less and less time with them and usually had some place to go, especially on weekends, and so they were excitedly happy to be going out with their son, their pride and joy. Tonight was going to be a real family night. It was going to be a family celebration, and they were going to go there as a family.

When Harry finished eating, he patted his stomach and told his mother that it was delicious. Youre the best cook in the world, Mom, smiling at her.

Thank you, son, I'm glad you enjoyed it, beaming as she picked up the plates. Coffee?

Yes, please.

They sat smoking and drinking coffee, music from the radio faintly audible in the background, each one enjoying the others company and conversation. Three people sitting at a dinner table, a man and a woman; a husband and a wife; a father and a mother—and their only child, a young man who adds joy to their lives. The atmosphere was calm, relaxed, the cigarette smoke drifting almost straight up, moving abruptly only when the air was disturbed with sudden laughter. There was love at the table.

When they arrived at the party, Mrs. White took Harry from one old friend to another, introducing her son proudly, telling them of his fine position and future and what a wonderful son he was, his mothers and fathers pride and joy, Harry smiling enthusiastically when old friends shook his hand, smiled and told her she was fortunate, yes indeed, quite fortunate to have such a wonderful son, a regular chip off the old block, eh? Looks just like his father, doesnt he? Spittin image. But he has your eyes, Sara. Yep, he sure does. No mistaking that. Could tell he was your son a mile away in a blackout. Sara White beamed, and indeed, you could see her smile a mile away in a total blackout.

And Harry followed his mother obediently, and happily, feeding off the joy that his being there made possible. He was making her happy and this in turn made him happy, and making his mother happy was something that he would try to do from time to time—or at least want to try—but somehow he could never seem to accomplish it, at least not on a consistent basis. For some unknown reason something always seemed to happen to prevent him from bringing the smile to his mothers face, or if he did, he usually did something that would, at least, turn down the corner of her smile.

But tonight he was not going to allow that to happen. He felt good, loose, relaxed, and was going to make this her night. And he smiled appropriately, at the proper time, and answered the usual queries with a bow, a smile, a quiet laugh and then an, Of course, now I remember. Sure. Mr. and Mrs. Lawry—or Little or Harkness, or whatever or whomever. It did not make any difference, the anecdotes were all pretty much the same about how he looked and what he did when he was two or three or four or whatever cute or fanciful age they remembered. And as Harry and Mrs. White left one couple to go to another, Harry knew that they were smiling and saying what a nice guy he was.

Harry pretty well had his smile fixed for the night, so even after his mother finished with her introductions he continued to smile through the room full of familiar and unfamiliar faces. When he spotted his grandmother, his smile broadened and he put his arms around her and kissed her and kept his arms around her for a few moments. How you doin, grandma?

O, just fine, son. You know, you cant keep the ol girl down, her eyes sparkling.

Thatta girl, kissing her on the forehead.

How are you, son? Everything going all right?

Yeah, just great. Couldnt be better.

O, thats good to—

HEY! HEY EVERYBODY!!!!

the oldest son of the golden anniversary couple waved his hands above his head, quiet for a minute . . . we have to give a toast. Hey Mom, Pop, come over here. They walked across the room, dressed in their finery, faces and eyes glowing, as pleased and excited as children on their first Christmas morning as they stand, amazed, looking at the tree, the balls, tinsels and lights, the stockings and presents and feeling the excitement of Christmas all around them. The son stood behind them and put his arms around them. Now everybody take a drink if you havent got one. The other children passed around with trays of manhattans, and then they went to stand near their parents. Mr. and Mrs. White joined Harry and his grandmother. O.K., everybody got a drink???? Good. He raised his glass high, the others joining him. A toast to Mom and Dad for fifty short and beautiful years of marriage. For loving each other and loving us, and making the world a better place, and a little more crowded—chuckling and laughter—we all wish you all the joy of Gods blessing . . . your five children . . . your twelve grandchildren . . . your twenty *great* grandchildren . . . and all your in-laws and out-laws. YEAH! SALUTE! LUCK! YAAA! SALUTE!!!! and everyone cheered and sipped their drink or emptied their glass and continued cheering as each one of the family kissed the golden and radiant couple, and with each kiss another cheer went up. When the endless parade finished, the Anniversary Waltz was played and they spun around the floor, slowly, but joyously, and everyone reached for someones hand as they watched the couple dance, their eyes looking into each others with the fire of endless joy as husbands and wives, parents and children, hugged each other and watched with moist eyes.

Harry had his arm around his grandmother while his mother held his other hand. When the song ended, everyone cheered and the golden anniversary couple bowed slightly, like timid children, and were eventually absorbed by the people. You know, son, looking up at Harry with a hint of tears still in her eyes and the softness of fond memories on her face, your grandfather and I would have been married fifty years this October if he were still alive, God bless his soul.

Harry smiled at her for a moment, then took her half empty glass and put it on a table along with his. Comeon grandma, lets dance. They joined the others who were dancing, and Mr. and Mrs. White beamed with pride as they watched them merge into the crowd; then they too joined the dancers.

It seemed like every time Harry put an empty glass down,

someone was handing him another drink, and so he felt looser and looser and looser. And so was his grandmother. The half of a manhattan she had went directly to her head and she was dancing, sort of, with an old friend, kicking and wiggling in a confused version of a Brooklyn cancan. Harry joined the others, including his parents, who were clapping their hands as they watched her dance, but after a few minutes she stopped with a long *wwwhhhheeeewwwwwwww*, and sat down, enjoying the laughter and attention.

Harry continued to circulate among the guests, calculatingly sipping on his drink, slowly, not wanting to put an empty glass down and have another full one shoved in his hand. He was starting to feel the drinks and wanted to be careful. He put a cigarette out in an ashtray on a coffee table, and when he straightened up, he almost fell into the arms of a woman who was more than feeling her drinks. When he bumped her, she instinctively reached out and put her arms around him to keep from falling, Harry supporting her by holding her under the upper arms. When they finished with their, ooops, sorry . . . look out . . . are you all right? and stopped swaying back and forth, Harry withdrew his hands, but she continued to keep hers on his shoulders. Gee, I'm really sorry. I hope I didn't mess you up or anything.

No, no. No harm done, smiling, everythings fine.

Whats your name, tilting her head to one side, looking into his face, her lips slightly parted.

Harry. Harry White, returning the smile and look.

Mines Gina. Gina Logan. It used to be Gina Merretti, but thats a long time ago, gesturing with her hand. You can call me Gina.

Glad to meet you, Gina, nodding his head and smiling.

Harry, a quizzical look on her face, thats not so bad.

Thanks, laughing.

Why dont you dance with me, Harry? Come on.

O.K., why not? shrugging his shoulders, then putting an open hand on her back as they eased themselves into the group of dancers.

Harrys reaction to Gina was Pavlovian, and his evaluation and assessment of her attributes were instant. She was probably in her forties, early forties, but looked at least five years younger, maybe even more, even though it was obvious she had a little too much to drink and it altered her appearance. All in all she was not a bad-looking head—her left hand clung to the back of his neck, moist and warm and alive—and his eyes roamed approvingly over the parts of her boobs visible above her low-cut dress. He tried to penetrate the darkness between them, but was unable, and so he simply used his imagination, and experience, to mentally construct the roundness and fullness of her boobs and the purplish-brown nipple in the middle. Twenty years, or so, ago, she was real cunty Italian—his open hand pressed against the bareness of her back and his cheek was brushed by her black hair—and still had that look in her eyes and ass—and krist, her box was hot as it rubbed against his crotch while passing from one thigh to the other. He could feel the cold, metallic security of her wedding ring on his neck—he knew that somewhere between those luscious tits were a couple of short, black hairs, and he would love to jerk them out with his teeth—youre a good dancer, looking up at him with half-closed eyes and half-open mouth, I like the way you move your body—he could open her zipper just a little and slide his hand down her back and under her pants to that nice round ass and just lay his hand between her cheeks, feeling the small beads of sweat, and feel her ass grind his hand as he kept her tight against him—you make it easy. I fit right in. My husband doesnt dance. Used to a little bit, but no more. Says hes too tired. Well, I guess he works hard, (not as hard as my dick). But you need a little fun once in a while too, looking up at him again with the same open invitation, if you know what I mean? Yeah, smiling and nodding, I do. And anyway, who knows what hes doing right now in Poughkeepsie? (POUGHKEEPSIE! Holy shit!) Whats he doing there? really and truly wondering. Business. Always business.

The music suddenly stopped, and Harry became conscious

of his hard-on. It did not embarrass him, but this was not the kind of party where he could walk her into a closet or the cellar and throw a quick hump into her, not that he was particularly fond of quickies, having given them up with his teens, but he was feeling the drinks and the urgency of his stiffened dick, and the image of the back yard and the huge shade tree quickly flashed through his mind. He disengaged his arm from her hands and excused himself. I/ll be back in a minute. He went to the bathroom and closed the door, then splashed some cold water on his face. Maybe I should take a cold hip bath, hahahaha. He dried his face, looked in the mirror, then at his crotch, then back in the mirror. Well, I guess everythings under control. Krist, I/d like to fuck that broad.

He left the bathroom and stood for a moment looking around the room until he saw Gina with a couple of people in a corner. She was profiled toward him and the light seemed to shimmer on the roundness of her ass. He leaned in that direction—a stiff dick has no conscience—then suddenly turned and walked back in the direction of his grandmother, and sat down beside her.

How you doing, ol girl?

O, just fine, son. Having a grand old time. Its so good to see so many old friends, and to watch the young folks have so much fun.

You mean teenie-bobbers like you? smiling and looking out of the corner of his eye toward Gina, wondering if he should at least try to get her phone number for future reference. Wondering, too, exactly what Ginas relationship was with the rest of the people and who might find out if he copped her drawers and what would happen. His folks would probably die from humiliation and—

Come on May, this is my dance. An old friend, of many long and friendly years, stood in front of Harrys grandmother with his hand extended.

Well, allright Otto, if you insist, but youre going to have to help me get out of this chair. Otto tugged, Harry pushed, and they all laughed.

Harry watched them dance, a bit of an eye still in the direction of Gina. He smiled, and glowed inwardly, as he watched them move around the floor, their movements slightly stiff from age, yet projecting a nobility as they danced with each other and their memories.

He watched and smiled, yet his eyes slowly and inexorably strayed toward Gina until the dancers were just a blur in the corner of his eye and his mind seemed to be lighted by the light reflecting from Ginas ass and boobs as she—Krist, shes not only somebody's daughter, shes probably somebodys mother. Uh, uh. No good. Bad news, man. Later for that shit. The folks would be destroyed. Forget it!

Harry started to sing the words to the old ballad that was playing to himself and concentrated on the dancers and the people around him. When his grandmother finally plopped herself back in her seat with a sigh and a laugh, he took her hand in his, kissed it and held it tightly, but gently. You were great, Grandma. You really do know how to trip the life fantastic. They laughed. Harry loved his grandmother and was suddenly overwhelmed with realizing the fact that some-day, soon perhaps, she would be dead. He kissed her hand again.

When Mrs. White suggested that they leave—Mothers getting tired, and it is getting a little late, dont you think so, Mother? Yes dear, I am. I guess Im just too old and pooped to pop, laughing and smiling up into their faces and enjoying her joke completely—she asked Harry if he would drive them home? Harrys mind was filled with Ginas ass as he leered at her from the corner of his eye, feeling the sweat from between the cheeks of her ass between his finger tips. Uh? What? fumbling, stumbling, eyes blinking rapidly for a sec-ond, concentrating on his mothers words as she repeated her question. O . . . O, yeah, sure. Lets take the old girl home.

When Harry went to bed that night he left the blinds of one of his windows open so a piece of sky was visible over the corner of a building. He lay on his back, remembering. Scenes and images floated comfortably through his minds eye and there was no need to fight to keep the image of Gina from his mind. He was involved with his family and the warm flow that flowed through him, as if something had been injected into him, as he remembered his familys happiness: the way his parents danced and looked at each other, the way his grandmother laughed and cried as she watched her friends waltz on their fiftieth anniversary—Jesus, the old girl is really something else—but mostly the image that he dwelled on and caressed more than any other was his mother kissing him good night with her happiness not only reflected in her eyes, but just sparkling from her finger tips. Thank you for coming with us dear, it really made our night complete. And you made your grandmother so happy— Yes son, patting Harry on the back, then squeezing his shoulder, it was great that we could all spend the entire evening together. It was quite an occasion. Yeah, it sure was, smiling at his parents, squeezing his father's arm, then kissing his mother on the cheek, I had a ball. . . .

Harry continued to enjoy the feeling he got from remembering the scene, knowing he had made his folks happy, until the images started to overlap and fuzz out, then he closed the blind and plopped back into bed and drifted into a restful sleep.

The next day, Sunday, Harry strolled up to Caseys and got there shortly after his Irish friends who rushed from the twelve oclock Mass to get there when the bar opened at one. He hung around for a while, then left to go to a movie with a couple of the guys. After the show they went to Fin Hall, a small, neighborhood dance hall.

Before they had been sitting at their table long enough to change the temperature of the chairs, Harry was dancing with a woman who was there with her younger sister, just passing the time while her husband was away on a short fishing trip. After a few dances Harry returned to the table and told the guys he would see them tomorrow, and left with Irma.

Jesus Krist, you see that? I aint even decided who I want to dance with and hes coppin some broads draws, shaking his head and looking at Harrys back with awe and wonderment.

I tell you that guys incredible. If theres only one broad in the joint that can be made, Harryll sniff her out.

Yeah, even if she dont know it. They laughed and enviously watched Harry work his way through the people around the edge of the dance floor, his open hand on the small of Irmas back.

The way Irma figured it, they had plenty of time. Her husband usually got back about five or six in the morning, but never before two, and that was only once. Harry was still bubbling with the energy of joy, and he tossed his clothes on a chair and literally dove onto the bed with a flump and a squeal, and lunged at Irma, who was standing at the side of the bed, her panties still on and in the process of taking off her bra. He grabbed her around the waist and kissed her on the small of the back, then cupped his open mouth where the roundness started to swell and blew hot air on her flesh. Irma squeaked, sighed, oooood and panted all at the same time and floated to the bed as Harry yanked her down beside him. She put her arms around him as he kissed her neck and then her boobs and worked the tip of a few fingers under her panties and weaved his way through the brush to the promised land. Irma swayed and rolled and undulated and grabbed frantically at Harrys head and arms and shoulders and back and the sheets and anything else she came in contact with as she floundered and flailed from all the sudden attention.

Suddenly Harry remembered whats-her-name sitting on the park bench waiting for him—Mary, yeah, thats it—and he suddenly started to chuckle, his face buried between Irmas boobs. Her left hand was ensnarled in Harrys hair, and she gave a slight tug. Gee, thanks a lot. You know, I really could use a good laugh. Harry looked at her and really laughed and there was so much joy on his face that Irma started to laugh too, thats the funniest thing I ever heard, lying back and rolling her head back and forth, laughing, her hand still entwined in Harrys long hairs while his had her by the short hairs. I think so too, shaking his head back and forth, his eyes tearing, and they continued to lie there, hand in hair, laughing, until Harry finally stopped shaking his head, took a deep breath, and filled his mouth with tit. That not only stopped his laughter, but was equally effective in stopping hers.

Harry continued to think of Mary from time to time, and somehow the idea of her attitude toward her husband, the coldness that obviously existed between them, and the fact that she was sitting on that bench waiting for him and he knew it, kept his excitement at a peak level for hours. When Harry was finally ready to leave, close to three in the morning, Irma just lay in the bed watching him dress and muttering, Jesus, you really know where its at. You should talk to my husband and give him a pointer or two.

Why I would just love to, laughing and giving his clothes one last tuck and tug. Maybe I/ll come around next week and we can play Monopoly. Irma laughed, weakly, and rubbed her stomach gently with her hand. Harry waved goodbye as he left the room, and Irma fluttered a hand in response.

Harry stood on the street for a moment, breathing the fresh air. After a couple of days on a fishing boat, that bedroom should smell natural to her husband. Harry laughed out loud and started walking. His step was brisk and buoyant. The air and the night were refreshing, and the sky had a glitter or two of star. It was a beautiful night, a beautiful world. This was probably the best weekend of his life. . . . Yeah, of anybodys life. Harry was one with himself, his fellow man and God.

Monday morning the jostling of the subway helped unglue Harrys eyes, hair by hair, as he hung on a strap and drowsed at signs, advertisements, faces, backs of heads, newspapers, magazines, and his vague reflection in the window. When he extricated himself from the man-made mess of men and machinery, he walked as briskly as possible to the coffee shop in his building and got a large container of coffee, with extra sugar, and a cheese danish.

Actually it wasnt a bad day at all. There was enough work to keep Harry busy, but nothing that made inordinate demands upon him; and he was young and healthy and was able to snap back rapidly from a night of frolicking and cavorting. At lunch time he briefly thought of whats-her-name and wanted to find out if she was sitting on the bench, waiting, but wasnt in the mood. Instead he called down for lunch and stayed in the lounge, stretching out and resting his fire-engine-red eyes.

The rest of the afternoon went by rather rapidly, all things considered, and Harry jostled home and spent a quiet evening of watching TV with the folks, which made them happy, and went to bed early. Didnt do much today, but we/ll give it hell tomorrow.

Ah yes, a good day tomorrow, today, Tuesday. An educational ride to work, reading a little of the *Daily News*—sports and page four, the Jewish *Daily Forward*, *The Enquirer*, *La Prensa*, the *Times*, *Newsweek*, *The New Yorker*, Mad Magazine, Harold Robbins, Albert Camus (Camus at eight oclock in the morning on a crowded subway?), Lady Clairol (does she or doesnt she, only her gynecologist knows for sure), a crush-proof box (hmmm, now thats interesting), and a dark brown mole with at least five rough black hairs growing out of it and feeling their way around like antennae, and assorted hacks and coughs. Harry emerged from the hole in the ground a true cosmopolite and survivor of the tunnel of darkness. He stood on the corner for a moment, midst the beeps and honks and zipping and rushing, breathing deeply, then sallied forth to do battle with the giants of industry.

An energetic morning and the solving of a few not-quite-so knotty problems, and then the ringing of the dinner bell as it growls in an empty stomach. Lunch. And whatever happened to whats-her-name?

Hi, how are you? smiling and bending slightly.

Well, hello stranger, eyebrows slightly raised in a questioning look, this is a surprise.

Mind if I sit down?

Its a free country and a public bench.

Harry sat next to her, balancing his lunch on his lap,

(37)

chuckling to himself at her obvious hostility and the reasons for it. I/ll tell you, its good to be home, Mary looking at him suspiciously, after a job like that.

You were out of town? the hint of hope in her voice obvious.

Why else do you think I didnt keep our lunch date? smiling into her face. You dont think I forgot, do you? She shrugged almost apologetically. Got a sudden emergency call shortly after I left here and had to fly to Chicago.

Really? her face softening into a smile, and you just got back?

Late last night. I would have called your office, but of course I didnt know who you worked for.

O, well, thats not important. You know, I usually sit here anyway, smiling, the tension now gone from her shoulders.

Good, a warm squeeze of her knee, then a bite of his sandwich as he smiled at her.

The breeze warmed, and the reflections in the lake were friendly, as were the birds that flew and hopped by, and an occasional squirrel zipped by, then posed and wrinkled his nose. A delightful day, a delightful time of chitchat, of mirth and laughter, a delightful hour and a half. After Harry dropped their paper bags in the trash can, they walked slowly up the walk, Harrys hand lightly on her shoulder. He stood on the corner until she had entered the building, then zipped along Fifth Avenue to his office.

Forty minutes late. An eyebrow or two seems raised a wee bit. He seems to attract just a little more attention than usual as he hurries to his desk. Is there a frown, perhaps, on an executive face behind a closed door? O well, if so, it will soon be gone. No one is going to hang him for being a few minutes late. He/ll get his work done without any trouble, and it wont happen again. So wipe that frown off and relax. Everything is all right. I can take care of things. And anyway, life is just a bowl of berries.

Lunch the following day was even more delightful. There was no hostility to overcome, and they were relaxed and cheerful. Harry wanted to be certain to get back to the office a few minutes early and openly checked the time, telling Mary that he had to be certain to get back to the office before two as he was expecting a very important call from Chicago, about that emergency job I had to fly out there on.

What is it thats so important, anyway? You never did tell me what it was all about.

O well, its just a system to coordinate a couple of existing national, and international, communication systems into one instant network for the distribution of telemetry data and related fixed logs—

O.K., O.K., laughing and waving her hand, forget it. He joined her laughter and stopped telling the story, but continued to check his watch.

Checking his watch was not an affectation, but a necessity. He enjoyed the game he was playing so much that he could, as he had the day before, forget time completely, and he did not want to do that. Toying with Mary rekindled that spur of excitement in his gut, that twinge that came from expectation and apprehension, but he did not want to jeopardize his job for the game, no matter how much he enjoyed playing it.

Harry White got back to the office almost five minutes early and sat smugly at his desk, painting smiles of approbation on the frowning faces of yesterday.

Part of the game with whatser-name was, naturally, to let her dangle. And the longer she dangled, the greater the excitement, the tighter that worming twinge became and the more it spread itself out in undulating rings through his body until it reached the tips of his fingers.

And, of course, the longer she dangled, the more anxious she became. He wanted her to fumble around, as she was starting to do, awkwardly looking for ways to tell him she wanted to see him again, and not only for lunch; trying to find out where he lived (she asked him, today, how long a subway ride he had each day, and he told her he took a bus, about twenty minutes) and what he did with his spare time, and where he went and with whom. . . .

Harry parried each reaching question easily, though he did admit that he was not married, which obviously pleased her as Harry knew it would. And, with each answer Harry whetted her curiosity, and so their little repast by the lake, or short strolls by its edge, were a time of fun, games, excitement and relaxation for Harry. And it was obvious that Mary enjoyed these times too. Perhaps even more than Harry, and obviously in a different way and for different reasons.

One of the things, an important one too, that made it easy for Harry to continue this game indefinitely, something he had never done before, was the fact that he enjoyed her company, at least for the short time they spent with each other. And that time never amounted to more than a few hours a week because one of the elements of Harrys game was never to see her more than two days in a row, and never more than three days a week. After a few weeks the game became a game and in addition to his other goals, Harry wanted to see just how long he could keep the game going . . . or perhaps it would be more specific to say to see how long he would want to keep it going. Ah well, only time would answer that question. Only time, happy time, would show when Harry would allow whatser-name to seduce him. Ah yes, I/ll tell you something, its lovely to watch spring slide toward summer in Central Park, to see more leaves on the trees and bushes with each day, and more eagerness in her eyes. Ah yes, Harry knew that it was true, that New York was, indeed, a summer festival.

And festive it was by the lake in Central Park, Mary talking more and more about her husband and her discontent and disillusionment with her marriage. Harry wisely refrained from attacking her husband, which would have forced her to defend him and start talking about what was nice about him, but he did stop defending him and offering excuses and/or explanations for his conduct and lack of concern and attentions toward her. As a matter of fact he just listened, a concerned expression on his face, as Mary allowed that her husband was an asshole, a big-mouthed son of a bitch. He never, not once, has he ever sat and listened to me . . . like you do—a tower-of-strength and understanding expression on Harrys face—he just turns on the television or walks out of the room and if I walk after him and try to make him listen to me, if I try to get him to understand that Im a human being with feelings and needs and things, he just calls me a dumb broad and goes out with the boys. Oohhhh, shaking her head agitatedly, there are times when I think I would shoot him if I had a gun.

O, you wouldnt want to do that, touching her hand solicitously, you would just go to jail and deprive me, and the rest of the world, of your company. Mary smiled at Harry, then suddenly frowned as he said he felt sorry for her husband.

Feel sorry for him? Hes the one who is always going out with the boys, who comes and goes as he pleases, who gulps down a meal I sweat to prepare, then belches in my face and leaves. Just like that. He goes, wherever he goes, no thanks, no nothin, and leaves me alone with the dishes. See if I ever slave over a stove again. Hes lucky if he gets a TV dinner.

You dont understand what I mean, patting her hand and smiling, I mean its a shame that he denies himself the extreme joy, and excitement, of listening to you, and watching the light dance in your eyes when youre excited.

O, do you really mean that, that its exciting to listen to me?

Of course, chuckling and looking into her eyes, why would I say it if it wasnt true?

And so the game continued, Harry getting more and more excited as he watched her excitement grow. There were times when Harrys nose seemed to twitch as he smelled a bitch in heat, and so the combination of the game he was playing, and Marys squirming struggle with herself and her neglect by her husband, made Harry aware that the game would have to end soon. Or at least this stage of it.

And then, In the Merry, Merry Month of May, except that it was June by now, Harry finally responded to a gambit by Mary. They were sitting on their bench, chatting, and Harry finished his sandwich and was crumbling the paper when Mary reached over and brushed the crumbs from his lap, spending extra time, and effort, on a persistent crumb on the upper, inner part of his thigh. Harry sort of chirpped inside his head, and raised his leg slightly against her hand, then put his open hand on hers, caressing it strongly as he looked deep into her eyes, his lids slightly squeezed and his nostrils just barely flared. He felt her hand twitch as the tip of his tongue just managed to squirm its way through his lips.

We cant go on like this, Mary, slowly sliding his hand off hers and reaching up with his other hand and rubbing the back of her neck. For a couple of seconds her eyes closed as she surrendered to his hand, then they opened partly as she looked at him (krist, this bitch is horny).

What can we do?

Harry just stared into her eyes, enjoying the game and hoping he did not bust out laughing.

When? moving her hand against Harrys hand, Harry chuckling inside, enjoying his small victory of having her ask him. He applied a little more pressure to the nape of her neck, and her eyes rolled back for a second and her body swayed with pleasure.

Tomorrow night, after work.

She nodded her head and continued to sway with his hand. I/ll tell my husband Im going out with the girls from the office.

Harry nodded, sort of tap dancing in his head, with a smile as his umbrella, and wondering what her reaction would be when he announced a change of plans tomorrow afternoon.

Ah, tomorrow . . . another day, another lay . . . hahahaha, why not? I/ll tell you about tomorrow, what they say about it is a lie. It does come. It always comes. Haha, and so do I. And Mary? Quite contrary? Ho, ho. Why not? Im sure she/ll come . . . if I invite her . . . hahaha, would you like to come, my dear? Hey Louie, come again on the rice pudding. Be my guest. Yeah, tomorrows another day . . . with a razzmatazz and a twenty-three skiddoo. Trip down the path with those pretty maids all in a row. Nope, she aint contrary at all. Hahaha. To-*mor*row is a-*noth*-er day. . . .

And what ill tidings bring ye to she? Be it tidings of pain or joy? Ah, yes, pain or joy? How can I answer? With a wave of the hand? A shrug of shoulder? A nod of head? Or shall I answer with that beast of beasts, another question? If you will, a question. How beats her heart? How quickens her breath? And tell me, does not her pulse pound and throb through her veins? And how quivers that succulent mound of Venus between soft thighs? Surely the pounding pounds and the throbbing throbs, and the tingle doth crawl beneath her flesh. I/ll tell you what I bring the anticipating maiden—the joy of pain and the pain of joy. . . .

Yeah, youre goddamn right. Right up the old gazoo, the moist and hungry gazookus.

The next day Harry left the office early and met Mary on the corner. Tom, what are you doing here, I—

I have to talk with you, Mary, grabbing her arm and directing her up the street.

Mary looked at him, bewildered and surprised. Whats wrong? You look so intense, and—concerned. (Ah, very good Dr. White. Just keep that expression for a few minutes and we/ll be back in the saddle again.)

I got a call from Chicago an hour ago and I have to fly out there tonight.

O, no! Not tonight Tom, the light draining from her eyes.

And I have no idea how long I will have to stay, the look of concern now coupled with frantic despair—and hunger. He looked deep into her lightless eyes. This was the penultimate stage of the game. In a few minutes she would be taking off his clothes and devouringly pulling him on top of her.

Mary returned his stare, then noticed a sign on the side of the building across the street, HOTEL SPLENDIDE. Tom, look, and he turned and looked at the sign, then back into her shining eyes.

O, and sing a song of sixpence, a pocketful of rye, and all that sort of stuff. That broad was hungry, really hungry. So much so that Harry got the fright of his life and for a second not only regretted the entire game, but almost prayed for deliverance. They did not have too much time (much less than she knew), and when round one was finished there was not the time for a cigarette and banter, wanting to get in as much as possible (O, thats funny, a real bon mot), and she started to gobble his bird and a chill pierced him as he thought she was some kind of cannibal who was going to eat him, but for real, but after a shriek she apologized and her table manners improved, and Harry breathed a sigh of relief and with a wave of the hand he wished her *bon appétit*.

Time was short and the desires long, but they did the best they could with what they had. And, all things considered, they had quite a lot. They definitely were not disappointed with their *LAprès-Midi dun Fuck*. Eventually when time, and job consciousness, intruded upon their hasty liaison, they left bed and board (Sorry you have to eat and run. [O, thats a good one.]) for the shower.

The shower was a large, flat sprinkler head protruding from the wall over the bathtub, which gave a feeling of openness to it. They soaped each other and rubbed and lathered and, from time to time, Harry would slip the soap up out of sight, and soon they realized that time and job would have to wait just a little longer and Harry helped Mary stretch out in the tub and mounted his maiden fair, the water falling and sprinkling itself on his back and tinkling on the tub as he sang merrily his lay, with his big toe stuck in the drain. When the song was over (but the melody lingers on), they both stretched out on their backs and let the water plop on them, and slid up and down in the tub, laughing.

But, alack and alas, times thrust is inevitable, and so the cleansing rain of summer was turned off and bodies briskly rubbed with inadequate towels. When they finished drying, Harry took the towel from her hands, slowly slid his hands across her body while looking into her eyes, then pulled her close to him and nuzzled her hair and neck. Youre a magnificent, woman, Mary, and kissed her on the shoulder, the neck, the lips.

O, Tom, her eyes closed, swaying with a feeling of ecstasy, my precious Tom, I love you.

Neither one reacted to the statement, but Harry continued

to kiss her for another few seconds, then they dressed and left to fulfill their commitments to job and time.

When they parted at the corner, Mary looked up at Harry with eyes that were aglow and dreamily twinkling. You will come over to the park when you get back, wont you?

Of course, smiling gently. He squeezed her hand. Goodbye Mary.

So long Tom.

Harry walked back to the office knowing that he would not have to check up on her to see if she was sitting by the lake, waiting. She/d be there, for a long time. And who knows, he might go back someday. Yeah . . . the next time he wanted a box lunch, hahahaha. But she was all right, that broad, at least while shes hungry. Hungry hell, she was starving. But shes got an insatiable appetite. And not for the old zortch. Love. Yeah, thats what she wants. A little T.L.C. Some affection and understanding. I bet she could be a pretty good wife—but not for me. Its too bad, we could have some good lunch hours (or two), but thems the breaks. But she/d probably change after she wasnt so hungry, after she had had a few good, steady meals.

Well, anyway, thats the end of that little scene. Sure was a ball while it lasted. Glad she didnt get too mushy. A pretty straight broad. Bet it was the first time she fucked around on her old man. Wonder what hes going to think when she comes home tonight with her skin and eyes glowing? He probably wont even notice. He must be some kind of jerk. Maybe shes right and hes just an asshole. But you can bet your sweet ass that that glow will be gone in a couple of weeks. Poor bitch. Feel sort of sorry for her. Probably curse my ass. . . . But someday she/ll thank me. At least now she knows she doesnt have to sit around and wait for her old man. Now she knows she can spend a night with the boys too, hahaha. . . . Yeah, I probably saved her a lot of time and trouble. Who knows how long it might have taken her to find out she can play around too.

Harry disembarked from the elevator, waved at the receptionist and strolled to his desk. Before he could sit down, Mr. Wentworth's secretary was standing beside him. Where have you been?

Out to lunch. Why, did you miss me, Louise?

No, but Mr. Wentworth did—Harry looked at his watch—and was pretty mad when he left.

Krist, it is late, isnt it?

Frankly, Im surprised you bothered to come back at all, or are you just early for tomorrow? laughing quietly.

Thanks, I need your cheerfulness, frowning. What did he want?

The figures for the Compton and Brisbane proposal. We found most of the information on your desk, but the calculations and data sheets and a few other things were missing.

O, krist, his previous elation drained, they should be right here, opening a drawer and pulling notebooks and a few folders out and putting them on the desk. What did he want them now for, assembling papers hurriedly, he said he didnt need them until tomorrow.

Evidently there was a sudden change, shrugging her shoulders, and he had to meet with the client this afternoon. You/d better get them ready, he said he would call if he had to have them. He thought he— O, theres the phone.

Louise left, and Harry continued to arrange the papers, hoping—almost praying—that Mr. Wentworth would not call. He suddenly felt nauseous as he realized that that might be him on the phone now. He turned and looked toward Louise, who was nodding her head and writing on a pad. He tried to get her attention by increasing the intensity of his stare, but she continued to listen and take notes. All of a sudden his insides were in a turmoil, his bones and flesh seemed to be knotted with anxiety. For krists sake, Louise, look up, will you? Harry could feel his toes twitching and his eyes starting to tear slightly from staring so hard. Damn it, clenching his jaw tightly, is he on the phone????

Louise hung up the phone, looked at her notes for a few seconds, then noticed Harry staring at her. She returned his stare for a second, wondering what was wrong with him, then realized why he was staring and smiled and shook her head no. Harry felt a sudden relief, as if he had just had a reprieve, but then realized that it was to be short-lived, as if he had been taken away from the gas chamber at the last moment, but was already on his way to the gallows. He shook his head. Jesus krist, whats going on? This is crazy. He looked at the mess he had made with the papers, then closed his eyes, took a deep breath and was determined to slow down and just take it easy and get the papers ready. He looked at them for a moment, then carefully and methodically started to assemble them properly.

Louise stopped at his desk on her way out. You look like youre ready to spend the night.

Well, I thought maybe I/d stay around for a few minutes, looking a little sheepish and embarrassed, just in case Mr. Wentworth called.

I dont think he/ll call now, not if he hasnt called already.

Yeah, youre probably right. Guess I/ll pack up.

Goodnight Harry. See you tomorrow.

Yeah. Good night. Harry straightened up his desk and got ready to leave, but decided to stay until five-thirty. He felt that if he somehow stayed that extra half-hour, it would make everything all right, that somehow it would erase what had happened today.

Happened???? Yeah, what in the hell did happen? What is all this bullshit about, anyway? Im doing my job. What do they want from me? Krist, youd think I killed someone, or something. Has it just been *one* day? *Jesus.* It seems like years ago since I stood on the corner and waited for whatser-name. . . . Somethings wacky. Just cant figure it. One day . . . I do a good job. They dont have any right to get on my back like that. O balls. Be damned if I know what it is, but something sure as hell is wrong.

He left the office and walked along Fifth Avenue for a few blocks, his head tumbling with images and words, then got on a bus and rode to Forty-second Street. He got off and walked west to Times Square. The crowds seemed unusually oppressive and his ears hurt as if there were some sort of pressure behind them, as if they were about to be pierced with an ice pick, and his eyeballs felt like they were being pressed by two large thumbs.

He stopped at Grants and had a couple of hot dogs and clam juice, then continued down Forty-second Street until he turned into one of the movies. He did not know exactly what was going on on the screen, but it helped relieve the pain in his head. He had reviewed the day so many times, trying desperately to make some semblance of sense out of the events, that he was slowly becoming mentally exhausted, and whatever was happening on the screen absorbed enough from the surface of his mind so that he got relief from the pressure.

After a few hours he left the theater and went home. Every now and then the clacking of the subway train seemed to say *Comp*ton & Brisbane, *Comp*ton & Brisbane, and he would have to shake his head and concentrate on the people in the train or the advertisements until the noise was just the usual click, clack.

The following morning Harry got to the office early to be certain to be there when Mr. Wentworth arrived. He double-checked the Compton & Brisbane folders to be sure they were ready, then tried to get involved with another job, but found it impossible to concentrate as he involuntarily continued to look toward the door, his right leg bouncing up and down on the ball of his foot.

He did not want to be drinking coffee and eating his usual danish when Mr. Wentworth came in, so he passed them up this morning, and now he wished he had something to wash that metallic taste out of his mouth and feed that active hunger in his gut. It seemed like every part of his body was itchy with apprehension, even the tips of his hair. He tried to freeze a look of deep and absolute concentration on his face, but it felt like his skin would crack.

Thank God, Wentworth finally got there. Harry could feel his pulse in his temples and the sweat on his chest and under his eyes; could feel his heart pounding in his throat and his stomach twisting and turning. He followed Mr. Wentworth with his eyes, ready to smile if he should look at him, but he just continued to his office.

Then Harry waited.... And waited.... For eternal minutes. He could not believe that time could move so slowly, or that he could feel so sick. He had to constantly swallow his nausea, and those thumbs on his eyes were pressing harder and harder. He sat waiting for Mr. Wentworth to buzz him, his foot bounding uncontrollably, all the power of his mind focused on the control of his anal sphincter muscle. His skin felt as if it were being flushed with molten lead, and he knew that any minute he would leap up from his desk and start to scream and scream and scream and he fought hard to swallow his scream over and over again along with his nausea. He could feel the sweat stinging the small of his back and the toes in his right foot started to cramp, and when the buzzer finally screeched in his ear his skin almost peeled from his bones.

Come in here White. Harry could not believe it, but he was actually dizzy when he stood. What the hell is wrong? This is insane. He tried to adjust the serious business look on his face, but his mind and body were so alive and active with emotions that he had no idea what he looked like, but knew he felt like a leprous sheep being led to slaughter. He was so overwhelmed, not only by all these feelings, but also by the fact that he should be experiencing such feelings, that he was almost unable to get from his desk to Mr. Wentworths office. He again tried to pull on a look of self-assurance and entered the office.

You picked one hell of a time to screw off, White!

Im sorry Mr.—

Never mind the stories. I dont have time for them. Fortunately I was able to talk their people around not needing the data I did not have with me yesterday, so we have not lost the account, yet—a sigh inside of Harry went kerflop—no thanks to you. But time will only tell. Now, heres the data I took yesterday, tossing a couple of file folders on the desk, get all the information properly assembled. I am going to meet with them again next week. I had to do a back-breaking selling job, yesterday, to get that appointment, so make certain everything is ready. Got it?

Yes sir. I/ll—

I will be dictating some extensive notes to Mrs. Wills today, and she/ll give you a copy of them when they are transcribed. I want you to be absolutely certain that you incorporate the salient facts properly in our summary.

Yes sir, nodding his head, I/ll—

I want this proposal so perfect that it sells itself. Got me? Perfect!

Yes sir, nodding his head and picking up the files.

And one more thing, Harry standing erect and trying to look alert. This business of strolling off in the afternoon— Harry swallowing hard and praying for survival—it has ended. You understand? Ended!

Yes sir, standing stiff, afraid to move.

You are one of the brightest young men we have here, leaning back in his chair, but I dont give a damn how bright you are, youre not doing the corporation any good when you are not here. You understand me? A slight nod. You can have a great future here. You have all the equipment to go right to the top of the ladder . . . the very top. *But*—and this is the most important thing in your life—you have to want it. You have to want it more than anything else. Thats the key to success. It is available, but it is not going to be given to you. We can give you the opportunity, that is all. You have to do the work. Do I make myself clear?

Yes sir. Completely, hoping that the end was near so he could collapse at his desk and breathe.

Good. Now go ahead and do the kind of job I know you are capable of doing, and give it to Mrs. Wills when you are finished.

He made it. He was sitting at his desk and his body and mind were slowly, but steadily, relaxing, and his breathing came easier and he sat for many minutes, shaking his head in disbelief—disbelief that the turmoil was subsiding, and disbelief that he could react the way he had. He was still trembling, slightly, from fear.

When he thought he had sat at his desk long enough to impress anyone who might be watching, he went to the mens room. He bathed his face with cold water, then sat on a commode, with the top down, for a few minutes to relax. He wished he could take his clothes off and take a cold shower and put on dry clothes. After a few minutes he nodded his head, got up and went back to his desk and applied himself to his work. There was not too much more he could do on the Compton & Brisbane proposal until he got the notes from Louise, so he involved himself in another project. As he worked he slowly became aware that both his legs were bouncing up and down, and that he was feeling very squirmy in his crotch. He unobtrusively reached down and scratched his crotch a few times, then rubbed it and became aware of the fact that he had a painful hard-on. He suddenly started thinking of Mary and wondered if he should go over to the park—she/d be there in a few minutes—and take her to the hotel, but he quickly nixed that idea. He had to be here today, no matter what. But krist, he was horny. He never felt like this before. At least not that he remembered. The feeling overwhelmed him. He tried to concentrate on his work and all he could think of was his erection and the squirming in his crotch, and when he looked at the papers on his desk, he kept seeing Marys hairy bush and feeling the flesh of her ass between his teeth, or one of her tits in his mouth, and he fidgeted in his seat until he could no longer stand it, then guiltily looked around before getting up and going to the mens room and masturbating. When he finished he sat on the commode, his pants around his ankles, his head hanging dejectedly, sweat dripping down his face, swallowing a vile and bitter nausea he had never tasted before, trying to remember the last time he jerked off, but unable to. He turned red with guilt and remorse and shook his head, perplexed, wondering why he felt the way he did.

Screw it. He stood up and dressed, washed his hands, splashed more cold water on his face, then went out to lunch.

He lost himself, and his thoughts and feelings, in the crowds on the streets and in the stores, before eating a sandwich in a coffee shop, then drifting with the crowds again. He continually glanced at his watch and made sure he got back at least five or ten minutes early.

When he got back to his desk, he felt weary and confused, but at least he was not battling an onslaught of unfamiliar feelings, and so he was able to lose himself in his work. In the middle of the afternoon Louise gave him the notes, and so he was absorbed in them for the remainder of the day and in fact was surprised, pleasantly, when Louise tapped him on the shoulder at five and told him it was time to go home.

Already? Boy, time sure does fly.

Yes, especially when you bury your head in work the way you did today. You know Harry, leaning a little closer, Mr. Wentworth really likes you. He thinks youre the brightest, most likable, young executive the firm has ever had.

Thanks Louise, looking at her with an expression of genuine humility and gratitude, that helps.

Just thought I/d mention it, smiling. Good night.

Harry gathered the papers together and left the office. His pace was lighter and quicker as he walked to the subway, it seeming like a lifetime ago that he dragged himself along the street to the bus and then along Forty-second Street. The reason for his lightness was the intense relief he now felt after enduring the dreaded confrontation with Mr. Wentworth, and the mildness and brevity of the reprimand. And, of course, Louises comment didnt do any harm. But the feeling of relief was actually secondary to the feeling of excitement that was responsible for the quickness of his pace and the crispness of his thinking.

What Louise had said about his burying his head in the work was true. And it worked. It eventually shoved all the other matters that were jumbling around in his brain aside and took over completely and he was once again the sharp and promising young executive. And to narrow it even further, the only thing he was conscious of now was the Compton & Brisbane account. Sometime during the afternoon, not long before he knocked off for the day, some of the information in the notes Louise had given him started to fit with something he remembered from the previous specifications and he hurriedly checked and dashed off a few equations. He thought he had found a way not only to save time, perhaps a week, but money as well. . . . He wasnt certain, but perhaps a few hundred thousand dollars. The excitement made him oblivious to the jostling and bumping of the subway. He could not wait to get back to work tomorrow.

The next morning he was involved with his new idea before he finished his coffee and cheese danish. By ten oclock he knew he was right. He stopped for a moment, then assembled the papers in the proper order and reviewed the proposal from the beginning to be absolutely certain he had not overlooked anything, and to collate more information to support his idea. By midafternoon he was ready to present his idea to Mr. Wentworth.

Again he was overwhelmed by how rapidly situations can turn themselves around—one day he was terrified by a prospective interview with his boss, and today he was anxiously anticipating it.

He had prepared a rough graphic summary of his idea, using the appropriate charts, and laid it out in front of Mr. Wentworth, and then went over it, step by step, referring to the clients data and spec sheets, and to their own experience and expertise.

I think youre right Harry. It sure as hell looks that way. We will save from five to seven days and at least a few hundred thousand dollars on the initial outlay. And who knows how much after that. Combine that with the edge we have going in, and no one can compete with us. Harry, patting him on the back, you did a good job. I am proud of you.

Thanks Mr. Wentworth, smiling, thats good to hear.

You know—the old brain clicking away—I think we can save some additional monies and time by incorporating a few procedures from an existing job, and do the same for another one that should be coming up next year. In any event, that need not concern you. You go ahead and have this proposal prepared as you have outlined and we will be in business. They smiled at each other and Harry gathered up his papers and Mr. Wentworth patted him on the back as he left.

The following days flew by as swiftly as a flying arrow, or as swiftly as an arrow can fly through the heat and humidity of a New York City summer. Harry spent the weekend on Fire Island with some friends amid the usual Fire Island madness and hysteria. He swam, walked along the beach, strolled over the reed spotted dunes, stared out at the ocean, tumbled in the surf, soaked up some sun, played volleyball, endured the shrill cacophony of a few parties and screwed a couple of broads.

The following week there were a couple of rush jobs and Harry once again had his head immersed in work, and so the excitement continued to carry him through the days, the subway rides, and the nights, which he spent primarily at home watching the tube with his folks, or reading a book.

At the end of the week Mr. Wentworth brought back the signed Compton & Brisbane contract, and told Harry he was going to take him out that night as a small token of his appreciation. Im going to give you the full treatment, just as if you were a prospective client, and smiled at Harry and gave him half a wink.

Thats fine with me, chuckling and nodding his head.

They waited for the girls in their suite at the Plaza. They arrived at seven-thirty, and Harry knew that he definitely was going to have a good time. Harry, this is Alice and—Cherry. I thought you were the redhead type, so I asked Alice to see what she could do.

Hi.

Hello.

Hi.

Actually Im an any-head type, smiling, the others chuckling, but I must admit that Alice sure did just great.

Wentworth poured them all drinks, and they clinked ice cubes and sat around letting the cool drinks warm things up. This was Harrys first experience with a professional of any type, no less a member of the Public Relations Entertainment Committee—the take-your-clothes-off-I-want-to-talk-to-you, lie-down-so-I-can-hear-you-better faction. O well, thats show biz, of which theres no biz like.

After a drink or two they left for dinner, and Harry joined in the conversation, thinking about throwing a good one into this Cherry.

And he did. And a few more. It was the best night Cherry had since entering the Public (Pubic?) Relations field. After dinner they made the rounds of a few night spots and played a little kneesies and pinch assie under the table, then went back to their suite at the Plaza.

By the time they got back to the hotel Harry had worked himself up into a lather, and so before Cherry could get all her clothes off, Harry buried his face in her luscious crotch. When he came up for air, he helped her undress and they frolicked and cavorted until they finally went seepy, seepy bye bye.

The next morning Wentworth was pretty much the corporate executive as he paid the girls, in cash, and checked his pockets to be certain he was not leaving anything behind. As they stood at the curb waiting for cabs, Mr. Wentworth nudged Harry on the shoulder and screwed his face into a sly look. Pretty good night, eh Harry? Pretty good stuff. I hope you didnt find yourself out of your league.

No, it went all right, smiling and trying to look sly, at least as far as I know. Wentworth laughed and just before he closed the door of his cab he said, I/ll see you bright and early Monday morning, Harry.

Sunday night Harry ended up at a dance in Sheepshead Bay with some of his friends, and, as usual, he left after a short time with half of a marriage, the bottom half. Everything was pretty much the same, with one exception: he fell asleep. A fact he did not become aware of until he fought to keep his eyes closed Monday morning as the light stabbed at them, then suddenly realized that he was not at home. He looked around, then realized where he was and slowly remembered the night before. Somewhere around two or three in the morning, Olga (if thats her name) rolled him over on his stomach and started massaging his neck and shoulders, and that was the last thing he remembered. He sat up suddenly and looked at the time, then jumped out of bed and took a quick shower, then dressed, kissed Olga on the left cheek, or her ass, and left.

He rushed home to change his clothes, then rushed to the subway. He was a little breathless by the time he found a strap to hang on in the train, but was not too disturbed about being late even though it was just a short time ago that he had to endure a torturous reprimand. After all, after Friday night there should not be any hassle with Wentworth. If he asks me why Im late, I/ll just tell him I was with a broad and did not notice the time. But so he would not add insult to injury, Harry decided to forgo his coffee and cheese danish.

He got to the office a few minutes before ten, and for some reason the fact that he was less than an hour late was significent to him. He could see that Mr. Wentworth was already in his office, but that did not create any uneasiness. He sat at his desk and opened the file of the proposal he was currently involved in. After ten minutes, or so, Mr. Wentworth buzzed him, and he picked up the phone. Yes sir?

White, theres a time for play and a time for work, and the successful man never gets the two confused.

Click! End of message. It took Harry a few seconds to react to the silence, the stern voice and click still seeming to reverberate somewhere in his head. Especially that click. It seemed to have such a finality to it. Absolute. He hung up the phone and became aware of the hollowing churning in his gut. Jesus, not again. This is crazy. Feeling good, feeling bad. Feeling good, feeling bad. Somethings goofy here. . . .

O well, screw it. Its not all that important. I/ll just get to work and pretty soon this whole thing—whatever in the hell it is—will be gone. He buried his head in his work.

He kept his head there for the remainder of the week, making a fifty-minute hour out of his lunch hour. But then the emergency and urgency disappeared, and he soon started eating a quick lunch and spending the rest of the time walking along Fifth Avenue and through the stores.

From time to time, quite frequently as a matter of fact, he thought of Mary and the time in the Hotel Splendide. He was not so much interested in her—she was obviously trouble, and he studiously avoided the lake in the park—but those weeks certainly did give him something to do with his time. But he remembered, too, what happened later that afternoon, and did not want to go through that torture again. Not for anything.

So Harry would stroll aimlessly along the avenue and through the stores, always going in a direction away from the park.

3

One day Harry was looking around the mens department of a store, when a woman suddenly turned around and knocked into him, dropping her pocketbook, which opened, the contents spilling out. O, excuse me, Im sorry.

No, it was my fault, I shouldnt have turned so suddenly.

Here, let me help you, helping her pick up the contents of her pocketbook and noticing the sheen of her stockings as she knelt beside him.

Thank you, putting the last of them in and closing the pocketbook, Im really sorry.

No harm done, smiling.

I saw a sign that said sale, chuckling apologetically, and I guess I just started to charge like a bull in a china shop.

If bulls ever looked like you, I/d be a matador. She smiled in acknowledgment of the compliment and started to relax. Where is that sign you saw?

Over there, in the tie department.

O . . . yeah. Looking for something for your husband?

No, smiling, my father. Its his birthday.

Then why dont you let me help you? Im an expert on ties and fathers.

Really? smiling.

Absolutely. I have both. They both chuckled and went over to the counter and started looking. Now, I assume you want silk.

Gee, I dont know. Im such a ninny when it comes to things like ties.

Well, fear not, your problems are over. Now, what color hair does he have?

Well, squinting and twisting her mouth, its sort of dark with a little gray. Mostly on the side. Sort of distinguished you know.

Of course, your father would have to be, returning her smile. Does he usually wear gray and blue suits?

Ahhh . . . yes, I guess he does. How did you know? looking at him with astonishment, youre amazing.

O, gesturing, nothing to it my dear Potson. Now, here are some stripes that will go with any shade of gray or blue. Just about, anyway.

O, gee, at those prices I can afford to get him a couple of ties. Harry showed her various ties from the rack, and she looked, shook her head and finally told Harry she didnt know which ones to choose.

Well, we cant have a beautiful young damsel like you in such a state of confusion. Here, taking two ties from the rack, why dont you buy these? Im sure he/ll like them. Theyre perfect for any occasion.

O.K., her face bursting into a quick smile. She paid for the ties, had them gift-wrapped, and they left the store. Harry looked at his watch, then at her and shrugged. Looks like its time to go. Tempus sure does fugit when youre enjoying yourself.

I really cant tell you how much I appreciate what youve

done for me. I might still be there trying to decide which ones to buy.

O, it was my pleasure.

Well, you simply saved my life, looking at him with a smile of complete sincerity. I wish there were some way I could express my appreciation.

Well, the charming smile on his face, there is something you can do. You can have lunch with me tomorrow.

All right. That would be delightful. Where?

Well . . . how about across the street, at one.

I/ll be there.

Krist, she had a lovely smile. Sort of warm and . . . real . . . yeah, I guess thats what it is. Its genuine. He rushed back to the office and just did manage to get there on time—actually two minutes late—and had been partially involved with his work for a while before he realized what he had done, that he had made a date with her for tomorrow. A slight jolt of fear and apprehension singed his gut and grabbed his bowels. O well, whats the big deal. Having lunch with her isnt going to kill me. No need to get my bowels in an uproar over a couple of ties and lunch. He dismissed all concern with a wave of a mental hand. One lunch date never killed any one.

Especially when it is as joyful and exhilarating as this was. She was simply bubbling with enthusiasm and glowed when she told him how much her father liked the ties. And I know he wasnt just trying to make me feel good—you know how you can tell those things, Harry nodded—but genuinely liked them. He tried them on right away.

It was a delightful lunch. One of the most pleasant hours he had spent in . . . he couldn't remember when. They chit-chatted about nothing in particular, laughed frequently and, no matter what they talked about it was enjoyable and relaxing. When it was time to leave, Harry was so caught up in the lightness of the mood that he almost asked her if she would like to have lunch tomorrow, but stopped with the words half out of his mouth. How about Friday, you free for lunch?

Yes, I believe so.

Here again?

Sure. It seems nice enough. Just before she left she grabbed Harrys hand, the smile still on her face. Thanks again.

Any time, smiling, then waving as she turned to go.

Harry rushed back to the office, almost trotting the last half a block, and got to his desk a few minutes late again, but less than five. Thank God. No one seemed to notice anything. There didnt seem to be any frowns or stares of dissatisfaction behind those executive doors. Yet he had a vague uneasiness. There was something disquieting smoldering inside of him. But it was ridiculous to feel like that. After all, he was only having lunch with her. Whats the big deal. Shes nice company, is all. He wasnt going to let the situation get out of hand. There was nothing to worry about. He could control it.

The next day Harry found himself a little restless at lunch time, not that he was thinking so much of—krist, I dont even know her name. I/ll be damned. Thats kind of funny—but just not knowing exactly what to do with his time. The usual strolling through the streets and stores seemed inane and aimless. He walked a few blocks to a coffee shop he had never tried before and ate as slowly as possible, then walked back to the office, his head lowered slightly and looking straight ahead of him.

Their lunch the next day was marvelous and they laughed frequently and by the time they were halfway through lunch Harry realized that he had started the game. He was startled for a moment by the realization, then mentally shrugged and continued it. Helen was different than Mary, so naturally the game was a little different.

One of the differences was that Helen never mentioned her husband, and so Harry avoided that area too. Harry was curious about him, but figured that she would mention him sooner or later, and Harry just continued with the usual eye-fucking and open-hand-on-the-thigh routine, carefully interspersed with compliments and smiles.

Harry got back to the office ten minutes late and quickly buried his head in his work, trying to look as if he had been there for fifteen minutes. He wiped the pressure of work from his brow with the back of his hand; but although his head was buried in his work, it was not involved in it. He suddenly flushed slightly as he remembered asking her if she would like to have lunch Monday— That would be swell. Good. Here at one. He had meant to be casual and leave it, bumping into each other some time for lunch, or some such thing—or at the most to make a date for the middle of next week. O well, its no big deal. He let it get out of hand today, but he wouldnt let that happen again. Next week would be different.

And different it was. They had lunch every day, and Harry found himself thinking the night before of how he would smile or touch her, of what direction the game would take, only to find the next day that he was running after the game. And he made a few elementary mistakes at work. Things that he never had to think about before, things that he did automatically and now he was screwing up. Louise caught two of them and he quickly corrected them, but one got through to Mr. Wentworth and he looked at Harry with an expression of surprise that soon seemed to turn to disgust. Are you all right, Harry?

Yes sir. Fine. I just somehow—

Well, you sure as hell dont act it lately. I suggest you get back on the track.

Yes sir, nodding and leaving Mr. Wentworths office.

What did he mean by that? Was he trying to tell me something? Jesus Krist, you cant crucify a man for being a few minutes late at lunch time. Harry corrected the error, then left for lunch. He waited for a few minutes, but Helen still hadnt gotten there. He looked at his watch. Ten to one. Krist, he must have left fifteen minutes early. Damn! O well, screw it. The work is done anyway. Or at least part of it. I can stay late if necessary.

Helen arrived and the game continued and Harry absorbed himself in it. When he got back to the office, he tried to concentrate even harder on his work and make up for lost time, but he found his mind slightly muddled. It was not that he was consciously preoccupied with other thoughts—it was just that he was looking at familiar things, knew they were familiar, but somehow they seemed vague and alien. He was forced to double- and triple-check procedures that he should have been able to do with no conscious effort at all. And though he was even further behind at five than he thought he would be, he did not stay late to finish. It was just impossible. And anyway, tomorrow was another day. He/d be able to take care of it then. After all, everybody has a bad day once in a while.

But they continued. Not that he could really call them bad days. But he sure as hell couldnt call them good days. As a matter of fact, he did not know what he could call them. Something was not right, that he knew, but he had no idea what was wrong. Whatever it was, it remained undefined and vague; and, actually, the only evidence of this a . . . malfunctioning was the fact that his work was not going as it should. Making errors where he never had before; taking longer to do routine work, and even finding it a little fuzzy at times; and an almost complete inability to bring anything new to his work. It was probably just the fact that there really wasnt anything new in his work right now. That was probably it. Different accounts, but the same basic routine. Yeah, thats it. As soon as something demanding comes along, I/ll perk up and everything will be all right. Nothing to worry about.

But thank God for those lunches. This week would have been one hell of a drag without them. Dont exactly know how we ended up having a lunch date each day, but Im sure glad it happened that way.

And finally Friday came and with it the end of the week and the knowledge that the following week would be better. At lunch that day Helen asked Harry if he would like to go to a show that night, we got a few free tickets at work.

Sure, I/d love to, wondering about her husband and what sort of scene they had, but determined not to bring up the subject.

That afternoon Harrys head was involved in the game, no

matter what he buried it in. He found himself tensing as he tried to concentrate on his work, more confused by his inability to solve simple problems than anything else. From time to time his head felt like it was going to burst, but then the feeling would pass and he would push the work aside momentarily, again, and think of the game and wonder about Helens husband and what he was doing tonight. Maybe this was his night out with the boys.

The dinner was delightful and the show was a comedy and very funny. When it was over, they walked along Broadway for a short time until Helen said it was time she got home. I dont have my walking shoes on, and Im tired and sore from laughing so much. That was a marvelous show.

Yeah, it was really funny. Where do you live?

Near Gramercy Park.

O well, thats nice and easy. We could even walk that.

No thank you, both of them laughing.

The light and enjoyable conversation continued during the trip downtown, and when they got to her apartment she opened the door, turned on the light and walked into the apartment, Harry following, accepting the tacit invitation. He looked around, then closed the door and finally asked her where her husband was.

O, Im not married, Harry looking at her bewildered and surprised. I just wear this, waving her left hand, to keep some of those obnoxious office wolves at bay, smiling then chuckling, and it works very well. Of course it doesnt stop them from asking, but I just tell them I have to meet my husband. Harry started to get over his shock and started to smile. Then I show them a picture of my older brother and tell them that he is my husband, see, opening her wallet and showing him a picture of a man who was obviously at least six feet two and at least two hundred and forty pounds of muscle. Harry burst out laughing. It never fails, and they both laughed loud and hard.

It was a lovely weekend. Saturday morning she made him the traditional breakfast of soft scrambled eggs, à la Sorrentino, and later in the day they took a ride on the sightseeing boat around the harbor. Then dinner, a movie, a walk (she wore her walking shoes) and back home. A simple, enjoyable and relaxing weekend; and when Harry left Sunday evening, with a kiss and a pat on her lovely ass, there was no mention of lunch Monday, or any other day. He left the apartment, left Helen and the weekend and, he thought, the game.

On the ride home he realized that he had spent the weekend with a single broad (unless that guy really was her husband), and it was no hassle. He did not spend much time with the thought, but simply allowed it to register and to file itself for future reference. If nothing else, it meant that he did not have to go out of his way to avoid them in the future.

His parents were sitting in the living room when he got home. He started to wave a cheery hello at them, but his mothers lost and injured look stopped him. You missed your grandmothers birthday party last night. She was seventy-five. Harry winced, and the pain was so sharp and instant that he could not speak. He stared at her for endless seconds. He somehow climbed the stairs to his room. Nausea twisted his gut and throat. He wanted to punch something . . . to wrap his arms around his head and yell . . . to tear the door from its hinges and crumble it . . . to cry . . .

anything . . .

some-

thing . . . but all he could do was to sit and shake and wonder what had happened and why. He loved her. Jesus Krist, he really loved her. Why???? Why????

There was no problem getting to work on time Monday morning and taking care of the work on his desk, which was routine. There was plenty of work to be done, but all of it was familiar; there was nothing new and challenging that would make tremendous demands upon him.

His lunch hours were routine too, walking and browsing through the streets and stores. Halfway through the following week he was bouncing his legs up and down as he sat at his desk, doing a lot of fidgeting and getting up occasionally to go to the water cooler, which was something he had not done before because he did not particularly like to drink water, but he wet his lips and actually drank a drop or two.

His restlessness made him leave a few minutes early for lunch and return a few minutes late. He found himself thinking about his feelings as he walked the streets, trying to analyze them until he became so involved with them that he started to feel a blackness wrap itself around his head and crawl through his gut, and he automatically reached out for the only answer he had ever found.

He had lunch in a cafeteria and looked around until he found a vacant seat at a table where a broad was eating. A little chitchat, a walk to her office and then back to work ten minutes late. Lunch did not stop his fidgeting, but it did stop the analyzing.

As days followed disquieting days, Harry continued to fidget and take extended lunch hours to afford himself ample time to reconnoiter unfamiliar ground, which kept him from looking within himself.

He also started neglecting his work and waiting until he was backed into a time corner before finishing a job, completing it at the last minute. He could feel that this would get him into difficulty, but he refused to define it when the thought started to materialize and dismissed it with a mental shrug. One Friday he was finishing a job that had to be ready by Monday, but imperceptibly he slowed down, took an even longer lunch hour and played around with the work the remainder of the day, figuring on finishing it in a hurry Monday morning. It was a simple, routine job, and the time pressure would give him something to look forward to on Monday.

Sunday night he met another Olga and did not get to work until a few minutes after ten Monday. Mr. Wentworth just looked at him as he walked into the office. It was not necessary for him to say anything, and Harry shriveled inside himself as he said good morning. He plunged into his work and the job was done on time, but the damage was done. Thank God it was time to go to lunch.

He was existing in a drift of confusion as he walked to the cafeteria nearest the office. Self-analysis was becoming a habit and he felt fuzzy as he tried to understand just what was happening and how and why. He could almost feel when it started happening—it wasnt so very long ago, of that he was certain—hoping that if he could just isolate that point in time he would see the why of the events and be able to change everything. Or if not the why, then the how, and then be able to prevent these things from happening. Yet the more he tried to find that point, and the closer he felt he was coming to it, the more vague and confused everything seemed to become, and all he could do was shake his inner head and allow all the images to tumble.

And when he did, he was left with a question like how could he be coming into work late suddenly, and when he did, why was Wentworth there waiting to pounce? And why should he be having trouble with his work? He liked his job and his work and he was burning with ambition. Nothing made any sense.

His mind was still a jumble of words, thoughts and images, when he found himself, tray of food in hand, smiling at a broad and asking her if this seat was taken.

No, nodding and continuing to eat and read.

Harry settled in and after a few minutes excused himself and asked her how she was enjoying the book. I remember reading a review, but Ive never gotten around to reading the book, smiling at her.

I like it. Its really interesting. Its—a—different.

Yeah, thats what I read. I didnt know it was out in paperback.

O yeah, for over a year I think, looking at the front of the book for the date of the printing. Yeah, here it is. Almost exactly a year.

What do you know? I wonder where Ive been, smiling and shaking his head, the confusion, fuzziness and conflict of feelings smoothing away as he continued to eat and talk.

After lunch he walked her back to her office, making certain, as he had done lately, not to make a date for the next day. He was only a few minutes late in getting back to the office and though he still fidgeted slightly, there was no turmoil inside and he went about his business at his newly acquired pace of indifferent slowness.

The next morning he was early for work, but still had to rush to finish a job on time, a job that he had had on his desk for over a month. That in itself would not have been a problem except that Mr. Wentworth called him about nine-thirty and asked him to do a rush job for him, and Harry had to explain that he had the other job to finish and he could hear the annoyance (disgust?) in Wentworths voice when he said he/d give the job to Davis.

Harry was almost muttering out loud as he went about his work. Something was all botched up, and he sure as hell couldnt figure it out. And what does Wentworth want from my life? Calls up at the last minute for a job, then gets bugged because Im working on something that has to be done this morning. I thought you finished that weeks ago. You did, eh? Well thats too damn bad. If you didnt keep yourself locked in your damn office all day, maybe youd know what in the hells going on out here.

So give the job to Davis. Who gives a damn? What am I supposed to do, cry because you give someone else a last-minute job? Up yours.

A quick trip to the water cooler and cold water hitting his lips, then back to the desk. He attacked the work and finished it rapidly and accurately then left for lunch, unaware that he was leaving twenty minutes early.

He walked rapidly for a few blocks, his inner voice mumbling and blithering, until he once again found himself standing with a tray of food and asking if the seat was empty.

Her boss was out of town for the week and she was in no

hurry to return to work and so they spent a leisurely time talking over coffee, then walking around for a while before returning to their offices. Before leaving, Harry asked her if she ate there every day, and she told him she did. Then if Im lucky, I/ll see you tomorrow.

Could be, smiling.

As Harry walked back to the office he felt a slight twinge of apprehensive nausea, but quickly shoved aside the vague thoughts that were trying desperately to define themselves. It was nobodys business if he wanted to have lunch with some broad, and whats the big deal? It aint interfering with anything, and it sure as hell aint hurting anybody.

He got back to the office even later than usual, and could feel the eyes burning into his back, and the clock, as if they were trying to brand him with the time. He squeezed his pencil hard as he rustled papers, announcing the fact that he had just returned, his inner voice telling all and sundry to go to hell, and that goes double for you Wentworth.

The next day he managed to keep his anger alive, having nurtured it from time to time during the night, but could not seem to focus it or direct it—it just seemed to be there, jumbling around inside him trying to find a way out. He slowly ate his cheese danish and sipped his coffee until it was too cold to enjoy, but continued to sip it anyway, not starting work until both were finished.

When he finally did start working, he attacked his calculator and almost shoved his pencil through the pad a few times, then jammed the papers into the proper order. He worked as slowly as possible, trying not to finish the job until late in the afternoon, but there was so little left to do that he finished before lunch in spite of his efforts. When he finished the goddamn job, he tossed his pencil on the desk and left for lunch.

She was just getting on line when he got there. As they talked and moved slowly along the line, picking up plates of food, the turbulence within him subsided, and when they were finally settled at a table, he quickly became involved with her. The strain drained from his arms and back and he could feel himself relaxing as they talked about nothing in particular.

Halfway through lunch he could feel a knot forming in his gut, a small one, and it started tugging at the back of his throat, and he could feel a change flow through him inwardly and outwardly. He could feel his thigh muscles twitching and he could feel his eyes closing slightly as he looked at her, the tip of his tongue wetting his upper lip, and his hand reached over and brushed a few crumbs off her lap and then his open hand was on her thigh and he looked more intently into her eyes, unclothing her and himself, feeling somewhere within him another Harry looking at what was happening and wanting to want to stop. She returned his gaze and put her hand on top of his and smiled in answer to whatever he was saying.

When they left, they walked along the street for a while, Harry leaning out of the way of passers-by and brushing her tit with the upper part of his arm and smiling into her eyes, and feeling that tug in his gut as the other Harry tried to pull him away from the game, but it was completely out of control and Harry was more a witness to his actions than the creator of them; and they talked about movies and then skin flicks, and Harry could feel the knot tightening, and the tugging increasing, and was aware, too, of the passing of time and an intense feeling of the intoxication of danger, but first and foremost he felt a rapport with his lust as he looked at her. He led her to the side of a building, out of the stream of people, and stood almost touching her as he told her that he would like to fuck the ass off her, continuing to look at her, the naked thrust of his lust exciting her; then, taking her hand, he led her to the Hotel Splendide, all his various feelings welling into one turbulence of excitement.

When they left, Harry went to a nearby bar and sat in the corner trying to disentangle the mass and mess of feelings within him. He did not understand them. It was as if he was sorry for not getting back to work on time, as if he had done something wrong, but did not know what; having a vague desire to change something, but not knowing what. He finished his drink and thought about going back to the office, but the mere thought made him turn red and he could feel his skin flush and the sweat form under his eyes and at the base of his spine. He could not go back to the office a couple of hours late. He tried to force himself, but the ability to move had been taken from him. He was paralyzed. He ordered another drink, then decided to call and tell them he was sick and was going home. He called Louise and told her he had gotten violently ill after eating and was on his way home, that he had spent over an hour in the rest room and this was the first chance he had to call, and he could feel that other Harry watching him and could feel his head shaking and he finally mumbled a goodbye and hung up the phone.

He slowly sipped his drink and thought of getting drunk, but somehow the idea not only did not appeal to him, he did not know exactly how to go about it, never having been able to force down enough liquor to get drunk. When it started to make him woozy, he stopped.

As he sipped his third drink he tried to find something to rage about, something to isolate and attack, something that would prove to be the reason for the disturbing and unfamiliar feelings burning through him, but there was no coordination within him between desire and ability. Eventually he gave up trying and finished his drink and left.

The next day he left the house at the usual time, so his mother would not question him, then called in sick. He still could not accept the idea of explaining his absence the previous afternoon, and even in the quiet of his room he could not fabricate a story that he would be able to relate believably. By taking off today there would be no doubt that he really was sick, and they probably would not question him.

He went to Forty-second Street and sat through a couple of old westerns, then walked up to Bryant Park and sat on a bench, avoiding all eyes, even those of the pigeons. He felt strangely conspicuous and had the vague feeling that people were looking at him and wondering what he was doing there. He stayed there as long as he could, watching the pigeons peck away at food thrown them, vaguely hearing the music of the recorded concert and trying to get involved with the way in which the sunlight glanced off the leaves of trees and slanted through the branches, casting moving shadows . . . the flowers, shrubs, statues . . . to no avail. No matter how hard he tried to stay on the bench and wish time by, he could not and had to get up and walk around the perimeter of the park, keeping his eyes on the path.

He continued walking until he reached the library and went inside hoping to get involved with something in there, but all he could do was wander aimlessly through rooms and tiers of books until he once more found himself in Bryant Park. He walked to Forty-second Street, then down to Times Square and another movie. He tried to sit through both films, but had to leave after seeing the second half of one and the first half of another. He rode the train back to Brooklyn and went to Caseys.

He walked to the end of the bar, where Tony and Al were sitting. Holy Krist, look whos here. It must be Sunday.

Yeah, or six oclock. Hi, whatta ya say?

Hi.

Holy shit Harry, whats the occasion, your boss die or something? both of them laughing as Harry pulled up a stool and sat.

Up yours Al—hey Pat, give me a beer. Youd better give them one too, they look like theyre waiting for a live one.

Thats the kind of talk I like to hear, quickly draining the glass and pushing it forward.

All shit aside though Harry, whats the occasion?

Nothing. Why? Cant a guy take a day off without everybody going apeshit?

Yeah, sure, laughing, but not you. You never take a day off and then come here.

Well, I am today. Im taking a day off and Im going to have a couple of beers.

Yeah, how come?

I thought I/d do a survey.

Yeah, what kind of survey?

An investigation into the nature of being a bum, and I cant think of anyone better qualified to help me than you guys.

Hey, I resemble that remark, laughing, Pat joining them.

You think just because I dont go to an office every day— Whata ya mean, aint this our office—

Yeah, all of them laughing. You think because I dont ride the subway, I dont work? Look, I bet I work harder playing the horses than you do at your job. They all laughed again.

Yeah, I bet you do.

Speaking of jobs, how come you took a day off? Aint you afraid your job will disappear?

Harry smiled at their laughter. I thought I/d live dangerously.

Well, I always said, you hang around Caseys long enough and youll see a miracle, and Im seeing one. Harry taking a day off from work and sitting in Caseys. This calls for a toast. Tony raised his glass, then Al raised his. To Harry the Hump, and they drained their glasses, then put them down on the bar as Harry smiled, trying to stay involved in their game to keep from going back inside himself.

Hey Pat, give us three more.

Hey, man, why dont you come to the Fort with us tonight? There should be some good fights.

Yeah, the main events got a couple of welters that look pretty good.

Yeah? shrugging, maybe I will.

Harry drifted through the day, sipping on his beer, staying with his third one for an hour, Al and Tony trying to get him to keep up with them. Harry listened, smiled, laughed, talked, not completely involved with any of it, but not involved with that twinge inside either.

He went to the fights with them, and a couple of other

guys, after stopping in an Italian restaurant, and could feel himself relaxing slightly as they sat in the outdoor arena. It was a clear night and there was a pleasant breeze from the harbor and he got caught up in the horsing around of the guys, and then the action of the fights. Most of the prelims were pretty good bouts, one was really good, a knock-down, drag-out kind of fight, but the main event was a real winner and Harry got completely caught up in the excitement and was standing along with everyone else and yelling and cheering.

After the fights, they all went back to Caseys, but after a short time Harry waved goodbye and went home. He lay in his bed thinking about the day, then yesterday and the past weeks and months, and suddenly a cold knot twisted in his gut and he involuntarily raised his knees to relieve the pressure, and when the knot finally started dissolving, he no longer reviewed the day or any other part of his life, but closed his eyes and, with the aid of the beer he had drunk, drifted off into a shallow sleep.

If, indeed, such restlessness could be called sleep. He was not twisted, turned and tormented during the night, but was part of a continuing dream—maybe it only occurred once and he dreamed that it happened over and over again—that did not drag him from unconsciousness, but kept him just on the brink of wakefulness so that his mind and spirit never got the complete rest they needed. It was such a simple dream that it almost did not seem worth dreaming. A dream that is going to keep you from getting the proper rest should at least be a little spectacular, or loaded with sexual symbols.

Certainly not as simple as driving along the street in a normal flow of traffic and seeing the brake lights go on on the car in front of you and you lift your foot from the accelerator and it gets caught under the brake pedal and you get closer and closer to the car in front of you as you struggle to get your foot out from under the pedal so you can jam down on it and not hit the car in front, and, of course, everything is happening in slow motion and it seems like you go through this time after time and you never hit the car in front of you, but you never find out exactly what happens either. . . .

Harry did not remember the dream in the morning, though he had a vague idea that he had dreamed something, but he felt sluggish and more or less dragged himself through his shower and shave. His step, as he went down the stairs to the kitchen, was slow and flat.

As was his voice. He could hear it when he said good morning to his folks.

Are you all right, Harry?

Yeah, sure Pop, why?

Well, I dont know exactly, its just that you seem sort of out—well, out of sorts lately. I cant quite put my finger on it, but you just dont seem to be yourself.

Gee, trying to manage as sincere a look as possible, I dont know. Theres nothing wrong.

Harry bought a paper and tried to concentrate on it as he rode to work, but his mind kept drifting back to his fathers question and he kept asking himself if something was wrong. What could be wrong? Things werent going exactly right lately, things were getting a little goofed at work and Wentworth seemed to be getting on his back, but there was nothing wrong. At least not that he could pinpoint. He tried to get involved in the comic strips, but the vague uneasiness persisted and he kept dismissing questions from his mind. If anything was wrong, it wasnt his fault. That he was sure of.

Harry had been sitting at his desk a few minutes when Louise came over and asked him how he was feeling.

Pretty good. I think I/ll live.

Well thats good to hear. Have a stomach virus?

He suddenly felt trapped and had a second of panic until he remembered that he had told Louise that he had gotten sick after eating and had to go home.

(75)

Yeah, I sure did. Couldnt stray too far from home, smiling at her knowingly.

I thought you might be coming down with something.

Why? frowning.

O, you just didnt seem to be your usual self. You know, not as relaxed and sort of preoccupied. But Im glad youre all right now, patting him on the shoulder, then going back to her desk.

Harry puzzled over his coffee and cheese danish and wondered what in the hell was going on, why people were sticking their noses in his business. He wished to krist they/d keep them where they belonged. The only thing wrong with him was them.

He worked aggressively that morning and by the time he became aware of people coming and going and realized it was time for lunch, he felt relaxed. He looked at the work on his desk. He had done a good mornings work. Damn good. The Wilson job was all ready to go and neatly packaged.

He nodded at the work he had done and left for lunch feeling exhilarated. He started walking along Fifth Avenue, but by the time he reached the first corner the exhilaration was replaced with that vague uneasiness, and he turned and went to the coffee shop in the building to eat lunch. When he finished, he went back to the office and spent the remainder of the hour in the lounge.

For the next week, until the company outing on the following Friday, Harry had his lunch sent up from the coffee shop and spent the hour in the lounge reading, having absolutely no desire to go out for lunch, unable to force himself even if he thought of trying. He had gotten a few science fiction books from the neighborhood library and read them on the subway as well as at lunch time, and they seemed to absorb the energy from the surface of his mind and he could ignore any twinge he might feel.

Although he wanted to, he could not keep up his aggressive attitude toward work. He would manage it for an hour or two, but that was all, and then usually because he had fallen behind schedule again and had to work frantically to finish the job.

From time to time Harry White would start to question himself about his inability to work consistently as he once had, and his inability to leave the office for lunch, but as soon as he could feel these questions vaguely forming, a fear gripped him and he shoved them aside and inundated his mind with something, anything, else to avoid facing those questions.

The day before the company outing Mr. Wentworth called Harry into his office. Harry knew it was serious when Mr. Wentworth told him to sit down, and something inside him turned over and a slight twinge of nausea tugged at the back of his throat. I wanted you to hear this from me, Harry, rather than at the banquet tomorrow night. As you know our firm is growing rapidly, and, I say this with pride, growing at a very accelerated pace. As a matter of fact our growth over these last two years has been phenomenal.

Thats wonderful, trying to look dutifully impressed.

Thats right, it is. Now, because of this growth a need for more executive-level personnel has developed, and just recently the title of junior vice-president was created—he looked at Harry for a moment, leaning back in his chair. Harry could feel the ball in his gut leap up and jam itself in his throat—and its been given to Davis—plop, down it goes, twisting his windpipe and groveling around in his bowels—upon my recommendation. And I want to tell you why. You are sharper than Davis—Harry could feel his eyes blinking, and he hoped to krist he wasnt going to cry. He didnt really want to, but he could feel a pressure behind his eyes and could feel a tired sadness veil itself over them, and he tried desperately to keep the proper expression on his face, whatever in the hell that was. He sure as krist didnt know—you have more imagination and have the capability of being more aggressive; in other words, you have all the attributes of a successful corporate executive (o for krists sake shut up and let me get out of here) except the most essential, leaning forward to emphasize the point—consistency and reliability. I would like to see you as junior vice-president, I think you could give a lot to the firm, but I cannot depend on you. Davis may not have much to get him beyond a junior vice-presidency, but he is reliable and consistent. He is a family man, with three children. A man who has settled into life and does a good job *every* day. You see, thats the important thing. He doesnt skyrocket one day just to fizzle out the next. And thats more important than aggressive imagination to the firm at this point in time, and in this particular position.

Now, I do not know whats been happening with you lately, but I cannot rely on you the way I could. When I need something done, I want to be able to push this button and know that it will be done, no questions, no delays. Lately I cant even *find* you when I need you, so obviously youre no help to me when something suddenly needs attention. You seem (holy krist, stop the shit. Let me get out of here) to have acquired an irresponsible attitude, and you can take it from me, there is nothing more detrimental to a successful career. Personally, I think its time you thought about settling down, raising a family, accepting the responsibilities of a man. Theres nothing like it for giving you a clear perspective on life and clearing away the fog from the goals we want to attain. Personally, I think its the incentive you need.

But these are not the only reasons I recommended Davis for the position. You see, I have not changed my opinion and/or the evaluation of your ability. I think you have unlimited potential and can be a great asset to the firm. A great asset. But you are going to need a change of attitude to realize that potential, and I am hoping that this will shake you up enough to realize that you are jeopardizing a great future and that you will change your attitude.

I believe in our firm. I believe in it completely and absolutely. We are growing and will continue to grow as long as men are willing to dedicate their lives to it and give their absolute loyalty to it. Theres no other way. It is all in the attitude,

Harry. And I want you to be the asset I know you can be. Being passed over for a junior vice-presidency now is nothing, if you will just take my advice and change your attitude. You got me?

Yes . . . yes I have, Mr. Wentworth. I—

Good. Think over what I said. You know, Harry, someday you will thank me for this. You will look back on this day as the turning point in a spectacular career, Harry nodding his head and blinking his eyes rapidly. O.K., end of lecture. I will see you tomorrow.

See me tomorrow, going back to his desk and plopping in his chair, his eyes still blinking rapidly, the twisting ball still bouncing from his gut to his throat and lodging and tugging, see me tomorrow. Some day youll thank me for this. What kind of shit is that? Who the hell does he think hes talking to? I break my back for him and look what he does. . . . O screw it. He went to the mens room, pissed, splashed some cold water on his face and killed a few more minutes until it was time to leave.

The science fiction books didnt seem to help much during the ride home, as he wondered who Wentworth thought he was coming on so high and holy. You/d think I was the only one who played around with the broads. Who is he to talk???? Yeah, who are you to cast the first stone, you and your public relations team. . . . Ahhh, screw it . . . its not the only job in the world . . . they need me more than I need them . . . just see what happens if I dont take care of the work . . . yeah, how long would Mr. junior veepee last then . . . ah, I dont know . . . I cant seem to figure . . . shit! What the—why cant they just get off my back . . . ahhh . . .

Tony, Mike and Steve were going to the ball game that night, so Harry went along with them. From time to time, during the night, Harry would find himself reaching down into the dark hostile corners of his mind to abuse Wentworth and let him know what an asshole he was, and he was going to show him, but he had already dissipated a lot of his energy, and found himself partially involved in the excitement of the game, and so that inner hand was unable to bring the hate up into the light of the night.

4

It was a perfect day for an outing, and the Wooddale Country Club was the perfect place. There was an eighteen-hole golf course, sunken gardens, a huge pool, impeccable grounds surrounded by pleasant woods, and all the other facilities and amenities of an exclusive country club.

Most of the others sat around the tables in the sun, or on the shaded patio. A few were on the tennis courts and Harry watched them for a while, then drifted along the fringe of the wooded area.

He enjoyed the time alone, not because it made him feel any closer to the trees that surrounded him, the birds that chirped and flew through the branches, the green spotted earth under him or the sun and blue sky over him; nor because of a fear of people or an inability to socialize—he had no real problems in that area—but rather he enjoyed the self-satisfied feeling he experienced as he looked around at the vastness of the club, knowing there were people throughout the grounds involved in various activities and feeling that they were aware that he wasnt there and were wondering where he was.

He stood in the shadows of the trees and looked out at the bright sunshine on the sloping grass that ended at the sunken gardens and the edge of the pool, a feeling of power surging through him. He half-closed his eyes and looked at the images within him, feeling the destiny that would bring him the money, property and prestige he desired and knew he would have someday.

The line between the shadows and the brightness was sharp, and the transition abrupt as Harry stepped into the almost tangible substance of the sunshine. He could feel the suns heat on his face while still feeling the coolness of the shadows on his back, but by the time that brief instant registered on his consciousness, it had passed and he was feeling the suns brightness and heat on his back too.

He walked toward the pool, where half a dozen or so people were lying around, swimming, or stretched out in the sun. As he got closer to them, he noticed a girl in a bikini standing alongside the pool and could feel himself staring at her. He could hear the voices of the others, the sounds of tennis from the courts a few hundred yards on the other side of the pool, the occasional yell and splash of someone jumping into the pool, yet he was completely preoccupied with the girl in the bikini and the way her boobs seemed to ooze out of her top and the way the bottoms seemed to hang miraculously from below her hips in a narrow band just under the slight swell of her belly. . . .

He stared at the water dripping down to her navel and thought of a keyhole and blinked from the brightness of the sun and the electrical shocks of his lust. Krist, he/d like to ball her right there, right now. She took her bathing cap off and shook her hair loose before lying down on a towel beside the pool. He could tell her pubic hair was thin and did not cover a large area.

He stood so his shadow covered her body. She opened her eyes and raised her head slightly. Youre in my sun.

O, Im sorry, and he stepped aside and watched his shadow slowly slide across her body and onto the grass. Theres nothing worse than a sun stealer.

Thanks, smiling, eyes still closed, right now Im primarily interested in getting dry before lunch.

Well, with the sun the way it is and a suit like that, it shouldnt take long—

Hi Harry. Why dont you come in. The waters great.

Hi Steve, Joan, waving his hand, not right now. I/ll wait till after lunch—

For some reason, frowning, Im confused about that business about drying and the suit.

O, well, I only meant that its the suit that takes the longest to dry and you dont have that much suit to get dry, the laughter in his voice obvious and she responding to it with a chuckle.

You no like?

O, on the contrary, laughing and squatting beside her. Im Harry White. I dont believe Ive ever met you.

Im Linda Sorrenson, turning her head toward him and opening one eye, Im Mr. Donlevys new secretary. I only started a couple of months ago.

You have been with the firm for a couple of months and I havent seen you before? My God, I must be going crazy. I/ll never forgive myself. Where have you been all this time?

Right at my desk where I belong, turning over on her stomach, her head turned facing Harry and looking up at him and smiling.

Well, I have an idea Im going to be involved with Donlevy quite a bit in the future. She chuckled and Harry looked across the grounds toward the buildings. It looks like theyre getting ready for lunch. Maybe we should start strolling over.

O, I dont think I want to bother. Im a light eater.

You dont have to worry about that, laughing.

O, yes I do. Its not easy to stay bikini size.

Well, you should come along anyway. If nothing else, youll like the way they lay it out.

Really?

Yeah. Its a buffet and it looks lovely, standing and stretching for a moment, youll like it, believe me.

She looked up at him for a moment, then rolled over. O.K., youve talked me into it.

Harry extended his arm and she grabbed his hand and he tugged her up, her momentum stopping her just inches from him. You look familiar, smiling at her.

Not too familiar, I hope, taking her hand from his and rolling her bathing cap in her towel.

They walked across the grass, Harry walking beside her, part of him following and watching, his eyes caressed by the swing of her hips and ass as they flowed with her movements.

They sat on a shaded patio and ate their lunch, some of the others sitting at tables in the area, but most of them remaining in the air-conditioned dining room. Louise and Rae joined Harry and Linda, setting down plates that were filled with a variety of foods.

You dont mind, do you Harry?

Do you have a reservation, smiling at them.

Of course he doesnt mind, Louise, why should he want to sit alone with a beautiful young girl? Oi, I hate you already, Linda looking a little surprised, such a cute figure, Harry and Louise laughing. Even before I was a grandmother I didnt have such a figure.

Have another blintz and relax.

Harry, you should only *plotz*. They all laughed and lunch continued amid the clicking of fork on plate and laughter.

After lunch Harry put on his trunks and joined the others around the pool. He jumped in and swam to the other end and stood beside Linda. You look vaguely familiar, smiling through the water trickling down his face.

Not too vaguely, I hope.

O, not at all. Not at all, and he splashed her and she splashed him and they tumbled around in the water laughing.

Someone came up with a beach ball, and the swimmers formed a large circle in the pool and the ball was tossed up in the air and knocked from one to another, the first one to miss being dunked by the others. Most of the players tired of the game after a while, and Harry continued to fool around in the pool with Linda.

Davis and his wife joined the others, and when Harry first noticed them walking toward the pool he felt that twinge twist his gut and he stood still with the water just under his chin, moving his hands to help maintain his balance, feeding the churning in his gut and staring at them, automatically and unconsciously sizing up the wife with her obvious inches of flab strapped in her one-piece suit, sneering at Davis, already going to pot, and his skinny hairless legs. But she isnt so bad, not bad at all, especially when you consider shes had some kids, and a little belly aint bad, as long as they dont have any wrinkles in their ass—

Hey Harry, get out of the way, Harry not hearing a sound, you deaf or something?— Yeah, thats not a bad idea . . . Ive never fucked a junior veepees wife—

Hey move, tugging his arm, Harry turning and looking at Linda questioningly, they want to race.

Huh???? O, moving to the side of the pool with Linda.

You must have some very strong powers of concentration. What?

They were yelling at you and you didnt hear a word.

Im studying Yoga, smiling at her and watching the Davises out of the corner of his eye. He helped her up onto the side of the pool, then joined her just as the swimmers dove into the pool and raced toward the other end. There was cheering and yelling for a moment, and it separated Harry from the Davises.

Want to get out and lie in the sun?

In a minute, looking at Linda and feeling his face smile,

but not really feeling a part of that smile. I want to get a few kinks out.

Linda left, and Harry lowered himself under the surface and swam to the other side of the pool, then swam the length of the pool a few times, feeling a small knot of energy that he sensed he had to exhaust, and halfway through the third lap he could feel it dissolve, so when he reached the end of the pool he hiked himself up and out and joined Linda.

He stood over her dry back and let a few drops of water splash on her.

Ooooo, thas cold, you rat, twisting over and away from the water.

You spend an hour in the water and then scream when you get two drops on you, laughing and sitting beside her.

That is funny, isnt it? laughing and readjusting herself on her towel.

Boy, that was good, stretching out on his stomach and looking at her face cradled on her arms only a few inches away from him. A good swim is just about the most relaxing thing in the world.

Yes, it is. It makes you feel kind of dreamy, her eyes closed, her smile in her voice.

You sound like youre going to sleep.

Hhhmmmm. Wake me up in a little while so I can get some sun on my front too.

Whats a little while?

O you know, when Ive had enough sun on my back.

O, O.K., aware of the nearness of her, and smiling.

Harry didnt sleep, but he drifted within himself, hearing, but not really listening to, the sounds of swimmers and others around the pool, their voices blending in with the noises to form almost a single sound, with different parts, that absorbed the surface of his mind as did the Forty-second Street movies; and Davis and his wife were not allowed to enter his mind, his senses filling that part of his mind, and he was drowsily aware of the feel of the sun on his back, the smell of the grass and earth and the feel of them and the towel under him, the brush of flies and other insects that investigated his back and legs, but mostly of Linda and the feeling of her lying next to him, feeling that same sun on her back and the little bugs leaving his skin to touch hers, and the smell of dampness that floated from her as she stepped from the pool, the smell of water and skin and air that mingled together to excite him and stay within his mind even now when the sun made dampness a thing of the past.

He remained consciously involved in these feelings and sensations, and then he slowly became aware of something else, of another feeling . . . a feeling of relaxation. He sort of chuckled within himself as he realized he did not feel like this when he said a swim was relaxing, but he did now. Thats funny. Funny too how you can know theres a whole lot of people around you, yet you can feel distinct from them. Nice to float and drift and feel the ground under you. . . . Really nice. . . .

Good water . . .

nice sky . . .

and trees. . . .

He heard Linda take a deep breath and sigh slightly as she rolled over onto her back.

Time to move ?

Huhmm.

How come?

The back is done, and she smoothed out a place for her head by moving it back and forth, then settling in her little niche.

Well, I guess its time for me to roll over too.

Harry could feel the brightness of the sun on his eyelids, but soon adjusted to it and started to drift down into the hollow of sleep within him, and he droned deeper and deeper within himself until the drone was almost silent, then wakefulness suddenly jabbed him. He squinted his eyes open and rolled over onto his side. He could hear that no one was in the pool, and it was much quieter than before. He looked around and noticed that most people were lying in the sun and a few were playing cards.

Time to get up.

Hmmmmm, stirring.

Youd better get up if you dont want to get baked.

She rolled over on her side and half opened her eyes, then blinked them rapidly and tried opening them again.

I thought you had some sort of built-in timer so you wouldnt stay in the sun too long.

I havent been in too long.

Yeah, but if I didnt wake you, you wouldve been burned to a crisp.

Well, I didnt say exactly how I would wake up, did I? smiling, there are all kinds of alarm clocks.

O, I see, laughing, you set *my* timer.

Well, you did wake me up when I was done, joining him in laughing—

Hey Harry, how about some rummy? You too Linda, we need a couple of hands.

Harry looked at Linda and she answered with a why-not shrug and expression, and they joined the others and sat around the towel that was being used as the playing area. Do you know how to play five hundred, Linda?

I think I remember.

I see youre keeping score, Tom.

Naturally Harry, what else? They laughed and chuckled as they played, and halfway through the game the women changed places so they would be evenly exposed to the sun.

When the game was over, which Tom won amid yells of fraud and demands to have the score sheet audited, they went, along with the others, to dress for the cocktail hour and dinner.

When Harry got to the bar, Mr. Wentworth called him over and introduced him to Mr. Simmons, the president. Its good to meet you, White. Walt here has been telling me some good things about you, an arm around Harrys shoulder, and I like to make a point of meeting, and getting to know, our up-and-coming men, the new blood thats the backbone of our firm.

Thank you Mr. Simmons, I hope to be able to make some major contributions to the growth of the firm.

Good, good, thats the kind of attitude I like.

You want a drink, Harry?

Scotch and water.

Wentworth waved for the bartender, and when he brought the drink, he handed it to Harry.

Thanks. The way I figure it is simply that the more I can help the firm grow, the more I can grow along with it.

Thats right. Its like I always say: The more important the firm is to you, the more important you are to the firm. They looked at each other and nodded in understanding and approbation.

They remained in a small group for a short time, Harry a little surprised that he felt fairly comfortable with Wentworth, there being no anger bubbling within him. He meant everything he said: he did want to contribute to the firm and become a successful corporate executive, and he did like the firm and his work and would be perfectly content to stay with them the rest of his life, the life that he had planned and projected, the life that included not only a title and success, but a large home, automobiles, boats and all the other accouterments of success, like membership in an exclusive country club like Wooddale.

Harry sipped his drink and sincerely listened to their sincerity, almost feeling a part of the conversation and the two men with him, but vaguely aware of a feeling of separateness. He quickly, and automatically, brushed it aside and replaced it with a swelling and glow that came from the fact that he could feel the others in the room watching him talk with Simmons and Wentworth as equals, and knew, too, that they were in awe of him and envious.

Their conversation finally terminated and Harry drifted among the others, feeling a little heady and superior, and had a feeling that he was just a little taller (in some cases much taller) than the others. He also felt suave and enjoyed shaking his glass and hearing the ice cubes tinkle.

He walked up to the Davises, pulling his shoulders back just a bit more as he approached them, and looked at her intently as Mark introduced him. Honey, this is Harry White. Harry, my wife Terry.

Hi, its a pleasure.

Hi, Mark has mentioned you often.

O, he has has he, looking at him and smiling, then looking back at her, nothing good, I hope. Mark has mentioned you, too, but he never said that you were so beautiful, Terry blushing slightly. Mark, you old devil, no wonder I havent met her before. If I were married to you, looking at her intently again, I/d be afraid to let you out of the house, his face opening up into a friendly smile, Marks a lucky man, and Harry continued to look at her for another second or two, feeling a slight twinge inside and wanting to follow where it would lead him, but others came and joined them and so he drifted away with a feeling of relief.

Eventually he came across Linda sitting with Rae and Louise. Three lovely young ladies all alone, this is my lucky day.

Join us?

Thanks, Louise.

So listen to Sir Finklestein. You think Im going to believe your looking at these ancient ruins when such a beautiful girl like Linda is here?

Everyone laughed as Rae looked at them with a huge impish grin. They joked and laughed until it was time to eat, then got up and followed the others into the main dining room.

Harry was once again conscious of Lindas presence, and as they walked to the dining room he could feel the way her thin dress clung to her body. They sat near each other at one of the long banquet tables, Rae and Louise on one side and Harry and Linda across from them. He was still aware of it as they sat at the table, her bare arm just a few inches away from him.

The friendly chitchat, and Raes humor, prevented Harry from becoming completely, and exclusively, preoccupied with Linda, though even with the joking and laughter, he was constantly aware of her presence and a feeling that was new and vague, that seemed to come from her. He felt attracted to her, yet, at this particular moment, there was no knot of anxiety in his gut or tightness of apprehension. He gave fleeting moments of thought to this feeling, but the closest he could come to defining it, in any way, was simply to be aware of the absence of certain feelings he usually had. For the most part he simply tried to enjoy what was happening (or *wasnt* happening) as they proceeded from soup to the dessert, which Rae kept claiming she was not going to eat, then started nibbling at with looks and sighs of approval.

Youre going to hate yourself in the morning.

O Harry, youre awful.

So whats so bad? I wont get on the scale for a few days and I/ll think thin.

They continued chuckling until Mr. Wentworth stood, tapped on his glass for a moment and asked for everyones attention. The room became silent and everyone turned toward Mr. Wentworth. Thank you. He looked around the room for a moment, a large smile on his face. I trust you all enjoyed the dinner—there were bursts of verbal approval and applause—and, Mr. Wentworths smile broadened, the relaxing cocktail hour—more applause, laughter and the energetic nodding of heads. Mr. Wentworth was silent for a moment as he looked around the room. Now you will get the tab. . . . Im going to make a speech—there was a splattering of applause and a self-conscious silence for a moment, and Mr. Wentworth chuckled and waved his hands. No, no, please dont worry. I would not ruin a good meal like that—more chuckling and laughter. All Im going to do is introduce our president, Clarke Simmons, turning toward him and extending his hand, then applauding as the others joined him.

Clarke Simmons stood and listened to and acknowledged the applause for a moment, smiling broadly, then raised his hands for silence. Thank you, thank you very much. It is indeed a pleasure to be with you on this festive occasion. And like my good friend Walter, looking toward Wentworth, I do not want to ruin a good meal with unnecessary words. He smiled and was silent until the chuckling died down. However, I do want to thank each and every one of you for being faithful employees and the type of individuals who meet their responsibilities with enthusiasm and energy and who helped make this the best year in the firms fifteen-year history. And in keeping with that tradition and the growth that it has fostered, I want to make a brief announcement about a new position that that growth has made possible and necessary . . . and to introduce the gentleman who will be our new, and first, junior vice-president—Louise and Rae quickly looked at Harry with large congratulatory smiles on their faces, and Louise started to reach for Harrys hand but he quickly lifted it off the table to scratch the back of his neck. I must confess that this bright young man has not as yet been advised of his change of status, and so it will come as a surprise to him and his lovely wife too. Ladies and gentlemen, I want to introduce our junior vice-president, Mark Davis—ooos and ahhhs and Mark Davis looking around surprised, happy, startled, smiling, and his wife bouncing up and down in her chair, clapping her hands vigorously and screeching hurray and pushing her husband toward President Simmons as those nearby shook Marks hand and patted him on the back as he hesitatingly moved forward and grasped the outstretched hands of Clarke Simmons and Walter Wentworth, and some of the people started chanting, speech, speech and others joined the chant as Mark Davis stood between Wentworth and Simmons, each with an arm around the new junior vice-president's shoulder, and a few flashbulbs popped as pictures were taken for trade publications, and eventually the applause and chanting for a speech died down so Mark Davis could speak, and Louise and Rae looked at Harry with frowns and disbelief and questioning expressions and Harry fought like a sonofabitch to keep a goddamn smile on his face and shrug away the tacit questions and accusations of Louise and Rae and not let his skin crack open from the heat that seemed to be pounding through him and the nausea that was suddenly twisting his gut and constricting his throat, and Wentworth and Simmons sat there with those grins on their faces as that jerk Davis made some kind of dumb remarks about how happy he was and how he would try to live up to the responsibility of his position—*new* position, jerk—and he had to thank his wonderful wife for all the help she/d been and for making it possible for him to do the kind of job that got him this—and he continued to thank people with a bunch of meaningless tripe, the gutless wonder, and he finally sat down and everyone clapped like a bunch of mentally retarded seals, and Harry could feel Louises and Raes eyes burning into him like two mothers who had just been told that their son was a mass murderer, and he had to stand in front of them and open the zipper on his chest and let everyone look inside of him and see the ugliness and rottenness that was hidden there and was slowly festering and explain himself and why he was sitting there while that ass-kissing Davis was taking all the bows and his fishmonger of a wife was screeching and hanging from his neck like a syphilitic albatross as if that dumb sonofabitch had actually done something to be proud of when he was lucky if he could brush his teeth and comb his hair without getting the comb and brush confused, and Harry was grinding his teeth as he smiled, gently, at Rae and Louise, and felt as if his legs were going to run away from his body and he shrugged again and wanted to laugh but was afraid he would puke all over the table and he tried to force an attitude of nonchalance and let his two surrogate mothers know that he could have had the job, but turned it down as it might interfere with his future, but he couldnt say it, but only imply it, because he couldnt let the word get around, but anyway it was no big deal and there are bigger things ahead and Davis needs it with all those people he has to feed, the poor sucker, and thats the real reason they gave it to him anyway, and anyway, who gives a damn about the whole damn thing, and the muscles in Harrys shoulders and the back of his neck felt like they were about to snap and the pain became so intense that Harry thought he would either faint or jump up on the table and scream, and the goddamn smile seemed to be cemented on his face and Louise and Rae didnt seem to be talking to him and there was a slow awareness of something new happening, something in addition to the renewal of the voices chatting and chuckling and laughing, and out of the corner of his eye he became aware of movement and then the sound of music, dance music, and he blinked his eyes a few times and it seemed to crack the cement slightly and slow down his heart just enough so that it wasnt pounding in his ears, and then he heard a semblance of words as Rae told him to get up and dance already, what are you, some kind of schlemiel, youre just going to sit there like that? And he heard Linda laugh and felt himself rising on legs that were weak from painful muscular spasms, and tears came to his eyes as he stood and tried to walk and he blinked away the tears rapidly and chuckled as he stumbled, hoping to hell that his legs wouldnt collapse, and he supported himself by leaning on the backs of those sitting as he worked his way to the dance floor and gropingly led Linda in among those stumbling around the dance floor, allowing himself to fall against whoever was near until his legs finally started to strengthen and he could stand and move without fear of falling, but fortunately the dance floor was too crowded for that and it was a simple matter to bounce off other couples until he could stand, without aid, on his own two feet, and it was as if an endless wind had slowly seeped from inside him, cracking away the cement that had been holding him, and his smile, in place, and he pulled Linda closer to him and put his cheek against her ear and felt the softness of her dress against him and the heat of his breath as it filtered through her hair back into his face.

What were all those looks about before?

What looks?

What looks? Rae and Louise looked at you as if something weird was happening and they expected you to explain it— Linda laughed, or as Rae would say, explain me?

Harry was regaining his composure as they lost themselves among the dancers, feeling anonymous and inconspicuous, and his face fell into his relaxed smile. Who knows? Whatever it is, its not worth talking about now. Lets just enjoy dancing. Linda smiled and tilted her head in a shrug, and Harry pulled her back to him and they continued to dance.

When they got back to the table, some of the people had already left and they decided to have another cup of coffee before leaving, Linda having accepted Harrys invitation to have him drive her home.

When they drove past the gatehouse, through the huge stone columns and past the iron-grill-work gate, then turned onto the narrow road leading to the highway, Linda looked through the rear window at the darkened and shadowed grounds, and the dotted lights of a few cars as they moved along the narrow road toward the gate. A turn suddenly removed the grounds from view, but Linda continued to feel the pool, the sunken garden and sloping green ground and trees, and the sun and laughter. She smiled as she turned around and sort of wiggled into her seat. Louise and Rae certainly are nice ladies. I dont think I have ever laughed so much in my life. She looked at the silhouetted trees and the bright moon and stars. Gee, its a beautiful sky. The moons almost as bright as the sun, but the sky is softer now. Like velvet. She settled deeper into her seat and sighed softly. Sort of a perfect day. I really had a marvelous time. I guess it would be almost impossible not to have a good time there, its such a beautiful place. Linda chuckled, I didnt realize it, but I was born for country club living . . . gracious living as they say. Dont you agree Harry? Dont you think its a beautiful place?

Yeah, but its all over till next year. In no time we/ll be back in the stink and sweat of the city.

Linda chuckled and looked up at the velvet soft sky as Harry felt the telegraph poles chopping by. That may be, but it certainly is beautiful right now.

Linda turned on the radio and tuned in a quiet-music station and nestled into her seat and the warmth of her feelings, her gentle smile and attitude remaining as the trees turned into distant smoke stacks and cluttered buildings. Harry anticipated bumps in the road and fumes from the smokeless stacks. I suppose Davis will have to move to the suburbs now that hes a big man. Some elegant cardboard box in Levittown— no, no in Jersey. Yeah, some anthill in Jersey.

What? Linda became aware of Harrys voice, but the bitterness had not as yet registered. She was still feeling the gardens and the sun and the laughter.

You know, when you have a high class title like junior veepee, you have to live in the suburbs. Linda looked at him, her smile still on her face, and blinked a few times. I mean, after all, a junior anything cant afford Central Park West. And anyway, its no good to get that close to Park Avenue, you might get some stupid ideas. Of course theres Connecticut, but the carfare would put him in the poorhouse. No, its got to be Jersey. In some miserable tract where everything freezes in the winter and they have a two-man volunteer fire department. And they can sit around and bullshit about the house theyll have some day with a lawn with automatic sprinklers and an azalea bush next to the front door.

What in the world are you talking about? chuckling and shaking her head.

What? Our new giant of industry. Our vice-*prezeeeedent*. That worldbeater, Davis.

O. You really had me confused. I had no idea—

Did you hear that speech he made? Jesus, what a bunch of bullshit.

I didnt notice anything wrong, peering at Harry and frowning.

Are you kidding? Krist, he sounded like he had just been given the Nobel prize, or at least the Man of the Year award:

and I want to thank my sweet wife, who has stood by me (while I kissed ass) and has always encouraged me and given me—achh, what a bunch of shit.

Youre serious, arent you?

What do you mean?

I mean youre really upset by his promotion. Youre really angry.

About his promotion? No. Who needs it? Thats not it at all. Its just all the fuss over nothing and that dumb broad of a wife of his getting up there and squealing like a stuffed pig—

My God, you really are angry. I think youre jealous.

Are you kidding? turning his head to look at her, his grip tightening on the wheel, jealous of *him*? O, you have to be kidding. Ive got more going for me in my little finger, sticking it up in the air, than he has in that empty head of his. And I sure as hell wouldnt want to wake up in the same bed with that wife of his. Jesus, what a dumb broad.

I thought she looked very sweet, looking at Harry earnestly, very petite and pretty.

Yeah? Well, better him than me, shaking his head, and junior veepee sure isnt anything to write home about.

Me thinks the lady doth protest too much, looking at Harrys face in the blinking light from the street lamps. Youre the one whose making a big thing out of nothing, Harry.

He looked at her face for a moment. She was obviously relaxed and sincere. She wasnt putting him on. Listen, let me tell you something. If I wanted to be some kind of flunky junior veepee, I could get it in my sleep. Davis may be a nice guy and all that, but hes a simple-minded shit, his voice becoming louder and more intense, and anything that dumb bastard can do I can do a thousand times better with a finger up my ass whistling Dixie, and if you think Im just going to be some kind of schlunk while that ass-kissing sonofabitch gets somewhere, youve got another guess coming and youd better hang around and see whats going to happen because Im going to be long gone while hes still a junior vice stuck in some crummy shack in the Jersey swamp somewhere and— Harry breathed deeply and clutched the steering wheel and blinked his eyes rapidly for a moment. The rage in his voice was obvious to him now and it scared him. And, too, he could sense the pettiness of what he was saying and he was starting to cringe, inwardly, from embarrassment. Ah screw it. Its not worth getting bugged about. He clamped his mouth shut, then pushed in the cigarette lighter. When it popped out, Linda held it while he lit his cigarette. He nodded and mumbled a thanks, still fighting the embarrassment twinging inside him, worrying and wondering what Linda was thinking, afraid to look over and try to determine by her expression what was going on in her mind.

Linda stretched out and turned her ear to the soft music coming from the radio, a satisfied smile once more softening her face. Long before Harry started his tirade, or before they had even started the drive home, a part of her had reviewed the day and decided that it was a good day, a day to be enjoyed and that nothing could ruin it . . . or anyone either. She had listened more with curiosity than real interest and had no intention of going to the trouble of remembering what had been said, but was content to allow it to drift away with the scenery and the passing of time.

The radio suddenly went dead as they entered the Lincoln Tunnel, and Harry tried, desperately, to join Lindas light chitchat, but found conversation almost impossible and was aware of the sweat dribbling down his sides, and he cursed the guy in front of him under his breath for not moving faster so they could get out of the tunnel and she could go back to listening to the radio.

When they finally left the tunnel and merged into the New York traffic, Harry started to feel a little better. But the closer they got to Lindas place, the more apprehensive he became. He just did not feel like sitting around and bullshitting with some broad and he knew he didnt feel like putting the make on her, and all they would do would be to sit around and talk about the day and how nice it was and all that sort of shit and jesus krist he sure as hell wasnt in any mood for that.

He parked in front of her building and Linda looked up at the third floor. The lights are out. I guess my roommates asleep already. Sorry, smiling, but I wont be able to ask you up for coffee. I dont want to wake her up.

Thats O.K. Im kind of bushed anyway.

I had a wonderful time, smiling broadly and sincerely, and thanks so much for driving me home. Harry waited until she entered her building, then drove away, anxious to get home and get some sleep.

Krist, the following Monday was a drag, a big, fat drag. The closer it got to the time to get up, the more restless was his sleep. He tossed, trying to find a comfortable spot, but couldnt, and hung, imprisoned, in a gray and painful limbo between sleep and wakefulness. His body ached and burned with fever, yet his head, in reality, was cool. He tried hard, very hard, to believe he had the flu and should stay in bed all day, but sleep was impossible, and to lie in bed, awake, and relive the outing and the ride home with Linda over and over again was much too torturous, and so, five minutes after the alarm sounded he got out of bed and cooled himself off with a hot shower.

And the goddamn subway reeked like a sewer. All those goddamn animals jammed into the train like the ark . . . yeah, thats what they are, a bunch of stinking animals. Like a zoo on a hot day. Yeah, New York is a Summer Festival. The rotten bastards. I got their festival . . . with this kind of weather. Just lovely weather. So goddamn hot and humid it was like being in a shower, you sweat so much. And those assholes smell worse than animals. Never heard of soap and water and toothpaste. Jesus, what a stink. Ugly goddamn slobs. They smell like they rubbed their armpits with garlic and onions . . . and chewed on dirty underwear. Like that goddamn baboon over there. Looks real natural hanging from the strap. He/d probably love it if I threw a few peanuts atim. Jesus, I/d like to see the orangutan hes married to. Can just see them sitting around watching the boob tube, picking nits off each other and eating them. Shes probably as hairy as that dog over there. Krist, shes got a bigger mustache than Groucho Marx. Shit, shes got more hair growing out of that mole on her cheek than I have on my head. I/d hate like hell to see her legs. Hair probably hangs off in festoons. . . . Jesus, its hot in this rotten trap. The sweats rolling down my back like a river. Sweet Jesus, what a miserable way to live, starting off the day jammed in a train with a herd of stinking animals. . . . Shit, no animal smells this bad . . . or looks this bad. A bunch of goddamn peasant. . . . Slobs! Krist, look at the uniforms theyre wearing. The goddamn chimps in the circus are dressed better than these cretins. Those coordinated sets from Kleins basement. A dollar ninety-eight for the whole damn thing, including a free radio as a bonus. Red slacks! Red jacket! Pink knit shirt and a red asshole polyester tie. Krist. They must be twins, one guy couldnt be so dumb. And the broads. Jesus, what outfits. Uglys really in this season. Ahhhhhh, screwem. All but . . . Shit, maybe I should move to the city and get away from these rotten subways. Or maybe to the suburbs where you have a higher class of slobs riding the trains. Shit! Who needs it. Screw the suburbs. And these assholes. These low-life cretins. Screwim. Where they eat. . . . Suburbs. Shit! Who needs it. . . . Who wants. . .

He bumped and jostled through the sweaty tunnel with the decades of stink and graffitied walls and the tomblike tile and Neanderthalic slobs hacking up phlegm from the depths of their bowels and sucking on it before splattering it onto the tracks or into the shadows of the girders and stomping it into the pores of the cement and hiding it under last years dirt

and up into the joy of honking traffic and menagerie streets heated from a sun hidden by those goddamn slabs of steel and bullshit, but you know the goddamn thing is up there somewhere because its so hot and God forbid there should be a breeze to cool it off because even if one did try to sneak up on the rotten oven of a city, it would get cut off by one of those phallic symbols except in the wintertime when nothing seems to stop the wind from freezing your balls off

but even the streets are better than getting jammed in the elevator next to some broad loaded with cheap perfume that burns your eyes until they feel like two piss holes in the snow

and you finally get to your desk and start going through the garbage on it, waiting for the air conditioning to break down. . . .

A deep breath, a sigh, and a ahhhh, fuckit, and a new day, a new week, is begun. . . .

And anyway, whats the big deal, what in the hell is everyone griping about? I didnt really say anything out of line. I didnt hit anyone on the head or rape their wife. Maybe it doesnt sound so hot, *out* of context, but its easy to misinterpret a joke or an off-the-cuff remark like that. You know, youre driving along with the radio playing and theres the noise of traffic and the breeze coming in the window and youre concentrating on driving and you dont quite catch a word and you say something like, hes got a good head, and it gets all jumbled up in someones ear and its liable to sound like—a— anything, you know—like, he should drop dead, or something, I dont know, maybe thats not a good example, but you know what I mean, or maybe you do say something like, he should drop dead, but you mean it in a joking way and if the person could see your face they would know that you were joking, but they cant see your face in the dark and theyre not used to your sense of humor and so they take you seriously and by the time they repeat it, it gets all twisted out of shape and it takes on a connotation and meaning that has nothing at all to do with what you said and meant . . . you know what I mean, right? I dont have to go into detail and run the shit into the hole—

and goddamn it, what happened to the spec sheet for the Clauson job? I know fucking well right I had it right here last Thursday and now the son of a bitch is gone. If Louise took it, I/ll. . . .

O.K., O.K., so here it is. Somebody probably moved it while they were looking for something. I wish to krist people would leave my desk alone. . . .

And for krists sake keep those corny jokes to yourself. I dont have the time to stop and listen to every dumb joke some idiot heard. I have work to do. Some of these dumb broads think everyone is like them and theyre just here because they have nothing else to do and they dont give a shit about the job and only think about coffee breaks, lunch breaks and time off—

you know better than that, Mr. Wentworth. You know I wouldnt say anything like that about any employee. Jesus . . . Ah, you know. . . . Im not going to say that whoever said that I said that is a liar, but I will say theyre mistaken. . . .

I suppose it does sound like Im jealous, but I/ll tell you the truth, Linda, the Gods Honest Truth. Im not. For one thing I like Davis, Harrys face relaxed with a sincere smile, and respect him. Hes as hard a worker as you will find and has been a lot of help to me. And after all, hes been here longer than I have and . . .

No, no, not at all, Mr. Wentworth. I dont mind tying up the loose ends of his work. After all, we/re all here to do the best we can, right? And if . . .

Krist! Its amazing how people screw things up and make a big deal out of nothing. You make some idle chitchat to some broad and someone has to make a federal case out of it. And anyway, its none of your goddamn business. Why dont you just butt the fuck out of it. I didnt ask you for your opinion. If you dont want to believe me, then thats your problem. I know I didnt say anything and thats enough for me, and if you dont like it, then up yours. Go peddle your bullshit somewhere else. I dont need it. I do my job and I dont have to apologize to you or anyone else for anything! Anything!!!!

And then the ride home . . . clickity, clackity, fuckidy, shittidy, hackidy, coughidy . . . Thats it, chew on it, you son of a bitch. Roll it around in your mouth you—achh, what an animal. But at least the days over and I dont have to listen to that office bullshit and those dizzy broads talking about what a nice time they had Friday, and isnt it a beautiful place, and can you imagine, one man owned that whole place once, and wasnt the food wonderful, and, and, and . . .

Piss on it. I/ll go to a flick tonight with a couple of the guys, or something. It/ll be better tomorrow—it better be! Everybody shouldnt be so screwed up because of the outing and I/ll be able to get back into the swing of things—thank krist that hackin son-ofabitch got off, they shouldnt allow those bastards on the train—and see about coming up with something on this new Langendorff proposal and we/ll see what old Wentworth has to say then. . . . Yeah . . . It/ll be more than a night on the town. . . .

Harry abandoned himself to work with a drive that absorbed all his energy. He wasnt concerned about a title, he didnt need some dumb title to prove who was *really* important. And he wasnt going to say anything to anyone, but just go about his business and develop an idea that had been floating around in his head for a while and lay the best goddamn proposal on Wentworths desk that he had ever seen . . . or anyone else, with or without a title—Hahaha, I wonder if he/ll get a Bigelow on the floor????

He got to the office early and got immediately immersed in his work so that he was undisturbed by the usual morning chitchat and slow settling in, and stayed late, enjoying the quiet and solitude, and the quantity and quality of the work he produced during those few hours at night.

On a couple of days he spent most of his time out of the office collecting and collating information and checking previously submitted data. The longer he worked on the project the more completely involved he became with it, and when he got home late at night, he would sit quietly in his room and reflect on the days work, double-checking himself mentally to be certain he hadnt overlooked anything. And the more involved he became, the more convinced he was that he was right and that his idea was extremely workable, and the more he realized this the more excited he became, and a warm and wonderful feeling of smug satisfaction eased its way around inside him.

He went to the office on Saturday and by early afternoon he had become so intensely involved not only with the job, but with the projected results, that he became very excited and had to leave his desk and walk around the office for a while. Actually he strutted more than walked, and bounced on his feet as he had been doing at his desk.

He stopped in front of one desk and realized that it belonged to Linda, and simultaneously realized that he hadnt thought about her, or Davis, in days—it seemed like years. Jesus, that was only a week ago. Incredible. It seems so long ago that its almost a distant memory. Well, screw it, no point in thinking about her and Davis. Not now. Just get the job done. . . . Yeah.

He went quickly back to his desk and resumed work immediately, his right leg bouncing on the ball of his foot as if he were pumping fuel into himself.

By the middle of the following week he wrapped up the Langendorff proposal and two smaller Class A Linear-type proposals to illustrate how his new method would work on any-size proposal of this type. He also dug into the files and got out proposals from previous years for the same type of corporation. When he had everything assembled and ready to present to Mr. Wentworth, he was so excited that he found himself jumping up and down inside. Just looking at the job he had done thrilled him. He had to be careful in talking to Wentworth because he felt like bouncing in and slapping him on the back and asking him, hows tricks? Turned any good ones lately? Hahaha. Wait till you see what I got for you Wenty boy, youll shit a brick. A solid gold brick. We can really cut the competition now. What do you think of it, Wenty baby boy, you old son of a gun you, chuckling and guffawing, you think its worth a night on the town and a slooooooooooooooooooowwww blow job from one of your pubic—ah, excuse me, I mean public relations people? Or maybe the whole damn department, slapping him on the back and laughing loudly . . .

But how does *this* data give us the results we need for *this* computation?

Well, what I did was to interpolate this information, on a semi-decimal basis, with this current data. Then I coordinated it with the experience projected on *this* data and fed it into the IL30 computer, based on a one to seventeen ratio, which is *ultra*-conservative, and still came up with a low figure.

Wentworth leaned back in his chair for a moment, staring at all the papers and charts Harry had assembled, then leaned forward and continued to stare at them. Combined with the technique you used on the Compton and Brisbane proposal, we are untouchable in the Class A Linear field.

Thats right.

How do you know you are right?

I checked back in our files and reworked old proposals on this basis and *then* checked it with the actual experience, and in each case it worked out to less than a 1 percent differential of the actual cost of the completed job, including all the intangibles and unpredictables.

In other words, peering up at Harry, we can eliminate the ten to twelve percent error factor and still have a minimum of 8 per cent margin at the outside.

Thats right. Easily. Plus the fact that it takes half the time to work up one of these proposals.

When is the Langendorff proposal due?

The twenty-seventh of next month.

O.K., heres what you do. You take this, all of this, over to analysis and tell them I want these proposals, and procedure, ripped apart. I want them to chop it up from every conceivable angle. If there are any flaws in this idea of yours, I want them uncovered now. Got it?

Right, his insides burning with excitement and his arms and legs trembling as he gathered up his papers and charts and started to leave Wentworths office.

And Harry.

Yes?

Dont fumble the ball this time, a faint hint of a smile on his face.

I wont. Definitely.

Yeah, dont worry. Im not letting anything fuck things up. I sure as hell aint going to be sucking hind tit around here. Im on my way. Nose to the grindstone and a finger up my ass whistling Dixie. Yeah, forgot to ask him about the slooooooooowww blow job, or a little dancing cheek to cheek. Why not, ass is ass. Yeah, and a finger is a finger. Finger, schminger. Later for that. Got to sew this thing up. Yeah, tear it apart—chop it up—twist it and turn it, and when youre all finished, sew it up nice and neat and send it back where it came from. Right here.

He dropped in on the boys in analysis from time to time during the following week and each time was told the same thing: its still holding water. Eventually they could not think of any other way to attack the system, and so a report was forwarded to Wentworth detailing the methods used to try to refute the system, and the result: it is sound in theory and practice.

Harry was calmly excited when he had lunch with Wentworth. He enjoyed the slow walk through the office to the elevator; the chitchat as they walked to the restaurant; the waiting for the maitre d, the sounds of the dining room as they were led to their table, the adjusting of himself in the chair and the unfolding of the napkin; the smooth and quick efficiency of the waiter and the busboy; the sipping of his drink; the red, gold and beautiful script of the menu and leaned back in his chair as he leisurely read the menu, then nonchalantly laid it aside. It was a way of life to which he intended to become accustomed. Places like this were just one of the aspects—rewards—of the success he sought and was determined to attain. Harry White was excited and, for the most part, he felt at home sitting at the table with Wentworth, but a part of him felt like a visitor, the visitor that in reality he was, but someday he knew that he would feel as much at home here as Wentworth and the others he noticed as he glanced around the room. They looked like they were completely at ease and did not know what it was to feel like a visitor, and he was determined that someday, soon, he would fit in just like them.

In case you are wondering about it, Harry, I do not intend to discuss the Langendorff proposal—you read the report from the analysis boys—as far as Im concerned we/re going ahead with it, smiling and looking at Harry, as is. Harry glowed inside and fought to keep a relaxed smile on his face as the significance of Wentworths remark sunk in deeper and deeper, and he became instantly involved with the future and what it had in store for him and how the barriers to success would be disintegrated and he kept going up and up and up. . . . After the contracts are signed—and that seems to be an absolute certainty to me—I/ll see to it that you receive a substantial raise.

Thanks, smiling and making a conscious effort to speak as calmly as possible, I/ll always say yes to that.

Wentworth looked at Harry for a moment. But what I really wanted to talk to you about—again—is why I am not going to recommend you for a promotion . . . now. Harrys guts suddenly went flip flop and he hoped to krist his face didnt show it. Im not going to bother rehashing a lot of ancient history—and thats what it is as far as Im concerned—

but you know we have had discussions in the past about your inconsistencies. Ive told you that I think highly of you, and its true, I do. When you apply yourself to your work—what you have just done is a perfect example—you are the sharpest young man in the firm . . . and maybe not just with respect to the younger men. I can guarantee a future that is without limit if you will just apply yourself consistently. Anyway, waving his hand, we have gone over all that and I think thats enough said about that. The point is—to be specific and pertinent—that I know you can do a great job for a while—this isnt the first time you have done it—but how do you wear over the long haul? That, my young friend, is *the* question. Youre great in the fifty-yard dash, but thats not what we need. We need men who can continue to do it day after day after day . . . year after year. Now, I think you can do it, but Im not certain that *you* do. I think that somewhere in the back of your mind you doubt that you can live up to your potential with consistency. Harry could feel his muscles twitching and he was fighting desperately to keep the right expression on his face, if he could only figure out what in the name of krist was the right expression. Thats why I do not want you to get a promotion now. I do not want you to think you have won the race and start to rest on your laurels, as you have done in the past, and count the spoils of victory. You see Harry, there is no finish line to the race, except down and out. Every day is another race that demands another victory. So, I want you to prove to yourself that you can apply yourself to the work with consistency. And, leaning back slightly and smiling, I am even going to make it a little easier for you to do it by giving you some additional work. I know what its like to be bored. They both smiled, and Harry started to relax a little more. Consistency is the secret of success, Harry. Its the bottom line to the top.

Harry spent the remainder of that day vacillating between feelings of joy and disappointment, feeling resentful at being at the same old desk, then looking forward to the additional money and work. He applied himself to his work, which was anticlimactic right now, and stopped every now and then and looked around, feeling at one time as if he had been here his entire life, and then another as if it was all new, as if he knew he had been there before, yet somehow it all looked unfamiliar.

He thought of Davis, the new junior vice-president, and he twinged slightly and felt flushed, but then remembered the pending raise and the complimentary things Wentworth had said to him, and smiled smugly as he thought that he would probably be getting more than Davis even with his title. And his mind constantly kept taking him back to the restaurant and the sounds and the smells and the feel of the napkin on his lap and in his hand as he dabbed at his mouth from time to time, and to Wentworths expression and attitude. And he knew he wasnt bullshitting him. He was straight. And what he said was straight. Harry knew that. Deep down inside he knew absolutely that he meant everything he had said. And there was something about Wentworths attitude that made him feel good. Yeah, he was leveling with him, all right. There was no doubt about that. All Harry had to do was to stick to it and Wentworth would push him all he could. And there was really nothing to it. He didnt know exactly what had happened before to get him all screwed up and blow that promotion, but whatever it was, it was not going to happen again. He was going to see to that. He was going to get in here every day right on the button and do the best goddamn job Wentworth, or anyone else, had ever seen, and pretty soon . . . Yeah, who knows. No place to go but up. Forget about those crummy cafeterias, he knew where to go for lunch. And that bullshit of sending out for a quick hamburger when he was working late—no more of that. He knew how to live—how to really live. Central Park West isnt that far away. A nice little apartment up high enough so you can see the whole damn park or even the ocean. Thats the way to live. Have to get somewhere, you just jump in a cab. No more hassling those subways. It wont be long. Yeah . . . Harry stared in front of him, smiling and emotionally involved with the future and a feeling of warmth and well-being.

His smile broadened and he got up and walked to the junior vice-presidents new office. Hi. How you doing? I suddenly realized that I hadnt seen your new office, so I thought I had better get over here before you get another promotion.

They both laughed, and Davis got up and stuck his hand into Harrys as he extended it over the desk. Hi, Harry. How you doing?

Great. Just great. Boy, some office, looking around. Complete with painting and potted plant, eh?

Yeah, laughing. I guess when youre a junior vice-president, they think you need a little extra oxygen.

I guess so, both of them laughing and chuckling. Harry turned back to Davis with a serious smile on his face. What I really wanted to tell you is that I am really happy for you and if there is ever anything I can do—you know, maybe give you a hand or something—just give a yell.

Well, thanks, Harry, I really appreciate that.

Right. They smiled at each other and Harry cupped Davis on the shoulder and left.

Harry felt so good, and so excited, that he had to force himself to sit at his desk. He didnt know what he felt like doing, but he felt like doing something—anything.

His phone rang and he picked it up instantly. Hello Harry, this is Linda. Do you still have the Burrell file?

For a moment Harrys mind whirled around and he tried desperately to keep up with it. He knew he knew a Linda and a Burrell file, but he could not get them connected or related. Then after a couple of endless seconds, it clicked into place.

Hi. Long time no see. Yeah, as a matter of fact I do.

O good, I need it. Do you mind if I come over and pick it up?

Dont bother. I have to go over that way anyway. I should have returned it before this in the first place. Be right there.

He found the file and happily left his desk. At least he now had something to do and somewhere to go. He could not have sat still for another moment.

As he walked to Lindas desk his mind quickly flashed pictures of her lying beside the pool—and him—and of their dancing, and he remembered how she looked and felt, and he vaguely wondered whether or not her roommate was out of town.

Hi. Where do you want this? extending the file.

O, you can just put it over there with the rest of them, smiling warmly.

I hope they dont fall, adding the file to the top of the pile, they will crush you and we wouldnt want that.

Im with you on that. I/ll be finished with them someday, I hope, and get them safely off the desk. By the way, I hear that youve been burning the midnight oil over there lately.

O yeah? You must have been talking to Louise and Rae, chuckling and waving his finger at her.

Well, laughing, I did have lunch with them a few times.

Speaking of lunch, how about joining me tomorrow? I/ll spring.

I thought you gave up lunch hours.

Well, gesturing expansively, for you I/ll make an exception.

Thank you, smiling and chuckling, thats very generous of you.

Well, you know me, clutching his hands to his chest, Im all heart.

How can I resist an invitation like that—no, raising her hand, dont tell me, I know: easy. They both laughed.

I have to get back to my desk. See you tomorrow.

Lunch was delightful. It seemed like years since he had had a leisurely lunch, and he could not remember the last time he had lunch with a woman, or who it was, it was so long ago.

And whenever that last lunch was, and whoever it was with, he knew absolutely that it was not like this—relaxed, no pressure, no games, no maneuvering. Just an all-too-fast lunch hour with a lively woman (hmmm, what do you know, shes not a broad) and charming conversation.

I hear by way of the grapevine that you have something new cooking?

You mean a grapevine named yenta?

She chuckled along with him. I guess Rae and Louise do sort of take a special interest in you.

And a lot of other things, too.

Yes, thats true, but I really love them. Theyre so nice, so warm and—a friendly. Kind of motherly, I guess.

Yeah, chuckling, I know. But one mother is enough, I dont need two more—Harry suddenly laughed—wondering about our lunch and when we/ll get married.

Youre probably right, smiling, how many children do you want?

O, I dont know, why not start with ten?

Suppose we just get back to lunch, if you dont mind.

O.K., laughing along with her, that seems a lot safer.

But there is one thing that cannot be denied, and that is that they are a great source of information. Between them they know everything that is going on in the office, even if it hasnt happened yet.

Yeah, nodding his head, that sure is true—O, by the way, I wanted to apologize for bugging you on the way home from the outing.

Bugging me? Im afraid I dont know what you mean.

Well, you know, fidgeting in his seat and toying with his coffee cup, I, ah . . . well, I may have sounded a little negative about some things, and, shrugging his shoulders, the way I—ah—mentioned Davis and his promotion may have sounded funny— You know, in thinking about it I realized that it may have given you the wrong impression.

No apology is necessary, Harry, smiling warmly and reassuringly, as far as Im concerned. As a matter of fact I have no idea what you are talking about. I had a really wonderful time.

Good, smiling and sighing inwardly, Im glad to hear it.

But tell me about this new thing youre doing, Im dying to hear about it. Rae said that it was something, quote, spectacular and fantastic, already, end quote.

Well, it really isnt all that great, relaxing and enjoying the warmth of her smile and her voice, its not going to change the world. But, his smile broadening, it really turns me on. You see, one of the great things about this idea, moving and speaking enthusiastically, is that I think I can adopt it for areas other than what I originally used it for—at least thats what I am going to try to do—am trying to do. And who knows what may be developed if I keep— Linda laughed and Harry looked at her bewildered for a moment, and she reached across the table and squeezed his hands with hers.

Im sorry Harry, I didnt mean to interrupt or upset you, but I have never seen anyone so excited about his work before. I think its wonderful, just marvelous. You really do love your work, dont you?

Yeah, well, blushing slightly, I guess I do. It kind of grabs me sometimes, you know when theres a problem and you have to find an answer, Linda withdrawing her hands and continuing to look at him intently, smiling, or when you suddenly get an idea and you work on it and work on it and you twist it and yank it until it fits just right—Harry leaned back and chuckled, I guess I really do like it.

Yes, it certainly shows. But Im afraid we will have to continue this another time, its time to get back.

Thats too bad. The only thing I like more than my work is talking about it, gesturing with his arms and smiling broadly, to you. How about having lunch again, tomorrow?

Fine. I/d love it.

Lunch the following day was even more exciting, it being spent talking about Harrys work and what he had done and what he hoped to do and how good and, ah—sort of whole he felt when he was completely involved in his work; and of his ambitions and dreams of success. And the amazing thing, the thing that Harry White was not too aware of because of his involvement with himself, but could somehow sense, was that Linda not only listened intently, but was truly interested in what he was saying and thoroughly enjoyed the conversation—or perhaps it would be more accurate to say—monologue.

When he got back to the office, he asked Rae if she wanted to know what they had been talking about, or did she already know?

Of course I do—Louise was laughing—but Im not going to tell you. Youll have to find out for yourself, darlingk. So what do you think of boy wonder here, Louise? He thinks maybe we had a bugger gadget under the table. Harry and Louise burst into a loud guffaw, then quickly swallowed it to controlled laughter. So whats so funny?

Louise and Harry were still bouncing back and forth between deep chuckles and laughter. You tell her, Harry.

Harry wiped a couple of tears from his eyes and stopped laughing. You mean bugging device.

Eh, so big deal. Bugger or bugging, its the same difference.

Not quite, he and Louise started laughing again, theres a big difference.

So whos fighting? Let me tell you, bug or bugger, you tell a girl how wonderful you are and how far up in the world you are going to go, and then you let her catch you.

You should listen to her, Harry, its good advice, still laughing and chuckling.

You mean like advice to the lovelorn by Linda Lovely—or is it Linda Lovelace?

So what could I tell you? You name them, you pick them.

They all laughed, and Harry extended his arms in a gesture of submission. I give up. I dont know how I ever got involved in this, but Im getting out of here before you drive me nuts.

Thats not much of a drive, Louise was choking on her laughter and sputtering as she spoke. its a short putt.

Harrys eyes were tearing again from laughter as he walked back to his desk.

Lunch with Linda became almost a daily occurrence, and an extremely happy and relaxing one. Harry knew that they were simply going to eat lunch and talk and get back to the office on time, and so he was not afraid of things getting out of hand and thus getting back to the office hours late and getting in trouble with Wentworth again. He did not want that. Things were going well—as a matter of fact they were great—and he wanted to keep it that way. He really loved his work and actually looked forward to it each day.

And, he had no desire to roam around during his lunch hour and see what broads he could pick up or play games with. Somehow that whole scene seemed to be part of the distant past and only vaguely remembered, at times with a tinge of embarrassment, and at other times with the vague realization that if he were to pursue that again, it would not only mean the loss of his job, the work he now loved so thoroughly and that was so satisfying, but would also mean the loss of something else. Of what he did not know, but there was the vague feeling that he had better beware because there was something that was not only unknown involved with those actions, but something absolutely deadly.

And, of course, he really enjoyed Lindas company. She was different, unlike any broad—female—he had ever met. He didnt try to analyze the difference, or ponder about it in any way, but just allowed himself to enjoy the feeling. And, he was becoming more and more aware of how she was making him feel.

One of the things that he did think about from time to time, in an amazed sort of way, was how much he enjoyed just talking with her. They always seemed to have a ball just talking and eating their sandwiches and drinking their coffee in a crowded luncheonette or cafeteria. They somehow always seemed to have many things to talk about, and ideas to exchange, which was so new to Harry.

But the big thing, the really significant thing that he thought about over and over, and enjoyed more and more, was her laugh. It was the happiest laugh he had ever heard. It was so real. Like she not only enjoyed laughing, but enjoyed living. Many times he would laugh before she got to the punch line of a joke she was telling because she would start laughing halfway through it.

But it wasnt only the sound of her laughter, or what it did to and for him. It was also the sight of it. She just sparkled when she laughed, and her whole body, her entire being, seemed to be having fun. Her eyes just twinkled with little lights and even her fingernails seemed to glow. She loved laughter.

5

Friday they made a date to go swimming the following day. They got to the beach in the late morning and though the beach was crowded with the weekend relief-seekers, they had no trouble finding an unoccupied area more than adequate for their needs, and just a short walk from the surf. They spread their blanket, rolled their clothes up and put them under their towels, then went for a swim.

The water was cold when they ran in, but once the initial shock was over it was invigorating, and they stayed in for quite a while, swimming to the last float and back; diving into the waves or just jumping around in the surf. When they left the water, they trotted back to their blanket laughing and shaking water from their bodies.

They stretched out on the blanket, and when Linda was dry, she started to rub herself with suntan oil. When she had rubbed all of her body except her back, she handed the bottle to Harry and then stretched out on the blanket. Rub my back please, Harry.

Sure. Harry let a few drops slowly drip on her back and laughed as she wiggled.

Ooo, thats cold, Harry, dont do that.

Yeah, I know, laughing and pouring a little oil in the palm of his hand.

Youre awful.

Yeah, I know, chuckling as he slowly rubbed the oil in her back. You know, with bikinis like this you end up with an awful lot of back to rub. She chuckled, and Harry continued rubbing her back, loving the feel of her skin, so smooth and warm from the oil and the sun. He continued rubbing, almost hypnotically as he watched his hand moving over her beautiful back, his insides warming, too, from the sun and the excitement that flowed through his hand and up his arm. . . .

O, thats so good I could drift right off to sleep.

Well, laughing, it keeps me awake. He gave one final rub and was about to slap her on the butt, but didnt. He handed her the bottle, O.K., now its my turn, then stretched out on the blanket.

The day was a typical beach day, complete with sand kicked in their faces by kids running by. They swam, floated, dunked, jumped and dove; and had hot dogs with cold beer, and even some Turkish taffy.

They left the beach in the late afternoon, and the roads were crowded and at times the traffic barely crawled, but it just did not seem to bother Harry today. For one thing they were in no real hurry, and they chatted and laughed—Jesus he loved to hear her laugh—and though at times the traffic may have lagged, time didnt and it was an enjoyable ride home. It certainly was a lot different from the last time he drove her home. Its incredible, but that wasnt such a long time ago, yet its as if it were something from the vague and distant past. God, what a difference between that ride and this. Just no comparison. None at all.

Lindas roommate was away for the weekend, so they decided to eat dinner there. I/ll broil a few chops and toss a salad together and see what else is around.

Great. Thats fine with me.

Im going to take a quick shower and get the sand off. I/ll be out in a minute.

Harry stretched out in a chair and slowly became conscious of the fact that he was listening to the sound of the shower and then was aware that he was imagining it flowing off Lindas body, and he shook his head and blinked his eyes and dismissed the image. He didnt know why, but he did not want to get into one of those fantasies.

The shower suddenly stopped and in a few moments Linda came out of the bathroom wrapped up in a large terry cloth robe and rubbing her head with a towel. O.K., its all yours. You know, I think one of the best things about the beach is the shower when you get home.

Harry laughed along with her. Well, I guess thats one way of looking at it.

When he got out of the shower, all crisp, clean and cool, Linda was busy in the kitchen chopping, mixing and tossing. You know, youre right, that is the best part of a day at the beach. He went into the kitchen and watched Linda work for a moment. Man, you move around like you really know what youre doing.

I do, wrinkling her nose at him, then laughing, and I love it too. I think I was born to it. It really turns me on, to quote an industrious young man I know.

With a memory like that I/ll have to watch what I say. Anything I can do to help?

No, not really. Unless you/d like to have wine with dinner.

Sure, why not? How about a little Blue Nun?

No, I dont think so, a serious expression on her face, I thought we/d eat alone. Her face widened into a big smile, and Harry laughed.

Be careful, it can get to be a habit. They chuckled, and Harry asked her if she preferred any particular wine?

No. I really dont know one from another. What I usually buy is the ninety-seven-cent imported Bordeaux. It seems to be pretty good.

O.K., one imported and expensive wine coming up. Red or white?

Red. Its much prettier.

I dont think that thats how they figure it, smiling and enjoying watching her moving around the kitchen, but if you say so, its red.

When Harry looked at the table before sitting down, he had the feeling that it was magic. The whole thing. Magic. There were a couple of candles, a large salad bowl and two small ones, plates, silverware, napkins, an old wooden table, nothing unusual or exceptional, yet together Linda somehow made it seem so special. It was special.

This is incredible. How/d you do it? It seems like you were only out there a short time.

O, its nothing. Any great chef could have done it.

I guess youre right, smiling, it really does turn you on, end quote.

Dinner was delicious and delightful. When they finished, Linda brought out a bowl of fruit and some cheese. I hope you like stinky cheese. I love it.

They continued to sit around the table, drinking coffee and talking. Harry hadnt thought about how he felt all day. He did not even know whether or not he had thought about anything. He enjoyed himself and just followed those feelings without question. As a matter of fact, he could not remember, if he had bothered trying, when he had had a better time in his life. Not since he was a child had he been so relaxed. Part of the reason he had such an enjoyable day was that he was unaware of any of this.

But then he did become aware, slowly, of some sort of disquieting feeling within him. He felt ill at ease for no reason at all. The evening was continuing to go the way the rest of the day had gone and they were talking and laughing, but now he felt a vague tugging inside that was fighting against the momentum of the day, fighting to change the direction of what was happening. He became aware that what he was doing was unnatural for him. He had no business just sitting and joking like this with some broad. This was crazy. He had never done this in his life. There was something else that he should be doing, but right now he wasnt sure what that was. It was wacky. He could feel that he knew what it was he was supposed to do, that he should just simply do it, but at the same time he could not figure out what it was—or why—or even what all this was that was going on inside him. He was just becoming more and more confused by this conflict, and his confusion confused him even more.

And to add to all the confusion was the fact that he felt good being with Linda, just talking and joking and drinking coffee and nibbling on a piece of cheese. Smelly cheese. And she excited him and he wanted to reach over and touch her hand, but he couldnt seem to do it. Jesus, why should that be such a big deal? Why was he getting tight in his gut and feeling like something was going to happen? He started to become involved with that strange feeling and the fact that he could not reach over and hold her hand. And why should he want to hold her hand anyway? That was kid stuff, for krists sake. He somehow had lost control of the play. It never went like this. But how did it go? He couldnt seem to remember. Or did he? He could somehow sense how it should be going, but he seemed to be just sitting on the sidelines watching it go in the wrong direction. He almost felt like standing up and yelling, Hey, theres something wrong here. This is not the way. But he just sat and talked and joked and laughed and had the best time of his life as he fought the demon that was welling up inside him, growing and growling, and causing his inner eye to blink with dismay and confusion.

He got up and went to the bathroom and looked in the mirror and frowned at his reflection—or did his reflection frown at him?—and tilted his head this way and that and spread his mouth in a smile, then shook his head and chuckled softly, youre crazy, you son of a bitch. Youre out of your head. He looked back and forth at himself for another moment, then shrugged and left the bathroom.

He stood behind Linda for a moment, then put his arms on her shoulders and kissed her on the neck, and let his hands slowly slide down her arms. She seemed to lean into his kiss slightly, and as he continued to kiss her neck he became self-conscious and watched himself as if he were playing some sort of a movie role—or rather imitating some actor in a love scene. He felt stiff, awkward and unnatural, but forced himself to continue to kiss her neck and to glide his hands over her breasts. She very gently but firmly moved his hands away. He continued to breathe heavily down her neck, trying to work up more enthusiasm for what he was doing, and at the same time criticizing himself for such a bad performance. But he could not stop.

Lets go to bed.

Linda chuckled gently and turned and looked up at him with amusement. One minute youre laughing about *Abbott and Costello Meet the Wolfman*, and the next you want to go to bed.

Well, whats so strange about wanting to go to bed with a beautiful woman, forcing himself to try and kiss her again, but she gently rebuffed him and he sat down.

Nothing. Its just the timing that seems so strange. And funny.

He shrugged, trying to appear nonchalant, but still feeling awkward and self-conscious. I didnt know there was any special time.

Well there is, still smiling gently, the right time.

I always thought any time was the right time.

Perhaps for you, but not for me. And it does take two to make a couple.

Harry shrugged and tried hard to swallow the demon out of existence, but he couldnt. He didnt know what had happened and how they got to be sitting here suddenly talking like this, but he could not seem to stop himself from doing what he was doing, and he didnt know what else to do or say. Something was out of hand. It seemed like the only thing he could do was to sit here and listen to himself, and watch himself, and feel so goddamn twisted and weird inside that he did not know what the hell to do.

Im sorry if I bugged you—

You didnt bug me, Harry, still smiling gently—

but I didnt know you were saving it.

Linda tilted her head to one side and looked at Harry for a moment, then shook her head. Im surprised. Im really surprised, Harry.

Why? What did you think I was, some sort of celibate monk, or something?

Well, to be perfectly frank, I hadnt thought of it at all. But if I had, I must confess I never would have thought you were so . . . so—she shrugged her shoulders and shook her head—ah . . . I dont know exactly how to say it—Harry stared at her as if just staring might change everything, change what had been said, what was happening, and most important of all, change what Linda was about to say because he could feel in his bones that it was going to rip through him like a jagged piece of ice—well, I guess what I mean is that I never thought you would be so high schoolish.

Maybe youre the one who is high schoolish. Maybe youre the one—

Harry, the smile gone from her face and looking him in the eye, almost looking through him, twisting things around isnt going to change anything. And I really dont see why youre making such a big thing out of nothing. Is your ego so fragile that you cant take a no without becoming hostile?

Who in the hell is hostile? Just because you want to sit on it and try to hatch it sure as hell doesnt make me hostile.

Linda looked at him, no longer surprised, but annoyed and extremely disappointed. Im going to tell you something, Harry—Harry could feel himself cringing inside and wanted just to get up and go, or disappear or change everything, and

what the fuck is going on here anyway—not that I *have* to . . .
I certainly dont *owe* you an explanation for my behavior. It
is certainly *my* prerogative to say yes or no to whomever I
please. But I want you to know so you can get a few things
straight in your head . . . and maybe I want to tell you because
Im annoyed with your childishness.

You dont have to tell me—

I know I dont. But I want you
to know that I am not *sitting* on anything, or *saving* anything,
because theres nothing to save (Harry could feel himself getting warmer and warmer and he/d be a son of bitch if he
wasnt blushing. Shit! SHIT!) and there are no *hang-ups, no
repressions*, no deep, dark, ugly and sordid secrets being
wrapped in a cloak of wishful virginity (Harry was fucked.
Fucked! He couldnt protest. He couldnt move. He couldnt
seem to do a thing but sit and listen), just a simple decision
made by me, for me (if only she would yell or do something
that would let him get angry so he could break this fucking
inertia, but she didnt. She just looked him right in the eye and
firmly said what she had to say without even raising her voice),
a decision that came about not as a result of some ugly,
dramatic or traumatic experience, but simply through an
inner understanding of myself . . . an inner need. And it has
nothing to do with you, or anyone else as a matter of fact . . .
just me. You know, Harry, Im not a teeny-bopper or some sort
of liberated or frustrated female running amuck from bed to
bed. Im simply a mature woman, and the next man I go to bed
with is going to be my husband. *My* husband, smiling gently
once again, not someone elses. And he will be my *then*
husband, not my *future* husband. Im sorry I dont have a sordid tale of woe to tell you, Harry, Lindas smile was becoming
more and more gentle, that we could mull over and analyze—
Harry made a half-ass attempt at a shrug—but its just as
simple as Ive said.

Harry looked at
her smile and could feel that his face was stiffly blank, and his
head tumbled and twirled around inside, trying desperately to

think of something to do, some twist of the mouth, a nod of the head, a gesture of hand or a shrug or a smile, and though the turbulence within him continued, he just sat looking at her smile. Then he fumbled his hand to his watch and tried—hoped—to affect a slight tone of surprise. Its late. I/d better get going.

Linda remained silent, swallowing her disappointment, and watched Harry leave. And though she was disappointed at the way the day had ended, she was relieved when the door closed behind him. The awkwardness and embarrassment, and the tension they created, increased so rapidly, especially as they sat there silently looking at each other, that it became almost tangible and unbearable.

Linda continued to sit at the table and sighed softly, still a little shocked by the suddenness with which a lovely day had turned into something so —so sad. Yes, I guess thats the word. It too bad. Its really too bad. She quickly reviewed what had happened and what she had said and had no regrets. None whatsoever. No matter how she looked at it, or her feelings for Harry, which were deep and tender, she would still say the same thing again. There are just some compromises that cannot be made without compromising the foundation of your life. She sighed again and picked up the coffee cups and put them in the sink.

She looked around, then dumped the ashtrays and put them in the sink too, then put out the light and went to bed. She lay awake for a short time thinking of Harry, fondly, though greatly disappointed in him this evening, but accepting what had happened and the fact that it was over and done with and no *thing* and no *one* could change it. And, accepting, too, that she would not change what she had said, even if she could, the disturbance within her dissipated and she drifted into sleep.

Jesus krist . . . Son of a bitch. All screwed up. The whole rats ass thing is screwed. Just cant figure the son of a bitch out. Sitting there laughing and all of a sudden wham, its up yours. How in the hell did I let some broad bullshit me like that? I must be nuts. I shouldve just split. Hey, who needs it baby? Save it for someone else. Im not buyin it. See you later. Can you imagine that broad trying to lay that garbage on me? Who does she think shes kiddin? Just a big smile, a laugh and split. Or just pick her up and take her to bed. Thats probably what she really wanted. Coming on with all that *mature* bullshit and just sitting there waiting for me to call her bluff. Why didnt I do it???? Screw it. Why give her the satisfaction. Let her eat her heart out. Harry entered the Brooklyn Battery Tunnel and the sudden closing in, and the tile and the lights, got him remembering the distant past when he drove Linda through a tunnel and that son of a bitch Davis was bugging him, and he waved his hand in a gesture of dismissal and shoved all that out the window or behind him or some such place, any place, he didnt care, he just didnt want to be bothered with that now. . . . When he came back from the bathroom, he sat down and as he listened to Linda, he gently took one of her hands in both of his and looked up at her and smiled and then gently kissed her finger tips and slowly her voice trailed off and he got up from his chair and walked around the table, still holding her hand, and kissed her gently on the forehead and then the eyes and the mouth and he could hear her sigh, almost inaudibly, as she slowly stood and their bodies burned against each other and without a word he led her to the bedroom. . . .

Yeah, what is this shit you dont want to go to bed? You got to be kidding. . . . When Harry got back from the bathroom, they turned on the television and watched *Abbott and Costello Meet the Wolfman*, and they ate some more of the smelly cheese as they laughed and made comments from time to time, sitting on the couch feeling her warmth and listening to that lovely laughter, finishing the wine, then drinking coffee. They just sort of relaxed and laughed the night into a new day. . . . And Harry started to feel vulnerable as he drove along the Gowanus Parkway, the parkway seeming to be so sidelessly wide and lonely this time of night with just an occasional car going by. What a rotten day. What a rotten, stinking day. Try to swim and some jerk knocks into you, and when you try to relax on the beach, some mentally retarded brats go running around kicking sand in your face. The little bastards.

The mattress seemed hard and lumpy and he kept adjusting and readjusting himself, trying to find a comfortable spot in the bed. And the fucking sun will be up nice and early and shine right in my eyes. No point even in trying to get any sleep. Rotten son of a bitch. Screw it. Everything. The whole damn thing.

O Monday, rotten Monday! The subways, the heat, the humidity, the smell, the people. There ought to be a law against fat slobs riding the subway. . . . O, well, the hell with it. I just hope Rae doesnt bug me. I really dont need that. The whole office will probably know what happened Saturday night before I even get there. Should have known better than to take out a broad in the office. Too damn many yentas. Probably get the stares and the looks. Maybe Raes vacation started Friday. Eh, whats the difference. Let them talk. Big deal.

Fortunately for Harry he had a lot of work and was forced to concentrate on it rather than continually dwelling on Saturday night, constantly replaying the scene and rewriting the script, over and over again. The work was demanding and he stayed consciously involved with it, but yet there was a disquieting feeling within him. He was especially aware of this at lunch time as he strolled through the streets, his work no longer occupying his mind. At times the feeling would get stronger and he felt he almost knew what it was, as if he felt he should apologize, but he was sure that couldnt be true, so he just shrugged it away.

Gradually he became aware of the fact that he was following a broad whose ass, barely covered by a miniskirt, was winking and blinking at him. It was really a beautiful ass. Nice and round and firm and smooth. He just knew it was smooth and —he stopped suddenly and blinked and shook his head. Hey, what the hell is going on here? He looked at his watch. Damn! A couple of minutes late already. Goddamn it. He turned and rushed back to the office, getting back about five minutes late. When he sat at his desk, he found that he was out of breath. Five minutes was no big deal, but he had planned on getting back five minutes early. He sat quietly for a few minutes, then pushed everything out of his mind with his work.

The ride to work the following day was a little more comfortable. He was less apprehensive. No one had bothered him the day before. No one had said anything about Saturday night. Neither Louise nor Rae tossed any digs or had any cute remarks to make. And, thank God, he did not have to have any contact with Linda. That was the thing that really bugged him. Even now he flushed and squirmed slightly when he thought of confronting her. And it was ridiculous. Why in the hell should he feel embarrassed? He didnt do anything. Not a damn thing! There was no reason for him to apologize. There was no reason for him to get himself involved in that nonsense. Forget about it and concentrate on his job. He had a couple of problems on his desk that really turned him on, that really had him thinking. . . .

But maybe they had lunch yesterday and she told them about Saturday night and today theyll be ready with their little zingers or looks. Balls. I really dont need that kind of action. I/ll just bury myself in my work and they wont bother me. I/ll just make sure I dont end up on the elevator with them, or let them trap me into going to lunch with them. Harry knew what he had to do, and though he resented having to go to the trouble of doing it just so some old broads wouldnt bug him, he would do it anyway.

The morning went easily enough, and quite rapidly, as he stayed completely involved with his work. He thought of calling down for a sandwich and having a quick lunch at his desk, but decided against it and went out. After eating he decided to stroll around for a few minutes and get the kinks out of his neck. Actually, it was a beautiful day for strolling around. It wasnt too hot and humid and so it was comfortable in the shade, so he stayed on the shady side of the street and stretched his legs for a few minutes. . . .

I/ll be a son of a bitch, ten after. Damn it. Again he turned and rushed back to the office. How in the hell did it get to be so late? And he wasnt even following a broad. Just sort of roaming around, maybe looking a little, like any guy would do. Thats all. Not even— O, shit. Now the elevators got to take all day. He could feel his feet squirming around inside his shoes as he waited for the goddamn elevator to get down so he could get back to his desk. Shit. A quarter after. I/ll be a rotten son of a bitch. Its about time. He jostled himself into the elevator and rushed back to his desk and quickly surrounded himself with papers.

After a few minutes he glanced around and realized that Wentworth wasnt in the office. Thank krist for small favors. He relaxed a bit and concentrated on his work, but found himself stopping from time to time to look around. Everybody just seemed to be doing their work, yet he continued to get this feeling that somebody was watching him, though Rae and Louise never seemed to be looking in his direction. It was strange, and very puzzling, how the feeling just seemed to grow slowly until he found himself looking around, again, against his will. He didn't really want to keep looking around, and actually he wasnt aware he was doing it until he was doing it. Screw it. He just turned back to his work. Again . . .

And the damndest thing was that he still had that disquieting feeling after work too. He didnt exactly feel like someone was watching him as he rode home on the subway, but there was a vague disturbance sort of rolling around within him.

And the damn thing was still there after dinner. He strolled up to Caseys and talked with the guys for a while and listened to them bullshit about the horses and the ball games, not really knowing what they were saying, then went home early. He went to his room and tried reading for a while, then closed the book and squeezed it and shook his head. It was ridiculous. This whole thing was ridiculous. There really wasnt any reason why it should, yet something kept tugging at him in the back of his head. Shit! He tossed the book on the chair and called Linda.

Krist, it was a long time before she answered the phone. And the whole time it felt like his stomach was attached to his throat, and he was hoping she wasnt home, and at the same time he wanted to talk to her because he somehow sensed that that was the only thing that would calm this strange and disquieting feeling. It was an interminably long time before she picked up the phone, and by the time he heard her say hello, his fingers were starting to cramp from squeezing the phone so hard.

And then the fumbling hello, how are you? and the apology torturously squeezed out by the churning in his gut, and then the gradual relaxing until he was holding the phone loosely and was stretched out in his chair . . . and then the sound of her laughter and they chitchatted, and when they finally hung up he wasnt exactly certain just what he had said, or what she had said, but he knew that everything was all right. He was all quiet inside. Except for a little whirl of excitement, a whirl that seemed to grow a little when he thought about her laugh. Harry spent the rest of the evening thinking about Linda.

6

Wentworth wasnt kidding when he said he was going to give him a lot of work. He really piled it on, and Harry thrived. He stayed late quite often, not out of necessity, but simply because he did not want to leave a part of a job in the middle, and wanted to see it through to the end before leaving.

There was another significant change too. He was almost leading a life of celibacy—at least for him. Thats not to say that he took a vow or a pledge with a solemn oath and sent it out to pasture; he still knew what it was for, but for him there was a vast difference. There were some nights when he just stayed home and read or studied, sometimes a couple of nights in a row (his parents developing a sense of security and hope, seeing their son starting to settle down), and he kept his activities to the weekends. As a matter of fact, he let a couple of weekends pass without even a serious thought of copping some broads drawers—not many, but it did happen on occasion.

And then there was Linda . . . the Lady of the Laugh. The feelings Harry had when he was with her or thought about her perplexed him, primarily because he had never experienced such feelings. But with time they became more familiar and thus less and less disturbing until he was so accustomed to them that he found he enjoyed them. There was an excitement, yet there did not seem to be any tension. Actually, he could not tell exactly how he felt, but he did know how he did *not* feel. He knew what was missing, and what was missing he did not miss.

There were occasional lunches, dinners, movies or the theater, and on all those occasions, a lot of fun. Yeah, fun. Somehow that seemed like exactly the right word. It was not the hysteria of a Fire Island weekend, or the screaming at a ball game or the fights, or balling some chick and splitting before her old man got home . . . or any one of those other *fun* things. Somehow no way in which he had used the word before fit how he felt now, but yet fun was the only word that registered within him when he thought of their times together.

Fun . . . walking along the street looking or not looking, talking or silent . . . Yeah . . . Fun tossing nuts to squirrels. Fun seeing Shakespeare in Central Park. Fun arguing over politics with a bleeding-heart liberal woman . . . No, that cant be fun. It just doesnt make sense. Political arguments— well they certainly werent arguments, but whatever they were . . . yeah, fun. Thats the only word. Linda the Laugh is fun. Jesus krist, thats goofy. You spend time with a woman doing all sorts of things and only one word sticks in your head, fun. Goofy. But thats the way it is. Fun. Fun.

With the passing of time and the beginning of fall, Harry started back to school a couple of nights a week. One of his classes did not start until eight oclock, so on that night he had dinner with Linda and they lingered over their coffee, chatting, until it was time for Harry to leave.

Harry did well in school, better than he ever had before. It rather surprised him because he wasnt aware of trying harder than usual, or putting forth any extraordinary effort, yet his marks indicated that that must be what he was doing. He somehow felt more relaxed, unpressured and was intensely interested in what he was studying. It was obviously something that was going to help him up that ladder of success rapidly.

And his ability to concentrate seemed to have increased tenfold. There somehow didnt seem to be a barrier between himself and the work. He listened to the instructor and read the books and they made sense, and the material seemed to penetrate his head with a minimum of trouble, and stay in his mind. He spent many hours studying, but he wasnt aware of the time because he felt free of conflict and its resulting tension; and because he enjoyed studying, the time passed with speed and ease.

To see their son staying home frequently and studying, and so relaxed and content, truly pleased Harrys parents, but their big thrill came when he took them out for their anniversary. At first they were speechless and almost declined the invitation. Harry had never bothered sending a card in the past, or indicating that he even remembered the date of their anniversary. When one of them would mention that today was their anniversary, he would smile and say thats great, congratulations, and kiss them and then act as if he had dismissed it completely from his mind, which is actually what he did.

But this year he not only remembered it, but he was taking them out, alone. And he had even gotten tickets to a Broadway musical, which meant he had had to plan it in advance. Ohhhh, it was wonderful. Just so wonderful. Even the weather was delightful.

Their Harry took them to a lovely French restaurant and they had one of the most delicious meals of their lives, and they had a little wine with their meal, and Mrs. White felt so special and Harrys father laughed and chuckled and squeezed his wifes hand and kissed her on the cheek from time to time, and Harry glowed inside watching their excitement and happiness. In some inexplicable way he felt very close to his parents this night, closer than he had ever felt in his life. And knowing that he had something to do with the happiness they were experiencing filled him with a joy that he never knew existed. The fact that he was contributing to their happiness overwhelmed him, and bewildered him. He couldnt consciously draw the relationship between his actions and his feelings of well-being. But he didnt strain to understand. He just enjoyed the moment.

Unfortunately the evening was over much too soon. But the mother and father of Harry White would relive that evening many times amongst themselves and with their friends, sharing their joy with them and smiling broadly and deeply when telling them about their loving son.

It was more than an evening out. It was a confirmation. A confirmation of hopes and dreams—and more importantly, a confirmation of success: their success as parents and his success as a son. They felt justified in the way they had lived their lives; in the methods they had used in raising their only child. And justified in keeping their hopes and dreams for him: that he would be healthy and happy and enjoy a good life.

Of course his life was not complete yet, but someday, maybe someday soon, he would have a family and children. For years they had been afraid that they would spoil him because he was an only child and had actually looked into adopting a child, many years ago, but the process looked endless and hopeless, and so they never pursued it. But now their fears were melted with the warmth of the food and the music, and the warmth of the memory of the night. It would be cherished and relived over and over again.

Gradually, as time passed, Harry spent more and more of his free time with Linda, to the point of seeing her almost exclusively. Of course he still got laid occasionally, but it seemed like he could go weeks, sometimes, without even thinking about it. Between work, school and Linda there just did not seem to be enough time, or room, to think about the broads. He spent his lunch time quietly, usually with Linda, so getting back to the office on time was no problem. All the areas of Harry Whites life were running smoothly and routinely.

One day Wentworth asked him to join him for lunch again. When they had settled in their seats and ordered their drinks, he got right to the point. This is not for general distribution, so keep it to yourself, but there are going to be some significant changes made next year. Some rather large changes. We/re growing. Expanding. Especially our foreign operations. And I would like to see you become a major—*major*—part of the change.

Harry smiled and nodded his head, So would I.

Yes, smiling, Im sure you would. And I would because I believe you could not only be an invaluable asset to the firm, but to me personally as well. You see, I will be responsible for effecting those changes. Harry looked and nodded appreciatively. The waiter brought their drinks and they both tasted them before Wentworth continued.

Things have been going well these past months for you. At least I assume that from your work and your attitude.

Yes, they have. Very well.

Good. Good. Glad to hear that. But of course it has been obvious. They smiled at each other. Weve talked before and I do not want to go over old ground again and again, but I have the idea that maybe youre ready to move up—Harrys gut suddenly went flop and he could feel the excitement suddenly surge through him—or at least almost ready—Harry suddenly felt hollow. He wasnt sure what was going on now. Wentworth continued to look at him, and Harry didnt know how he was supposed to feel or how he did feel, other than confused. He took another sip of his drink and waited Wentworth out.

You have to be responsible to be successful. Without that you have built-in barriers. As an example in point, I am constantly entertaining other successful executives, and these men are like myself: responsible. We are family men with good, solid roots in our communities. We keep things in the proper perspective. We know how to—a smile and a gesture of the hand—relax and have fun, but . . . *but!* we go home to our families. The right thing, in the right place, at the right time. It is imperative that a corporate executive be a good family man and a responsible member of his community. Wentworth continued to look at Harry for a moment, then picked up the menu and started reading.

Harry, of course, was no dummy. He knew exactly what Wentworth was talking about. He had told him the same thing more than once before. In that world, as Wentworth saw it, you had to be a family man to be trusted. And Harry supposed he was right, at least to some degree. By being conscious of your obligation to your family you are less likely to become irresponsible at work, and to Harry that was of the utmost importance.

But that wasnt what Wentworth was really talking about *today*. No. He was talking about doing something about changing his marital status soon if Harry wanted to be an important part of the major changes that would be occurring soon.

And, the other thing that Wentworth was obviously reminding Harry of, in his own way, was the fact that he had the power of life and death over him with respect to his future with the firm. Harry had the choice of doing it Wentworths way and going to the top—and there was no doubt in Harrys mind that that is what would happen—or he could just flop around somewhere in the middle and maybe some day be a junior vice-president. The facts of the situation settled into place immediately. But whatever was going to happen wasnt going to happen until next year. In the meantime he would keep pushing the way he had. It was working so far.

7

The first Sunday in December Linda and Harry visited her folks. Rather than worry about snow and ice on the roads they rode the Long Island Rail Road. Linda was familiar with the hazards and unpredictabilities of this mode of travel and so they brought a thermos of hot coffee with them.

Harry looked out the window from time to time at the drab-to-ugly surroundings, conscious only of how good he felt.

"When I go to sleep, I never count sheep,"

Their breath was steaming from their mouths and they drew silly pictures on the window with their fingers, then breathed on the window and watched the pictures appear in the mist that formed from their breath.

"I

count all the charms about Linda. And lately it seems,"

Harry
looked at the funny little drawing and then at Linda. Whats
that supposed to be?

O, smiling, you should be able to figure that one out.

"in

all of my dreams, I walk with my arms about Linda"

Harry
smiled and shrugged. It beats me.

Linda laughed, Nanook of the north.

The steam puffed from their mouths as they laughed,

"and

after a while I will get to know Linda."

the sight and sound of
her laughter pulsing a warm glow through him.

Lindas father met them at the station and though it was only
a ten- or fifteen-minute drive to the house, the scenery changed
drastically, and Harry felt like he was driving through a
Christmas card. His smile seemed to start on the inside and
then flow up to his face. The snow was banked high on the
sides of the road and sloped off in pristine whiteness, and
icicles hung from the snow-covered trees and glistened in the
sun. And the sky— Krist the sky was beautiful.

"But miracles

still happen, and when my lucky star begins to shine

A light winter
blue, and crisp, with white fluffy clouds moving just fast
enough to let you know it was real.

When they got to the house, Harry was introduced to
Lindas brother and sister, her mother and an aunt—the
mothers older sister. They sat for a while drinking coffee and
warming to each other. Then it was game time. Harry, Lindas

father and brother went into the living room to watch the football game while the women remained in the kitchen to prepare dinner and talk to Linda about her fella.

Harry had a ball watching the game with them. They both knew and liked the game, so the running commentary was enjoyable. He had been a little apprehensive, afraid they might be like those crazy old broads in the office who hoot and holler during the World Series and seem to be especially delighted when your team is losing; then they ask you who is up, the Rangers or the Knicks? But this was different, and to top it off the game was really exciting, and so Harry didnt feel as if he was being constantly inspected.

And the dinner was positively delicious, and the conversation enjoyable. And when they finally left the dining room table two hours later, they continued talking and sipping coffee in the living room, every one feeling tranquil from the food and the burning and glowing logs in the fireplace.

Time slipped warmly and gently by, and it seemed that the warmth of the day, the home and its people, was infinite, and the mirth and laughter that tickled ones bones endless. God, it was beautiful. And no one would know what was said. But the feelings would be remembered, as feelings always are, long after the words and the circumstances have passed beyond recall.

And then the laughter was interrupted with the announcement that it was time to go, and the thermos was refilled with steaming coffee and Linda and Harry were bundled into their coats and there were hugs and embraces and pats on the back with more laughter, and kisses and the shaking of hands and, Goodbye, goodbye, dont forget to call as soon as you get home, dear.

I will, mother, dont worry.

And you come to see us again soon, son.

O, I will, smiling broadly, and thanks for a great day. It was really wonderful. And thank *you* for that great meal. You are a great cook.

Thank you, Im so glad you enjoyed it.

Well, goodbye.

Goodbye.

Thanks. See you again.

Soon.

Safe home.

Well, we/d better get moving, and the door was opened to the cold winter night and they rushed to the car and scampered in and the joy and jubilance were still in their voices:

Oooo, its really cold, brrrrr.

Boy, its really something. One minute youre in a nice warm room, and then, bamm, the north pole.

They laughed while Lindas father let the car warm up for a few minutes before starting for the station. The heater will be ready in a minute and then it/ll warm up in here.

They stayed in the warmth of the car until the train was in sight and then they hugged, kissed and shook hands, and Harry and Linda hustled to the station.

The ride back was a little warmer; they got to a car where the heaters worked and settled into their seats. They looked out the window, and as they left the lights of the station they were looking at each others reflection and smiled simultaneously and continued to look through each others reflection at the darkness. The night obscured the drabness of the surrounding area, and here and there patches of snow and ice sparkled as they reflected a nearby light. It looked enchanting.

Harry winked and Linda smiled, and then they both chuckled and turned from the window,

"We meet on the street."

Hello Linda.

They looked in each others eyes intently and smiled warmly. Harry took her hands in his and looked at them for a moment, then looked back into her eyes. It was a beautiful day, a truly beautiful day. I had a great time.

Good, her smile broadening, Im glad you did.

Harry looked down at her hands again, squeezed them gently, then smiled tenderly as he looked up. The only thing more beautiful than the day is you. Linda could feel herself flushing. Youre the most beautiful thing in the world. Harry kissed her finger tips, gently, ever so gently, then raised his head again. I love you.

The train clacked on and they continued to look at each other for a moment, both surprised by what they had heard. Linda had been wanting to hear it, and Harry did not know he was going to say it, but it felt right when he heard it.

Thats not a word to use lightly, Harry.

I know. I know its not. Youve never heard me bandy it about.

No, thats true. I havent. But it is a word that can mean many things.

I know. At least I think I know what you mean. This is the first time in my life I ever thought about it, I guess.

Linda looked at Harry intently, her expression extremely firm. What do *you* mean by it, Harry?

He blinked, a little surprised by his feelings and by what he was about to say. I want to marry you.

They continued to stare at each other for whatever length of time it takes for words to become a part of feelings, and for the feelings to register and turn into actions. The train continued to jerk and clickity-clack its way toward the City of New York, and gradually Lindas face started to relax, then beamed into a smile.

I would love to be your wife Harry, and she put her arms around him and kissed him and he started to giggle and kiss her and they both started laughing as they bounced up and down on the seat, their arms around each other. Linda pulled her head back for a moment and looked at Harry and shook her head, O Harry, I love you. Love you. Her eyes were tearing slightly and sparkled in the dull light of the train. She fell back into his arms and they embraced and hugged and kissed, then eventually they allowed a little space between them and Harry laughed and wondered what the other people on the train were thinking.

Theyre probably thinking we/re happy, and anyway, who cares what theyre thinking?

Harry poured steaming coffee into two thermos cups and the carefree, joyous lovers toasted their betrothal.

Lindas parents were overjoyed with the news, and they talked with them for many minutes before finally hanging up the phone. After a few more cups of coffee, and sharing the good news with Lindas roommate, Harry left.

On the way home he found himself instinctively reviewing what had happened. Everything seemed to have happened spontaneously—he hadnt planned on proposing to Linda, or telling her he loved her. He had never said to himself that he loved her, yet when he said it to her it felt right. And the idea of marrying her felt right. It was all a surprise and the reality was starting to settle in, but it still felt right. He felt—sensed— that it was the missing ingredient in his life, that this was what he needed to make his life complete.

Harry broke the news to his folks the next morning and was surprised at their reaction. His mother literally squealed with joy and hugged him and kissed him, O, thats wonderful son. Im so happy for you. I thought there was something going on with you and that Linda.

His father slapped him on the back repeatedly, Congratulations, Harry. Thats great. Thats just great. Every man should have a family. After all, winking at Harry, the rest of us have to suffer, why shouldnt you?

O, you phony you. You love every minute of it and you know it.

He laughed and kissed his wife, and then they both congratulated Harry again.

Harry was still chuckling to himself on the way to work.

That was the first time he had ever heard of a festive breakfast. His folks were so happy he thought maybe they were going bananas. Guess maybe this whole thing is right. Sure as hell made them happy. And that made him happy. Have to have Linda over for dinner Sunday. I hope Pop doesnt pound the shit out of her back. He almost laughed out loud, but checked himself.

He started to get apprehensive as he walked from the subway to the office. He was keeping to his new schedule, so he was a few minutes early and would not have to walk by an office full of stares, but still he knew that he was supposed to have some kind of an attitude, but what? And in a matter of minutes the office would be filled and then there would be the looks and the questions. . . . Harry frowned inwardly, maybe not. Its only Monday morning, you know, and it was only last night that this whole thing happened— Really? Is that all? Krist, can it only be a matter of hours? Sure doesnt seem that way. Well, whatever, it feels weird.

The morning was still young, many minutes from the first coffee break of the day, when Rae and Louise occurred at his desk. So good morning, lover boy.

Harry looked up quickly, then leaned back and laughed; they joined him.

Its about time. I was afraid you were going to let her get away.

Hey, what is this, some sort of inquisition?

So why not? Once it was your turn, now its ours.

Harry laughed along with them, then looked at Rae, You should only *plotz* . . . ten feet from the Fountainbleau.

It took Harry a few minutes to get back into his work after they left. Well, at least that was over with. The rest of it will be easy enough as far as the office is concerned. A few more congratulations and handshakes, but that will be easy enough to take care of. Harry was smiling inwardly and outwardly, and hummed through the remainder of the morning.

For the first time he felt a little conspicuous meeting Linda for lunch, but that soon passed. After all, this was the first time they met at the elevators on their floor rather than in the lobby, which really made their betrothal official.

Linda laughed, I hadnt thought of that, but I guess youre right.

Yeah, but the novelty will wear off in a few days and nobody will bug us.

We hope. She laughed, and Harry smiled as he watched her eyes sparkle. Krist, he felt good being with her. He never seemed to realize just how good he did feel. And it feels better and better and better. Krist, he was going to get married. . . . But it was all right. It really was all right.

Harry wanted Wentworth to know about his engagement, but for some reason he did not want to go into his office and announce it. He/d feel foolish. And anyway, hed find out sooner or later. Most likely sooner. Rae wasnt the only yenta in the office.

He was right. It was sooner. When he went into Wentworths office that afternoon, Wentworth had a smile on his face. I hear from Donlevy that youre engaged to his secretary.

Yes, smiling, that right.

Good, good. Im glad to see that youre maturing and settling down. Thats a wise move Harry, a very wise move. It will make all the difference in the world.

Harry sat at his desk thankful to krist that he wasnt a paranoid. It would be easy to get the feeling that people were doing nothing but sitting around and talking about him and his marital status. Makes you feel weird. Like they know something you dont know. And the way his folks acted you could think that maybe theyd been planning on what they were going to do with his room as soon as he got married and left, and lets hope its soon. Maybe we can help you pack. He shrugged and smiled, O, well, everybodys happy. And it probably *will* make all the difference in the world.

8

The wedding was set for the first Sunday in June, and Harry was so preoccupied with his work that he might not have been aware of the approaching date except for all the details that had to be taken care of, most of which were taken care of by Linda, but leaving enough for Harry so that he was reminded of the coming event.

In the middle of May he had a brief conference with Wentworth. Youre getting married soon, arent you Harry?

Yes. Ahhh, lets see. . . . Three weeks from Sunday, as a matter of fact.

I hope, a sly grin on his face, that you know how to enjoy a honeymoon.

Harry chuckled, Well, if I dont, I/ll just stick in there until I learn.

Wentworth guffawed, then laughed, Thats a good one. I

like that. They laughed for a moment, then Wentworth stopped abruptly.

O.K., Wentworth grinning slightly. I want you to enjoy yourself and have the time of your life. The firm knows how to show its appreciation for its valued personnel and youll be getting a five hundred dollar bonus to help you make this a memorable occasion.

Thanks. I didnt expect anything like that. Thats really wonderful.

Thats O.K., thats O.K., waving his hand in a gesture of dismissal, we want you to come back here with an abundance of energy. To put it briefly, those changes I mentioned a few months ago are about to happen, and you are going to be an integral part of them. We are developing a new division, on a multinational basis, and I will be the general manager in charge of the operation, as well as executive vice-president, and you are going to be my assistant, the second in command, a second vice-president—Harrys head jerked back and he looked at Wentworth, forcing himself not to stare like a jerk and jump up and down and say hooray—and then you will know what it really is to work. Wentworth grinned again, and Harry got up, realizing that the meeting was over.

Thank you Mr. Wentworth, I ah—I dont know what to say.

Just continue to do a good job, thats all.

Right, nodding his head.

And remember Harry, no one, pausing to allow the phrase to sink in, no one is indispensable.

Harry was so excited he could hardly sit at his desk. He was on his way, he was really on his way now. None of that junior bullshit that Davis got. Krist, half an hour until lunch. Goddamn, thats what I call a wedding present. He couldnt wait to get started on the new job.

At last it was lunch time, and he told Linda the good news and she was so excited she kept hugging and kissing him. O, Im so happy for you honey, Im just so happy. Wait until I tell the folks. Theyll be absolutely thrilled— Ohhh, Im so proud of you sweetheart. . . . Harry smiled and chuckled, his excitement being fed by hers. Jesus she had a lovely laugh, and everything sure was coming up roses.

The honeymoon was as a honeymoon should be—a good fucking time. There are many enchanting elements in a successful honeymoon, and Harry and Linda certainly found them in New Orleans, but if it doesnt make it between the sheets, then a honeymoon just doesnt make it. Without that, the most exotic land is mundane and drab, but with it, even so lowly a pasture as Secaucus is exciting and romantic. But when both come together properly, the result is synergistic and you have an experience, and memories, that will be cherished during the longest of lifetimes and will be reached back to as a source of comfort and future hope.

And the honeymoon of Mr. and Mrs. Harold White was, to say the least, idyllic. What can be said about New Orleans at any time, under any conditions? Its certainly more than Jeanette MacDonald and Nelson Eddy, or the Mardi Gras, or even old Satchmo himself.

And when you have just left New York with your new bride and everything is new and unfamiliar, and you are walking through the Latin Quarter on a June night and you feel the excitement in the air and in each others hand, then it is pure enchantment.

And what could be said about Harry in bed???? Actually quite a bit. And all good. But the big thing, from Harrys point of view, was the difference in how he felt, a difference that he gradually became aware of as the initial excitement faded and a more intense pleasure replaced it. He could not define the difference, or even isolate it as far as that goes; he just knew that this was not the same as it had been in the past. About the only way he could describe this vague feeling of his was that he felt like he was in no hurry to go.

One afternoon they were strolling along a boulevard, just

having finished a tantalizing creole lunch, when Harry kissed Lindas finger tips, then hailed a cab and they went back to the hotel. Later, in the early evening, while she was showering and slowly rubbing her body with the perfumed soap, loving the feel and smell of the soap and shower, and even the sound of the water, feeling completely luxurious, she smiled and chuckled inwardly when she realized that if she had had any idea, even the vaguest hint, that going to bed with Harry would be so exciting, she might not have said what she had about waiting to get married. She watched the lather slowly being rinsed off her body. No, no, there was no way she would have made that little speech. . . . But thank God she had. If she hadnt, she might not be Mrs. Harry White today, and she wanted very much to be just that. She loved Harry and loved being his wife.

Eventually, of course, the honeymoon was over, but the melody did linger on. They got back late on Friday night and spent the weekend calling family and friends and settling into their lovely apartment on Central Park West, and getting ready for the new life that was about to unfold before them. And on Monday it started to unfold.

Linda bore the brunt of it, but she didnt mind. Rae called her almost as soon as she sat down and wanted to know how she was; and all the other girls wanted to hear all about her honeymoon during the coffee break; and then there was lunch with Louise and Rae and more questions.

But Linda enjoyed it. She enjoyed talking about their honeymoon; it excited her to relive it by telling others about it. And, too, she realized that in a day or two it would be business as usual.

For Harry it was business as usual immediately, only more so. Wentworth asked him if he had had a good time, then went immediately into the mass, and mess, of work that was waiting. They spent most of the day in Wentworths office, sending out for sandwiches for lunch—Harry vaguely flashed on his dream of making his mark in the world and eating lunch in the finest of restaurants—and staying late in the evening, a procedure that would continue for quite some time.

Linda was disappointed that they would not be going home together, but then she realized that it would give her ample time to prepare a nice dinner and have it ready for Harry when he got home, and so she rapidly adjusted to the new schedule.

Harrys new position was taxing and demanding, but he thrived on it. So much of it was new, and unprecedented with respect to the existing procedures, that new systems had to be constantly developed and changes made in current ones. Everyday there were new problems, each with its own particular demands. It was positively exhilarating and exciting and absorbed all his tensions.

Working until 7:00 or 8:00 P.M. became routine, but most days Harry made certain he had lunch with Linda, even if he had to cut it short. And then four or five hours on Saturday became s.o.p., and so Linda utilized that time to do the housework she was unable to do during the week. Harry wanted her to get a housekeeper, but Linda wanted to do it herself. They were both settled in their routine, and their life, and marriage, moved along smoothly.

And their love life got better with time. Familiarity bred excitement. They loved discovering those little things, the touch, that made the other respond with a quiver or a sigh, and, in turn, having the discovery made.

Time passed gently and unnoticed except for the change in weather and the need for a coat. Then the Sunday paper started getting thicker as the ads increased, and then another holiday season was just around a windy corner. Lindas excitement grew daily as she looked forward to their first holidays as man and wife.

Thanksgiving was a feast and an occasion that was surpassed only by Christmas. Linda had been dreaming, planning and buying, and their apartment was alive with color and joy. They put the tree up a week before Christmas, and Linda turned the lights on as soon as she got home each evening. There was a wreath on the door and mistletoe hanging from the chandelier over the dining room table. There was a warmth, a glow, a—a spirit that pervaded the entire apartment and its occupants. Harry started feeling it as he got into the elevator and the feeling grew as he opened the door and heard the little bell on the wreath, and then it flooded through him as he closed the door behind him and went into the kitchen and saw Linda fussing with the pots and heard her voice, Hi, honey, how are you? And before he got his coat off, he kissed her; then he stretched out in his chair and looked at the Christmas tree and enjoyed his inner glow.

Christmas morning they sat on the floor, around the tree, tearing paper off presents like little kids, and *ooooooing* and *aaahhhhhhing* and squealing and hugging and kissing and laughing. . . . There was a lot of laughter.

They visited his folks, then hers, and when they got back home late that night, they were tired and exhilarated from the joy of a long Christmas day that exceeded anything experienced or anticipated. Harry tossed his coat on the couch and plopped in his chair. Linda folded herself on his lap and leaned her forehead against his for a moment, then kissed him. Merry Christmas, Mr. White, my handsome, loving husband.

Harry smiled and twirled a finger in her hair and kissed her gently on the forehead, the tip of her nose and her lips. I love you. I love you very much, Linda White. You are my Merry Christmas.

Lindas life was comfortable. She did not see as much of Harry as she would have liked; and did not fully understand his drive and need for success, but she accepted them and his schedule. And the time they did have together was truly theirs and very precious to her. There were rides and walks and shows and zoos and gardens and window shopping and dinners and nights just sitting at home and talking and laughing and feeling close in an inner and special way. There was, for her, a completeness about their life. And she was certain that Harry felt that way too.

He had a way of touching her and looking at her that made her feel special, that made her feel that no one and nothing else existed, and a gentle yet exciting glow would flow through her and shine in her eyes.

And, from time to time, she would come home from work and find a note or card from Harry, and the card might have a picture of one of those funny-looking characters who looks like she is going ten ways at once and it might have some dumb caption like, Hey, whats for dinner, or something equally inane, but she loved it. Sometimes she would open an envelope and find a note saying, Hi, I love you. Or, See you soon, Mrs. White. P.S. I love you, baby. She would chuckle and glow with delight and add each new card or note to her existing collection.

And, of course, it wasnt just the note or card itself that thrilled her so, that had her humming as she rode the elevator, and had her standing in the middle of the living room saying, Hello home. It was the idea that Harry would take the time out of his busy schedule to buy a card or write a note and then address an envelope and mail it. It just thrilled her to think of him thinking of her as she thought of him.

And though she was not in love with her work, like Harry, she did enjoy it and had no problems in the office, and the days just seemed to gently slide by and away.

But eventually a vague discontent started to gnaw its way into Linda Whites life. She knew the reason long before there was a conscious problem to be concerned about. She had always been aware that something was missing, and so when she became aware of a discontent within her, she knew what was causing it and so was not unduly upset or worried. Her only concern was what Harry would say, and she would find that out as soon as the time was right. In the meantime she just did not upset herself by worrying about it.

One bright, clear yellow-green Sunday in May, about a month before their first wedding anniversary, they were strolling through the Brooklyn Botanical Gardens looking at cherry blossoms. It was the first really warm day of spring, with a sky that was blue and a sun that you could feel thaw your bones—a day that comes only a few times a year when everything seems to be clean and crisp. The cherry trees seemed to be endless and they could feel the softness of the blossoms under their feet as they slowly went along the path. When they reached the end of the trees, they walked to the Rose Garden and sat on a bench in the sun. They sat quietly for a while, enjoying this land, this bit of enchantment, that seemed so far removed from the city that surrounded it. . . .

Linda caressed Harrys hand with her finger tips. She looked at him and smiled tenderly. He smiled too and kissed her on the tip of her nose.

Harry . . . I want something. I want it very much.

Its yours.

No sweetheart, smiling, Im serious.

But so am I, returning her smile and kissing her on the nose again.

O, you . . .

They both laughed and finally Harry said, O.K., what is it?

I want a baby.

Right now, mock shock on his face, and here?

Well, it just might take a little longer than that.

Thats what I hear, smiling warmly and tracing the edge of her ear with his finger, even for the birds and bees.

I dont know about the birds and bees—or butterflies either.

Harrys eyes were open wide with surprise, Or butterflies either?

Please dont tease me, Harry. I want a baby. Very, very much.

Harry put his hands gently on her shoulders and bowed his head slightly, Your wish is my command. It is done, fair lady.

It is? I guess Ive been misinformed all my life then. They laughed for a moment, then Linda suddenly put her arms around him, Ooooooooo Harry, I love you, and hugged him close to her.

Harry put his arms around her and kissed her on the cheek and the neck and the ear, I love you Mrs. White. We will make beautiful babies, Lindas eyes were closed and she was gently leaning into his kisses, and we may just as well start now.

I think we/ll have to wait, her eyes still closed, at least until we get home.

Chicken, still hugging and kissing her.

Animal.

They laughed and got up and started walking back, hand in warm hand, along the cherry-blossomed path.

That September, the twenty-third to be exact, Linda told Harry that she was pregnant.

Are you sure?

Absolutely, smiling, I got the results from the doctor this afternoon.

You mean you failed your rabbit test?

It depends on your point of view. I would say I passed it.

They laughed and Harry looked at her for a moment, then grinned broadly, Mama White. Well I/ll be damned. Isnt that something. When? How far along?

Six weeks.

You sure?

Uh huh. Ive been checking the calendar.

Harry laughed, You really do want a baby, dont you?

Linda shook her head, a warm, contented smile on her face.

Well, clapping his hands together, I guess the least I can do is take you, both of you, out to dinner. He chuckled, I cant get over it, Mother White. Isnt that something?

Yes, it is, smiling and nodding her head, Papa White, putting her arms around him and snuggling into him.

They were moved into their new apartment a few months before the baby was born. It was a beautiful place in the same building, but higher, with a luxurious feeling of space and a magnificent view of Central Park. There was a den for Harry for the times when he had work he wanted to do at home, and a maids room, but Linda insisted she wanted to take care of her child and her home and so declined the services of a live-in maid, but she did allow Harry to make arrangements to have a cleaning lady come in a few times a week to help her with the heavier work. Theres no reason for you to have to take care of a place this large all by yourself. And anyway, we cant have the wife of an assistant vice-president in charge of foreign operations doing menial chores.

Linda laughed and shook her ahead, All right, you win. But if I get fat and lazy, it will be your fault.

They looked at her belly and laughed.

Harry not only liked the apartment and the view, but loved the idea of living in a huge luxury apartment on Central Park West. It had been one of his goals—dreams—and now it was a reality.

The pregnancy was comfortable for Linda and the delivery without complications. Of course it was late at night when Linda told Harry to take her to the hospital—I think its time —and early in the morning when she finally gave birth to their firstborn, a healthy boy. Harry sat with Linda until she drifted off to sleep, then he went home and slept until noon before going to the office.

He was still a little groggy, but elated. He told Wentworth, who slapped him on the back repeatedly, Thats the way, Harry. Theres nothing like having a son the first shot out. Thats great. Great.

When Harry finished spreading the news through the executive suite, he got to work and soon was involved in it as usual, but he still felt that hot whirl of excitement inside him that made his face flash into a smile from time to time. Walt is right, it is good to have a son.

When he brought Linda and Harry Jr. home from the hospital, they put the baby in his bassinet and stood looking down at him for many minutes. He was amazing, absolutely amazing. Harry had never seen a newborn infant before. Hes so small. I cant believe how incredibly tiny he is.

He may look tiny to you, sweetheart, but he did not *feel* tiny to me.

Harry laughed and put his arms around her and hugged her gently and kissed her tenderly on the cheek. Its hard to believe that someday he will grow up and be a man, and everything.

Linda laughed and shook her head. Let me enjoy my son for a few minutes before you pack his bag and send him off to college.

O.K., laughing and hugging her, anything you say . . . Moms.

They were new parents. And proud, especially strolling through the park on Sunday. And Harry was timid, too. He could not believe the ease with which Linda picked the baby up, turned him over, and rubbed this on him and took that off him and just sort of tossed him around. Harry held him occasionally, but was always afraid that he might hurt him. He was especially afraid that he might stick his finger in the soft area of his head or break this or that. Linda laughed and reassured him that the baby was a lot sturdier than he thought. After all, you are his father, and she would cuddle up to him.

With the passage of time Harry became less timid, and Harry Jr. grew, seemingly in leaps and bounds, and felt more comfortable and secure in Harrys arms. It actually got to the point where Harry enjoyed holding him—for a few minutes. Harry thought of his son, and his wife, occasionally during the day, even while involved in his work. He liked the feeling he got thinking about them, and he enjoyed the feeling of anticipation he experienced on his way home at night. He enjoyed, too, kissing his wife when he got home, and putting his arm around her as they looked at their son.

Harrys hand slowly moved down Lindas back and he caressed her bottom and she cuddled into him and leaned her head against his chest. O, Harry, I love it when you touch me. Especially when you touch me like that, looking up at him and smiling, you sexy creature.

I am, eh?

Thats right.

Well, I/ll tell you something, his hand slowly following the curve to her leg, you have the prettiest ass in town.

Linda turned slowly until she was facing him and put her arms around his neck and leaned close to him and pecked him on the lips. I wish I could make that doctor understand how I feel. This six weeks before and six weeks after suddenly seems awfully long . . . and unfair.

Harry laughed and kissed her on the tip of her nose. Maybe we should just shake hands, *friend*, until then.

Dont you dare, pulling him close again. Put your hand back where it belongs.

Yes, maam, slowly sliding his hand down her back, you mad and shameless hussy.

O yes, I certainly am. . . .

One night Harry was waiting for Linda to come to bed, and when she came into the bedroom she was wearing the nightgown she had worn on their wedding night. It was thin and clung and flowed, and Harry tried to look at every curve as she slowly walked toward him. I havent seen that in a long time.

Yes, I know. Much too long, sitting on the edge of the bed next to him.

Hhhhmmmmm, that smells good. Whats the occasion for all this?

O, toying with his hair, nothing much. Its just that your son is six weeks old today, raising her head and looking into his eyes, Harry raising an eyebrow and then a slight leering smile spreading over his face.

This somehow seems very familiar.
O really, smiling coquettishly, I wonder why?
Looks like I/ll have to take it off . . . again.
Why waste the time????

                           Harry laughed and pulled her down
beside him.

arry had been very surprised
to learn how long they had been living a celibate life.
Six and six are twelve. Krist, that three months. Thats one hell
of a long time. It didnt seem possible, yet it had happened. Its
amazing how time flies. Three whole (hole, hahaha) months.

And during that entire time he had had no desire to go off
by himself at lunch time and browse through the streets and
stores. Since Linda had stopped working, he had lunch each
day with Wentworth, and/or some of the other top level
executives, in the type of restaurant that had always been a
part of his goal and dream. He enjoyed dropping his credit
card, nonchalantly, on top of the bill; and enjoyed the company of these men not only because they represented achievement, but because he knew that he would be returning directly
to the office. He did not have to be on his guard.

And, with this realization, came a feeling of security. Not

that it was specifically defined as such, but he enjoyed the feeling and found himself relaxing more. This too was a surprise as he was unaware that there was any tension at all within him, other than that due to his work. Yet it was obvious that he was more relaxed. He thought about it occasionally but did not bother trying to analyze it; he just drifted along with it and enjoyed it. And, now that their love life was back to normal, these feelings of security and relaxation seemed to increase.

The new operation at work had been running so smoothly that it had been many months since he had been late for dinner. On the occasions when extremely important representatives of foreign firms were in town for discussions and/or negotiations, he accompanied Wentworth, and the public relations people, but left when the business discussions were finished and did not get involved in the social activities. He also managed to nibble lightly at the food, so he could enjoy a late dinner with Linda when he got home.

And that is what he intended to do on the night when he had to entertain two representatives of an international conglomerate from Belgium. Wentworth was a master at entertaining, and, as usual, the restaurant was elegant and the women were glamorous without being blatant; and Harry was consciously enjoying his increasing feeling of ease and security. He knew there was no need to be on guard, so he ate leisurely and enjoyed the entire meal, and when Wentworth suggested they continue the party in the suite, Harry joined them.

The Belgians had selected their girls, and one of the others joined Harry on the couch. He had a drink or two and joined in the conversation and the telling of jokes and even danced a little with Marion. He enjoyed her company, but had no intention of taking her to bed. He was just going to hang around for a while to keep the party moving as it should, so there would not be an extra girl sitting around, and then he was going to go home.

Soon he found himself alone with Marion and he just sort of shrugged inwardly and said to himself, what the hell, one wont hurt. I wont even ball her. I/ll just get a little head and split. An hour later he left, first checking himself and his clothes carefully for lipstick marks.

The next morning he woke up before the alarm went off and curled up in bed, cringing inside. He could hear Linda breathing softly behind him and he wanted to turn over and see if she was looking at him, but was afraid. He felt strangely conspicuous lying in bed; he had a feeling like he was crying inside and had a strong urge to say over and over, Im sorry. He wanted to get up and get into the shower, but thought he had better wait until the alarm went off. Thats what he usually did in the morning. At least he thought that was what he usually did. How could he not know what he did every morning? It did not make sense. *Im sorry! Im sorry!* Why doesnt that goddamn alarm go off. . . . Jesus, my stomach is screwed up. It just keeps churning and feels so hollow. What in the hell is going on? This is crazy to suddenly feel so screwed up. Goddamn it, ring . . .

and the seconds ticked away until the alarm finally went off, and he quickly got out of bed and hurried into the bathroom and the shower. He felt better as the water soothed him and he looked at the frosted glass on the door. He stayed in the shower much longer than usual, but eventually had to leave its comfort and security.

He felt very shaky and edgy while eating breakfast and could not seem to look directly at Linda. Thank God the baby was making a fuss this morning and Linda could only talk to him over her shoulder or on her way into or out of the kitchen. He got through breakfast as fast as possible without being obvious. Actually he did not have to force himself to eat slowly as the food seemed to repulse him, and he had to force it into his mouth and force himself to chew it and then fight to swallow it and keep it down, studying the pattern on his plate the entire time. When he finally finished, he put on his jacket and managed to kiss Linda on the cheek before leaving.

Krist, it felt good to be in the elevator. . . . At least until it stopped and some fool got on and Harry looked down at his shoes and the cuffs on his pants, his insides screaming at the elevator to hurry and get the hell to the bottom. . . .

At last he was on the street. Damn, that nausea was really burning him up. Thats what he got for eating last night. Should have passed the goddamn food up. O screw it. Dont make a big deal out of a blow job for krists sake—*comeon, comeon, comeon, move it lady*. . . .

Ahhh, sanctuary. His office. The door closed. Stays closed if he wants. That feeling will go. Just get to work. Dont sweat it. Work and some Pepto Bismol will take of— Shit! Did he check his shorts? There was nothing on them anyway. How could there be? She wouldnt notice anything anyway. How could she? Just toss them in the bag and send them to the laundry. Must be all right. It has to be— The phone rang and he jumped and instinctively jerked back from the phone as if it were a hooded cobra. He stared at it for a moment. It rang again, and he snatched it up and almost sighed audibly when he heard Louis/s voice. He could not keep his eyes open for more than a second at a time, even after hanging up the phone, for many long and glaring minutes. . . .

And then his work wrapped itself around him and soon he was aware only of his work and his mind was filled with the responsibilities of his position, and that was all he was aware of until he was in the elevator on the way up to the apartment; then his feeling of self-consciousness started twinging him again. His mind kept trying to tell him that Linda was involved in taking care of Harry Jr. and her wifely duties, but he felt, from time to time, that she was noticing that he was not acting as he usually did, and so he tried to act normal and was aware of the fact that he was over-compensating and he would then make another re-adjustment and try to get back to normal, if he could just figure out what normal was.

Toward the end of the evening he was trying to interest himself in a television show when Linda came out of Harry

Jrs bedroom and put her arms around him and kissed him on the cheek. Harry could feel himself tense immediately, and his eyes closed automatically as he waited. . . .

Linda kissed him again. Sometimes I feel that I am neglecting you.

Neglecting me? trying to keep his breathing as quiet as possible.

Yes.

What makes you say that? trying to prevent his smile from becoming hysterical laughter.

O, you know honey, Harry Junior takes up so much time and I get involved in this and that and I sometimes get the feeling that Im neglecting you. That Im giving all my time to our son and the house and none to my dear, sweet husband.

Harry smiled and sighed inwardly with relief and opened his arms as she sat on his lap. Well, life has been extremely difficult around here lately, but I forgive you.

They both chuckled, Linda happily feeding her feelings of relief, Harry consciously trying to control his. You know sweetheart, I dearly love our son, but you are still *the* man in my life.

And, O God, she smiled so sweetly and the palm of her hand felt so warm and petal soft on the back of his neck, and Harry pulled her close to him and pressed his cheek against her breast and felt the rhythm of her heart quieting the nauseous turbulence within him, and he snuggled gently against her for a moment and tentatively kissed her neck and looked up into her eyes and smiled into their lovingness, feeling tears warming the back of his. eyes, then kissed her again and slowly rose from his chair and held that petal softness of a hand in both of his and kissed it, and smiled again at his wife, then led her to the bedroom and hugged and kissed her again before gently snuggling her into their bed.

Memories, like ancient history, can easily disappear when their pertinence to today is ignored, and then they eventually reappear and become current events. Harrys life remained in its well-oiled groove for a couple of months, until the next public relations evening. He called Linda and told her to go ahead and eat, but he would not be too late and would have a snack with her when he got home.

Even without the aid of liquor he was quickly caught up in the relaxing atmosphere of the restaurant, its trappings, the laughter of the men and women at the table, his own complacency, and became actively involved in the telling of jokes and anecdotes and unguardedly tasted and savored his way through the meal. On their way out of the restaurant, he made a quick call and told Linda they had run into a snag and that he would be late and not to wait for him.

He was actually surprised to find himself in bed with the girl. That was not what he had intended to do. He was just going to sit around the suite with the others for a while to make certain there were not any loose ends that needed tying up, and then go home. He had not even intended to be alone with one of the girls, much less go to bed with her.

But he had. And it seemed as if it had happened beyond his control, as if it had happened *to* him. The girl enjoyed his company. He was different from the johns she routinely was involved with. He was pleasant. He spoke to her and treated her as if she were no different from any other woman, and so her enthusiasm for his company was more real than professional.

And so she was smiling at him and rubbing his chest when he suddenly noticed the time. All the way home he kept inwardly shaking his head and trying to reconstruct the night. How did he get from the restaurant to bed? What had happened? How did it happen? He hadnt planned it. He wasnt even horny. He was just sitting there talking and eating and was going to make certain everything was taken care of properly and then he was in bed with this girl and he came to the further realization that he had just finished screwing her. Twice . . . Why? Why did he do it? What in the name of krist is going on? It doesn't make any sense. No goddamn sense at all. Whats happening to me? Mother of krist, whats going on? Goddamn it! GOD *DAMN* IT! ! ! !

Then the morning and the goddamn feelings of guilt and remorse that churn your sweating body and dull your mind without ever really identifying themselves, the feelings being pushed and shoved desperately down into the cesspool of the gut so they can become confused and absorbed by something else, anything else, so they do not have to be looked at and recognized and accepted for what they really are. Mother of God, please, dont let that happen. Dont let me come face to face with the truth. What in Gods name will I do with it???? About it???? No, let those feelings churn and twist and rip, but let them remain nameless, so the reason for them does not need to be investigated. Let it just be called pain. That is good enough. Let us not hold them up to the light and seek the truth. Please. I dont know what to do with it. I just dont know. . . .

And anotherstaring-at-the-plate breakfast—the previous one suddenly vivid in the mind, the memory alive with the little tricks and techniques used the previous time—and the torturous, and time endless, ride to work and the interminable ride in the elevator and walk to the office before the door is safely closed, and a grabbing of the head with the hands and then the sudden clenching of teeth and hands and the conscious effort to abandon oneself to work and then the blessed relief of the work filling all the areas, including the dark corners of consciousness, and the day eventually proceeding at its normal pace.

And then the awareness of the fact that the office is almost empty, the quietness forcing the head up from the desk. Time to go, but then mercifully finding something that can be done right now. Must stay a little while longer. No real need to call to say so. Just work for a while. Call later. Work. Work! Work!!!! And eventually the quick call, and then no more games can be played with time and the papers are neatly piled on the desk and the reluctant leaving of the office.

Jesus,

did I check my clothes? Must have. Of course. I did. I know I did. A teething baby—O thank God—and some sort of dumb show on television, and eventually two tired people sitting and talking about something for a while—what is unimportant as long as the time passes . . . passés . . .

and then the mercy of sleep. And forgetfulness. More ancient history . . .

Harry Jr. was about six months old when Linda was away from him for the first time. It was a special occasion and she took the baby to Grandma Whites (and Grandpa too, of course), and he spent the night with them. She took him to their house in the afternoon, and coming home, alone, to an empty apartment was strange for her. And though she was alone only for a few hours, she fidgeted and called the Whites a couple of times, both times laughing at herself, but calling anyway. She certainly was not worried about the little guy, and was very surprised at her reaction to his being away for what she thought of, in the beginning, as a few hours, but which evolved into being away from home for the entire night —and actually when you take into consideration the time traveling, he will have been gone for one whole day!

Linda laughed out loud when she realized that she was nothing but a worrywart. She had never thought of it before, and actually there was no reason for her to have given it a moment of her time. But she knew even now, so aware was she of his being gone and having just called the Whites for the second time, that as soon as Harry got home and they were alone together and then went out that she would relax and en-joy the evening, just as Harry Jr. and his grandparents were enjoying the evening.

And it was a special occasion. A very special occasion. There was to be a dinner at the Bankers Club for the Board of Direc-tors, a few of the top executives, and their wives. Even Harry did not know all the details, and told her everything he knew about it—that the new operation was going well, exceeding all expectations, and that the primary function of the dinner seemed to be to pat each other on the back for doing such a tremendous job. Harry had also been told that he was going to be given another promotion, which would be part of the congratulatory speechmaking.

Linda was ready when Harry got home, and he had to stop and just look at her, his inner excitement warming his smile and putting a gleam in his eye. God, she was beautiful. Everything about her sparkled—her eyes, hair, skin—and the simple lines of her dress clung gently to her curves. You know something, Mrs. White, youre a lie. Youre unreal. A myth.

I know I should feel complimented, smiling and tilting her head, but Im too confused.

Well, laughing and walking toward her, its just that I have always heard that a woman tends to get a little doughy, or at least a little flabby, and run-down at the heels after shes been married awhile and has had a baby, but you get lovelier and more exciting every day.

You know something, Mr. White, her hands clasped behind his neck, you make me feel lovely. Im just a mirror.

They laughed and got ready to leave.

Although Linda was the youngest person at the dinner, being many years younger than everyone else with the exception of Harry, she felt completely at ease. There seemed to be less than two dozen couples and the introductions were leisurely. Linda blended in perfectly, doing much more listening than talking, and was instantly liked by everyone. More than one of the women, who were old enough to be her mother, whispered in her ear that they were jealous of her, she was so young and pretty, and she chuckled along with them.

And, of course, Harry was told by almost everyone that he was a lucky man to have such a lovely wife. Harry smiled, laughed, and readily agreed that she was vivacious and charming, and gave Linda a little extra hug or squeeze.

One of the many things Harry loved about Linda was her

poise, and she really delighted him this evening. She was so extremely graceful as she was introduced to people and maintained a charming stream of conversation during dinner, listening carefully to what others said and asking the appropriate questions and paying the appropriate compliments.

What made him conscious of this was the fact that he himself felt ill at ease with the people at dinner. He said and did all the right things, but it was a strain because his insides were in conflict with his actions.

It seemed strange to him that he should feel as he did; he had met these men before—and even a few of the wives—and never had had a moments discomfort sitting around a conference table with them, but tonight he felt extremely self-conscious and nervous, these feelings being magnified by his trying to find a reason for them, and becoming more and more confused the more he searched. And so it became a vicious circle—the worse he felt the more he searched, and the more he searched the worse he felt. So he just endured, with the proper smile on his face and the appropriate words coming from his mouth.

The surprise that numbed all of his feelings came suddenly when the Chairman of the Board asked for everyones attention and started talking about the expansion of the firm, how it had grown and what the prospects were for continued growth and expansion—especially in the foreign market—and he started thanking various people, with an anecdote or two regarding each followed by the appropriate chuckling, and then Harry heard his name and the appropriate smile spread on his face, but then shock instantly set in as he heard that he was the newest executive vice-president, the youngest executive vice-president the firm has ever had.

Linda clutched his arm and he could feel her bouncing in her seat, O, honey, thats wonderful, just wonderful, and she kissed him; and he found himself standing to light applause and saying a few appropriate words. He thanked everyone for their kindness and the honor they had bestowed upon him; and he told them how much he believed in the firm and his own personal dreams of what the future could hold for them, and he reaffirmed his dedication to the firm; and then he thanked Wentworth for everything he had done for him ever since he had joined the firm—Harry kept noticing the nods and smiles of agreement—and last, but certainly not least, he wanted to thank his beautiful and loving wife, who had always been by his side and been a constant inspiration to him (Jesus, didnt that jerk Davis say that? How you doing, junior veepee, hahahaha), not that I always asked for it or wanted it —Harry smiled broadly at his Linda, and the others laughed appropriately—and once more thanked everyone and sat down as the others applauded enthusiastically and Linda hugged and kissed him. Harry laughed and kissed his wife.

The congratulations and handshaking and backslapping and hugging and kissing seemed endless to Mr. and Mrs. White, but they thoroughly enjoyed it, and when it had finished, it seemed to have lasted a matter of seconds. But the joy and excitement continued to thrill them as they said their goodbyes and held hands on the ride home.

Harry sat on the couch and Linda stood in front of him, smiling warmly and looking at him with obvious pride. She almost shivered with joy and pride. O, Harry, I am so excited, just so excited.

Harry smiled and took her hand, It is a little hard to believe, isnt it? I guess it will take a little while to fully sink in.

Well, in the meantime, sitting beside him, I am going to give my husband a kiss. They sat on the couch chatting, chuckling, holding hands and kissing, and luxuriating in the excitement of the evening.

10

O God, how in the name of krist
can this be true? It must be a dream. Please, let it be a dream.
Let the alarm ring and I/ll get up and go to work. And Harry
tried to wake himself, as he looked into the closed eyes of the
woman under him, and felt her moving in response to his movements, and her excitement. Krist, he could hear her moan.
You dont hear people moan in dreams, do you? And he felt
her warm flesh under his and he moved and rolled and thrust
and felt the roundness of her ass against the palms of his hands
and she moaned louder and louder and he wanted to just get
up and run but he could not and he seemed to be a spectator
as he fucked the broad and the brightness of the light coming
through the shades shoved the idea of a dream out the window
and he could no longer attempt to deny the truth and he
moved along with himself as he fucked her and suddenly there
were spasms through both their bodies and then the sudden
silence and immobility and he closed his eyes and shook his

head and felt a warm nausea roiling around inside him, and he rolled off her and quickly closed himself up in the shower stall, and jerked the faucets on and stood immobile as the water pelted him. At least he wasnt going to vomit. He knew that. But he also knew that he felt like he was going to any minute. What was he going to do? Who was she? O, krist, how did it happen? He/d have to hurry and get dressed while she was in the shower. He had to get back to the office. O, shit!

He left the shower and dried himself and wrapped a towel around him and went back into the room. She was still in the bed with the sheet under her neck. He was afraid to look at her—he knew he would not recognize her—but faced her with his eyes moving in other directions. She smiled, Turn your back so I can get up. *O krist, would he. Gladly. Gladly.* He turned and as soon as he heard the water running, he dressed and quietly left the room and the hotel. He trotted across the street and went through a department store in case she was watching somehow and wanted to know where he worked. He walked as rapidly as possible through the store and out the other side, seeking the sanctuary of his office.

How could it have happened? He was not thinking of picking up a broad. It was crazy. Nuts. Nothing made sense. He had left the office early so he could have lunch alone, for some reason not wanting to be with Walt and the others. And then he was screwing some broad in the hotel. It did not make any sense. What the hell happened? He just went down in the elevator and went out into the street and turned a corner and brushed someone and reached out to grab them so they would not fall, and then apologized and smiled, and she smiled, and then hes grinding on top of her as she moans. It cant happen again. It just cant. I have to control it. Control! Thats the answer. I just have to control myself.

The control lasted a week, the resolve even less. For a couple of days he ate lunch in his office, telling Walt and the others that he was in the middle of something and did not want to stop, but with the passing of each day the desire to leave the office increased, growing to the point where it was interfering with his work. He had to exert a strong effort to concentrate, and then he would suddenly get up from his desk and go to the window and look out, feeling imprisoned. After a couple of days he went out to lunch with Walt and Simmons. He could not find any reason to fight the urge. But he was careful and stayed close to the others and after lunch went directly back to the office with them.

But then he found himself thinking about women; or standing in the doorway of his office looking around and suddenly becoming very aware of the womens legs and the length of their skirts. He could not remember ever having done this before. It seemed like he had never thought about them. Even before he was married. The action seemed always to have preceded the thought. He had walked with them, talked with them, danced with them, been in bed with them, but he could never remember thinking about them. He went back into his office and tried to dismiss the whole stupid mess from his mind, and for a while his work was the only thing he was conscious of, but soon he would become aware of the fact that he was thinking of some unidentifiable broad. He tried to replace the thoughts with thoughts of Linda, but somehow that repulsed him and he went back to his work and the conflict.

A week was all he could take. He could not tolerate another day of inner turmoil and conflict that was so bad it interfered with his work—and that frightened him. He could not, would not, allow anything to threaten his position.

This time he knew what he was going to do, and so there was no trouble in consciously reactivating an old routine. Actually, the ease with which he could reach down inside himself for the ability to just stroll into the nearest cafeteria and pick up a broad and take her to a hotel and bang her sent a cold stabbing pain between his eyes as he sat at his desk thinking about it.

That night at home was awkward and tedious. He was conscious of all his actions and was constantly wondering if he was acting the way he usually did. He tried to act and to talk as usual; yet he knew he was stiff. And indifferent. Especially in bed. A couple of hours before retiring he started to complain about a headache and a stiffness in the back of his neck from overwork. Soon, but not too soon, they were in bed and the light was out and he was lying on his side and the day was almost over and eventually he stumbled into a restless sleep.

A week was still as long as he could go without picking up a woman. And now the frightening thing was the fact that he had accepted this, and on Friday afternoon he made some sort of excuse to the others and went to lunch alone. There was no attempt to fight it. He just scheduled his work around an extended lunch hour on Fridays. As soon as he had made the decision, he found that he was able to concentrate on his work.

Of course he did not get laid every Friday, but that was not important. The important thing was the routine, the game, which allowed him to be free from that constant conflict so he could concentrate on his work and maintain his position and responsibilities.

And soon he was able to accept this as a part of his life, but a part that was separate from the rest of his life. He no longer felt awkward at home on Friday nights, or any other night. It seemed to him that he was able to go home and act just as he always had. And why shouldnt he? He wasnt doing anything that every other married man didnt do, especially those in his circle. And, as far as he knew, all the women he picked up were married too. He didnt recall ever promising himself that he would be faithful to Linda, but if he had, hed been silly and immature. . . .

Well, maybe sometimes he did feel a little twinge of something, especially when he had to beg off having lunch with the others. It was not that they questioned him or objected, and he certainly was not afraid that they would ask him to resign because he took a little extra time on Fridays—his days of being a junior executive whose time is accountable were over—but he felt as if he was stealing the time from the firm.

Whatever that twinge was, it could be ignored. But the conflict that twisted him in half, and threatened his ability to work, could not be ignored. So Harry rationalized himself into accepting a new phase of his life. And with the passing of time he became comfortable with this new schedule, this new phase, and soon it had become integrated into his life to the point where he took it for granted, and his life, at the office and at home, flowed along comfortably.

And then one Wednesday afternoon he found himself following a woman into a department store. He watched her looking at bras and bikini panties and suddenly realized what he was doing and turned abruptly and went back to the office. He seemed to be running a foot race as he sat perfectly still at his desk. The panic stayed with him the rest of the day and he was unable to concentrate on his work. The only thing he was aware of was the intensity of his feelings, and his inability to identify the feelings increased his panic.

Halfway through dinner that evening Linda asked him if something was wrong.

Wrong?

Well, I dont mean like trouble. You just seem sort of preoccupied, and quiet. I dont know, leaning back and laughing, if youre really acting any different tonight or if its just that the baby is quiet and we/re getting to spend a little time together . . . quietly.

Harry could feel himself struggling into a smile. Well, Ive been thinking that maybe we should buy a house.

Isnt this rather sudden?

Not really. Ive been sort of turning it over in my head for a while.

Gee, Harry, youve caught me unawares, smiling, I dont know what to say.

It seems like a good idea to me.

O, Im not protesting or complaining, sweetheart, its just that it will take a few minutes for me to adjust to the idea.

I thought it might be nice if we had a yard . . . a garden or something where you could maybe putter around with some flowers and perhaps Harry Junior could just sort of romp around and you would not have to worry about him.

That does sound wonderful, her smile becoming broader, I would really love to have a little garden. Where were you thinking of looking?

Westchester. You dont have to go too far out of the city to find something nice.

The more we talk about it, wiggling around in her seat, the more I like the idea. Im really getting excited about it.

I/ll get in touch with a few brokers tomorrow and see whats available.

What type of house were you thinking of?

I dont know. I wasnt, I guess.

I hope we can find an English Tudor. I just love them. Especially with a few trees and rose bushes and a curving walk with lilies of the valley. O Harry, it sounds wonderful.

Well, it doesnt make any difference to me what kind of house it is. I dont know one from another, anyway.

Linda looked at him for a moment, You sure you want to buy a house?

Of course. I suggested it, didnt I?

I know, sweetheart, but you dont seem very enthusiastic.

I am, I am. I just have a lot on my mind, struggling to get that smile on his face again, thats all. And Im really happy that youre so excited about the idea.

I am sweetheart, I really am. But if you dont want to its perfectly all right with me. Really. I know how much you love this place and Central Park West.

I know, honey. Dont worry about it. I want to move. Believe me. I really do want to move.

Money was no object and so it did not take long for them to find exactly what they wanted, or to be more precise, exactly what Linda wanted, Harry not being too particular, being primarily interested in as complete a change of scene as possible.

It was almost an acre, with fruit trees, maples, a large willow, as well as shrubs and bushes. It did not have the path or winding stream, but it had more than Linda had dreamed, and the house itself was more than a dream. When she called her mother to tell her about it, her mother burst into laughter from time to time and told her to slow down, youre going as fast as a rabbit running from a dog.

O, but Mom, its so beautiful.

All right dear, I believe you. Its beautiful.

They both laughed and Linda continued to describe the house and grounds in minute detail.

Waiting for the paper work to be completed and for everything to clear escrow was probably the most anxious time of Lindas life. Each evening when Harry got home she asked him if he had heard anything further yet and he shook his head and told her to relax. It takes time. A few more weeks and everything will be cleared.

But I cant relax. I think blue curtains in Harry Juniors room would be nice, dont you? And gold ones in the living room to blend with the furniture, and maybe—

Hey, wait a minute, laughing and putting his arms around her. You keep going around in circles, and the first thing you know you will end up behind yourself and you may never get right side out again.

O, Harry, you nut, wrapping her arms around his neck and rubbing her nose against his, Im so excited I could burst.

O really, I didnt notice.

Harry, in his own way, was just as excited as Linda, but for a different reason. And it manifested itself differently, which was, in fact, the reason for his excitement. Just being exposed to Lindas excitement was enough to excite him, but the real reason was that his recent pattern had been broken and he no longer went strolling the streets on Friday afternoon looking for a woman, but spent his lunch hours with Walt and the others.

And, more than that, his mind was clear of the thoughts, and terrible conflicts, and his body was free of those bewildering feelings. He felt free inside and was able to concentrate on his work as before, and did not feel awkward or self-conscious at home. Everything seemed to be completely normal.

When he finally heard from the broker that the house was officially theirs, he started to call Linda, but stopped halfway through dialing. He thought it would be better if he were there to tell her just in case she fainted or burst a blood vessel. He laughed to himself, and from time to time during the remainder of the afternoon he stopped working for a moment and closed his eyes and leaned back in his chair and thought of the evening coming and how Linda would jump and shriek when he told her the house was theirs, and he had the damndest feeling all through him as he watched his wifes excitement in his minds eye and felt her pleasure.

For almost a week, or maybe more—she wasnt sure just how long—Linda refrained from asking Harry if he had heard anything further about the house. She realized that if she did not stop thinking about it constantly her preoccupation with the house would become an obsession and she would go crazy whether or not they did get the house. And so, no mention was made of the matter, and they were eating dinner and chitchatting when Harry said *en passant*, O, by the way, I heard from Ralph today and the house is ours, and then he put another piece of potato in his mouth and asked her how her mother was.

Linda stared for a moment and almost said that her mother was fine, then suddenly stood up and ended up on Harrys lap all in one impossible movement. O Harry, thats wonderful, hugging him, kissing him, squeezing him, wonderful. It really went through. O, I can hardly believe it. Thats wonderful. Its ours. I cant believe it. I just cant believe that it is really ours.

And the bank. Dont forget the bank.

O, youll own the bank someday too. I must tell Mom and Dad. And Harry.

Getting the house ready and getting ready to move was as exciting, in a different way, of course, as the first days of marriage (my God, thats more than two years already). They were both excited and involved in what was happening in their lives together, and they fed each others excitement.

Finally the day came when the house was ready and they moved; Linda took care of that while Harry worked. When he got to the house that evening, there were cardboard boxes and barrels every which where, but enough had been unpacked so they could eat comfortably and sleep.

Harry realized that Linda would need a car, now that they were bona fide suburbanites, so the first thing he did was to buy a second Mercedes. The second thing he did was to join the Wooddale Country Club.

Although Linda had project after project to pursue in the house or gardens, Harry was soon settled in and was completely oriented to the new home and the ride to and from the city. For quite some time Lindas constant enthusiasm kept him involved with the newness of their situation, but soon it became routine to him and he vaguely and gradually became aware of disquieting feelings drifting through him. He could feel a vague knowledge tentatively reaching up from his gut to his head and he tried to ignore it, but it persisted and though he could not define it, neither could he ignore it, and it continually prodded him like some irresistible force cloaked in the vagueness of the ancient past.

11

Now Harry accepted his involvement with other women philosophically. It was better than fighting that maddening desire that flushed itself through him. At least by not fighting the urge he could concentrate on his work and exercise control over his actions—a strange type of control.

For a while he would just walk around the street on an occasional afternoon, not really looking at the women, but just more or less browsing. But soon he was out almost every afternoon watching the women intently as he walked in the street or roamed through a store or just sat and absent-mindedly ate lunch. And it worked. This degree of indulgence allowed him to satisfy the disquieting feelings and to continue to live a normal life at work and at home.

But soon the control started to weaken and he was once again in a hotel room with a woman in the afternoon. He did not fight or question it, but simply showered and went back to the office and to work. And this seemed to satisfy that little knot in his gut, and it seemed to remain satisfied with just a once-a-month routine, the rest of the time spent simply roaming and looking, or with Walt and the others.

And though he was still able to maintain a limited degree of control over his actions, he did not seem to have very much control over his thoughts. He would be sitting on the train on his way to the office, trying to concentrate on the newspaper, and he would come across an article on the cost of medical services and then would find himself wondering what a gynecologist did when he was examining a beautiful young girl or woman. Did he bend over and kiss her while his fingers were probing? Did he examine her alone or did he and his nurse—he twisted the paper in his hands and opened his eyes as wide as he could and stared out the window, trying to shove thought and image from his mind, but somehow the clicking and clacking of the train on the tracks developed into the sensual moans of a woman and he kept seeing a young girl on the table with her feet clamped in the stirrups and the doctor and the nurse getting ready, and he shoved the picture out of his mind again and thought of something else and quickly jerked the paper open and quickly rechecked yesterdays closing prices and went over the endless listings, checking his stocks, and eventually felt free from the image, but it would suddenly pop into his mind from time to time during the day and he would again and again be forced to struggle it out of his mind and he would not go out to lunch but stay in his office as deeply immersed in his work as possible, but whenever he passed women in the office, or on the way home, he would find himself staring at their crotch and they became walking snatches and he would get so tied up inside his legs would feel weak, but at last he would reach the sanctuary of his home where he could relax and feel free of the tensions and nameless fears that twisted and plagued him these days and he could find the proper object for his lust.

Linda was sensitive to her husbands moods, and could feel, more than see, the change, the tension, in him. There was perhaps a little more silence than usual and a general quietness; and, of course, she was very aware of the difference in bed, the way in which they did or did not make love.

There were those times when Harry would be very blatant about being tired and having had a difficult day before they were finished with dinner, and when they went to bed she could feel the tension in him and wanted just to reach over and tell him he did not have to explain anything, that it was perfectly all right if he did not want to make love. But she was afraid it would embarrass him and so she did not, but just kissed him good night, without caressing him the way she wanted to, so he could relax and get the rest he needed.

And there were those nights when Harry would more or less be the same as usual except that she could feel he was forcing it, and though he looked tired and weary he said nothing, and she knew that when they went to bed he would be a little more forceful in his lovemaking because of the tension that had built up within him during the day. And though a small, secret part of her felt a little hurt because it knew that not all the excitement Harry felt was due to her, he aroused such an overwhelming excitement in her that this feeling was easily flooded away. This happened easily as she not only knew that she loved Harry, but also knew, without doubt, that he loved her, and if ever there seemed to be distance between them she knew that it was something that would pass rapidly and was simply due to the pressures of Harrys work. He is a very sensitive and brilliant man, and high-strung. And, after all, he is the youngest executive vice-president the firm has ever had, and you have to expect him to be a little moody once in a while. Its only human.

And Lindas days were so full she did not have time, nor the desire, to create problems for herself. Although she now had a full-time housekeeper, at Harrys insistence, she refused to have a maid or cook or nurse for Harry Junior. She was still a wife and mother and would continue to take personal care of her family. And though they had a gardener to take care of the mowing, pruning of the trees and other heavy work, the gardens were hers and she spent many joyous hours in them with Harry Junior, who was now walking and stumbling around and making all manner of sounds. They had a swing set in the back, and Linda would swing him on her lap and sing to him as they gently swung back and forth. He was growing like a weed and was Lindas little man.

The next time Harry had to entertain visiting representatives he stayed in the city all night. He had not planned on doing it, but it just seemed to happen that way. He found himself rolling on the bed with one of their public relations people, knowing that he still had time to catch the last train home, but also knowing that he was not going to leave. The decision came from outside him and was forced on him and he accepted it with no real struggle. Just a little dismay.

He was at his desk, with the door to his office closed, before eight-thirty the following morning, trying to unravel, again, what had happened and how it had happened. He felt a little sick and apprehensive, and the more he thought about it, the more he tried to understand how he had ended up there, the more confused and sick he got. Finally he took a deep breath and called Linda. He suddenly felt a fluttering in his chest. He jammed his jaws shut. He mumbled an almost prayer. He wanted desperately to say something pertinent, but he couldnt think of a fucking thing to say. Hello, how are you? What the hell is that? How in the name of krist was he going to make small talk feeling so sick?

Hi, honey, how was the meeting?

(Holy shit, he could hear the smile in her voice and could hear his son in the background.) Fine. All finished.

Good. Im so glad. I really missed you last night.

Me too.

Will you be home at the usual time tonight, sweetheart?

Yes.

O good. Have a good day, honey. I love you. Some small talk and she hung up.

She finally hung up. Finally, finally, finally. How fucking long did they talk. Seconds? Minutes? Ten thousand lifetimes—Yeah, yeah. I know it was the first time I stayed away since we were married. What do you think I am, some kind of fucking goon? And get off my back. Im no goddamn leper. I havent done a goddamn thing every other son of a bitch in this world doesnt. So up yours.

And thus his day started and continued with frenzied attempts to lose himself in his work; he sent out for a quick lunch or an apple so he could eat the forbidden fruit and purge himself. O shit! what the hell is going on? The door to his office remained closed. From time to time during the day he suddenly started shaking and trembling, but it quickly passed. O krist!!!!

Work. Work! Get your ass to work and forget all this bullshit. Work . . .

And so passed a murky and interminable day for Harry White.

And for Linda, the wife of Harry White, the day was intermittently cloudy. From time to time a feeling of profound sadness would drag heavily through her and she would stop and look around frowning, trying to understand why she should feel the way she suddenly did. She hadnt felt like this since she was a teen-ager, and that seemed like so many years ago. Since then she had had moments of slight depression and loneliness, but not since she was married. In thinking about it she became more and more aware of how much she loved Harry and what a wonderful life they had together. She certainly was not bubbling over with joy and good will every day, but there just did not seem to be any sadness in her life with Harry—until now.

O well, it was only natural to feel like this the first time Harry did not come home. After all, its an impossible trip at night and Harry had no choice. Nothing at all unusual about it. What really was unusual, from what she read and heard, was that two people (actually three counting Harry Junior) could be as happy as they are. A three-year marriage may not be a record, even in this day and age, but there did not seem to be many couples staying married that long who were as happy as she and Harry.

And it wasnt just the beautiful home and gardens—or even Harry Junior—she felt like this before they bought the house and before Harry Junior came along. It seemed like she felt like this since she had met Harry. Except, of course, that night when she turned him down and he left. That was the last time she could remember feeling lonely, those weeks that passed before he called again.

He excited her. And just thinking about him kept the excitement alive. And it wasnt just the excitement he aroused in her in bed, though she would quickly and happily admit that that had a lot to do with it and she could not imagine any man being a better or more exciting lover than Harry. Many, many times she thought about their relationship and what it was about him that made her so happy, and though there is always a certain amount of magic that can never be defined or even isolated, there were aspects of his personality that were precious to her.

She loved his laugh. It wasnt that it was exceptionally musical, or anything like that, but it was just so happy. It sounded as if all of him was having a good time. She could actually feel her eyes twinkle when she thought about it.

They twinkled too when she thought of his tenderness, of the way he held her hand or rubbed the back of her neck and shoulders, or kissed her ear lobe. . . . And the way he would smile and tap her gently on the tip of her nose for no reason at all—just sort of do it and smile. She closed her eyes for a moment and looked at his smile and felt his warmth. . . .

And under all of this she could feel his strength. A strength that was not verbal, but real and inherent in his actions and attitude. He knew where he was going and how to get there. He knew nothing could stop him. And she knew that no matter what happened she could always, always, rely on him, that he would always be there to give her the strength and support she needed. He was dependable and his spirit was indomitable. . . .

The more she thought about him, the warmer seemed the sun, and by the time she was feeding Harry Junior his lunch she was smiling and humming and thinking of what she could prepare for Harrys dinner.

12

Harrys life continued to be a series of little compromises, and reevaluations of ethics and situations; of readjustments to life and then unwilling and agonizing acceptance of them that necessitated little lies, which, in turn, demanded more lies and readjustments and reevaluations. And it was not with the worlds ethics and morals that Harry was compromising, but with his own. That is what produced the conflict. That is what created the pain.

And the most difficult aspect of this evolvement of Harrys life, the one element that was responsible for the confusion, was the fact that Harry had to deny, to himself, that these compromises and petty lies were actually happening. He had to somehow maintain, in his conscious mind, that nothing was wrong, that whatever was happening was normal and was simply a result of the pressures of his job.

After all, he was a

successful man: respected in his business; a good provider; a man of considerable means and still only thirty years old. There was no doubt in his mind, and in the minds of his associates, that he would be a millionaire someday. No doubt at all. How could there be anything wrong?

And he had a wonderful family that he dearly loved and treasured, and they loved him. When he got home at night his son ran (well, maybe he more tottered than ran) to greet him, and his wife always had a big smile and a hug and kiss for him. Success. Yes, he was truly a successful man. How could there be anything wrong?

There couldnt be. That was obvious. A man as young and successful as Harry White could not have any real problems, and whatever might be responsible for that twisting in his gut and that tension that made him feel like a wound spring that was about to snap, would disappear in time. In the meantime, there was nothing wrong with his picking up a woman occasionally, or spending a night with one of their public relations people. It relieved that feeling, and he was becoming accustomed to living with the undefined feeling of guilt and remorse that he awoke with the next morning. The important thing was not to allow anything to interfere with his ability to work, and that tension did just that. He was willing to do anything to relieve that tension. He must be able to work.

And so another readjustment and lie inevitably followed the others and he stayed in town when there werent representatives to entertain, but it was a reason that was accepted and was always readily available.

But now it was becoming necessary to stay in town more and more frequently. There was less and less control. After each additional adjustment and lie he was depressed for a day or so and it was a struggle not to be silent and sullen around the house. Then he would become his old self in his constantly changing life, and life at home, as well as in the office, would seem normal as his emotions started on another upswing. But then the timing of the pattern would change and further adjustments would be necessary as the periods of depression came closer and closer together. One week Harry found himself staying in town twice, and on his way home that night he bought a split-leaf philodendron. He wasnt sure why, but he just felt an overwhelming urge to buy it. It was not exactly like bringing it home for Linda as an atonement for his behavior (Jesus, with her gardens that would be like giving an Eskimo snowballs), but it was meant as some sort of a present.

The next day he found himself thinking about the plant and bought a book on the care of philodendrons. He browsed through the book on the way home and became fascinated by the many varieties of philodendron and related species of house plants. That weekend he bought another plant, a smaller one.

I didnt know you were a plant lover, honey.

Neither did I. Guess I just got a bug or something, smiling at her. Maybe I thought that if you were going to garden on the outside, I would garden on the inside.

A family that gardens together, stays together.

That sounds good.

We/ll just have to be careful that our thumbs dont get too green; they might quarantine us.

They both laughed and Harry stared at the two plants.

The following week he brought home another plant, a spider plant set in a beautiful porcelain pot and hanging in a macramé holder.

Dont you think it looks great hanging in this window?

Yes it does. That macramé and pot are beautiful. Where did you get them?

What about the plant, isnt that beautiful too? After all, you dont want to hurt the *chlorophytums* feelings.

You sound like a botanist.

Ive been reading my book on the train, smiling. Anyway, theres a large florist and plant shop on Fifty-sixth Street that has an incredible selection of plants and pots and everything else.

Well, hugging his arm, I never thought I would be naming a plant shop as a corespondent.

They laughed, each feeling tension draining from them, tension from a different yet similar source.

Harry bought two more books during the week and another plant and macramé holder on Friday. Buying a plant on Friday became a new routine, replacing the old one, and once again the undefined tension and anxiety were gone as he tended plants instead of women. In a few months there were plants hanging in front of every window. There were *Columneas, Episcias, ivy-leaved Pelargoniums* and even *Gesnerias.* On the floor in an assortment of beautiful pottery were *Dieffenbachia picta, Ficus elastica, Ficus lyrata, Schefflera, Podocarpus Chamaedorea seifrizii* and other palms, and split-leaf philodendron. There was even philodendron and ivy crawling along beams in the living room.

Harry had to get up earlier and earlier, as the collection of plants increased, so he could check each one and make certain everything was all right and see to it that they got the proper amount of light and water; and mist them so their air would be humid enough. And on the train he read his books along with the *Wall Street Journal.*

Inevitably, of course, he brought home an African violet. That weekend he built shelves across a couple of windows for his African violets. Soon there were Wedgewood, Cambridge Pink, Dolly Dimple, Norseman, Lilian Jarrett, Wintergreen and plain boy, girl, fluted, variegated, black-green and rippled leaves. He bought special brushes for cleaning the leaves, and propagated new plants from cuttings.

For a while Linda stood in amazement as plant after plant came home and the house started to look like the set for a jungle movie; and then there was the worry and work of keeping Harry Junior from knocking them over or from digging in the large pots. But it was worth it. Harry seemed calmer and more animated since he had developed this hobby and was more like his old self—not so moody or listless; and, of course, she was much happier as a result of this change. In addition, of course, not having to take clients out and stay in the city overnight helped too. And she loved plants and so there was no real problem in adjusting to this newest change of scenery.

You know dear, any more plants and we will be suffocated by an overabundance of oxygen.

Well, with all the smog and pollution, if we have enough plants we can insulate ourselves from the world.

A garden of Eden?

Sure, why not?

At last, thank goodness, Harry stopped buying plants. And it seemed to happen at exactly the right time. They looked lovely and certainly added something to the house, and Harrys happiness with them made Linda happy, but she did not think they could get another one in the house.

There wasnt room for another plant in Harrys schedule. Eventually he did not care for them in the morning during the week, giving them a quick check at night, and giving them his attention on the weekends. Gradually they were ignored at night and he might get around to watering them on Sunday, and not always then.

And the feeling of tension and anxiety, those squirmy feelings in his gut and arms and legs, returned and increased. He could feel himself withdrawing from his family slightly and fought against it, but had no idea what weapon to use since the enemy was unknown. He fought against the twisting of his mouth and forced a smile on his face and loaded his family in the car one Sunday for a drive. The day was clear and sunny and Harry Junior was in his car seat pointing and asking. Harry started to relax, listening to his son, his wife and her laughter and feeling the warmth of the sun on his face.

But he could not seem to concentrate properly on his driving. He seemed to be slightly startled by other cars, pedestrians and traffic lights. Then he became aware of why. He kept looking at the women on the street, or in other cars, out of the side of his eye, not wanting Linda to know what he was doing. He fought like hell against it, but he just could not seem to control himself. He started getting nauseous from the fight and the guilt. He could not figure out what was wrong. Why couldnt he keep his eyes on the road? He fixed his eyes on the road and concentrated as hard as he could on keeping them there, but some goddamn broad with her skirt up around her ass was walking across the street and he could tell she was going into a store just a few feet away and he would have to hurry if he was going to get a look at that ass and see if she had a nice set of boobs—a panicky look back at the road and as soon as it registered in his haunted head that the road was clear he tried to look at Linda out of the side of his eye to see if she had been watching his eyes to see where he was looking and then looked back to the road (suppose I had hit a car), and sweet Jesus he was going crazy and he locked his eyes on the road again and he could hear Linda and Harry Junior and he could even hear himself answer her, and these couple a cunts came out of a store and he could barely see them and he slowed down hoping they would come into better view but the jerks were just strolling along like a couple of snails and he did not want to lose sight of them but he had to make certain Linda was not watching him now that he was slowing the car down and he had to make believe he was looking at something on Lindas side of the street so he could see what she was watching and it seemed to be safe and he quickly looked to the other side but those dumb broads were still taking their sweet goddamn time and not moving an inch an hour for krist sake and he was going to have to make a turn and then maybe in the turn he could get a look at them and he had to make sure that Linda was just watching Harry Junior, and he went into the turn and they were lovely especially the way the breeze blew their dresses against their crotch and one wasnt wearing a bra and he could see the nipples of her tits sticking a mile out and her— A car from nowhere and Harry jammed on the brakes and his car started to skid and there wasnt any car and Linda yelled, Whats wrong? and Harry fought against the skid as he saw a car crashing into the side of their car and Linda and Harry Junior were a mangled mess and he could hear their screams and he got the car to the side and stopped . . .

and closed his eyes and fought against the tearing pressure behind his eyes and the knotted nausea in his gut that seemed to be reaching up to his throat. . . .

Linda looked at him for a moment, calming herself, confused and bewildered by the suddenness of what had happened and by the fact that she had no idea why it had happened.

You all right, Harry? Anything wrong?

No, no, shaking his head, fine. Im all right.

What happened? All of a sudden—

I dont know.

Is there something wrong with the car?

No, leaning back in the seat and taking a deep breath. I dont think so. My foot just slipped. Everythings all right. Just startled me for a minue. Thats all.

O, thats a relief. I thought maybe you had a sudden pain or something. Anyway, smiling broadly, Harry Junior enjoyed it. He had a fine time. Hes still laughing, arent you sweetie?

Harry listened to them and watched them for a moment and slowly the fear drained from his body and the turbulence subsided and he started on the way home. He drove over cautiously and was shaking inside, but had no further problems and had no difficulty concentrating on his driving.

Later that afternoon he was sitting and reading the paper when Harry Junior suddenly dropped one of his toys, and he jerked up out of his chair and hit his head on one of the hanging plants. He growled low and viciously and grabbed the pot and yanked the macramé off the hook and threw the plant out the open door.

Linda watched dumbfounded.

13

arry stayed in the city Monday night. The guilt and remorse the next morning were severe and painful, but not as bad as the constant fight against desire and those vague and undefined feelings of fear, anxiety and impending doom. And, in the final analysis, he had no choice.

The plants withered and died, some slowly, some rapidly. Linda had tried to take care of them for a while, but eventually it had became too much of a chore and she, too, ignored them, trying very hard not to notice their slow death, and not to resent Harry for it.

Harry tried to ignore the plants, and the many books he had bought, but was always dragged back to them by his guilt. From time to time he would try to make some effort to take care of them, but when he did he was overcome with inertia bordering on paralysis. When he got home at night, he instantly seemed to know—to sense—how many additional leaves had died that day. Everywhere he looked, no matter where he was, he seemed to see brown. Brown, brown, brown—in a thousand shades, in a thousand tones. Brown.

One morning he noticed that Linda wasnt smiling. He didnt know if it was just for that moment, that morning, or had not been for a length of time. He wanted to ask her if anything was wrong, but was afraid. He was afraid she would tell him, and he knew that whatever it was, it was his fault. A couple of times he almost got the question out of his mouth, but the words just died on the vine. He just could not sit there and listen to her tell him what was wrong and how he was responsible for the pain on her face and in her heart.

And his son . . .

O

Jesus.

He spent the morning interrupting his work and thoughts with the reliving of the morning; he had her smile when he asked her, and tell him that nothing was wrong. I just must have slept on my shoulder in a peculiar way and it aches a little, thats all, sweetheart.

You sure theres nothing I can do?

Positive.

And she smiled at him and he put his arms around her and kissed her, and kissed Harry Junior, and then hugged and kissed Linda, his dear, dear and beautiful wife, again.

His fantasy was interrupted by a call from Walt. He wanted to know if Harry could join him and Simmons for lunch.

Thanks Walt, but I think I/ll give it a pass today, Harry feeling off-balance.

You all right, Harry?

Sure, fine, his heart pounding, feeling trapped and panicky.

You dont sound right. And we havent seen very much of you lately.

Well, you know, Walt, Ive been real busy with the Von

Landor project, Harry painfully aware of the quavering tone in his voice.

Yes, I know, Walt obviously dubious. But don't forget, we see Von Landor tomorrow at one.

Right Walt. Harry started to sigh before he cradled the phone and instantly wondered if Walt had heard it, or if he could somehow hear it even after the phone was hung up. He turned his back on the phone.

He browsed the streets and stores at lunch time, but it did not give him the usual relief. He felt conspicuous. Almost as if he were lurking. He knew he could not continue to steal these lunch times, that his position and responsibilities prohibited it, but he could not stop right now. Later.

The afternoon was agonizing. He could feel the muscles in his legs twitch and his skin seemed to squirm. A dozen times, perhaps more, he picked up the phone to call Linda and tell her he would not be home tonight, but he didnt. He fought and fought and the conflict seemed almost to be eating him alive, so that there would be nothing left of him by evening. The battle continued to rage, and each time he reached for the phone, he forced himself to leave it alone. He had to go home tonight. He just had to. He felt as if it were a matter of life or death. At least this one time he could not give in. He just could not do it.

He did not realize just how incredibly tense he was until his body started to relax as the train left the station that evening. When the train had surfaced and was starting to trek its way to suburbia, he could actually feel his body crumbling, and he was suddenly afraid he was going to fall asleep.

During dinner that evening his eye kept being drawn toward a large *Dieffenbachia* that was completely seared and was the same color as the dusty soil in the pot. As he ate his consciousness became more and more filled with the damn plant and his goddamn hand started to shake slightly as he looked at that ugly dumb-cane son of a bitching plant and his stomach kept knotting and his teeth seemed to be attacking his food and he started slashing at his meat until he could not stand looking at the fucking thing and he got up from the table and hacked that goddamn thing right down!!! right down to the surface of the soil! hacked that rotten son of a bitch with his steak knife, hacked it, hacked it, hacked and twisted that ugly brown bastard and then stabbed the soil over and over again and again until he felt his throat constrict with fire and he stumbled over to a chair and sat, rigid, his eyes closed, his head hanging.

He could hear Harry Junior asking Linda why Daddy chopped down the plant and could hear the tremor in Lindas voice as she tried to hush him and get him to ignore what had happened and changed the subject and finally quieted him with some pudding.

Harrys body continued to tremble and pound with rage and he felt chilled and poisoned and just endured the evening until it was time to go to bed. After Linda had finished bathing Harry Junior, and had put him to bed, she went over to Harry and put a hand on his shoulder and asked him if anything was wrong? He shook his head. You sure theres nothing I can do? He shook his head again. She looked at him for a moment, then slowly took her hand off his shoulder and spent the remainder of the evening reading a book.

It was cold in the room. Harry could feel it in his bones. He never felt cold like this before. It was icy and tomblike. And his body still felt poisoned. They went to bed and Linda kissed him good night and he could feel her concern and worry and all he could do was crawl deeper into his poisoned iciness.

He felt as if he had been awake all night. It seemed that even if he did fall asleep, he dreamt he was awake and tried so hard to sleep that he would wake himself up and start the cycle over again. He felt exhausted when the alarm went off in the morning. He somehow managed to talk with Linda in the morning while he ate breakfast and she took care of Harry Junior. It was all hazy, but he knew it was real.

As he rode to work that morning the clicking and clacking of the train seemed to be saying, stupid, stupid, stupid, stupid, and it seemed to come up through the floor of the train and through his legs and body and pound into his head: STUPID! STUPID! STUPID! STUPID! STUPID!!!!

Yeah, youre goddamn right I am. I should have had more sense. It was a goddamn stupid thing to do. I should have known better. After all this time youd think I/d know better than to do it. God *damm*, thats annoying. Upset the whole house, Wonder what Harry Junior thinks? Probably nothing. But Linda . . . Jesus. Just not going to allow that to happen again. Just not going to do it. Had no business going home last night. I knew it. I just knew it would be a mistake. Should have listened to myself. Maybe now I/ll learn. The next time I/ll know what to do. I know what to do when I feel like that.

While still on the train he decided he was not going to spend the day in conflict. He was going to take a little stroll during lunch time. Nothing special. Just browse around and stretch his legs, so to speak. He nodded in agreement with himself and when he got to the office he went immediately to work and did almost a days work in a couple of hours. Around eleven-thirty he started feeling a little fidgety, so he stopped work immediately and stood in the doorway of his office for a moment and looked to see who was nearby, then walked through the office as if he were going to the mens room, carefully avoiding the area of Wentworths office, then walked down the stairs to the floor below, then took the elevator down.

He had been vaguely planning a more or less innocent walk. He had no intention of concentrating his eyes on the piece of ground between his feet, but neither did he plan to leer, or even look, at every woman that came within the scope of his vision. He was, as much as he could be, planless. Just stroll around long enough to relieve the tension and antsy feeling, then back to the office.

He did not plan on being in bed with this broad, biting her

neck as he fucked her. He knew how he got there, and part of what made him so sick was the ease with which it happened. A smile, a hello, a look and a little conversation and his cock is thrust up her flowing cunt and shes grabbing and groaning as if it were Judgment Day. And he comes, and it seems endless as he pumps his semen into that insatiable hole, and he waits for the feeling of elation, that feeling of relief that follows when more than semen is drained from his body . . .

but it doesnt come. Somehow his ancient and reliable solution does not work the way it did, the way it should. He expects the torment in his mind, the guilt and recrimination, the disgust with himself and the taste of vileness in his mouth, but at least his body was always relaxed. If nothing else, that. That release from the rusty tin cans and broken bottles that tore apart his gut, and the agonizing twitching that constricted his chest and muscles and made him want to scream and scream and scream. At least that should have drained from him.

He lay on his back for a moment staring at another ceiling. She was next to him. Actively still. He sensed an urgency under his agony, an urgency to get back to the office. It seemed somehow very important, almost an emergency, and he wanted to get up and get the hell out of there as he always had in the past, but he could not move. He felt his jaw clenching tighter and tighter. He could hear the clenching and scraping and splintering. Sweet Jesus, he felt sick. God *damn* it, what was wrong? He felt that his body was going to burst and disintegrate at any moment. It had not worked. O dear god, why didnt it work? He felt as if he were being flooded with tears. He could hear them sloshing around inside him. There was a pressure within him that he could not define nor understand. He only knew it was killing him and his answer was not working. A voice seemed to be raging inside him.

He rolled over and silenced the voice by stuffing his mouth with a tit. He sucked and nibbled and buried his hand in her soggy cunt and she wrapped her arms around him and clung to him like another layer of skin until he pushed her arms away and rolled her over and forced his cock in her ass and her screams and moans were muffled by the pillow as he tried to ram his pain into her and she met his thrusts with her own violent excitement and it felt as if she would snap his joint off and he wanted to stop but continued until they shook with spasms and were forced into stillness and he could feel his body slowly obtaining that sought-after and blessed emptiness. He could feel the self-hatred and loathing fevering his brain, and their vileness burning his throat, but it was worth it. He would pay that price. At least he could breathe. At least his body wasnt making him feel that he was losing his mind.

      The hot water of the shower felt good. Krist it was great hearing it and feeling it splat against his body and roll its way down. The nausea was tugging at his throat, but he could function through that. And right now he could yell at his head to shut up. Thats right, shut up! Go haunt somebody else. You cant get me. Not now. O god, the water was good. It flowed and flowed and flowed. . . .

      Then back to the sanctuary of the office. His office. A closed door. O dear God, a sanctuary. Work. Work! His beloved work. A haven. A place and something to get lost in. Sanctuary!!!!

      Lost! Ruptured! Just like that. A moment of a semblance of peace, and it is all disintegrated with the opening of a door.

      Where in the hell have you been, Harry?

Harry blinked at Wentworth for a moment, trying desperately to orient himself. Why? Whats wrong, Walt?

Whats wrong? Von Landor, remember? One oclock.

Von Landor???? O shit, was that today?

Yes, that was today. It is now three-thirty.

O, krist, holding his head in his hands, I completely forgot.

Thats obvious. But how in the hell can you forget something like that?—Harry shaking his head as he listened to

Wentworth—the biggest deal the firm has ever put together. Months of work. Jesus krist, Harry, this is your baby. You put it together from the inception to the whole package. The most brilliant piece of international syndicating that I have ever seen. That anyone has ever seen. And you get it all wrapped up and suddenly you dont show up for the last stage. I even reminded you yesterday and—

I know, I know, Walt. I somehow got confused and—

Are you all right? You look like hell.

What? O, yeah, yeah. Im all right. Just—I dont know, shaking his head, I cant figure—

Look, Von Landor is still at the Waldorf. He wont be leaving for a while. After we had been waiting for a while, I faked a phone call from Linda and told him that you were sick, but would get here anyway.

How did he take that? still holding and shaking his head.

He bought it. We dont have much to worry about. He wants this deal as much as we do. Thank God you did such a great job in wrapping up this package—but never mind that. Lets get over there.

Right, Wentworths urgency clearing his head.

I/ll have my girl call him and tell him we/re on our way over. He called his secretary and made the arrangements, then looked at Harry. We wont have any trouble convincing him youre sick. What is wrong with you?

Harry shrugged.

O well, we can go into that later.

Harrys business mind took over and the necessary papers were gathered together in seconds and they were on their way. Wentworth was correct; there was absolutely no doubt in Von Landors mind that Harry was ill when he looked at him.

Harrys business genius seemed to have a life of its own and functioned perfectly, and everything was completely consummated in ample time for Von Landor to make preparations for leaving. They walked him to the limousine and shook hands and watched the car merge into the traffic. Wentworth was beaming when he slapped Harry on the back. What do you say we go back, nodding toward the hotel, and have a drink? We have some celebrating to do. Harry nodded and they walked past the smiling doorman.

Wentworth was buoyant and exuberant. Come on, Harry, smile, for krists sake. This is a great day. This deal is going to mean millions. Millions, Harry. And thats just the beginning. Just the beginning, Harry, and this is your baby. You should be bubbling like champagne, for krists sake.

I know, Walt, but Im much too tired to bubble.

In a couple of weeks Von Landor will be back and we/ll be in the board room putting our signatures on those documents.

Maybe I/ll bubble then, a weak attempt at smiling.

Come on, empty that glass and youll feel better. Wentworth indicated to the bartender with a wave of his hand that he wanted two more drinks. This calls for at least a small celebration. You need to relax. I can see it in your face. Youve been working too hard. We are going to go out tonight and I am going to help you relax. What say, old sport?

Harry nodded his head.

Good, slapping him on the back and picking up change from the bar. I/ll call some relaxers.

Harry watched him go, overwhelmingly and nauseously aware of the fact that there had been absolutely no resistance to his suggestion. He had surrendered to it before there was an urge, before there was any hint of desire, before there was a need. He was aware of a sense of loss, of a profound sense of sadness and irretrievable loss.

14

$\mathbf{L}$inda finally cleared all the plants from the house. For a while she had a vague hope that their presence in the house might reawaken an enthusiasm in Harry, but that hope withered with the leaves of the plants. Each day one or two more were beyond revival, and she stored them in a corner of the garage. Eventually all were undeniably dead and piled in the corner, the macramé also piled nearby.

For many weeks after the last plant had been buried in the garage she would look around the house at the evidence and memories of the plants, painfully aware of their absence.

She also became aware, with the passage of time, that she was responding more and more to Harrys moods. She could feel herself being pulling up or dragged down by his emotional pendulum. She tried hard to resist, but she continually found herself being swept along in his emotional wake.

Linda was at a loss to explain Harrys erratic behavior and

mood changes, and for the longest time she tried to ignore them in the hope that whatever was wrong would remedy itself. But now that it was having such an adverse affect on her she felt that she had to do something, but she had no idea what. She loved her husband and had unshakable faith in his love for her, but this feeling of hopelessness was unbearable. She wanted to help, but how? Whenever she tried to ask him what was wrong and whether she could do anything to help, he always said no, there was nothing wrong, just working hard. Or sometimes he would add that he was sorry if he was upsetting her, and he would put his arms around her and hug and kiss her. And she would respond to his reassurances and affection and forget everything until the next time his mood plunged down and dragged her with it.

From time to time Linda would try to pinpoint just when it had all started so she might be able to determine the cause, but it was impossible. It seemed to have happened so gradually and imperceptibly that it was impossible to go back to some point in time and say, There, thats where it all started, and then reconstruct the circumstances of that particular time and then know the cause and thus the answer to the problem. Sometimes it was impossible to realize that it had not always been like this, but then she would remember the first three or four years of their marriage and remember how different Harry was then. How most of the time his attitude and manner had been light and happy—yes, almost carefree. But even so it was not always possible to define the exact and precise difference between then and now. Except, of course, that there were those sudden flare-ups, and those depressed moods when he said almost nothing at all for days, and an overall feeling, admittedly very vague, that he was, at times, apologizing for his existence. As if, by action and implication, he was constantly saying, Im sorry.

But these speculations she had to dismiss from her mind, since they were confusing and just did not make any sense. She could find no reason, in fact, for believing that any of these things were true. Yet, from time to time, these vague and uncomfortable feelings would swell within her and she would start speculating once again and finally end by remembering how much she loved him, and his tenderness toward her and Harry Junior. Eventually she always returned to the definite and incontrovertible fact that they were very much in love and eventually everything would be all right. It had to be.

In the meantime, though, another undeniable fact had evolved—she had to talk to someone. For quite some time this fact tried to define itself in her consciousness, but as long as she could believe there was no real problem there obviously was nothing to talk to someone about. But as the acceptance that there was a problem grew, so did her need. She thought about whom she should talk with, not wanting to worry anyone, and one day the question was answered simply when her mother called. After saying hello and asking Linda how she was, she asked her how Harry was?

Fine.

No, how is he *really?*

Why do you ask? You sound serious.

Well, dear, I am. Whenever I ask about him I get the feeling that youre trying to hide something; and lately you havent been sounding like your old self. Now, if theres something wrong and you dont—

O no, Mom, its nothing like that—

You know I dont want to interfere in my childrens lives and if—

I know that, Mother, and I dont feel as if youre interfering in any way.

Well, if I am, you just tell me and I/ll—

No, Mom, honest . . . but youre right, there is something wrong—but not between us. I really dont know what it is.

Is he sick, dear? When was the last time he had a check-up?

I don't know—no, I dont think so. But I dont really know.

Well, what exactly is the problem?

Well, thats just it, Mom, I dont know. Sometimes he seems to be all right, but then he gets moody and seems a little jumpy and nervous and sort of—well—preoccupied, I guess. I dont know exactly how to explain it, Mom. I guess its more of a feeling than anything else. Like I said, sometimes hes a little irritable—nothing bad, dont misunderstand—but nothing you can put your finger on.

I understand how you feel, dear, but you dont have to protect him from me. Im not going to condemn him for acting human.

They both laughed, and Linda could feel the tension starting to drain from her body. I didnt think you were going to attack him, Mom, I just didnt—

I know, dear, you just didnt want anyone to think there was anything wrong with the perfect man you married.

They laughed again, and this time Linda could feel and enjoy the laughter. O.K., Mom, you win.

You know, dear, Ive been married to your father longer than I care to admit—except that it has been a happy time, at least for the most part—and our life together has not always been calm and serene. There are times when that father of yours is a veritable bear, just ranting and raving and— Well, to use a euphemism, there are times when hes a son of a bitch.

Linda burst into a loud guffaw and then laughed for many happy minutes and stopped just short of hysterics. O, Mom, still giggling, youre awful.

Well, to quote the younger generation, Im just telling it like it is. Anyway, dear, are you sure you havent been fighting, or that theres—

No, Mom, honest. Its nothing like that at all. To be perfectly frank, Im not sure whats wrong at all. Harry is just not himself. Thats about all I know.

When was the last time you were alone together?

Well, we did go to a movie a few weeks ago.

No, I mean away some place. Just the two of you.

O, God, I dont know. I suppose its—

If you have to suppose, then its been too long.

Linda was chuckling with genuine mirth. That sounds like some of that homespun philosophy.

Well, my dear, that may be true, but thats the way to keep the home spunning, chuckling, Linda continuing to laugh. Anyway, thats what I think you should do. Some place you havent been before and far enough away so it will be a complete change of scenery.

It sounds wonderful, Mom. It really does. I can just feel that youre right.

And dont wait too long, dear. The sooner the better.

O.K., Mom, the first chance I get.

Linda thought about where they might go for the rest of the day, and when a cold, gray rain started falling, and she came across an ad from the Jamaican Tourist Bureau in last Sundays *Times*, she knew where she wanted to go, and this seemed like the perfect time to suggest it. She left the full-page picture of sunny Jamaica on top of the pile of papers.

After Harry got home and had shaken the rain from his clothes and plopped in a chair, she handed him the ad before he had a chance to establish any particular mood.

It looks lovely, doesnt it?

Yeah. On a day like this even Miami Beach would look good.

Well, laughing, I dont think the weathers that bad. But I do have an idea.

Yeah, whats that?

Why dont we—just you and I . . . alone . . . together—fly down there for a couple of days? White sandy beach—

Huh? What?

Blue sky, emerald sea—

What are you talking about?

Jamaica. Us. Alone. Together. You getting the picture?

How can we? I have work and theres Harry Junior and—

And nothing, sitting on his lap and putting her arms around his neck. Mother would be delighted to take care of Harry—

Whose mother?

Either of ours. Theyre both goofy about their first grand-child. Really, honey, lets do it. Im sure you could take a day or two off from work. I cant remember the last time weve been alone together. What do you say?

Well, I don't know. I—

Please . . . Come on . . . We need a few days alone. We really do.

Harry looked at his wifes smiling face and into her shining eyes and put his arms around her and wanted to bury his face in her neck and cry . . . just cry. Thats all. Cry and tell her over and over that he loved her and was sorry and as God was his witness he loved her and did not want to hurt her. He hugged her to him and felt his warm breath on her neck. He swallowed his tears and felt them churning in his stomach. O.K., honey, I/ll make the arrangements tomorrow. We/ll go this weekend. He hugged her again, trying to create the hope that the white sand, the blue sky and the emerald sea would kill this thing within him.

The few days before their departure were nerve-wracking and agonizing for him. He wanted desperately to be with Linda and recapture that elusive something he felt was slipping away, but at the same time he was afraid he would destroy it completely. What would he do if the insane (Is it really ??? No, just a figure of speech; what other word would you use?) urge came over him there? Here he was safe. He could find relief easily without anyone (Linda) knowing. But what would he do on some dumb little island? Where would he go? What excuse could he make? How could he keep it a secret? The whole thing seemed impossible. There was just no way he could spend four interminable days and nights on that rat little island without either going stark raving mad or destroy-ing his marriage. . . . Krist, he did not want to do that. He did not want to lose his family. He/d die without them. He knew it. What in krists name could he do? He couldnt cancel the trip; Linda was planning on it. She was just bubbling and bouncing all over the house. He didnt know how or why, but it was obvious that it was very important to her that they go. He was stuck. Irresistible force and immovable object. He could only pray that he survived the trip.

The first time they walked onto the beach an incredibly cold chill twisted Harrys gut and the only thing that kept him from running back to the hotel was the overwhelming nausea that almost cut off his breathing. He staggered to an abrupt halt and swayed back and forth for a moment.

You all right, honey?

Huh? O, yeah, fine. Its—its just so bright l couldnt see for a moment.

Here, youd better put on your sunglasses.

Thanks, putting them on and continuing to walk toward the water, then stopping. I think this is close enough.

Whatever you say, sweetheart, dropping her things on the beach and getting ready to go into the water. Isnt it beautiful? —Harry nodded—I just cant wait to get in the water. Come on, slowpoke.

You go ahead. Im going to just sit for a minute.

O.K. Dont melt, and she ran to the water and dove into the surf and waved to Harry.

Harry waved as he struggled to breathe. He was feeling sweaty. He didn't know what the hell was going on. All manner of things seemed to be struggling through his mind and body, but the only thing that he seemed to be aware of, that seemed to saturate his consciousness, were the goddamn broads in their bikinis. He knew, or at least part of him did, that the beach was not crowded, that there could not be more than a hundred of them on the beach. He could see that. He could see that plainly. But that was not what registered. All he could see were long legs and round asses and tits that looked like they were trying to squirm their way free from almost non-existent restraint, and the gentle rise of flesh below the navel that glistened and shimmered in the sun, and then that incredible and bulging mound of Venus and little bits of sparkling hair that seemed to flutter and wave invitingly, and Harrys gut tightened more and more as he sat with his legs raised and his chin resting on his knees, his arms wrapped around and clutching his legs, staring at all the cunts grinding and undulating their way out of the water and across the beach, and Harrys chills shivered in him as the sweat slowly crawled across his face. . . .

He heard Lindas voice and she waved to him as she walked slowly toward him, the water glistening and rolling down her body to the glaring sand. He stared at the roll of her hips as she came toward him, and when she bent over to pick up the towel he leered at the nipples of her tits, then stared at the inside of her thighs as she dried herself briskly with the towel.

That was marvelous. Just fantastic. You have to go in the water, Harry, you just must. Its absolutely invigorating.

Thats not the only thing thats invigorating, pulling her down next to him and putting his arms around her and kissing her neck.

Be careful, Harry, leaning into his kisses, her eyes closed, youre getting me all sandy.

Thats all right. A quick shower will take care of that. I feel a little sandy myself. Come on, lets go.

Harry always brought Linda to peaks of excitement when they made love, but through her excitement she could feel a desperation within him, but easily pushed this knowledge aside, attributing it to his tension. And as the days moved along, she was convinced she was right, since Harry seemed to be a little less tense each day.

They made love frequently, during the day and the night, Linda especially enjoying the times during the day because of the novelty and the feeling of freedom it gave her. It helped her feel free of obligations and everyday routines, as if, for now, she was in another world.

And they danced and held hands in the moonlight and sailed across lagoons under the bright Caribbean sky. Im so glad we came here, Harry.

I am too, sweetheart. Its a beautiful place. Almost as beautiful as you.

She snuggled into his shoulder and felt the warmth of his love and the dark velvet sky.

Harry felt himself relaxing almost to the point of giddiness. He was constantly holding Lindas hand, even in their sleep. He would awake, his fingers interlocked with hers, and he would kiss her hand until she started to awaken, and then he would roll over on his side and kiss her beautiful face. He just could not get enough of his wife. He held her hand in the dining room, on the beach and as they strolled through the tropical gardens. From time to time he would kiss her tenderly on the cheek or finger tip. This world was lovely, calm. You had to walk and talk and think slowly or you would pass it by. Each evening there would be an orchid waiting for Linda on their table, and they would beam at each other as the maitre d pinned it on Madams dress.

Inevitably there was the final evening and the last day of their brief vacation. They held hands as they boarded the plane and all the way to New York.

When they got home, Linda called her mother to tell her they were back and that they had had a wonderful time. I/ll tell you all about it tomorrow when I pick up little Harry, but you were right, Mom—absolutely right.

They spent the remainder of the evening on the couch watching something or other on television, Harrys arm around his lovely Linda, and her head nestled on his chest.

15

He was back in the pit, only this time it was smelly and vile. He went straight to Eighth Avenue, south of Times Square, and made the rounds of a few bars until he found a thirsty lush and bought a bottle and they went to her sour, roach-infested room. He could feel the sooty grayness crawl under his skin as he looked at the scummy walls and floor, and felt the gritty sheets as their foul stench reamed his nostrils.

He fucked the sodden piss/sweat smelling mess next to him and then fucked her again before she drank herself to sleep. He could have left and stayed somewhere else, anywhere else —perhaps have even made the last train home—but he stayed. In the dim light that just managed to penetrate the soot on the window overlooking the air shaft he looked at the thing, whatever or whomever it was, next to him (white sandy beach, blue sky), thinking of ripping her off the bed as you would an old and crusty scab. Krist, what a hopeless and helpless bloated mess of pathetic flesh. He somehow knew that she was younger than he was. Maybe not much, maybe only a year or two, but younger. She looked and smelled like something that had been left on the beach (emerald green sea) by the receding ocean and was already starting to rot in the heat of the tropical sun.

A rotten drunk. A disgusting drunk. Living in a hovel not fit for a rat. The roaches he could hear scuttling across the bare floor were probably fighting to get out of this filthy pest-hole. How could a human being allow herself to degenerate to a state like this? It was inconceivable. She might even have been attractive at one time. He looked at her greasy hair and in the dim light he could see a large pimple on her shoulder, and remembered the crud under her fingernails. His leg started to cramp and he knew he had to move it, but fought against the need because he did not want to be made aware of the filth he was lying between. Eventually the cramp forced the movement and his body moved through the swill as he continued to look with disgust at the booze-reeking mess beside him. He raised himself on an elbow and looked down at her. He stared at the gray skin on the gray sheets (O Harry, Ive never seen such a beautiful orchid. Its never seen anything as beautiful as you) for an indefinite and interminable length of time. His eyes burned and begged to be closed, to be jammed shut in sleep and ignorance so everything seen could be denied or at least shoved aside for now. His body, too, ached for sleep or some sort of rest. He felt himself sinking lower and lower on the bed, his eyes shutting out more and more until his head was almost on the rag of a pillow, and he jerked it up, and his eyes open, and tried desperately to keep them open and his head as high as possible, but, O God, he wanted to sleep. He wanted so desperately to simply plunge into sleep. Instantly. Oblivion. That, at least, is what this hulk beside him had. Oblivion. O dear God, what a gift. Nausea was twisting and grinding him and his nose and throat burned (they stood in the surf holding hands, the soothing water and sand caressing their feet as they watched the sun sink into the sea) and he struggled to swallow through the taste of bile. He had to move. He had to get up and bathe—o, dear god, he had to bathe, to plunge himself in the water—and get dressed and get out of here and maybe get some rest . . . yes, some rest . . . Jesus, God, some rest. Why in the hell couldnt he move? He had to get up —and out. (Come on, I/ll race you to the float.) He jerked himself around and up and cringed as his body scraped through the sheets and his bare feet touched the floor, and he immediately stretched up as far as possible on the tip of his toes. He darted to the bathroom, trying, in an insane ballet, to keep his feet off the floor as much as possible. He felt the cold, slimy tile under his feet and looked around, in the dimness, at the bare bathroom. He hesitated for a moment, then turned on the light and instinctively leaped back. He quickly saw the shit- and pukestained commode and the dried vomit on the rust- stained bathtub. How in the name of krist can anyone sink so low to have to live like this? Animals dont live like this. Then it suddenly struck him that he was there. The scabby hulk couldnt help it, but he— He quickly jabbed at the light switch and started vomiting almost simultaneously. It splattered off the side of the tub onto his legs and the floor. He leaned over the tub until he was finished vomiting, swearing, crying, raging and pleading within himself as he bent so as to prevent any more vomit from splattering on him. When he stopped, he wiped his legs with toilet paper and instinctively started to wipe up the mess he had made, then suddenly dropped the toilet paper and backed out of the bathroom and hurriedly dressed and scrambled from the building.

        He thrust himself through the street, trying to breathe deeply, but unable to rid himself of the smell and taste that burned through him to the marrow of his bones and the pit of his gut. He looked up and down the dreary streets frantically and finally got a cab and went to a Turkish bath.

        He stayed in the steam room for hours visualizing the poison oozing from his pores, constantly swallowing, not because of the bile that soured his taste, but because of something that was trying to worm its way up from the depths of the darkness within him. He continued to swallow and to shove this demon down without ever acknowledging its existence.

On the way home that night he bought a box of chocolates for Linda. She was surprised by the gift and upset by Harrys appearance. You all right, Harry?

Yeah, sure, why do you ask?

O, you look a little pale, like you might be coming down with something.

No, yawning and shaking his head, just a tough day.

They tried to act normal, but Harry was fighting sleep but did not want to go to bed too early. He could not let Linda know how tired he was. He sat in his chair trying to think of something to say, fighting his exhaustion and the need of his eyes to close, but he could not get more than a couple of words together and just stared at the television and prayed that it would soon be late enough to go to bed.

Linda tried to reawaken the joy and closeness they had shared on the island but could not create the necessary degree of enthusiasm. She made the attempt many times during the evening, but Harry was silent and unresponsive and looked so haggard and exhausted—and . . . and . . . well, haunted. She did not know exactly why that word popped in her head, but she had to admit that it did describe how he looked. She did not like the word either because of the implication. It made her feel very uncomfortable. Especially when she thought of the present Harry had brought home that night, the box of chocolate-covered nuts. It puzzled and upset her. From time to time Harry would bring home a little present for her, but he had never brought home a box of candy. Especially a kind she did not like. Harry always made fun of men who brought home boxes of candy or bouquets of flowers. He said they were always apologizing for something. Yet that was what he had brought home. Not a lace handkerchief like before, or a Peanuts book or some silly little thing he had found. This was the thought that disturbed Linda and that she tried to keep from her mind.

She was also profoundly disturbed because when they had returned from Jamaica Harry was so relaxed, and they were so happy, that she believed that whatever had been wrong was a thing of the past and that they would continue to live the happy, carefree days of a second honeymoon, but now things were suddenly worse than they had been and Lindas sense of equilibrium was shattered.

Harry no longer left the office alone for lunch, but only in the company of his colleagues. He could not risk a reoccurrence of what had happened with Von Landor. Fortunately no real damage had been done, but the next time it might be disastrous.

But the occasional nighttime excursions continued, and as they did the fear increased. From Eighth Avenue he went further west to the waterfront, or in the opposite direction to the East River. He knew that fights, and occasional knifings, were not unusual, yet Harry found himself inexplicably and irresistibly drawn back there.

But it was not the fear of being physically attacked or beaten that troubled him. What really made him suddenly burn and flush was the fear of contracting a venereal disease. He had not made love to Linda since returning from the Caribbean because of that fear. Many times he thought of going to a doctor for a test, but just could not do it. How could he go into a doctors office and ask for a blood test? The doctor would want to know why. He would ask questions. What could he say? What excuse or reason could he give? Suppose they found out who he really was? He'd give them a phony name, but they would know he was lying. Suppose someone who knew him saw him go into the doctors office? They might ask him why he was there or mention it to Linda or someone at work. Jesus krist, what a fucking mess that would be. No. No, if he went to a doctor it would have to be in some asshole place in the Bronx. At night. But even then he could not be certain that he would not be discovered.

And anyway, what would be the use? Even if they told him everything was all right, it wouldnt help because deep down inside a part of him knew that he would just go back to those places and so the whole cycle would start over again. There just wasnt any hope. There was no answer.

Linda tried, desperately, to continue to believe that it was the pressure of work that was bothering Harry, but it became increasingly more difficult. She still believed that he loved her, but suspicions, or rather vague misgivings, about another woman kept fighting their way into her thoughts. She battled them as soon as they started, but she could not ignore the occasional box of chocolates, and what it represented, and the change in Harrys behavior and appearance. The haunted look increased, and he was not only more morose most of the time, and quiet, but he was always apologizing for something. And not just in words, but in actions and attitude. She had the inescapable feeling that he was apologizing for his existence and was pleading with her, and Harry Junior, to tolerate him. He seemed to be constantly in pain.

And he never touched her. He not only did not make love to her anymore, but did not kiss her hello, or goodbye, and when she kissed him he turned his head so the kiss landed on his cheek. He never held her hand or touched her on the shoulder. He treated her like a leper. She would shake her head in disbelief and confusion and tears would slowly form in her eyes and roll down her cheeks and she would sob, and the nights when she was alone, she would cry herself to sleep.

She finally swallowed her pride and told her mother what was happening, or what she thought was happening, and was so confused and incoherent that her mother was shocked and disturbed. She had never seen her daughter so distraught. She calmed her down and they spoke as calmly as possible and for the longest time her mother was paralyzed by Lindas pain, but was able to console her. She finally suggested to Linda that perhaps she should ask Harry if something was wrong. You know, dear, its just possible that hes sick and doesnt want to worry you.

Why would he do that? Im going out of my mind the way things are now. It would be a blessing to know that it was as simple as that.

I know, dear, but youre dealing with a man and men are not very logical in these matters. They have some sort of dumb idea that theyre supposed to prove theyre men by suffering in silence, she started laughing, and driving us crazy with the noise of it.

Her mothers laughter forced a smile to Lindas face. I hope its just some silly little thing like that—I dont mean I hope hes sick, but I just want—

I know, dear, putting her arms around her daughter, I know what you mean. Why dont you just ask him? Maybe this whole thing can be cleared up with a few words.

I hope so, Mom. I pray to God youre right.

Linda felt better than she had in months that night, but she just could not seem to find the proper time to ask Harry if there was anything wrong. But that was all right; there was no need to force it. She would simply wait for the right time and then ask him. In the meantime this hope and resolve helped lift her spirits, and so she continued to wait for the right time.

Harry started staying at the office for a couple of extra hours at night, occasionally, until he had to rush to catch the last train. On those nights he might nibble at a little food when he got home, somehow force himself to talk with Linda for a little while, then go to bed.

His work seemed to be the only thing that kept him from springing apart, the only thing he could still lose himself in. Day by day he felt himself getting tighter and tighter inside and the pressure that seemed to squeeze his body increased until he felt that these forces surely would destroy him.

He was having lunch with Walt on a daily basis, not only as a precautionary measure but because in the back of his mind he had the hope that he might be able to talk to him and tell him some of the things that were bothering him, at least enough to relieve some of the pressure. And though he had a deep affection for the man, he just could not say anything. He was afraid, among other things, of jeopardizing his position. When Walt asked him how he was, he treated the question, and answered it, rhetorically and nodded and said all right, for fear that if he said anything, anything at all, he would not be able to stop and all the ugliness that had been festering in the blackness of his mind would come spilling out. And so he remained silent, and the knot got tighter and tighter.

At lunch one afternoon, in the Bankers Club, they had just been served their soup when Harrys cuff caught on his knife, and when he lifted his hand, the knife splashed in his soup. Harry started trembling and his head shook so rapidly that his vision blurred to the point of almost disappearing, and he suddenly clasped his hands together and raised them over his head and smashed them into the soup as he screamed, AAAAAAAAAAAAAAAAAAAAAAAAAHHHHHHHHHH-HHHHHHHHHHH, and the soup splashed over Walt and he raised his hands defensively, For krists sake, what in the hell are you doing? and shoved his chair back and Harry leaned his elbows on the table and grabbed his head with his hands and moaned and started sobbing and the waiter and the maitre d came rushing over, Is there something wrong, Mr. Wentworth? Is Mr. White all right? I dont know, confused and bewildered. What are you doing, Harry? Come on, help me with him. Walt put his arms around Harry and helped him to his feet and with the aid of the waiter and maitre d they took him to an office. Harry and Walt were left alone. Harry sat and Walt stood in front of him. They were silent. . . .

After many minutes Walt offered Harry a glass of water. Harry shook his head. Wentworth held the glass in his hand and continued to look at Harry, who was holding his head in his hands and leaning his arms on his knees. Walt was concerned. Beyond business matters he had a personal affection for Harry. He stood, silent, and waited.

Eventually Harry raised his head and shook it slightly. Im sorry, Walt. I don't know what. . . .

Walt shrugged awkwardly. You all right, now?

Harry shrugged his shoulders and looked up at Walt with a lost expression on his face. Walt looked at him for a moment, then tapped him gently on the back. Come on, lets get cleaned up.

Harry was as indispensable as a man could be to the firm. He was a brilliant executive, and still in his early thirties, with many productive years in his future, and had probably not reached his full potential yet. And so the firm intended to do everything possible to protect its investment in Harry; and, on a more personal level, Walt was not the only individual interested in Harrys welfare. And so they insisted that Harry go to the Fifth Avenue Hospital and get the finest medical attention available.

When everything had been analyzed and evaluated by the specialists, the diagnosis was that he was suffering from the results of strain and anxiety but that there was nothing organically wrong. So an appointment was made with one of the most respected psychiatrists in the city.

While in the hospital Harry nurtured a secret hope that they would find something wrong with him that would explain those strange feelings he had and the need he had to do what he did. He was disappointed when he was given a clean bill of health though relieved at not having a venereal disease.

If only they could have found a brain tumor that was creating pressure on his brain that would explain everything. And then all they would have to do would be to cut it out and everything would be all right. But no tumor existed. No malfunctioning of the central nervous system. No excessive pressure of the spinal fluid. Nothing. Just him. Nothing.

Shortly before he left the hospital the psychiatrist visited him and they chatted briefly, and then he asked Harry what his problem was.

Harry felt defenseless and wanted to just blurt everything out, but something quickly closed it off and he shrugged and said, I seem to have sexual problems. Harry trembled inside as he heard himself say this and waited for some sort of reaction from the psychiatrist. Maybe he would find a way to get the truth out. It could be hoped for. But at the same time Harry was fighting desperately to prevent it. He wanted this man to help him, but there were certain things he just could not tell him. He could feel the sweat rolling down his back. Maybe he had said too much already. He wanted to take back what he had said. He wanted to tell this man that he was only kidding. Why did he say that? How did it get out? He was trying to think of some way to correct or retract what he had said, but he heard and saw the man laughing.

Dont we all.

Harry could feel himself grinning stupidly. He felt a little faint.

Sexual problems of one sort or another are the basis of many, if not all, of our problems. Its simply a case of finding out what their causes are and then we simply look at them and understand them and with self-awareness they are no longer a bogeyman.

Harry heard his voice but was not sure he was hearing all the words correctly. Actually he did not care. Above the panic that had shivered him when he heard his reply to the doctors initial question was a vague feeling that maybe this man would be able to give him the answer he needed. Even if he could not ask the question. Whatever the question was.

Here, here is a prescription for Librium. Just take one three times a day and you will feel much better.

Harry nodded and accepted the slip of paper.

I will see you at three oclock next Thursday. In the meantime you just relax.

Linda had an interview, too, with Dr. Martin, before Harry was discharged from the hospital and felt reassured and optimistic by the time the interview terminated. The psychiatrist had already been advised of Harrys brilliance and success in business by his associates, and when Linda told him of their marriage—she was too embarrassed to admit her suspicions—and their relationship in the marriage, he smiled and told her the prognosis was excellent. I really do not anticipate any real difficulty in getting to the root of your husbands problem.

O, that certainly is good news, Doctor.

I have a great deal of experience in this area—dealing with repressions and subconscious conflicts. As a matter of fact I have published many papers on the subject.

Its hard to believe that Harry has any conflicts.

Dr. Martin smiled benignly. To the untrained and unspecialized eye perhaps, but to someone like myself. . . . He shrugged slightly and leaned back in his chair. You see—I will try to keep this as simple as possible—we have all suppressed things from our childhood, things that go back beyond our memories. Sometimes they give us trouble. I have been successful in cases that were far more difficult than your husbands. He is an extremely successful man and, from what I have been told, his future is unlimited. He, in all probability, will one day be one of the most outstanding businessmen in the country, a man of tremendous influence. Linda smiled and nodded with obvious pride. And there would seem to be no real problem at home; you love each other and your son. So, it is simply a case where I must help him to understand how his mother and his childhood have created conflicts in his subconscious that have resulted in anxieties and his present condition. And, all things considered, I anticipate no problem in your husband sublimating the underlying tensions that are a product of those repressed feelings. I hope I have explained it in such a way that you understand what I said?

Yes, I believe so, Doctor.

Good, good. And do not be disturbed if your husbands behavior seems to be a little—ah shall we say, unusual? It may take a little while for him to adjust to the therapeutic process.

Yes, I think I understand, Doctor.

Good, good. You just leave everything in my hands and everything will be back to normal.

Linda wanted very much to believe Dr. Martin; she wanted reassurance. She also wanted very much to believe that the cause of Harrys recent behavior was some unresolved childhood problem and that their marriage was not endangered.

Harry came home from the hospital with a vague and desperate hope. The medication that the doctor had prescribed seemed to take the edge off his feelings; his skin did not feel quite so alive and he did not feel so squirmy inside, and in the back of his head was an attempt to believe that Dr. Martin possessed a panacea. It might take a little time, but someday (soon, he hoped) they would dig back into his childhood and he would remember something suddenly and the doctor would say, Thats it, thats where it all started, and his troubles would be over. That would be the day. The day that he would be free. Yeah, that would be the day.

Harry continued to cling to this idea even though things seemed to get progressively worse the longer he continued his therapy with Dr. Martin. They went deeper and deeper into the past and he remembered things that were not a part of his conscious memory. He relived experiences that had long been forgotten, remembering how he felt at the time and even the smells. They got deeper and deeper into the problem, which seemed to interest Dr. Martin profoundly, but there were no answers for Harry, and so he was forced to continue to seek the only answer he had ever found that relieved him of those intolerable feelings.

On the evenings that he went to the doctor, he left, after the session, and went immediately to some rats nest on the waterfront and fucked some pukey broad and then had to force himself to go home. Day after endless and painful day he would resolve to lie on that couch and tell Dr. Martin everything that was happening in his life. Tell him all the things he had done and was doing. To make a clean breast of it. But he not only found it impossible to get the words out, but did everything possible to avoid even approaching that area of his life, as if he were defending his right to continue doing the thing that was killing him but that was, at the same time, the only thing that would relieve the unbearable tension in his body and mind.

Again the fear of syphilis haunted him and made his home life more frigid than usual, and the old fear of discovery, and the feeling of hopelessness, prevented him from going to get a blood test. The pain of despair became so intense that he tried to open the gate and allow the poisonous flood to flow forth and he blurted out that he had been unfaithful to his wife.

Does this bother you?

Yes, it does . . . very much.

Why?

Why?

Yes, why? Why should this disturb you so much? You are trembling.

I dont know, shaking with confusion and fear, it just does.

Do you know any other men who have been unfaithful to their wives? his tone, as usual, cold and detached.

What???? I dont understand. I—

Are you the only man who has been unfaithful to his wife?

No, no, certainly not. But thats not the—

Do you have a mistress?

A what? I—

Do you have a mistress? A girlfriend?

No, no, of course not. You know—

You love your wife?

Yes. I—

Then this extramarital activity of yours is just of the usual variety.

Well, yes, but I—

In other words your liaisons with other women are the usual thing that last for an evening. The type of affair that millions of men indulge in.

Yes, yes, I know that, but I love my wife and I—

The interesting thing is that you should make such an issue of something that is so usual. Yes, it is extremely interesting that you should feel so guilty. Do you have any trouble performing with these women?

What? What—

Do you ever have a problem with impotency? How about with your wife?

No, no, thats not the—

What did your mother tell you about infidelity? Did she tell you it was a sin?

What???? I dont know, I dont know. I cant—

Were you ever caught masturbating?

Masturbating? I dont know what—

Were you ever told that it would make you stutter or make you go blind?

I dont remember anything like—

Can you remember your toilet training?

What? I dont—

Were you forced to sit on the toilet after each meal until you had a bowel movement?

Jesus, I—

When did you stop wetting the bed?

Harry wanted to
scream and cry and run and curl up in a ball and roll away or
fade into the wall and when the session was finally terminated
he took a cab to the nearest subway station and locked himself
in a public toilet and cried and cried, under the roar of the

trains, until he felt exhausted and there just werent any more tears, and no energy or resources to manufacture more.

Lindas hope was constantly decreasing as Harry became increasingly morose for longer periods at a time, the periods coming closer and closer together. And her fears and anxiety increased as her hope decreased. She fought with herself for weeks about calling Dr. Martin, not wanting to be an interfering wife, but eventually her desperation overwhelmed her judgment. She kept her voice and manner as calm as possible, but her insides trembled. She tried to reassure him that she was not trying to pry, but she was worried because her husband seemed so depressed and seemed to be staying away from home more and more often.

I wouldnt worry about that, Mrs. White. A man in your husbands position has enormous responsibilities, responsibilities that do not end at five oclock.

Yes, I realize that, Doctor, and I—

I assure you, I will take care of everything. There is no need for you to concern yourself.

Thank you, Doctor. I do not want to be an alarmist; its—

Yes, yes, I know. Your husband seems withdrawn and silent and you are worried.

Yes, and—

Such behavior is normal in therapy. Your husband is simply going through a period of transference. You just leave everything to me.

O, I dont mean to—

Good. I have to hang up now. Good day, Mrs. White.

Linda sat with her hand on the phone for many minutes. She tried to think herself into moving, but her hand refused to release the phone. She stared at it, trying desperately to revive a feeling of hope, but all she could feel was a void.

Harry was still able to function at work, though his work was not up to his standards. He had to reread documents and letters and, even after that, sometimes they still did not make sense, but by putting in additional time he just barely managed to keep up.

His associates, especially Walt, were concerned, since the evidence of the strain Harry was working under was becoming more and more obvious. They too were reassured by Dr. Martin and told that it was necessary for Harry to continue working. I appreciated your concern, Mr. Wentworth, and the concern of the firm, but a vacation at this particular time is not just what the doctor ordered, if I may introduce a bit of levity, hahaha. It is important that he be able to sublimate.

Fine. We/re really glad to hear that. Hes extremely valuable and we do not want to jeopardize his future. He is very important to the firm.

Yes, I am fully aware of that.

And, smiling and shrugging slightly, I guess I have more than a professional interest in Harrys welfare. I guess its obvious that it is also paternal.

Yes, yes, nodding his head, but dont worry, I will keep your Mr. White functioning.

And Harry continued to function at work, locked in his office, his oasis, his haven and refuge, envying the others who were free to come and go as they pleased, when they pleased, and wishing to krist that he could just stay in his office and then be picked up and placed at home and then back in the office, but he knew that he could not avoid leaving the office from time to time, that he could not avoid those trips to those phlegm-spotted bars to find another filthy mess to spew his poison in and then try to vomit the hell and rottenness out of his gut. . . .

O jesus, the rottenness . . .

The black, festering rottenness that chewed him up and the stench from his own gut that constantly hung in his nostrils. And the more time he spent on the couch the worse it got. The blackness that he felt squirming through him was slowly starting to wrap itself around his head and squeeze it and squeeze it until he thought he would lose his mind and he had to go out into those streets and fuck another pimpled cunt.

He tried to tell Dr. Martin, but somehow it just didnt come out. During the day, and especially in the cab going to his office, he would go over and over in his head what he was going to say, how he was going to tell him everything he was doing, how he was going to spew forth the evil corrosion of his soul (O jesus, he wished he could get that slime out), but somehow they always got involved with the past . . . his mother and his childhood.

The thing that kept him going to Dr. Martin was the vague hope that he would reach deep down and pull this vileness out of him. He wished to God it would happen soon. He couldnt stand this much longer.

                        Nor could he stand to see the pain in Lindas eyes . . . those eyes that looked so hollow lately. Eyes that seemed to be getting duller and duller . . . And a mouth that was constantly pinched with pain. Her laughter . . . Dear God, it had been so long since he had heard her laughter, he wasnt sure if it was a memory or a myth. Laughter . . . . Love?????? He loved her. And little Harry. He knew he did. . . . Or had. O God, whats happening? All he wanted to do was go home and put his arms around his family and hug them and kiss them and push his sons hair from his eyes and hold his wifes hand and kiss her finger tips— thats all he wanted to do. Jesus, krist, is that so goddamn much to ask? Whats wrong with that? Why???? Why???? WHY???? cant I do it? Why do I cringe when he comes running over to me and hugs my legs? Why do I have to push him away? Why are you doing this to me, God? I cant look her in the face anymore. I cant lift my head. Cant eat. He doesnt even come over to me anymore. He doesnt talk to me. I cant talk to Linda. O krist, she hates me, I know she hates my stinking guts. If I could just die. Just somehow not wake up. I wouldnt have to see her face or hear his silence—O jesus, I love her. But how can I? Look at her. O Jesus, I didnt mean to do it. Im sorry honey. Holy fuck, Im sorry. If I could only twist my head into a pulp, or just not see her eyes. I didnt do it. Please, tell me I didnt do it. I did not sink those eyes into her skull and take the life out of them. Please, I did not do it. O dear God, I didnt do it. I didnt. . . .

And again, he silently went to bed, keeping his back to Linda, hearing her voice and wanting to turn and say I love you and kiss her good night, but grunting something unintelligible and trying to push himself instantly into sleep, hoping for a soothing oblivion, but immediately conscious of the sick pain in his body, the twisting and knotting chills, the ache and cramp in his jaw— And he wrapped his arms around his pillow and pulled his knees up almost to his chin

and could hear her breathing. It was low and barely audible, but he heard it as a groan that iced the marrow of his bones and he tried to shut his ears against it, but the dull, low moan stayed in his head and he could feel her . . . he could feel her! She was there. In bed with him. He wrapped his arms around his head and clutched tighter at the pillow as he felt her in the bed with him. She was there . . . behind him. . . .

And she didnt move. She just lay there. . . . But it somehow felt as if she were coming closer . . .   closer . . .   and maybe she was going to touch him and his jaw felt as if it would suddenly snap and he fought and clung and was finally dragged into a half sleep that seemed like a dream, to dream a dream that seemed to be real, and he fought against the reality of the dream, trying to avoid it by going to sleep, and his body shook and he shivered and groaned and screamed inside his head but the dream persisted, and persisted in its terrifying reality, and he looked at his daughter getting ready for her fifth birthday party and she was in the tub taking a bubble bath and she was drying herself and he was staring at her naked body and he wanted to turn and leave but his head was locked, it wouldnt move, so he could only stare at her and his head yelled over

and over again and again and again a wailing and pleading
NO NO NO NO NO NO NOOOOOOOOOOOO
and finally his scream
spewed out of his mouth and his body jerked up and Linda
put her hand on his shoulder, You all right sweetheart?
Can I get you something? and he could only shake his
head and grunt and shiver and allow his head to slowly de-
scend to the pillow, and curl himself up again and fight the
tears that pounded against his eyes and chest, that welled up
inside him so he had to fight to breathe, that made him jerk
with the fear that he was drowning in his own juice. O God, if
he could only turn over and reach his hand out to hers . . . .

or cry . . . just cry . . .

or maybe just sink into
the ground and allow his body to be eaten by the maggots and
worms. Anything . . . . . .

Anything

16

There are limits. Limits of time. Limits of circumstances. Limits of endurance. Linda had reached hers. Time had run out. She could no longer sit passively by as the man she loved kept constantly rejecting her and humiliating her by treating her like some sort of unwanted encumbrance or excess baggage that he obviously wanted to get rid of, but did not know how to go about doing so and therefore continued to punish her with his cold indifference. She did not know the reason for Harrys behavior, but she was not going to sit idly by and allow herself to be treated like this.

She visited her mother and hesitatingly told her what was happening in her life and marriage, constantly breaking into sobs and crying and shaking her head—her mother embracing her and trying to soothe her childs sadness and pain—

looking at her mother completely bewildered and shaking with grief and frustration and moaning over and over that she didnt know what was wrong. I just dont know what is happening, Mom—

I know, dear, I know—

I dont know what is wrong . . . I just dont know—O Mom, help me . . . help me. . . .

You have a good cry, darling, and she hugged her little girl close to her, feeling her sadness and pain, and her tears wet and warm on her breast.

When Linda had finally calmed enough, they discussed the situation and decided it would be best if Linda simply told Harry how she felt, and perhaps, just (hopefully) perhaps, there might be a simple and logical explanation for his behavior and he would reassure her. And if not . . .

well, then maybe it would be best if Linda and Harry Junior spent a little time visiting her family. Lindas mother thought that it might be better to wait a day or two, when youve calmed down more, darling.

No Mom. I cant wait. I cant put it off any longer. I have to find out now. I cant wait. She left her son with his grandparents and went home determined to talk with Harry.

That evening, as soon as Harry sat down, Linda said there was something she wanted to discuss. She had spent the previous hours trying to think of some way to simply, and easily, say what she had to, but the more she thought about it the more confused and pained she became, so she simply blurted out that she was going to spend a few days or so with her family.

Why? an immediate and terrifying panic exploding within him, an instant welling of tears that pounded against his eyes, and the shattering fear that he would be alone and on top of that the god-awful dread that she would tell him *why*, and he would not be able to live with what she would say and yet would have absolutely no defense against her words.

Why? Because there is something going on that I do not understand and that I cannot live with.

I dont understa— What do you mean? his voice pathetic, pleading, unconvincing; his shoulders even more rounded and stooped with dejection.

Your behavior, Harry, Linda trying desperately to retain her firm resolve to talk this through and take the appropriate action no matter how painful it might be for her—Harry shaking his head and looking more at the floor than his wife—you . . . you treat me like some sort of object of scorn, keeping her voice low and her tone as inoffensive as possible and trying to ignore the pleading look on his face, you dont talk to me, you dont touch me no less kiss me, and if I ask you something you just grunt and turn your back on me—you are always turning your back on me, Harry, as if youre ashamed of me or tired of me or cant stand the sight of me or as if I did something terrible to you and you have some sort of resentment or hatred for me—Harry, are you seeing another woman?

Harry shook his head and stammered and sputtered but could not seem to create the force necessary to dispute the accusation because he knew if he tried she would ask some sort of simple question that he simply could not answer and he might end up telling her the entire truth and just contemplating that possibility froze and paralyzed him with fear. He continued shaking his head with the same pathetic expression on his face. Why do you ask? I dont—

Because of your behavior. There just doesnt seem to be any other explanation, and Linda could feel a terrible twisting of dread within her and though part of her wanted to get this problem out in the open there was an even stronger urge not to know the truth, not to have Harry suddenly blurt out that he was seeing another woman and wanted a divorce. She did not want to lose him, she just wanted him to change, to once again be the man she married five years ago. Perhaps if I spend a little time with my family, you and Dr. Martin can work out whatever the problem may be. I hope so, and she looked at Harry, waiting, and hoping, he would ask her not to leave and reassure her that everything was all right or somehow would be, but all he did was to sit and stare at the floor, his head seeming to sink deeper and deeper into his shoulders. Harry, dont you care?

He wanted desperately to reach out and ask—beg—her not to leave, but felt completely enervated by the overwhelming pain of despair and the pitiful and incomprehensible demoralization that had wrapped itself around him, more and more tightly, like a serpent.

He could feel her staring, and the longer he sat there staring at the floor, the more impossible it was for him to raise his head and look into her eyes.

Linda waited endless years for his protestations, and eventually the silence forced her into action. She went into the bedroom and hurriedly packed a few things. She started to say something before she left, but her eyes started tearing and an overwhelming sense of sadness constricted her throat. She left.

Harry heard her breathing, her sighs, her movements as she packed her bag, then felt her standing near him and staring, then heard her walking across the floor, heard the door, then the car slowly fade in the distance . . .

and nothing happened to stop her. And nothing happened to stop him from just sitting. And staring. And hoping pathetically he would sink further inside himself and suddenly wake up from this nightmare . . . But he knew that would not happen. That was just a dream.

Linda drove slowly down the circular driveway, the crunching of the gravel sounding loud and piercing and, somehow, ominous. She constantly glanced in the rear-view mirror, and stopped a few times and looked back at the house, hoping to see Harry in the doorway or running down the driveway waving at her to come back. O merciful God, she did not want to leave. She had resolved to leave if necessary but she had felt certain he would not let her, that he would explain away all her fears and refuse to let her go. She stopped at the entrance to the road. There was no traffic. It was silent. She strained to hear the sound of feet pounding on the gravel, running feet that would get louder and louder—but it was silent. The gradual sound of an approaching car. Then the sound grew more distant. The gravel was silent. Still. Linda wept. She was actually leaving. There was nothing stopping her from turning onto the road and driving away. O God, she did not want to go. She rummaged blindly through her pocketbook for a handkerchief, then threw it aside and trembled with a moan and rubbed at her face with her hands, trying to clear the tears from her eyes. She was no longer leaving for a few days. Inside she felt like she was leaving forever. She would never see Harry, or her home, again. It felt as if there were a form of death waiting for her if she drove away. There was a terrible and abysmal hollowness within her that was rapidly filling with tears. Her bones seemed to be slowly dissolving and she found it impossible to move, to put the car into gear . . .

to take her foot off the brake . . .

to put her foot on the accelerator . . .

to push down on the gas . . .

to turn the wheel . . .

to thrust herself at the wheel and yank it . . .

to turn the car onto the road . . .

the road that would take her away from . . .

from her life. . . .

O God . . . O God in heaven . . .

and still there was no sound behind her . . .

no sound of someone running down the gravel driveway

no voice

pleading for her not to leave

                            no waving hand beckoning for her
to come back

                    to come back . . .

                                    back. . . .

      The car moved slowly onto the road, and instantly
the driveway and home were out of sight. There was just a
road in front of her that soon would merge with a highway.
The shadows deepened and stretched further and further
across the road as the sun continued its rapid descent.

  There never is a real difference between ancient history and
current events. There are only variations; the theme is always
the same. The pressures within Harry were so intense and
built up so rapidly after each release that his night visits to
hell were happening more and more frequently. He did not
stay in the city most of the time, but would wait for the
pathetic alcoholic sponge next to him to pass out and then put
a twenty-dollar bill in the top of the empty bottle and take
the last train home.

                    It did not work that way this time. They
were waiting for him in the hallway. He was hit on the back
of the head, punched and kicked. They grabbed his money
and split. The first thing he saw when he regained consciousness were roaches scurrying across the floor and under the
ripped and rotting molding. The stench of urine burned his
nose and the cuts on his face. He sat up and leaned against
the wall and tentatively touched the painful areas of his head
and face, then looked at the blood on his hand. He looked
around, his vision wavering and going out of focus; then his
vision cleared and he could see where he was and remembered
what had happened. He saw his wallet on the floor with his
cards and papers strewn around. He picked them up and put
them in his pocket. He slowly got to his feet. The right side
of his face pounded and burned. He couldn't bear to touch it.

He staggered to the street and took a cab to his office building and borrowed money from the security guard. He continued to the train station, using one hand to hold a handkerchief lightly against his face.

The trip home was long and agonizing. The house was still empty. He was suddenly hollow. Rubbery. There was a tomb-like atmosphere in the house. He fell in a chair. He called out, not really believing she would be there—yet—

His voice sounded hollow and listless as it probed the rooms. . . . O please come back . . . please. . . .

Tears stung his battered and bloodied face His head throbbed. Burned. His body felt as if it were crumbling into itself. He called a doctor who lived near by, a member of the club he played golf with frequently. When he got to the house, the doctor looked at Harrys face for a few seconds, then called the hospital.

Is that necessary, Bob?

Definitely. Routine and necessary in a case like this. Come on, I/ll drive you over. Wheres Linda?

Visiting her folks, feeling himself flush and burn.

Do you want me to call her?

Tomorrow, shaking his head. How long will I be in the hospital?

A day. There are tests that must be taken to be certain everything is all right and that you dont have a concussion or a fracture.

When he was checked into his room, Bob stopped by to see him before leaving. Ive ordered a little something to help you sleep. I want to be sure you get a good nights rest. And dont worry about anything. I/ll call Linda tomorrow.

Harry shook his head and remained morosely silent.

I/ll see you in the morning, Harry.

Harry shook his head.

By the time Linda got to the hospital, early the next afternoon, Harry looked much better. The dried blood had been cleaned off and the cuts had been stitched. Yet his appearance shocked and frightened her. The drive from her parents house to the hospital had seemed endless—a couple of hours of torturous anticipation and anxiety. Bob had told her that the preliminary reports indicated that everything was fine, that there were no serious injuries, but still her mind put her through hell. She remembered every story she had ever read or heard about people being mugged and losing an eye or going blind or being paralyzed or any number of other dreadful things happening to the victim. And words like *injury*, *suffered* and *victim* continually rang in her head.

And intermittently forcing itself to her consciousness was the embarrassment of receiving the call from Bob at her parents home, and waiting for him to ask why she was there and if there was any problem between her and Harry, but there wasnt any question in his voice (at least she didnt think so), and all he did was tell her that Harry had been hurt and reassure her that he was all right. Yet still, from time to time, she could feel herself flush with embarrassment as she drove to the hospital.

She battled, too, with twinges of guilt, thinking that if she had not left, this would not have happened, and she kept reminding herself that that was ridiculous, and, perhaps it is, but if I had been home I at least could have taken care of him—but you couldnt have done any more than Bob, and actually less, after all he is a doctor—I know, I know, but at least I could have been there. . . . O, I dont know, I dont know . . .

and Linda tried to shout her mind quiet or still it with tears, but the confusion, anxiety, apprehension and fear continued to stab and twist themselves through her.

She walked rapidly down the corridor toward his room, and her momentum carried her within a few feet of his bed before she stopped. Harry looked at her and tried to smile, but immediately and involuntarily winced from stiffness and pain, and this propelled her forward and she put her arms around him and hugged him, tight, O Harry, Harry Im so sorry this happened, are you all right? And she suddenly realized that she might be hurting him and her arms sprang apart and she stepped back, O sweetheart, Im sorry. Did I hurt you? That was stupid of me. Im sorry. I—

No. No. Its all right. It looks a lot worse than it really is anyway. He looked at her, trying hard to smile and swallow all the terrors of guilt and humiliation.

Linda, her eyes moist as she stared at him, was suddenly frozen between desire and conviction, but it seemed like ages since she had seen her husband, the man she loved, and he looked so helpless, so vulnerable—so—pained that her resolve was slowly, but steadily, being dissolved by her desire and his pain. She sat on the edge of his bed. Are you really all right sweetheart?

Harry could feel his head nodding and he wanted desperately to reach out and grab her and clutch her to him and kiss her and hug her or just touch her—her hand, cheek—just to touch her and tell her he loved her, but all he could do was nod his head as all his desires welled up inside him and battled the demon that was getting unconquerable strength from his guilt and humiliation, leaving a black pit of despair in his gut. He turned as Bob came into the room.

Hi Linda, how are you?

I dont think I know, shaking her head and attempting to smile.

Well, dont you worry, squeezing her shoulder and smiling, everything is fine. It looks like this husband of yours is going to live. Linda sighed and inwardly felt such a sudden relief that for a moment she thought she would either crumble or faint. There are no fractures or concussion, addressing himself to Harry, no cardiac involvements or other complications.

Cardiac?

Bob smiled reassuringly and put a hand on each of their shoulders. Nothing to worry about. With some people, especially older people, an experience like this can affect the heart, and so we routinely check that too. Anyway, youre in good shape, for the shape youre in, chuckling and squeezing their shoulders, youre lucky.

Linda smiled, and Harry tried to but could not quite force a smile.

When can he come home?

Right now if you want. Just take it easy for a day or two.

A sudden panic shot through Harry. I/ll be able to go to the office tomorrow, right?

I guess so, if you dont push too hard. Take a later train so you wont have to navigate through the rush-hour crowds. O.K.?

Harry nodded.

Good. Come in to the office in a week so I can take a look at you.

Thanks.

Thank you, Bob, I really appreciate everything, smiling and squeezing his hand.

Thats all right Linda. After all, thats the least I can do. He lets me beat him by a couple of strokes every time we play, and he laughed. Dont forget, a week.

Bob left. Linda and Harry looked awkwardly at each other for a moment.

Well, I guess I had better get dressed.

Harry sat down as soon as they got to the house.

Can I get you anything, sweetheart? Coffee? Juice?

No, no thanks . . . honey, smiling faintly. Harry felt tired—exhausted. He suddenly felt too tired to feed the battle within him, and so a sort of truce was declared. He felt a tenderness flow through him. I guess I just want to look at you.

Linda sat on the arm of the chair and took his hand in hers. He looked at her hands for a moment, then lightly rubbed her hand with the tips of the fingers of his other hand—then leaned his head against her arm, feeling the fragile smoothness, delicacy and warmth of her hands, and, for now, feeling quiet inside.

For the remainder of the evening there was very little movement, and sparse conversation, in the White home. Although Harry had only suffered a few cuts and bruises, the trauma of recent events had left them emotionally drained and with a desire to avoid any serious and probing conversation. They went to bed early, each enjoying the best rest they had had in many nights.

By midmorning the next day Harry was squirming in his chair and was almost tempted to go out for a walk, but instead he kept to his recent routine of staying in the office during the day and relaxed by promising himself he would go find some pig that night, maybe over on the west side near the docks. He had nót forgotten what had just happened, but the knowledge that he had been beaten, and that Linda might leave again, had no power over his actions. A power greater than he seemed to be pushing him toward the gates of insanity or death.

He stopped in a restaurant for a light dinner and was waiting for the line at the cashier to thin out, feeling that leaden grinding in his gut, the apprehension and anxiety, knowing he should be going home and knowing he would not. He suddenly closed his hand around his check and put his hand in his pocket and waved in the direction of the people at the cashier. I/ll wait for you outside. I need a little air, and he walked out. He wanted to run to the door and down the street, but forced himself to walk slowly and normally the interminable distance to the door, then forced himself to stand there for a moment, then left the restaurant, turned and walked slowly, ever,

ever

so

slowly

to the next corner, then turned and walked a few more feet, then stopped and leaned against a building. His heart was pounding so hard he could barely breathe. His whole body, his entire being, was alive with feelings that were about to overwhelm him. He could not believe the pounding within him. That twisting in his gut that seemed to be tugging at the back of his throat. He knew he had experienced these feelings before, but so long ago, in some ancient and forgotten past that there was only confusion when he tried to identify them. He did not try very hard because he felt it was useless; he had never stolen anything before so naturally he would never have had any feelings like these. For a second he wondered why he did it. What would have happened if someone had suddenly grabbed his arm at the door? Or if they were to grab him now and perhaps call the police? He looked around and swallowed hard and rapidly. Krist, his stomach was alive. Then he knew the feeling. It flushed through him like fire. The fear and speculation about being caught disappeared. Nothing else existed except the excitement flowing through him. The same excitement as the first time he was going to get laid. He hadnt been sure he was going to get laid. Tony told him this broad was a sure piece, but he had been told that before. He remembered he was afraid he might shit his pants that day, or piss them. But he didnt. Thats how he felt. That same excitement before and after. That same apprehension. The same sweat. The same taste in his mouth. The same exhilaration. Harry White stood straight. He smiled. He looked around happily. Krist, he felt good. He felt the check in his hand in his pocket. He took it out and carefully folded it and stuck it in his wallet, then took it out and dated it before putting it back. He not only felt exhilarated, he felt free. Yeah, free. Son of a bitch. Son of a fucking bitch. Yeah. Free. There was a hint of a spring in his step as he walked to the station to get a train home.

When Harry called to say he would be late, Linda thought her heart had actually stopped for a moment. She continually nodded at the phone and finally managed a few words. She felt so sick when she hung up that she just sat for many long and agonizing minutes, shivering. She could not believe that he would let anything keep him from getting home on time tonight, her first night home since—since staying with her folks.

She repeated over and over to herself that she was afraid because of his physical condition that perhaps there was something wrong that did not show up in the tests—a—a—well, a clot or something like that . . .

but she knew that that was not the reason. She knew that she was not afraid of losing Harry to a blood clot or some obscure physiological condition.

When Harry got home, hours before he was expected, Linda was startled and surprised. Then it registered. Through the maze and turbulence of feelings it finally registered. Harry was smiling. Through the bruises and patches he was smiling. . . .

They sat and talked for a while, drank coffee and nibbled on some cheese and crackers. Smelly cheese. The release from dammed tensions and fears was such an incredible relief that they readily ignored their hysteria.

That night they made love. Then they lay in each others arms and spoke of the night, of the stars, of their lives and mostly of their love . . .

then softly and gently sank into a restful sleep.

Harry was more than exhilarated—he was manic for many days. He felt like a new man, yeah, a *Novus Homo*, a man released—reprieved.

His life got back to normal rather rapidly. The door to his office was now open most of the time. He got home on time except for rare and legitimate occasions. He went out to lunch with Walt and the others most of the time. The quality and quantity of his work increased. And all with a sense of freedom. Whenever that gnawing started in his gut and his skin seemed to become alive with ants, and those vague and undefined anxieties started to haunt him, he simply went out and had a free lunch. Just like that. So simple he found it almost impossible to believe. But there it was. And there he was. One free meal and he felt fine. He was amazed that he was able to do such a thing. But he was. There it was. He was doing it. From time to time he thought about being asked why he had not paid his check and he would pursue the thought just long enough to experience the thrill of apprehension, then dismiss it from his mind before it prevented him from walking out with a wave of the hand, You take care of it Henry, I/ll meet you outside. And, anyway, he could always say it was an oversight, that he was preoccupied and did not realize what he had done and simply pay the check with the proper reassurances. Actually, who was going to believe that a man in his position would try to leave without paying the check?

Linda became aware of her voice as she once more went through the house singing, and as she walked around the garden talking to Harry Junior, telling him the names of the different plants and flowers. She was startled by the sound of her voice initially, and then by the realization that it had been some time (my God, how long?) since she had stopped singing.

She could also hear, and feel, her enthusiasm being rekindled; and was startled, too, by the evidence of neglect obvious in her gardens. She happily and energetically trimmed, pruned, spaded and weeded as she answered Harry Juniors endless stream of questions.

And with the passage of time, and the passing of fear and anxiety, there came an awareness of just how frightened and anxious she had been. It was only with the release from her fears and anxiety that she became aware of the extent to which they had been haunting her for what seemed to be an eternity. Her only point of reference to time was the chorus that lilted through her head, telling her things were just like they were a year ago.

A year ago? Could it really be that long since the feeling

of despair became stronger and stronger and her husband, whom she adored and loved, became more and more of a stranger? Could it really be that long? How did she survive? How did *they* survive? Of course there had been times when things were fine—moments and days here and there—but in looking back the pain seemed so bad she could not imagine surviving it for a week, much less a year. Well, whatever the truth might be, it was unimportant now. However long was immaterial. Things were back to normal. They talked and joked and laughed and Harry put his arms around her and kissed her and hugged her and whispered in her ear and they made love . . .

and then held hands and thrilled to the softness of night. And Harry did not suddenly bolt up in the middle of the night looking as if he had come face to face with death. There was joy and love and happiness in their home once more. Yes, things were back to normal, thank God. And, she was pregnant.

17

Harry was happily surprised to
find out that they were going to have another baby. It would
be nice for Harry Junior to have a little sister. And, he agreed,
that they really did not want to wait any longer to have a
second child. As it was, Harry Junior will be five when the
baby was born. I think thats a large enough difference in ages.

Harry started looking forward to seeing the glow in Lindas
face and eyes that came with pregnancy, and feeling the baby
kick and protest at being confined in that small dark place.
It would not be long before the baby would fight and wiggle
its way to freedom and the light. Just a matter of time.

And it is just a matter of time until history
once more becomes a living reality. The reality came for
Harry one day when he walked out of a restaurant without
paying the check, and did not realize that he had done so.
There were no wave and faked instructions to bring the action

to his consciousness. He had walked a block or so before he became aware of what he had done. Actually the first thing he was aware of was the fact that the accustomed feeling was not there. There was no feeling at all. Not even a vague memory of apprehension or anxiety before leaving, or the slightest hint of excitement now. He just felt flat. Deserted.

He closed his office door and thought about it for a moment, but soon had to stop as his body started to shrivel with dread. He could only think that somehow this meant he would go back into the living nightmare, and he would rather kill himself than do that. He couldnt. Not now. He dismissed the matter from his mind and buried himself in his work.

But the thought and fear nagged at him on the way home, fighting for recognition, but he shoved them down out of sight and sound. The next morning he told Linda that he was going to work late, and when he saw the expression that suddenly clouded her face, he quickly added that he would not be too late, that he would wait to eat and have a late dinner with her.

A couple of hours after everyone went home that night he roamed through the office. In all the vast expanse of offices and space, he was the only one there. It was a strange and almost eerie feeling.

He browsed through offices and desks and was amazed to find money, jewelry, watches and a hundred and one little odds and ends.

He walked to the floor above and went through a few of the offices there. Again he seemed to be alone. It was quiet. Tomblike silence. He could hear himself breathing—then he heard the sound of an elevator and he froze and waited until it had obviously passed the floor he was on. His legs and knees felt almost rubbery. His gut churned and twisted. That thrill and excitement were there again. All of his senses were not only alive, but magnified.

He roamed through the office, opening and closing desk drawers, at first very carefully and quietly, and then in a more natural and open manner. He collected a total of seventeen dollars and thirty-seven cents, almost half of it in change. Small change. He walked down the stairs, slowly, to his office, then took the elevator down to the ground floor. Conscious of the weight of all the change in his pocket, he could feel his heart pound and ring in his ears as he said good night to the security guard. He had thought of putting the change in a bag and dumping it down a sewer immediately, but decided instead to carry it all the way home. Just feeling the coins in his pocket kept the excitement alive. The feeling of elation was intense. The following day he stopped in a bank and got a supply of coin wrappers.

Dr. Martin was delighted with the tremendous improvement in Harrys condition. It was obvious to him that he had penetrated Harrys barrier and that the process of sublimation had been successfully accomplished and that they could now delve deeper into Harrys childhood and his Oedipal involvement without any trauma. Yes, Dr. Martin was extremely pleased indeed and smiled and glowed inwardly and puffed on his pipe as he listened to Harry.

Although Harry was coming home late occasionally, Linda was not upset now. Actually it was no different than when they were first married, almost six years ago, except, of course, the trip home was longer. Everything else was the same. Harry was cheerful, and they had their evenings and weekends together, and she was able to give all of herself to him and wait for him with open arms.

And there was life in her belly. A life that she could feel and see. And Harry would put his ear to her growing belly and tell her she was right, it sure sounds like a girl to me honey. And as her belly, and the life within her, grew, so did her glow of peace.

Through exploring his own office building Harry found many ways to obtain access to other buildings, even those with security guards. It was simple to determine the approximate time that they made their rounds, if ever, and adjust the time of his explorations accordingly. On one occasion he stayed in a mens room for more than an hour, waiting until he was certain the office was empty. As he sat in the small cubicle, time felt heavy and endless. Then he became aware of the increasing feeling of excitement in his legs and loins, and the rumblings of the fear of being caught in his gut. He allowed himself to become consciously involved with the feelings, and the sensations, caused by the sweat sliding down his back, and he lost his sense of time and caressed himself with the feelings that throbbed through him.

He walked through offices, opening and closing drawers, making just a little more noise each time. At first he just took some of the money he found lying around because it was completely unidentifiable. No one could stop him on the street and arrest him as a thief for the few extra dollars in his pocket, even if he did have an inordinately large amount of change. But eventually the excitement started to wane and he started walking around the offices as if he owned them, making as much noise as he wanted. Then he started taking little objects such as rings and watches and kept them in his pocket until he was almost home; then he threw them away.

As the months crowded into each other it became more difficult to replace the tension in his body with excitement. He started taking larger objects from the offices, such as adding machines and calculators and various office machines and equipment, making certain he carried them at least two blocks before he left them on the street. One night he took a typewriter from the tenth floor of a building, and before he was halfway down the stairs, he thought he would have to leave it. His arms ached and started to cramp. His hands felt like they were being cut. His heart pounded and his eyes were almost blinded with sweat. He started stumbling and teetered on the edge of a step and could feel his body slowly leaning forward, ready to topple down the stairs and maybe get his head crushed by the typewriter, and he fought desperately against the forces of gravity and finally staggered back and banged against the wall and just stayed there, panting. . . .

He did not want to leave the typewriter there. He thought that maybe he should just put it down for a minute and rest. Yeah, just a minute . . . just a— No! No! He would never get it up again. He knew that. Definitely. And he had to get this thing out of the building. He had to. He leaned against the wall, feeling the sweat roll down his face and watching it splat on the typewriter. Every goddamn muscle ached and he felt like he could not last another second, but the excitement was so intense he was actually rolling his hips slowly and rhythmically. . . .

He licked his lips over and over and pushed himself away from the wall and slowly descended the stairs, leaning against the wall, tentatively putting one foot down, and then the other, reaching for the next step, counting each one carefully so he would not suddenly pound into a landing. Eight steps, a landing, turn, another eight steps to the next floor. Three more floors to go. Impossible. The machine hung from his hands. He rubbed against it. He rested on the landing. His body screamed to put the fucking thing down and go. But he wouldnt. He was going to get it down and out of the building. He would not give in to the pain. He would endure. Another eight steps. Turn. Eight more steps. Two floors to go. His rib cage felt like it would splinter. He wanted to at least rest. Jesus he had to rest. He kept going. He could not stop. He would never start again. He had to keep up the momentum. Eight slow steps. Searching and finding each one with a probing foot. A landing. Slide along the wall. Head pulled forward. Sweat blinding him. Drops floating on the keyboard. Down the steps. Down the steps. Down the steps. Another floor. Just one to go. Sweet Jesus. Still one more. Almost slides to the floor. Inches along the wall. The machine cutting into him. The steps are further apart. Cant find them. Down. Down. A landing. Thank krist. Slide, slide. Eight more steps. Find the fucking step. The step. Just a few more. Almost down. One more—THERES ANOTHER ONE!!!! Holy shit! He almost fell. He leaned against the wall, straddling two steps. He peered over the machine. Four more. How the fuck can that be? Should only be eight. Why twelve? Cant make it. Cant do it. Cant turn. Cant get straight. Have to turn. Find the next step. Where is it? Have to get down. Thats right. Twelve in the first staircase. One more. One fucking more. Down. Down. Down, goddamn it. Made it. The door. What the fuck! Cant open it. Cant pull it in. He leans. Tentatively. It moves out. IT MOVES!!!! He peers into the lobby. Staggers through. More doors. Leans them open. The street. The open fucking street. Cold. Move. Staggers along street to corner. Leans against building. Turns and moves. Move further. Move, goddamn your ass. More. You can do it. More. Body screeching. Be a fucking man. Move. Down the street. Yeah, here. Here. Stops. Lowers machine to the ground. Stand. Panting. His body and clothing saturated with sweat. Wipes head, then takes handkerchief from pocket and wipes face. Made it. I/ll be a son of a bitch. I made it. Yeah, hahahahahahaha. Still laughing as he starts walking. Stops for a moment and feels crotch. I/ll be a son of a bitch. That goddamn typewriter got me horny. Better than sniffing bicycle seats. Laughter. Laughter and a slow walk to the station. His body weak and exhausted, but the adrenalin high, blood pulsing through his veins to the strained muscles. A feeling of intense and almost unbearable stimulation and excitement. He remembers Finn Hall, the American Legion, Knights of Columbus and a hundred and one nameless and forgotten dance halls where he danced and talked and laughed and looked into a pair of eyes and put his open hand firmly on an inner thigh, then slowly walked from the dance hall into the street and took a cab to a house, wondering if an unexpected husband would be there or would suddenly come home while he was still there. Jesus krist, he feels great. Every bone and muscle in his body aches and screams and he feels great. He feels magnificent!!!!

Harry had stayed in an office so long the night before that he almost had missed the last train home, yet he had felt flat when he left and now, only halfway through the morning, his body was starting to cringe from a free-floating anxiety. Another small change in his routine was needed. He wouldnt be able to wait for a week or two as he had hoped, or even a few days. He would have to go out again tonight. With that decision came almost instant relief as the apprehension and anticipation grew.

But there was also another kind of anxiety. Linda was in her ninth month and could be ready any day. Any day or night. He wanted to be with her. This he wanted desperately. To be able to take her to the hospital and be there when the baby was born so he could hold his wifes hand and kiss her forehead when she came back from the delivery room. Harry Junior was already at his folks house, and Lindas bag was packed and ready. Jesus he wanted to be with her, but he knew he could not go directly home tonight.

What he could do though would be to start earlier—an instant flush of excitement bolted through him. Yeah, before he could be certain everyone had gone home. Jesus—he was squeezing his thighs together and tensing his muscles—that should do it. He was familiar with the schedule of most of the security systems in the large office buildings; they did not vary much from one another. He would start early and see if he could miss the guard by only a few minutes. Jesus krist that sounded great. He could feel the lump in his gut and at the back of his throat. His body jerked spastically for a moment, then he attacked his work for the remainder of the day.

He did not have to wait until the security guard was almost due to satisfy the craving within him that night. He had been walking through an office for a few minutes when he turned a corner and almost tripped over a cleaning lady. He grabbed her arms to keep her from falling and she started apologizing while they were still tottering and he instantly went hollow as he looked at the woman looking at him and he thought he would puke and shit and panically tried to get his legs to move and he clutched the woman and screamed at himself to stay, dont run, and he realized his hands were clamped on the womans arms but he couldnt release them and she kept saying she was sorry, are you all right? I hope I didnt get your clothes dirty and Harry clung and fought and nodded and shook his head and the pounding of his heart almost drowned out her voice and somehow she managed to free herself of his grip but he couldnt seem to open his hands and he felt his face shattering into a smile as he asked her if she was all right and he stuffed his cramped hands into his pockets and the damn woman wouldnt stop apologizing and Harry wanted to get the hell out of there and he kept smiling and smiling at the stupid lackey and finally started easing away with that same goddamn smile stuck on his face and the deafening pounding in his ears, its all right, no trouble, no trouble at all, and he finally turned and walked away slowly and felt himself get dizzy as his vision blurred and he opened the door to the stairway and walked down the stairs and down through the basement and out to the street, then turned into and alley, still conscious of the people and cars passing just a few feet away, and threw up and stared at the pool of vomit at his feet as he leaned against the wall and felt his body tingle with that excitement and he felt the air suddenly rush down his burning throat and he retched again, then once more, then slowly stood erect, hearing the voices of the people passing by and wanted to shout and laugh and pound people on the back and wish them a happy birthday or happy new year or happy Chanukah or some damn thing or maybe do a soft-shoe and sing a song or two and open the jailhouse doors and follow that yellow brick road to Oz and goose Frank Morgan and maybe pull a fuse or two from his wizards machine and everybody trip off into a technicolor sunset because by krist he felt great and all he needed was to whip out his sword and yell to the masses of churls rushing up and down the street to bring him giants, by jesus krist thats what he needed GIANTS!!!!

GIANTS!!!!

or perhaps a baby. Yes, by God, a baby. A jewel of a girl to go with his son and heir. He wiped his mouth and face with his handkerchief, then his shoes and pants legs, tossed the handkerchief into a garbage can with finesse, then rushed to the corner and took a cab to the station.

He got home just in time. He took Linda to the hospital and stayed in the waiting room for a short time, until the nurses finally convinced him to go home, that it would be hours at least and there was no point in his staying there.

The excitement that had been driving him disappeared instantly when he closed the door behind him in the empty house. The place suddenly seemed huge and had dozens of dark corners. He turned on the television and tried to force his attention on it, but his mind kept drifting back to the barren house, the dark corners and Linda. If he closed his eyes for a second, he would see her body in a casket, so he would get up and walk around and refill his cup with coffee, then sit back down and try to concentrate on whatever it was he was looking at, and eventually he dozed off in the chair for perhaps a few hours and was awakened abruptly by the telephone. He could come to the hospital now. A routine delivery and mother and daughter were doing fine.

He forced himself to drive carefully and not exceed the speed limit. He could feel the elation pounding through him again. Mother and daughter doing fine. Fine. Everything was fine. For a year now, or however long it was, everything had been just about perfect. Ever since he started stealing—not that that was really stealing. A few pennies here and there. And the machines belong to large corporations and were insured and no one really was hurt by their loss, if they were in fact lost. They were probably found the next day and returned. No, it really was not stealing. Not in the real sense of the word. And even if it was, it was no big deal. No one was being hurt and it certainly was solving his problem. Things in his life had been just fine, splendid, since he started. That was the important thing.

Linda had a bow in her hair. A pink bow. She was propped up slightly in bed when he went into the room. She glowed like a thousand stars. He kissed her. Again. Then again and held her hand and smiled at her. They just smiled for many long, loving and beautiful moments. . . .

You

lost some weight. She squeezed his hand and glowed brighter.

18

Harry had to terminate his relationship with Dr. Martin. He had wanted to terminate it for quite some time, but knew he would have to face protests from the doctor and his colleagues.

It was not an arbitrary decision. Harry had had hopes when he started therapy, but it had become obvious to him that he would not be able to continue. It was a feeling that was so strong and so deep that it had become an absolute conviction. He just could not spend a few hours each week consciously searching for, and living in, problems, problems that continued to disturb him when he left the doctors office.

He knew he would have to wait until the proper time to start his withdrawal. After things had been going well and he was feeling, acting and looking better, he asked Dr. Martin if he thought that it might be a good idea if they cut the therapy down to one hour a week, that he felt he would get enough strength from the doctor in that hour to carry him through. Dr. Martin readily agreed—the process of sublimation seemed to be working very well—and so from then on it was simply a case of waiting for the proper opportunity to decrease the treatment further. Eventually it was down to once a month, and then complete termination, with the understanding that Harry would call the doctor immediately if he started feeling anxious or upset in any way.

Harry had waited for exactly the right moment to take the final step. The international syndicate that Harry had conceived and helped organize with Von Landor had proven to be a tremendous success. So much so that a subsidiary syndicate had been formed and was now functioning successfully. The innovations and imagination that characterized the project were so remarkable *Fortune* had done a full-length article about Harry White, one of the brightest young men in American business. In the article Harry was quoted as saying that there was a time when he had had a few problems that caused him anxieties and tension, but a Dr. Martin had helped him cope with these problems, and, as you can see, I am certainly capable of functioning at absolute peak efficiency now. It was after the publication of this article that Harry and Dr. Martin terminated their relationship with a handshake and smiles.

As a result of the termination Harry felt a sense of release. He felt free to indulge his own answers rather than search for problems. In many ways he was more relaxed after the termination. He had known he could not tell Dr. Martin what he was doing, though he had felt obligated to do so. He had been constantly on guard to be certain he did not say anything that might somehow lead to his being forced to tell him the truth. And, underneath it all, had been the urge to tell him everything—and so he had been involved in additional conflicts.

One Sunday Harry told Linda he was going to take her for a drive. I want to show you something.

They drove through a less populated area, then through the gate of an estate that was completely hidden by huge trees. Harry parked in front of the house. O.K., everybody out.

What is this Harry? Who lives here?

A friend. Come on. I want to show you something.

They walked around to the rear of the large Colonial stone house. There were gardens that gradually sloped into endless trees—primarily birch.

O Harry, this is beautiful. Absolutely breathless. I have never seen anything like this in my life. How many trees are there?

A couple of acres.

My God, its incredible. What is all this? Why did you bring me here?

Its Whites Woods.

Whites Woods? I dont understand, shaking her head in complete confusion.

Its called Whites Woods. Or if you prefer longer names: The Woods and Estate of Mr. and Mrs. Harold White, gesturing with an arm and bowing slightly.

Mr. and Mrs. . . . You mean this, waving her hand and looking around, all of this . . .

Thats right. Its ours.

Linda sat on a stone bench by a lily pond and briefly returned the stare of a frog sunning himself on a pad. I dont know what to say. Its overwhelming.

Well, its ours. All of it. And up there, back in the woods—you can see it from that balcony up there—theres a small stream of cool, clear water. A veritable babbling brook.

I just cant imagine it. I just cant imagine this—all of this—being ours.

Well, its not as big as the Wooddale Country Club, but it will do for now. Come on, I/ll show you the inside.

Harry stirred slightly when Linda got up at night to feed the baby, but went right back to sleep. But even if he did not get enough sleep, that would not explain his feeling so goddamn edgy. He thought of his success: the money, the feature articles about him in *Fortune*, *Wall Street Journal*, *Dun & Brad*, their new home and Whites Woods, and his family. He had everything, including the respect of his peers. What in the fuck was wrong? clenching his teeth and squeezing his hands into white-knuckled fists. Thinking of all these things —the possessions, the accolades, the love—did not help. He had money, property and prestige, but he still felt that vague discontent and edgy tension gnawing at him.

He had discovered a relatively safe way to relieve these feelings, certainly superior in every way to the previous solution he had utilized, but now that was starting to prove as fickle and unreliable as the first. It still worked, but for shorter and shorter periods. Lately he had been timing his little projects so that he would be leaving just as the security guard was entering. Jesus, the excitement was great. Actually it was better than fucking some broad. And he did not have the fear of disease. But he was running out of methods to keep the excitement at the pitch necessary to relieve him of the gnawing tension.

He went back to the same office three consecutive weeks, and each time he could feel more and more sweat rolling down his back. They would have to have additional men on guard sooner or later, or at least change their schedule, but after three weeks everything was exactly the same. The fourth week he did not enter the building through an alley and the basement, but through the front door and smiled at the guard as he signed the register and went back to the same office. He emptied the petty-cash box and left a thank-you note, then went down to the lobby and signed out, smiling at the guard once more and wishing him a happy evening.

The exhilaration from this venture was intense, but after a few days he was fighting that same edginess and was developing a problem concentrating on his work.

Pilfering offices was just not working anymore, and he once more started drifting from the midtown area toward the waterfront. He set up an elaborate system for finding the best place and for determining the police schedule and how to get in and out in just minutes, or less, before the police were scheduled to make their rounds. This preliminary stage continued for many weeks and the old release and excitement surged through him as he walked through the gray and littered streets; he was once more able to concentrate properly on his work.

The first place he broke into was a small printing shop. He pried open a rear window and crawled through, carefully tucking his tie in his shirt first so it would not get caught on anything. He walked carefully through and around the cluttered area, eventually searching the office and emptying the petty-cash box. The entire structure wasnt much more than a shed and had a chilly and gloomy atmosphere. He walked around, looking at the material being printed, and at his watch. When he knew the police would be in the vicinity within a few minutes, he left the shop, closing the window, then stopping and going back and opening it again before walking down the alley.

He walked slowly along the street, toying with the clump of bills and change in his pocket. His pulse quickened, but his pace did not, as the prowl car passed him and continued down the street.

He went back to the same area a few more times the following month. Then he had to go to another area and another, and make the trips more and more often. In just a matter of months he was desperately trying to think of some way to keep himself relieved of the tension and satisfy that discontent and keep that excitement alive. Then one night he broke into a small dry cleaning plant and left just as the prowl car was turning onto the block. He walked slowly along the street and then flagged them down and asked how to get to a fictitious address. But it didnt do anything for him. There was no surge, no twisting of apprehension as he approached the car, no excitement, no release.

The next day he sat in his office, with the door closed,

trying to literally lose himself in his work, feeling as if he were being tugged and yanked apart. He wanted to go right home that night, but knew that he wouldnt, and as long as he fought that fact he continued to feel torn. Slowly, as the day progressed, he stopped fighting the inevitable and accepted the fact that he would have to find another place to break into that night, and he gave an inner sigh of relief and he was able to concentrate fully on his work.

He did not consciously plan on where to go, but more or less allowed himself to be led by some inner force. He ended up in the dark and stinking rear of a meatpacking plant and somnambulistically opened and closed doors and drawers and looked, then left, and walked listlessly through the streets until he eventually stood on the edge of a subway platform.

From time to time he automatically looked down the tracks and into the darkened tunnel for the the lights of an oncoming train. Soon he saw them. He continued to watch, then stared. He stood frozen, leaning over the edge. He could hear the train. It got louder, and louder, the lights closer. Suddenly it seemed to break through some invisible barrier and thrust itself at the station. Harry continued to stare, his eyes and ears hypnotized by the onrushing train, and he could feel himself being drawn toward the tracks and could feel his body slowly being pulled forward into the path of the oncoming train so that he would be shattered into dozens of pieces and his rotting brain splattered all over the station, and he quickly wondered what it would be like just to leap in front of the train, and at the same time he knew he was going to leap in front of it, that he could not stop himself, and it felt right, it felt good, it felt exciting, his whole body trembling and screaming as the train roared closer and closer and he leaned further and further over the edge of the platform and the train shot past him and his vision suddenly became a blur of windows and heads and bodies. . . .

He got on the train and rode to Grand Central. It would be over an hour before he got home, but the time passed almost in an instant. He had never experienced such a sensation in his life. He couldnt sit. He had to stand and hold on to a pole. Never had such excitement pounded and pounded itself through him as it did now. God in heaven, what an experience. What an incredible experience. It was, for Harry, so fantastic that he could not think about it. Not now. He could only experience it. He understood nothing. Was aware of nothing other than how he felt. Wanted nothing. It was as if he were separate and distinct from himself. He simply clung to the pole. Somewhere within him he was experiencing the answer of answers. It whirled through him. It pounded through him. It screamed through him. He held on tight to the pole. Sometime, soon, he would know what was being told him.

He no longer had to steal. He no longer had to worry about following women through the streets or spending time in rat-infested rooms. It was not a conscious realization, but an inner knowledge, something that he somehow accepted axiomatically.

But the inner man knew that when you take something away that a life is dependent upon, you must replace it with something of value. And that something of value was evolving like a fetus in the dark security of the womb. And Harry nurtured it slowly. And caressed it. Allowing it to seep slowly into his mind. Not forcing it, but allowing himself to be tantalized by the little hints of where it was going. This life-changing something remained undefined for many, many weeks, and as he continued to surrender to this inner feeling, Harry became more and more withdrawn and gave the appearance of extreme serenity. There was a constant smile on his face that reflected an inner glow, as if he had a secret no one else was privy to.

And there was an excitement too. An excitement that grew and grew as did the fetus. An excitement of anticipation and apprehension that was incredible, that was unlike anything he had ever known or dreamed of, that was undefinable, it had to be experienced. He could not consciously define, as yet, exactly what was going to happen, but his gut knew, and with the passing of each day he came closer and closer to knowing. And the closer he came, the more intense became his excitement.

When he finally did realize what he would be doing, he was surprised that it had taken him so long to become aware of it. It all seemed so logical and simple. And obvious. And with the conscious realization came a new surge of excitement, an overwhelming thrill. If he could feel so relaxed, so free, so complete while only aware of something happening but not what, then how great was his excitement now, now that he not only knew he would be killing someone, but would be contemplating each and every action before, during and after. Just the briefest thought of, the most cursory glance at, the situation almost paralyzed him with excitement. God, what joy. What exquisite joy. And he could go back to this thought any time he wanted to. Whenever the edginess was starting to affect his work, or he got that goddamn antsy feeling, he could just stop, thats all, just stop and think of how he was going to kill someone. He did not have to go anywhere, do anything, just stay wherever he was at that particular moment and contemplate the execution and he experienced not only instant excitement, but instant relief from the gnawings that had haunted him. Just like that. Anywhere. Instead of taking a cab to Grand Central, he started riding subways just to test the efficacy of this new answer. He would allow himself to be shoved in the train with the others and be jammed up against a door, or would hang from a strap, crushed by the surrounding bodies, and simply think of what he would be doing someday, and then he was oblivious to his surroundings. He simply experienced an inner feeling of peace and power. Incredible power. Undeniable power. Power that made him invulnerable to the lashings that he had been cringing from.

And with this new consciousness came the pleasure of being able to make a game out of it. At least for now. Someday the killing would have to be a reality, but for now just the contemplation of it exalted him. That was one of the great things about this experience. He could delay the action almost indefinitely, and it added to the excitement. Nurture, pet and caress the anticipation. That was the thing to do. And he would. He would tantalize himself just as long as possible. Someday the act would be a part of history, but now he would just dangle it in front of himself. He could create his own suspense. And master it!

19

It was many weeks before Linda
sensed a change in Harry. The caring for two children made
demands on her time and energy. Harry insisted that she get
additional household help, but she still maintained that she
was the childrens mother and insisted that she was the only
one who would take care of them.

She wasnt certain what the change was, but she liked it.
It was true that Harry had become quieter again and did not
joke and kid as much as he used to, but she enjoyed it. She
liked the quietness. Taking care of two children can help make
you appreciative of a little quietness.

But as the weeks became months she began to feel that
Harry was more withdrawn than quiet. He still smiled and
chatted, but something was different. She could not isolate
what it was, but whatever it was disturbed her. There was no
reason for thinking that something was wrong, yet that was

how she felt. It was very disquieting because she almost felt threatened.

One of the things that made it impossible to discuss this with someone else, or Harry, was the fact that there was nothing tangible to point to. He did not abuse her—or ignore her. There was not that cold indifference—but at the same time he just did not seem to touch her as much as he used to. Or was that her imagination? Sometimes she was so tired from getting up at night with the baby and taking care of the children all day that she could not be certain if all this speculation was due to her imagination.

Then she would think about it again and realize that it must be her imagination. There couldnt be anything wrong. After all, what was so strange about people becoming a little more quiet with time? Especially when you have two children and are so busy during the day. She would chuckle to herself and playfully reprimand herself for getting so caught up in her life, and work, and the children, that she could forget that Harry was a very busy man with tremendous responsibilities and naturally would look forward to a little peace and quiet when he got home at night. She chuckled again, After all, we/ve been married eight years and are not as young as we used to be.

Harry rode the subway a couple of times a day now. Not only to prove he could detach himself from the hordes around him, but because he loved the thrill and feeling of power he experienced when the train came flying into the station and he stared at it as it approached, pulling him toward it, the roar filling his ears, and feeling the sudden gust of wind as it roared by. He could smell the air that was packed in front of it and could almost distinguish the color of the eyes of the motorman.

But the passing of time and change are inevitable, and Harry started feeling that time was running out. There was a limit to how long he could play this little game—this he always knew—and he was fast approaching that limit. Thinking, contemplating, planning were no longer ends in themselves. The action had to be taken.

How he would kill someone had been obvious to him for months. It was simple. And there was no danger of being caught. Most murderers (the word sounded strange, and he knew it did not really apply to him) were caught, or at least identified, because the motive was obvious. But even if it wasnt, they were always personally involved with the victim, and there was no way that involvement could be concealed.

A man is obviously involved with his wife. If she is killed, he is always a suspect. He is always investigated thoroughly. And they usually find a girlfriend. Or an insurance policy. Or something to prove he would profit from his wifes death. Always an obvious motive.

And most killings were stupid. Lacking in imagination and intelligence. Usually committed in a fit of temper or despair. The connection between victim and perpetrator obvious within minutes of the discovery of the body. Actually, from what Harry had learned through reading a few books on the subject, a mentally retarded orangutan could solve most murders (he hadnt meant to use that word again). They usually solved themselves.

But Harry was not going to kill for profit—at least not in the usually accepted sense of the word. There would be no monetary gain. No gain in power or influence. No fulfilling of a vendetta. No wounded pride or broken heart . . . no personal connection. So there was no danger. No fear of exposure. He would not have to taunt the police and court apprehension as he had with the buglaries (strange how foreign that word sounded, as if it had nothing to do with him). There just wouldnt be any way he could be connected with the killing. It was that simple.

A complete stranger. How can you be caught if you kill a complete stranger? Who knows how many times that has happened? Thats right. I bet it has happened. Many, many times. And not just the psychopathic murderers who roam cities killing aimlessly. Or the Jack-the-Ripper type who choose a particular type for his victims. But those one-time situations. From time to time there must have been individuals who wondered what it would be like to kill someone and then went out and killed a stranger. They never get caught. Its almost impossible. Only fate could change that. And Harry knew that fate was indifferent and would not oppose him.

He wanted to also make this an act of charity. At least as much as possible. Someone had to die, so it might just as well be someone who would not miss living, or be missed. He looked at all the dreary and harried faces on the subway platform. What could life possibly hold for them? Wearing tattered clothes. Ripped shoes. Grease-rimmed shirts and blouses. They probably lived in some roach-infested trap. They obviously did not live, they merely and barely existed. They had forgotten how to smile. If, indeed, they ever knew. He would be doing them and the world a service.

He stood jammed in the rush-hour crowd on the subway platform. The sound of trains rushing through the tunnels and screeching to a stop at the station was drowned out by the pounding of his heart. The sound flooded through him. His head felt as if it might burst. His eyes felt as if someone were shoving two huge thumbs against them. All of his body seemed to be stuck in his throat. He had to concentrate on his anal sphincter muscle. His muscles tightened until they felt like bands of iron about to snap. He could hear the train in the distance. It sounded louder. And louder. He could not breathe. He was chilled with sweat. His hands and feet were numb with cold. His head shook with terror. He almost lost his vision. The train grew louder. It started to roar and scream at him. The person in front of him became a blur. He could feel the platform trembling as the train got closer and closer until all there was was the roar of the train and Harry screamed under the roar *AAAAAAAAAAAAAAAHHHHH-HHHHHHHHH* as he shoved the body in front of him and the train thudded into it and the screams and screeching mixed with the roar of the train and the steel-on-steel screech as brakes were suddenly applied and the window of the motormans cubicle was covered with his vomit and the passengers screamed and yelled and moaned as they went plummeting forward and the parts of the body splattered and rolled and bounced along the tracks and platform and people were sprinkled with brains and bones and flesh and blood and Harry almost fainted and started to stagger away from the crowd so he could run up the stairs but he couldnt move more than a few feet at a time being crushed by the hysterical crowd and the thudding and screaming inside his head his legs almost paralyzed from terror and ecstasy, and he inched his way along the platform and eventually a few feet up the stairs and he could see the blood splattered against the pillars and on a womans face who was screaming hysterically as she wiped and clawed at her face and others tried to keep her from tearing her own flesh from her face and somewhere in the darkness of the tunnel and on the shiny steel of the tracks was the body of a stranger and it was spread over more than a quarter of a mile of track and tunnel and platform and people and soon the roar in Harrys head took the form of words and he tried to understand the words as he stood on the stairway looking at the people pushing shoving vomiting and the transit police trying desperately to fight their way through the crowd to the train to find out what had happened and what they should do and Harry squinted hard as he tried to listen to those words and then finally he understood them and he almost screamed with joy as he looked down on the chaos as emergency crews tried to pry open the doors to get to the motorman who had passed out and was slumped over the controls his head resting in his own vomit and the people in the train fought and strained to stand and they pounded on the doors and screeched out the windows as some tried to climb through the windows and they clawed at each other to get through the tiny openings and hands and arms were thrust through the windows and people on the platform yanked the pleading passengers through and Harry wanted to shout the words to the madness below him but only mumbled them to himself as he inched his way up the stairway being shoved aside by a trio of policemen thrusting their way through the crowd and its done its done its done. . . .

Harry remained a part of the chaos and madness for more than an hour and then reluctantly drifted away after the last siren and ghoul had left. He stayed in the vicinity of the top of the stairs, surveying as much of the scene as possible. Police and medical people were jamming their way into the station, followed by newsmen, photographers and then the TV people with their cameras and mikes. All the accelerated activity, the hysterical screams, moans and people fainting continually fed Harrys excitement and maintained it at such an intensity that for the entire time he was there he thought his legs might fold at any minute. He felt as if he were suffocating and, from time to time, that he might crumble in a faint like so many others, but he remained jammed in the crowd with the screaming police and paramedics fighting their way through and then coming back carrying people who were unconscious from a coronary or simply from hysterics. Occasionally he would get a glimpse of some of the people they were carrying out and he almost collapsed when he saw brains splattered all over their face and clothes, and with all the noise and screaming it seemed like the only words he could distinguish distinctly were, They had to wipe him up with a blotter.

As the last of the authorities left and the crowd started to thin, Harry could see wet spots on the platform, pillars and sides of the staircases, as well as the tracks, where the workmen had watered and scrubbed. The last of the newspaper and television reporters left after interviewing and filming dozens of eyewitnesses to the bloody tragedy.

Soon there were only the usual noises (*they wiped him up with a blotter*) of trains rumbling into and out of the station and of people talking and rushing by. Harry forced his body into motion (*its done, its done*) and climbed the stairs to the street and took a cab to Grand Central station.

The high pitch of excitement stayed with him as he rode the train home listening to the wheels singsong, *It is done, it is done* . . . *with a blotter, with a blotter* . . . *it is done, it is done* . . . *with a blotter, with a blotter*. . . .

When Harry walked into the house that night, Linda was stunned by his appearance. He looked pale, almost gray, yet was flushed, and his eyes had the glazed stare of someone ravaged by fever; when he moved, it was as if he were being moved by some outside force or control, as if weirdly detached from himself. He was, in fact, almost unrecognizable as her husband. She felt a twinge of panic as she watched him sit down.

You all right, sweetheart? You look feverish.

I dont know, shrugging and shaking his head.

I was almost ready to call the police or the hospitals. You are so late and you didnt call. You always do when youre going to be late and when I didnt hear from you I thought maybe you had an accident or the Lord knows what happened to you. O Harry, Im so glad to see you, hugging him and kissing him, can I get you a cup of coffee or something? What happened, honey, I was frantic with worry.

Train was delayed, mechanically putting his arm around her waist and resting his hand on her hip.

Lindas attention was suddenly drawn to the television when the newscaster said something about a terrible accident on the subway, and the camera followed paramedical personnel down the stairs to the subway platform and suddenly there was Harry on the screen for a brief moment—Harry, thats you—and the camera continued among the shrieks and clamorings of the crowd as the newscaster continued to describe the scene following the tragic accident. O my God, thats awful. You were there, Harry. O how dreadful. No wonder you dont look well.

Harry stared at the television set, transfixed by what he was seeing, hearing, remembering and experiencing.

He remained in a semicomatose state the remainder of the evening, and Linda, realizing what was wrong, did not disturb him as he half watched television, believing that after a good nights sleep he would be all right.

Harry bolted up in the middle of the night, and Linda quickly reassured him, Its all right, Harry, its only Mary. I/ll take care of her. Shes just teething. He sat on the edge of the bed feeling his stomach thrusting itself against his throat and his head was like a ramrod starting to splinter its way out. Suddenly he jammed his hands over his mouth and hurried to the bathroom and started puking while still a few feet from the commode, bounced against the wall and slid down to the floor, still retching, and sat on the floor and hugged the cold porcelain of the bowl and continued to puke and retch, the spasms coming so rapidly and fiercely that he found it almost impossible to breathe and his feet and legs started to cramp. It continued forever. . . .

After a long, painful, time Linda put her cool hands on his forehead and rubbed the back of his brittle neck as he continued to retch with the dry heaves, a little green bile occasionally dribbling from his lips as he leaned against the upturned seat for another eternity until he finally stopped from exhaustion. . . .

He pushed and pulled himself up and rinsed his face with cold water. He stretched out on his back in bed, enjoying the hollow metallic feeling that seemed to go from his mouth down to his knees. Linda looked at him with an expression of fear that bordered on panic as she brushed his hair back from his forehead. He looked at her and smiled, feeling lightheaded, euphoric and almost unreal. You look like a canary thats just been swallowed by a cat. Linda reacted instantly to his smile and words and smiled and tilted her head. You looked like you were dying.

No, chuckling and putting his arms around her, just something that didnt agree with me. He pulled her closer to him and kissed her on the cheek and the neck and caressed her with his hand and slowly, slowly moved her nightgown higher until it was a wispy frill around her neck and he caressed her stomach and thighs with his hand as he kissed her breast and excited the nipple with his lips and tongue and leaned his body against the warmth of her and made long and luxurious love to his wife . . .

                                                                    then
drifted into an exhausted and restful sleep . . .

                              and awoke leisurely from the insistence of a painful erection and reached over and toyed with Lindas ear lobe and gently kissed her to a state of partial wakefulness and pressed her body with his until she awoke and once more made love to her with an urgency he had never experienced and a passion whose control over him was almost frightening. He felt and experienced each and every move with heightened sensitivity and pleasure that were magnified by the sensation of fear, a fear of infinite power, a fear that forced him on and on long after desire had melted and flowed from his body.

Linda was in a state of surprise the next morning that still affected her slightly by the end of the day. She took Harry Junior to school, then roamed through her gardens and Whites Woods. She sat beside the little stream that trickled through the trees and over the rocks, hoping she could dissolve the vague uneasiness she felt by remembering the pleasure of their lovemaking. But remembering the lovemaking actually made the uncomfortable feeling worse. Again she felt there was something wrong, and this time the feeling was stronger than ever. Actually she was fighting a premonition that was trying to tell her that there was some sort of emergency. Linda looked around at the trees and the hint of sky flashing through their limbs, and thought and pondered and became more and more confused and disturbed and finally dismissed everything simply as a result of the horrible experience Harry had had yesterday; obviously, the emotional strain had been so severe that it had not only affected Harry, but had also affected her. She remembered hearing that parts of the poor mans body had been strewn across the station and the people who were there. Maybe Harry had been one of them. She wanted to ask, but was afraid that if he had, it would be too painful a question for him to answer. She finally decided that all this speculation was too painful and dangerous. She left her little stream and went to the shed and got her gardening tools and went to work.

Harry did not have to remind himself about the horrible accident. It was done for him. Everyone seemed to be talking about it. The headlines screamed it. People stood a foot from the edge of the platform. It seemed like the entire city was conspiring to keep that hollow, metallic feeling alive in him, and to keep him remembering, and experiencing, that accentuated excitement of yesterday. Other feelings were trying to be felt, and heard, but they remained buried under the others. At least for the present.

With the feelings and the remembering of the horrible accident came the realization that he not only would not have to worry about those filthy pits he had found himself in, and about contracting a disease, but now he would not have to rummage through offices or dirty factories. He knew, absolutely, that an important and irrevocable change had occurred in his life.

As the events of the preceding day were forced upon him, he reviewed them with an almost scientific detachment and objectivity—an attitude he was able to maintain for many months. He could more or less reminisce and feel free from the compulsions that had previously plagued him, and experience the intense excitement that reliving the scene precipitated.

Then the power of time started to define the vague feeling that had been lying restlessly under the others. And as it started to force itself onto Harrys mind, he fought it down and tried to annihilate it, but it would not die. It wanted to shout at Harry that he was guilty, but was content to murmur indistinctly, and so Harry struggled in ignorance and fear and inevitably the edginess and squirming under the skin returned, but now it was magnified by the wheels of the train as they went over the same tracks every day—the same tracks, the same tracks . . . *it* is done, *it* is done . . . *with* a blotter, *with* a blotter—and the battle inside Harry White slowly built up in intensity and the tension increased slowly but steadily.

Linda felt, then noticed, the change in him. There seemed to be an unusual tenseness about him. His movements and re-actions were quick, almost spastic. At first she thought it might be because he was preoccupied with some business problem, but in the past, whenever that had been the case, he had worked late and been a little withdrawn. Now he was coming home early, and had done so for many months, and did not seem to be withdrawn or preoccupied, but extremely sensitive, a sensitivity that with time was developing into irritability. He was not nasty to her, or to the children, but she could see that the childrens noise grated on him as if his nerves were on the surface of his skin and raw, and that he had to fight with himself not to yell at them more often than he did.

She became increasingly concerned and worried. She did not want to act like an interfering or nagging wife, but she did ask him one evening if he was all right, and he answered with a sharp yes and immediately changed the subject.

Eventually she came to realize that she was preoccupied with what was troubling him, and was becoming so tense that she would have to bring the subject up again. She waited until the children were asleep, then asked him if he was feeling all right.

Fine.

She hesitated for a moment, afraid to continue, but more fearful of remaining silent. Are you sure, sweetheart? I mean is there something wrong that you are keeping to yourself so I wont worrry?

Theres nothing wrong. Why you being so insistent?

Im sorry, honey, I didnt realize. But I am worried. Why?

Well, you seem so nervous . . . as if something is troubling you.

Nothing you need worry about.

Linda hesitated for another second, then precipitated herself into continuing. Do you think maybe you should give Dr. Martin a call?

What for? looking and sounding surprised.

I dont know, dear, his name just sort of came to mind.

Look, theres nothing that I need to tell him, and theres certainly nothing *he* can tell *me*. Now, if you dont mind I would like to get off the subject of my health.

Linda tried to think of something light and frivolous to say, but nothing would come to mind. After a moment or two she got up and took a bath and tried to relieve her anxiety with bath oils and hot water.

The wheels of the train continued to chant to Harry, *It is done, it is done . . . with* a blotter, *with* a blotter, but as the months droned on, the refrain lost its impact on Harry. The feelings of relief and excitement slowly drained with time and left him with the old edginess and anxiety, which were becoming more and more intense. And they must be becoming obvious—Linda was asking him if he was all right. He didnt want to chase her away, but he could not stand being questioned. For a while he could remember the intensity of the feelings after the subway incident and the memory absorbed all the tension and anxiety, but gradually it reached the point where it not only did not do that, but also added the heat of guilt. He would start remembering the mention on the newscast of the mans family—*it* is done, *it* is done . . . *with* a blotter, *with* a blotter—and cringe and flush and feel extremely conspicuous. For the longest time remembering shoving the body in front of him charged him with the excitement necessary to relieve him of those gnawing feelings, but then the thud and screams started becoming louder and louder and soon the body was reaching out and grabbing Harry and pulling him with it.

And then a new plague was visited upon him, or rather wormed its way up from the depths to his consciousness. A faint whisper that became a roaring certainty. He could feel it throbbing through him and for the briefest of moments he tried to fight and deny it, but then he simply surrendered to the undeniable fact that he was going to do it again. It was inevitable. With the acceptance of this came another realization: there would be no satisfaction in doing it the same way again.

Harry encountered great difficulty in thinking about how it should be done the next time. After thinking about it for a moment or two he started to get nauseous and even trembled slightly. Then he became aware of the reason why it would not work doing it the same way again. Not enough personal involvement. There had to be more personal contact. Yes, that was the solution. He had to be personally involved. More *completely* involved.

Once again the excitement of anticipation pushed aside the tension and anxiety and he felt free. But there was an inner knowledge that he could not think about it too long, that if he did, those old feelings would be back to plague him.

This last thought was frightening because there was one more inescapable fact that he was forced to accept: each time those old feelings came back now they were much worse than they had been the time before. He knew, too, that he had to try to keep them buried, at any cost, bcause if he did not, they would destroy him. Beyond any doubt they had to be controlled.

20

When all the other matters had been clarified, he knew almost instantly where and how the next one would happen. He watched people crowd into the elevator and he knew it would happen in a crowd. He did not even think of a subway. He had not been in the subway since that day.

But there were many places that were almost as crowded. Places in the open. The stadium after a game. Many places. But there was only one place that was truly in the heart of everything. One place that was crowded almost twenty-four hours a day. One place that was known all over the world. The perfect place. Times Square.

And it would be with a knife. Very long and very sharp. He had to penetrate the thick layers of winter clothing before penetrating the body. It should be neat and clean. With the abundance of winter clothing there should be no evidence of bleeding. A chefs knife of some sort. He would carry it in a thin paper bag. Yes, that would be perfect. Conceal the knife. And be inconspicuous. Never be noticed. Should probably be someone tall and big. Can hide behind him. Never be noticed. I dont know? Maybe thats no good. Perhaps the knife should go up high. Bump into someone walking toward me. Try for the heart. Can—No. Thats no good. I would be seen. Even someone short would mean I would have to raise my hand. No. That wont work. No room to really move in the crowd. Must be a simple thrust. Someone too short and the knife might get tangled with the ribs. Must be careful. Must penetrate immediately. No room for maneuvering or time for probing. A thrust. Quick. All the way in. Yeah, deep. Deep. Try and hit bottom. Feel it against the sides. Warm and soft. Twitching. Moist. Then wet. It will have to be from behind. Someone big. A twelve-inch blade should do. Deep enough for anyone. Under the ribs. And up. Lean on it with my weight. Feel his body tighten. And moan. Breathless. Panting and moan. Yes. From behind. A quick thrust. Deep. Can hear it go in. All the way in. . . .

He continued to think and plan, the lump in his chest getting larger and larger until he could hardly breathe. He could feel his face flush and his legs and stomach tighten and knot, and he knew that his legs would not support him if he tried to stand. He had to stop indulging in the thrill of the plan and start to put it into execution.

He spent some time in a cutlery store carefully inspecting its assortment of knives. When he decided on the one he wanted, he had them put it in a plain brown paper bag.

He walked unhurriedly through the crowds in Times Square until he saw the man he wanted. He was big and broad and was wearing the clothes of a hard hat of some kind. His jacket came down to his waist and did not look too thick. He walked close behind him. He was about a head taller than Harry. He walked aggressively. Harry looked at the bottom of his jacket. He could see the broad, thick belt the man was wearing. He would have to be careful not to hit the belt. Right above it. Excitement pounded through Harry and almost blinded him. He could hardly move. He wanted to wait for the right time, but he knew he could not wait much longer. The people continually bumped past him, and every now and then some one would get between him and the hard hat and he would have to quicken his pace and weave in and around people in order to get back in the right position. He could feel his arms and hands trembling as he rushed to get closer. He had to keep swallowing hard. The intensity was rapidly reaching the point where he knew he would slowly fold in a bundle on the street. They crossed the street and he had to run quickly around a car that was slowly moving through the crowd; he bumped into the car, and the driver jammed on his brakes and yelled at him, but he continued after the hard hat, limping for a few moments. Then there was a sudden surge of people and they were pressed tightly together and Harry grabbed the handle of the knife with both hands and jabbed it in the guys side, just under the ribs, at an upward angle, leaning against it with all his weight and hearing it crunch in. He seemed to be leaning against him forever. He could feel the people around him, he could feel the body stiffen and jerk up and back and could hear the deep-throated moan and could even feel the heat from the body and could feel his hands cramping around the handle of the knife and could feel the edge of the jacket rubbing against his knuckles and smell the cement and sand on the jacket, and he knew he was all the way in, all the way in, and the body was starting to lean heavily against him and he knew that he had to let go of the handle and move away but somehow he could not seem to do it and it seemed like he was there for hours but he still clung to the handle feeling the hard hats pulse throbbing through to his hands and the man leaned more and more heavily against him and he finally slid his hands off the handle and stepped aside as he saw the hard hats hands twisting and grabbing at air and heard the moaning roll through his head and down into his gut and he bumped into someone rushing by and spun aside and continued along Broadway concentrating as hard as possible on maintaining a normal pace in the evening rush of people hustling through Times Square on their way home and he was aware of a bit of commotion behind him as he heard the dull sound of something hitting the sidewalk and a few, Hey, look out— Whats a matta, ya drunk or somethin?, and he continued through the crowd feeling the blood pulse behind his eyes and fighting to keep his knees from buckling and feeling on the very brink of exploding. . . .

His heart was still pounding as he rode home. The wheels were clacking loudly, *done* again, *done* again, and he was answering *go*ing home, *go*ing home, and when he got home, he went right into the shower and stayed under the water until it was no longer hot enough, just letting it bounce and roll off him and trying to ignore that little irritation in the back of his head but unable to because he knew it was true, that he would have to do it again, and he could feel the beginning of a plague in the pit of his gut and he knew it was only a matter of time, a short time, before the demon would be eating him again and he would have to find some way to relieve himself of the twisting tension and gnawing anxiety.

The battle within himself for control of himself started much sooner than he had anticipated. After the subway incident it had been many, many months before he had started squirming again, and it had been about a year before he had had to do it again. This time it was only a matter of weeks.

He no longer had control over when he thought about what he had done. Most of the time he could suppress it with his work, but at other times it was suddenly in front of him, and now he was constantly turning the hard hat around to get a look at his face or, worse, there were times at night when from the blackness of his sleep a face drifted before him or simply suddenly occurred and just hung there with a mouth open in a silent groan, the features constantly melting into each other and changing while remaining the same. He would struggle to scream it away, but felt himself pinned to the bed in a painful and grotesque silence until he finally yelled himself awake and sat on the edge of the bed, nodding and grunting away Lindas questions and attempts to comfort him.

In spite of himself and his constant battle, he found himself thinking of the next time and tried to shove the idea out of his mind and to pull a shade down from some place in his head to cover it, but then his mind would thrust him in the midst of the crowd watching the St. Patricks Day parade down Fifth Avenue and he would feel the muscles in his toes tighten and curl and he could hear his teeth grind and feel the sharp ache in his jaws as he fought against the image but it continually came back to haunt him and he dropped the paper bag in his hand and tried to shove his way through the crowd but the damn bag was always back in his hand and the handle seemed to have been molded especially for his fingers, it seemed to be imbedded in them as if it were growing out of them, and no matter how hard he tried he could not rid himself of the dreaded knife and he put his hands behind his back and pushed through the crowd, but he could still feel the knife, and he attacked the work on his desk until the image of the parade and the bag became obscured in the dark corners of his mind and sometimes nonexistent . . .

and then he would sit on the train at night and feel and hear the drumming of the train: *it* is done, *it* is done . . . *with* a blotter, *with* a blotter . . . *done* again, *done* again . . . *going* home, *going* home . . . *done* again, *done* again, *done* again, *and* again, *and* again, *and* again . . .

and he knew that the face would come in the middle of the night and hang in front of him and constantly melt into itself while remaining unchanged with that horrible mouth hanging open in an agonizing and silent scream and gradually he became more and more afraid of falling asleep, thinking that staying awake was the only way to fight it, and he stayed awake later and later reading a book or pretending he had important work that had to be done, or just lay in bed with his eyes forced open waiting to just pass out and hoping that would keep him from seeing the face, but he still saw it, not every night, but often enough to be afraid of sleep, afraid not only because of the agony in the face, and the silence of the open mouth, but because he knew that one night the mouth would speak, to him, and he did not want to hear what it had to say, and so with the passing of each day, and night— *and* again, *and* again, *yet* again, *yet* again, *yet* again—he felt more and more haunted, and looked more and more haunted, and started looking constantly at the calendar, counting down the days until St. Patricks Day, when those goddamn assholes had to put on their green ties and dumb fucking hats and eat that watered-down corned beef and cabbage slop and get drunk and piss green, and as the days and weeks passed he started looking like a man ravaged by a rare and insidious disease as he fought to stay awake and pull a curtain down over the dark corners of his mind again, and again . . . yet again. . . .

And Linda could only watch and worry and pray. She knew, not only from Harrys previous reactions, but primarily from a deep, inner conviction, that it would be useless to talk to him, to ask him what was wrong. So she watched, in silence, as some unseen force ate away at the man she loved. She seemed almost hypnotized by the slow and steady change. When they talked to each other, it was as if his voice was coming through a tunnel and there was a stone coldness in the sound of his voice, and she felt, so deeply and painfully, that he was not really a part of the conversations, that his thoughts and attentions were somewhere else.

The one element that made her resolve to stay, no matter what, was simply that she knew, instinctively and absolutely, that there was not another woman. It was a thought she did not have to battle simply because it did not enter her mind.

From time to time she would try to build the resolve to smash the barrier that was being created between her and Harry, but somehow the impetus could not be sustained and a strange and unfamiliar type of lethargy set in, and so she could only watch and worry and pray.

It was not until March 16 that Harry realized St. Patricks Day would be on a Saturday. He had looked at that date on many calendars a hundred or more times these past weeks, yet it was only now that the *day* of the week registered in his haunted mind. Saturday! My god . . . Saturday!!!! His stiffened body almost dissolved in a flood of relief. He could stay home. He did not have to be in the city. He did not have to go near the parade. He could keep himself locked in the house. Did not have to go near the station, or even hear a train. He was safe, at home. He heard the phrase go through his head and he almost chuckled, safe at home.

He was a little more animated at breakfast on the morning of March 17, far more so than he had been in many months. Linda reacted immediately and hummed to herself as she prepared breakfast for her family. Harry ate more that morning than he had since— Linda could not remember when. He had a couple of eggs, Canadian bacon, home fries and toasted English muffins. Harry Jr. had the same thing as his father though not as much.

It almost looks like eggs Benedict.

Yes, smiling, I guess it does. Its just sort of spread around and lacking a few things. Its delicious. Isnt it, son?

Yeah, Dad, it sure is.

The light laughter and chuckling continued as the children finished and went to watch their cartoons. Linda and Harry sat at the table drinking coffee and chitchatting for the first time in so long that it seemed beyond Lindas memory. The sun was not only shining outside today.

Harry Jr. yelled excitedly that there was a parade on television, hurry, hurry. Harry and Linda joined the children and watched the diminutive mayor, who had been made an honorary Irishman, complete with green teeth, lead the parade down Fifth Avenue. There were endless lines of drum majorettes in green skirts, green boots and green hats twirling green batons; and the people jammed along Fifth Avenue, watching the parade, had their green ribbons and pins and pennants announcing ERIN GO BRAGH, and green ties and green socks, and, Harry was certain, there was someone with green under-wear and before the day was over he would undoubtedly dis-play his finery. And, of course, there was the inevitable fool or joker or rotten Protestant with an orange tie, who, before the night was over, would be covered with his own blood.

Harry chatted, sipped his coffee and laughed at the inanity on the television screen, but his chatting and laughter grew progressively more derisive, then steadily decreased until he was completely silent and was grinding his jaw and clenching his fists as he stared at the dumb fucking donkeys with their goddamn pope-loving bullshit, and he felt like yelling at the television that if they chased the fucking priests out of Ireland instead of the harmless snakes, the people would be a lot better off, especially if they spent their money on food and birth-control pills instead of whiskey and that corrupt and insidious church and asshole parades where all they did was prance up and down the street like the aborigines they were, especially those green-hearted men in blue who loved nothing better than to get some poor, hopeless and helpless black man or Puerto Rican and split his skull open with their clubs for no reason at all other than that they felt like doing it, and dump the body in a garbage can and then push an Abe Relles out the window so the important people in the city wouldn't be in-convenienced and . . .

Im going for a walk,
and
he walked through the trees, his trees, his own private and personal woods—*yet again, yet again, yet again*—trying to fill his screaming head with the sound of birds and fill his eyes and his knotted and screaming body with the new, green life of spring, but somehow the green was still bullshit and his gut and loins ached and twisted with weakness and he could still hear the dumb fucking drums pounding and pounding as those rotten cunts kicked and twirled, and goddamn it he had trees. . . . . . You hear that? Goddamn, motherfucking trees and theyre mine, every motherfucking one of them, and I dont need any goddamn parade and green booted broads—*yet again*

—and where are the birds, goddamn it, why dont they sing???
Sing, you sons of bitches, sing—*yet again, yet again*—do you
hear me????   SING!!!!

Why, in Gods name, wont
you sing to me?   Please.   O, please, sing to me. Fill my
head with song and drown out the screeching of the crowds,
those monstrous crowds all jammed together, jammed together so tightly—*yet again*—that a man could not even fall
to the ground—*yet again*—if he were to faint or have a
stroke or—*yet again*—No! NO!!!!—*yet again*—please . . .
please . . .

He
knelt on soft green moss and looked at his hands and at the
trees whose branches were crowded with new leaves and buds,
some more yellow than green, the sun shining on their crispness, and looked up and through the many limbs reaching and
stretching through space, and at the light slanting through, and
started to raise his arms, then dropped them and got to his
feet—*yet again, yet again, yet again, yet again*—and walked
through his woods, touching the trees and caressing them, trying desperately to fill his head with the sound of the birds he
knew were there (he could see them, goddamn it, why was he
still hearing that asshole crowd?), and he put his arms around
a white birch and hugged it and pressed it to his breast—*yet
again, yet again, yet again*—and clung to it desperately as he
tried to still the yelling and pressing closeness of the crowd
with the serenity of his woods, but he could feel the bodies
tugging and yanking at him and feel the sick turmoil inside him
while his head yelled, screamed and pleaded for peace, and he
felt the soft, cool whiteness of the birch against his cheek and
the sorrow welled up in him until he once more felt like he
was drowning in the flood of his own fears, and he yelled at
his woods HELP ME! GODDAMN IT, HELP ME! And he
hugged his birch tighter and wondered why it did not help:
how can all this be mine and it does not make it better? Behind
me theres a house, a beautiful house with a loving family, and
my gut is filled with rats and maggots that are chewing me

up alive. A garden, my own woods with a stream, and inside Im churning with broken bottles and rusty tin cans. It doesnt help. Nothing helps. What else is there??? And Harry clung more desperately to his birch, his lovely, young white birch— *yet again, yet again, yet again, yet again, yet again*—feeling the rottenness of decay growing within him and trying to spit it out but only able to endure the foulness with which it filled his mouth, yet again. . . .

Linda smiled and hummed her way through the day, and the house was filled with warm sunshine until Harry came back from his woods. Linda watched him walk to a chair and sit, and she went hollow inside. Everything turned gray and proceeded to get darker. She continued to function through the day, feeding the children, washing faces and answering questions listlessly, feeling somehow that it was all part of a hopeless sham and berating herself for having allowed her hopes to get so high so easily. She just could not seem to keep from hoping, but now some force far greater than she, seemed to be mocking her.

The stifling grayness affected the children too. They rebelled against Lindas bristling swipes with the face cloth and started bickering with each other, and Mary started yelling and whining and crying incomprehensibly, and Linda yelled at them and asked Harry Jr. what he was doing to his sister? Nothing. Im not doing anything—Mary screamed and stomped her foot—Be quiet, for Gods sake. Harry, you leave your sister alone—But I didnt do nothing—Mary screamed something—I did not, you liar—Dont call your sister a liar—Well she is— And you leave her alone—But I didnt do—Mary screamed louder and louder—Didnt, didnt—If I have to come in there, youre going to be sorry—Mary screamed and screamed and screamed—Give me that, you brat—Thats it! I am not going to tolerate this any longer, and Linda slapped them and sent them to their rooms and they continued to yell from behind closed doors and Linda tried to pour herself a cup of coffee and she was trembling so badly that she spilled the hot coffee on her hand and dropped the cup and she started shaking so violently she had to lean against the wall to support herself, then she went into the bathroom and leaned against the closed door and wept

and Harry wished—*yet again, yet again*—to krist he could do something about what was happening . . . anything about anything, but all he could do was listen to his grinding jaws and clutch the arms of his chair and feel the world slowly—*yet again*—crumble and melt into itself like the face that occurred in the night.

Things got progressively worse the following week. The bickering and screaming and crying and yelling seemed to start even before Harry got out of bed, while he was still trying to fight his way back to sleep and not wake up, but the noise forced him from the bed and by the time he got to the breakfast table it had reached a peak and then suddenly abated slightly as he sat down, and Linda spoke softly to the children and encouraged them to eat and be quiet and leave each other alone and Mary didnt like her cereal and Harry Jr. toyed with his and spilled some on his shirt and Linda shook with rage but controlled herself and wiped the cereal off his shirt and ominously told him to be careful and to hurry and finish his breakfast or he would be late for school and he said he didnt like the cereal and then yelled at Mary to stop kicking him and kicked her and Mary yelled and started crying and kicking and Harry Jr. yelled and started kicking and Linda yelled at them to shut up, and Harry sat drinking his coffee staring straight ahead and Linda stopped their kicking, but they continued to yell and Harry Jr. said he didnt want the cereal and threw his spoon down and Linda told him that he had better stop and start eating and he yelled NO, NO! and Mary started screeching and Harry Jr. continued whining and Linda yelled at them and Harry suddenly slapped his son and knocked him off the chair

Instant silence as Linda stared in shock, her mouth hanging open, and Mary blinked rapidly and Harry Jr. looked up in astonishment, his silent mouth open, the marks on his face becoming angrier and angrier as he lay on the floor frozen, seemingly not breathing, as was everyone else, then Mary started to whimper with fear and Harry Jr. scampered and half crawled to his room before starting to cry and howl and Marys whimpering grew louder and louder and Linda instinctively put her arms around her and stared at Harry in bewildering astonishment and Harry got up, his head screaming, and pleading for forgiveness but unable to speak or comprehend, and he saw Lindas eyes and the pleading question in them and wanted to shout I DONT KNOW WHY! but could only avert his eyes as quickly as possible and leave.

Yet again,
yet again, yet again, yet again—Harry tried to relieve the turbulence within him but there was nowhere he could direct his mind, and he could not keep it a blank. It jumped and jumbled from women to those foul-smelling traps he had ended up in, and his nose burned as he relived the stench, and he was dragged through the offices and his petty pilfering, but that was a bore and ineffective and he was dragged protesting back to the subway platform and Times Square—*yet again, yet again*—and the face melting into itself with its mouth hanging open in an agonizing and silent scream and the face of his son, the screaming red marks of his hand on his face, his mouth open and the silence stabbing through Harry—*yet again, yet again, yet again*—and it seemed as if there was no place for Harry to go without animating the agony within him, and no matter how hard he fought against it he continued to find himself on the subway platform and walking through Times Square and his sons eyes burned him and everything inside him started sinking and he could not swallow away the foul leaden taste in his mouth and he tried to turn away from those images but they persisted and he would feel the guilt torment him and ooze through his pores and trickle down his sides and back in an agonizing insectlike crawl—*yet again, yet again, yet again, yet again, yet again*—and the *Wall Street Journal* didnt help nor could he become absorbed in the

scenery flickering by through broken fences and telephone poles and wires or in the sudden darkness of the tunnel as the train plunged underground, and the people seemed to be crushing up against his cab so that he was almost tempted to walk part of the way up to his office to avoid the elevator but forty-three floors were too much so he endured the ride finding it more and more difficult to breathe, and when he got to his office he closed then locked the door and sat at his desk uncomfortably conscious of his damp clothing irritating his body and still feeling crushed, sitting behind his huge desk in his large luxurious office, and he looked over his shoulder and through the huge window at the city and drew the drapes and tried desperately to dispel the forces that were crushing him but he could not find any defense against them, almost thinking of praying but quickly shoving the embryonic thought into some dark corner and trying to break loose from the tightness by inhaling deeply but unable to breathe deeply enough to break through the constriction and relieve the irritating oppression in his chest—*yet again*—and his son looked at him and the finger marks smoldered their way into his flesh and Harry grabbed his head and shook it and moaned low as he fought the suffocating feeling, as he forced air down his throat in staccato gasps and he trembled and fought his way through the day by forcing himself into his work again and again and again and again and again, yet again. . . .

He seemed to age daily, almost hourly, the week preceding Palm Sunday. The haunting pressure within was almost equalled by the pressure without from work. A multinational organization was attempting to weaken, and ultimately destroy the corporations international syndicate. Harry, and the other members of the board, knew that he could develop the necessary strategy to preserve the integrity of the syndicate, but speed was of the utmost importance. There was a cutoff date, April 15, and if the reorganization plan was not ready by then, everything Harry had worked so hard to create through the years would suddenly disappear and the firm would be in financial chaos. And so he tried to continue to resolve his inner conflict by abandoning himself in his work, but that too was steadily eroding as a solution. He still managed to work, but his haunted mind made a mockery of him. He not only worked with lethargic ineptness that was incredible for him, but was constantly aware of the terrors in his mind, the terrors that were eating away at his flesh and boring into his bones.

He had lunch with Walt and Clarke Simmons every day that week, and each lunch started in exactly the same manner: How is it coming, Harry? Fine, nothing to worry about, and he would cringe inwardly as he heard himself lie, and he prayed that he would survive one more lunch so he could get back to the sanctuary of his office, resolved to attack the job with his former vigor so there really would not be anything to worry about. And then they would ask him how he felt, You dont look good at all. Well, I seem to have a slight touch of something, but its all right. It will pass.

Walt and Clarke were concerned when they looked at Harry, who was obviously fighting some sort of virus, but they just reminded thmselves that he could do the job—he had in the past and there was no reason to think he wouldnt now.

Harry accepted the song of the tracks and allowed it to lull him into an almost pleasant drowsiness. He ignored the papers —*yet* again, *yet* again, *yet* again, *yet* again—and allowed the clacking to drone through him. When he stood up to get ready to leave the train, he no longer stretched his neck up and his shoulders back, but strained to his feet and hunched forward like a man two inches taller than the ceiling.

A feeling of hopelessness and terror seemed to precede him, as he trudged up the walk to his house.

Linda tried to occupy her mind by keeping busy and taking care of the children, and fought with herself not to ask or tell Harry anything. The most painful things for her were her feelings of hopelessness and lack of power. She desperately wanted to help the man she loved, the man who was slowly deteriorating before her very eyes, but though she constantly racked her brain, she could find no answer. No answer for

Harry—or herself, but she knew she had to stay and keep trying.

Harry remained mute when he went to bed, trying desperately to ignore the fact that Linda was getting thinner and more haggard-looking each day, until he yelled himself awake in the middle of the night, sweat stinging his eyes, and tried desperately to breathe and destroy the image that hung in front of him, the image of that goddamn face melting into itself and the mouth hanging open in that dreadful silent scream . . .

and then his sons face drifted from the mouth, eyes staring in questioning horror and faint wisps of smoke drifting from the finger marks in his cheek . . .

and then he would become aware of a hint of light somewhere in the darkness behind the melting and constant faces, a light that seemed to be an eternal distance away yet he sensed that it could instantly blaze in front of him and suck him up in its vortex. And he fought against the light, trying to deny its existence as it slowly dragged itself closer and closer like some hulking creature with a twisted or crushed leg and he tried to scream it back and out of existence and the faces continued to melt into themselves until he was once more awake, wiping the stinging sweat from his face and sitting on the edge of the bed, trying to ignore the darkness that surrounded him and equally afraid of the light, clinging desperately to some semblance of strength, but the terrors in his mind simply mocked him and he sat crushed between the powers and fears of light and darkness until he fell back exhausted and slept for a few pitiful hours, then dragged himself from bed to start another day like the one before that would end in a nightmarish night like the one he had just survived.

For Linda White the days were barely tolerable. The sun was bright, the sky clear and new life was budding and blooming everywhere, yet there was no joy in her life. Easter had always been a special time for her, and she had been looking forward to buying an Easter outfit for Mary, but now she had to force herself to go shopping and then she just bought the first thing that seemed to fit.

The children, too, had been looking forward to Easter. This would be the first year that Mary would be aware of her Easter basket and she was all excited about the Easter bunny; and Harry Jr. was looking forward to the Easter vacation and stay-over visits with both sets of grandparents, but the forboding atmosphere in the house was dulling the sharp edges of their joy.

Linda tried to shop to get baskets, jelly beans, chocolate rabbits and marshmallow chickens, coloring for eggs and the other Easter goodies, but kept putting it off one more day, unable to find or create the necessary energy to go and so she stayed in the home she so dearly loved and cherished, feeling more and more trapped the more she procrastinated, and more and more depressed, telling herself that tomorrow would be different.

Palm Sunday came into being with a bright sun, a clear sky and the refreshing coolness of early spring. Linda and the children were outside, and Harry sat alone in the house half hearing and half ignoring the television that was telling him about the events of the day.

He started to focus his attention on the television as he heard the phrase, special program, repeated a few times. Then the screen was filled with people crowded on the street. Thousands of them. Harry could not tell where they were, but wherever it was, it was absolutely packed. And there seemed to be a park in the background. He was suddenly and intensely curious about the reason for all those people being there. And then he became aware of the voice of an announcer informing him that it was Central Park in the background and he was looking down Fifth Avenue, and the building the camera would focus on from time to time was a hospital, the same hospital Harry had spent a few days in. He stared at the endless mass of people, his curiosity increasing—and, as you can see, there are literally thousands of people here on this glorious Palm Sunday waiting for the appearance of Cardinal Leterman. Some people have been here for hours, getting here early so they could get a good vantage spot from which to view the Cardinal. And this is, indeed, a beautiful day for a homecoming—can you get a shot of the park, Phil? Yes, thats it. As you can see there is green everywhere and even the ducks in the lake seem to be aware of the solemnity of the occasion as they glide across the surface of the water. It is a truly beautiful sight, the gentle rolling softness of the grass and the magnificent skyscrapers in the background with the blue sky and those white clouds rolling by and— O, yes, isnt that a beautiful scene, the buildings and sky reflected in the water of the lake—the camera kept coming in until the screen was filled with the familiar lake and the background clearly reflected in the water— Wait, there seems to be some activity in front of the hospital, ladies and gentlmen. Cardinal Leterman may be coming out now—the camera focused on the entrance to the hospital— I can see—yes, yes, there he is, ladies and gentlemen—a roar suddenly burst from the crowd and the people were jumping up and down to get a better view and others were on the tops of cars and everyone was screaming and most people were waving crosses of palms— theres an aide opening the door and the beloved Cardinal Leterman is standing just outside the hospital waving to the people, smiling, and it looks like there are tears rolling down his face as he reacts to this unprecedented and absolutely incredible and spontaneous outburst from thousands of people of all faiths. And that is one of the most marvelous and significant things about what is happening here today, ladies and gentle-men. This demonstration of love—just listen to them—and affection for one of the most revered and respected men of the cloth in the world is not based on dogma or theology or even religion, but is an outpouring of the hearts of people of all faiths: Protestants, Jews as well as Catholics, and people of other faiths and, I am sure, those who profess none in par-ticular. This certainly is an unequalled testimonial to the life of love, devotion, kindness and service that this man has lived these past seventy-five years. As you can see there are endless flashbulbs going off, and the people are so eager to demonstrate their love and enthusiasm for this great, great man that it is taking a strong force of New Yorks finest to protect Cardinal Leterman from his admirers— Wait just a minute, ladies and gentlemen. He is raising his hands for silence, a hush has fallen over the crowd, and as you can see on your screens there are tears of love and gratitude— Ladies and gentlemen, Cardinal Leterman . . .

    My fellow children of God . . . My life has been filled with countless riches through the blessings of Jesus Christ, our Lord, but surely this day must be the richest of the rich. Truly my cup doth run over. Surely no man can be more blessed than I, and surely no man can be less deserving than I for I am no more than a sinner. No more or less, perhaps, than anyone else, but still a sinner. Yet our merciful God in heaven has bestowed upon me countless gifts, including the gift of life, and has shown me a way of life whereby I can, in my small and humble way, try to glorify His name. And though I am not worthy of His gifts, I can but accept them and say may Thy will be done and not mine, and hope, and pray, that I may be an instrument of His peace. . . . As you know, just sixty-four days ago I was stricken with a heart attack and was rushed to the hospital, where I was pronounced dead on arrival . . . yes . . . dead! Yet today I am alive through the grace of God and the ministrations of the dedicated and devoted men of medicine. And how fitting it is that I should once more walk these beloved streets on this day, this day that commemorates the ride of our Savior, Jesus Christ, into the holy city of Jerusalem on that first Palm Sunday, aware that he was reaching the end of his ministry on earth. It came to pass that he was betrayed and suffered on the cross, and endured the Passion, so that we might know that through death in Christ we may all find eternal life. I am today a living miracle. A man back from the dead . . . Next Sunday, Easter Sunday, is the most important day in all Christendom when we celebrate the triumph of life over death. And so that I might in some way give thanks to the Almighty for the miracle of my rebirth, and give praise to our Lord and Savior, I will serve Communion in Saint Patricks Cathedral on that most reverent of days, Easter Sunday. . . .

Ladies and gentlemen, I can hardly talk. There is not a dry eye anywhere to be seen. Cardinal Leterman is crying as freely as the rest of us and his face is one big smile as he blesses the people and is helped into his car. As you can hear, there is still a hush over the crowd, and as you can see, they are all standing absolutely still in complete reverence for this man who is so universally loved that he has been called not only a man of God, but a man of the world, loved by one and all regardless of what God they may worship. His car is slowly pulling away from the curb and— O, my God, ladies and gentlemen, people are starting to peel away from the crowd and lay down their palms in front of the Cardinals car. In all my thirty years of broadcasting I have never seen anything like this in my life. The Cardinals car is just barely moving and men and women and children are stepping into the middle of the street to lay down their palm leaves. This is the greatest demonstration of love I have ever seen, and needless to say no one is more deserving of it than Cardinal Leterman. As far as the eye can see down Fifth Avenue people are laying down palms and bowing their heads as the Cardinals car slowly passes by, the Cardinal giving the people his blessing. . . .

Harry stared at the television screen as the car of Cardinal Leterman slowly moved along Fifth Avenue and eventually the scene faded and the station identified itself and a studio announcer informed him that he had just seen a special program presented by the stations news bureau and the voice quickly faded into a hum and Harry continued to stare in front of him, not noticing and not listening. . . .

It droned on and on and Harry was aware only of the hollowness within him that grew and grew and seemed to twist itself around his throat, trying to tug it down into that grinding, sickening and bottomless pit. He lay his hands upon his stomach and rubbed firmly, unconsciously trying to stuff the hole in his gut and stop the wind from blowing through.

He sat and stared, his hands stuffed in his gut, for a short, painful eternity. Various images flipped and jerked on and off the screen as a series of commercials followed each other, but he did not see nor hear them. He stared. He stared from a hollowness into a hollowness. He stared from a pit into a pit—from a conclusion to a beginning. . . .

He stood . . . slowly. The hollowness deepened. The pit deepened. His mouth was flushed with lead. The initial movement was painful. He stopped. His head whirled. He clutched his gut. He moved. Got a jacket. He left the house.

The train—*yet* again, *yet* again, *yet* again, *yet* again, *yet* again—the city and an endless subway ride—*with* a blotter, *with* a blotter—and a walk to the playground, and Harry, who had been playing in right center for the pull hitter, ran with the thud of the bat toward the right field fence. The Swenson coaches were waving their arms and screaming at their teammates to run, run ya son of a bitch, and the man from third had already crossed the plate and the man from second was halfway home when Harry leaped in the air and crashed into the fence, his glove hand high over his head, just a fraction of a second before the ball, and the ball thumped into his glove. As he bounced off the fence he held the ball with both hands and cradled it in his gut as he rolled over on the concrete, unwound and stood and threw the ball to the first baseman, who easily doubled the man off first and then whipped it to the second baseman for a quick and simple triple play. The entire Swenson team, and their fans, stood in openmouthed disbelief. Harry grinned from ear to ear as he trotted off the field, the Casey team and fans yelling, cheering, whistling and jumping all over him and thumping and patting him on the back and throwing their gloves at him, and when Harry got up to bat there were two men on base and the pitcher looked at him with obvious rage and threw the first pitch at his head and Harry jerked back his head and smiled at the pitcher while the Caseys yelled and screamed and called him a punk headhunter and the Swensons yelled, no hitter, easy out, and Harry stepped in and took another pitch in tight but the next one got away from the pitcher and Harry leaned into it and sent a rifle shot over the center fielders head and the ball rolled to the farthermost corner of the field and the Casey coaches had their hats in their hands as they waved the runners around the bases and Harrys hat leaped from his head as he rounded second and he gave an extra burst as he saw the coach waving him on and around and he thundered down the third base line and bounced on home plate as the second base-man picked up the ball in short center and threw it over the head of the catcher who just stood there and let it fly into the backstop and Harrys teammates and fans mobbed him again and thumped and pounded and slapped and yelled and screamed and hollered jubilantly and Harry could feel the pride in his eyes as he saw it in their eyes and he smiled and laughed and yelled along with them, and the gray fence felt chilled as he leaned against it and looked at the gray sidewalk and gray concrete of the playground and the sky was turning a gunmetal gray and as the sun got lower and dimmer the breeze seemed to increase and the chill penetrated him as he leaned against the gray wire fence around the playground and he stared at and through the playing field and he knew it could not possibly be ten years later but it was and no matter how he thought about time or changed the point of reference it was still ten years and now a decade later there was something wrong and thinking about it was futile and how much longer could he fight it whatever it was, and he looked at the grayness around him and felt it seething through his body and no matter what happened or did not happen he was still on this side of the fence and there was no way he could get to the other side again . . .   never! the grayness made that obvious and undeniable, and Harry finally turned and left the gray fence and gray playground and walked down the gray street, his eyes seeing every crack and little imperfection in the concrete

down the steps covered with gum and cigarette butts into the gray subway hole—*yet* again—and the lonely ride to the end of the line and out to the ending of a day and through a gray wind blowing through a mocking Coney Island, and he stood on the boardwalk with his face to the wind and looked at the meeting of gray water and gray sky and the gray sogginess of the surf and sand and leaned against the railing for another eternity feeling his body shiver with a chill but refusing to be a part of the gray cold that shook him and stood with his hands in his pockets, his fists clenched, and stared at the intermingling and changing grayness until once again the darkness surrounded him.

He moved through the gloom and mocking glare of the ancient and occasional carnylike lights that were still scattered around the once popular playland. It was like living in the midst of the ruins of ancient history, like having been displaced in space and time, looking at the splintered and poster-plastered fronts of closed stands and rides remembering in spite of circumstances the gaiety and laughter of lifetimes lived long ago and hearing the lights and excitement in his head but being completely detached from them as if it were a stranger who laughed and sparkled with joy. There were the memories of foamy root beer and his grandmother and grandfather and saltwater taffy, but the memories belonged to someone else, someone who was still living here in this ancient age. Maybe the colors of the remaining lights were still the same garish colors of those ancient time but they felt gray and, as they split the darkness, all they did was to make the cracks in the sidewalk plainer.

He checked into a drab hotel and sat, fully clothed, on the bed and leaned against the headboard. He fought against sleep and those faces that hung before him, and the light that was now taking the form of another face and drifting toward the others, but from time to time his head fell forward and was dragged into sleep, then jerked awake as he struggled to free himself of the past and the future.

It did not seem possible that he could be there, that what had happened really had happened and was not a dream from which he would awake and find everything as it should be. But this was not the case. And though he tried to resist, there was an inevitable force tugging him deeper and deeper into his blackness and he could sense the futility of the fight.

He was Harry White, Executive Vice-President, and had been for quite a few years. He was respected and admired by his peers. A man of influence. He had a wife and a son and a daughter. A beautiful family that he loved and that was very precious to him. And they loved him. This he knew. He had a beautiful home in Westchester. He was a success. Harry White was a successful man . . .

and,   O God, he just wanted to die . . .

to find relief from this cancer that was eating him . . .

just a little relief . . .

thats all . . .

just

a

little

relief

He spent the next day sitting on the boardwalk, staring at the ocean. The cool breeze whipped up white caps and scudded sand across the beach. From time to time someone would walk by, but Harry remained deeply isolated within his loneliness and the despair of shame. He stared at the horizon and vaguely heard the surf and the sand scratching against the boardwalk and sank deeper and deeper into the jaws of his demon.

When he had not returned by midnight, Linda called the police, then Walt. The police were kind and courteous, but answering the questions was still painful for her. Yes, he had been acting strange lately, as if there were something on his mind. No, she did not know what might be wrong. No, she did not think he was seeing another woman. Yes, he had seen a psychiatrist, Dr. Martin, but he hadnt been going to him for some time. No, I have no idea where he might be or if he left the house of his own free will and she gave them a photograph and Walt got there and answered their questions and told them the thing that was on his mind was an important business problem and impressed them with the urgency of finding Harry immediately and eventually the police left and Walt remained with Linda until he was certain she was all right, then he too left and Linda finally went to bed and cried herself into a fitful and restless sleep.

The following day Lindas mother and Harrys mother came to comfort and help her. They all tried to keep themselves occupied so as not to think about Harry, but they were constantly noticing the look in one anothers eyes and the fear and anguish behind them.

Wentworth related the events, such as he knew them, to the other members of the board at a hastily called meeting. It was immediately decided that Walt would review what Harry had done to date and see what he could do to continue the work. In addition, an emergency call was placed to Von Landor. In the meantime, all possible pressure would be applied so the proper authorities would intensify the search for Harry and locate him as rapidly as possible.

The sun had long since disappeared from sight and memory, and Harry continued to sit on the boardwalk and stare straight ahead. He seemed somehow to be locked in that position. The wind increased and now the sand rasped against his face and the surf pounded in the gray distance. Eventually he wearily stood up and turned his back on the unseen horizon and walked back to the hotel. He sat on the bed, leaning against the headboard and staring at his shoes . . .

then took them off and undressed and got between the sheets and pulled the covers tight against his neck and slept.

The next day he checked out of the hotel and started to make an endless round of stores and shops, both large and small. He roamed back and forth across the island of Manhattan, along the avenues and side streets, moving as slowly as possible. He only had one item to buy and had plenty of time to find exactly the right one.

His family waited. Hoping. Trying to get through each tense and endless day. They leaped to the phone when it rang. Linda continually tried to believe there was hope, but everything inside her was dead. She mouthed the words for the others. But she knew. She just knew.

Time no longer had any real meaning for Harry. The time of day and the day of the week were mere designations. Hours passed and days passed. On Saturday morning he found exactly what he wanted. The gold plating on the long carved handle was exquisite. It was stunningly beautiful resting on the purple velvet in the case.

He walked up Fifth Avenue to Central Park and sat by the lake with the gliding ducks and reflection of the skyscrapers. He sat. All day. And stared. Stared with the same numbness with which he had stared at the ocean, walked the streets and gone through the stores and shops. A numbness that alienated him from his feelings. It was the numbness and alienation that allowed him to do what he had to do. . . . That numbness . . . Deadness. The deadness that kept him alive. Allowed him to move. But sweet and eternal death, how long would it last? How long would he be free from the black and bottomless pit of Harry White? He sat. Listening to the faint churnings in his head. Feeling the difference when a dark cloud covered the sun. Then it would move on. It was warm. The sun. His bones could feel it. Funny. Seems like years since he felt heat. Or cold. He sat. Stared. The ducks rippled the skyscrapers in the lake. They melted into themselves. Harry shuddered. They never became completely whole. Almost. Then another ripple. And melting. He stared. Sat. And stared. The sun on his face. Flashing from the water. God is in his heaven. Shit! So is Ra. RA! RA! RA! All the same shit!!!! The sun moved through

the lake. Behind trees. Long shadows. Chill. Chilling. All
shadows. Squint of sun . . . Colder . . . Darker . . .
                    Night!
                                Black night . . .
                                                      Black
night! Black night! Black night!
                                        Ice . . . In the bones.
Ice. Frozen marrow. Grinding cold. Dark. Black night. Lights
twinkle in lake. Like Xmas. Yellow light near bench. Hangs
over Harry. His shadow folds under bench. Under him. Behind him. In him. Lights in lake twinkle. Grinding cold. Quiv-
ering. A moon ignores him. Looks at self and smiles. Lake
ripples with many moons. The black night is thicker. Yellow
light on bench. Alone. No one. Alone with the night. Alone
with the lake. Alone with the moon and twinkling lights.
Alone with him. The cold firing his feelings. The cold bringing life. Life! LIFE!!!! O Jesus, no. NO! NOOOOOOO!!!!
                                                            His
head fell forward and he wrapped his arms around it as it hung
from his neck. . . .
                    Why does it have to be????   Why?
          Why?
                    He clutched his package to his stom-
ach and bent over and rocked back and forth, back and forth,
back and forth again and again and again

                                            yet a-
gain as his gut and groin became alive with those feelings of
ancient history and he shivered for many long and painful
seconds upon seconds that piled into an eternity and he could
feel the tugging at the back of his throat and he could feel the
faces melting and the third one coming closer and becoming
more and more distinct and he could feel the laughter of his
children and the softness and warmth of his wife and the pain
in her eyes, and his frozen and aching body threatened to
snap as he forced and pushed himself to his feet and leaned
against the bench trying to straighten his body but staying
bent and gnarled in the yellowness of the lamp on the edge of

the path and he felt the screeching within him and the terrible conflict as he became a battleground for the hounds of heaven and the hounds of hell and the hounds of hell were ripping and tearing his flesh and growing wilder and more insane from the smell and taste of blood and the hounds of heaven stood in absolute silence and immobility waiting and the hounds of hell looked mockingly and tauntingly at them while tearing and ripping more flesh from the entrails of Harry White because they knew they were safe, that they did not have to fear the hounds of heaven, who could devour them with quickness beyond the measure of time and restore the bloodied and festering battleground to its proper state, because they knew the hounds of heaven had to be asked to join the battle and they knew that that plea would never come and that the hounds of heaven would have to wait and watch in absolute silence and immobility while they continued their ripping and tearing of the flesh of Harry White and rolled their crazed heads in his blood, their eyes inflamed with their madness, and they moved defiantly and mockingly toward the hounds of heaven and spit the blood and splattered flesh of Harry White in their faces and wailed and bayed with defiance as the hounds of heaven stood in absolute silence and immobility waiting and enduring and hoping they would hear the word that would al- low them to dispel the blood-crazed madness that was rending and destroying and mocking them as well as the flesh they were tearing, and they waited and waited for the word, hearing the anguish of Harry White as he was being devoured and hoping that his pain and suffering had been enough so he would scream out for help but the hounds of hell came closer and splattered them again with the mutilated flesh of Harry White as he clutched his package close to him and walked slowly up the familiar path to Fifth Avenue and then turned and started walking in the direction of St. Patricks Cathedral.

He walked alone. There were automobiles. But he walked alone. There was an occasional individual or two. Yet he walked alone. There was no one with Harry. Except for the inner man, and there the battle continued. But here, on the avenue, he was alone. Harry White walked, and stood, alone.

And in his loneliness he could feel himself once again being crushed by the crowd watching the St. Patricks day parade. Parade? Today? When? When was Fifth Avenue a sea of green with bands and policemen and sanitation men and drum majorettes and two-bit politicians????

Centuries? Eons????

A lifetime   ?

He walked around the cathedral, painfully bending his head back from time to time to look up at the spires and gargoyles. The massive structure seemed almost to penetrate the heavens and looked as if it could not be disturbed, as if it would remain securely and imperturbably there for eternity.

He stopped next to the steps and waited, then climbed the steps and waited in the darkness next to the massive doors. He leaned against the stone and the cold pierced him to his bones, but soon he adjusted to it and clutched his package and huddled deeper into his heavy jacket. He settled himself into the cold darkness and waited, staring at the spot between his shoes.

Time moved slowly but inexorably. But time was meaningless. There was a time when time had been of the utmost importance, when there had been some sort of vague timetable in the back of Harrys mind, a schedule for success, a schedule that he had bettered. He had arrived ahead of time. There was a time when the schedule, that timetable of achievement, had been everything, but then as he achieved his various goals, they became increasingly meaningless, and still he pushed and pushed, but where? He had arrived. Where now? Where?

Yes, once time had been an important and tangible substance in his life, but not now. Now he would just lean against the wall and look at the spot between his shoes and allow time to pass and sometime it would be morning, Easter morning, and the doors would open and he would enter the cathedral. All that would happen. Sometime. Time was no longer important. Not now.

As the night progressed toward morning, the cold became more and more penetrating, but he remained immobile. As the sun approached the horizon on this day of Resurrection, a few others joined Harry outside St. Patricks Cathedral. A couple of attempts were made to engage him in conversation, but he either ignored them or shrugged them aside and remained isolated from the others who stood with him in the cold darkness of Easter morning.

As dawn approached the line grew longer and soon there were hints of light in the sky and then there were sharp shadows as the sun moved through a cloudless and undisturbed sky. The conversations became more animated and joyful as the warmth of the sun reached those waiting. There were constant glances at watches, and sounds of early morning traffic helped bring in the new day. Harry was vaguely aware of TV crews setting up their equipment, and he heard someone mention that the service would be televised all over the world, that probably 200,000,000 people would be watching as Cardinal Leterman served mass. Then the sound of the huge carved doors being opened made the new day official. It was now Easter Sunday.

Harry clutched his package and entered. He walked slowly and unerringly to the seat he had picked out in his mind. He walked to the first row of pews, then moved to the left, and sat. And waited.

The area between his feet changed in texture and color, but it was all the same to Harry as he stared and clutched his package under his jacket. He remained oblivious to the hushed movements of the people entering the church and kneeling and praying as they fingered their beads. The organ was very low and blended in perfectly with the sounds of the worshipers.

The spot between Harrys feet became brighter as the sun continued to rise, and the stained-glass windows glowed with life, and the warmth of the life of love in the glass filled the massive cathedral and warmed its heavy stone.

THE LORD HAS INDEED RISEN, ALLELUIA.
GLORY AND KINGSHIP BE HIS FOR EVER
AND EVER

The suns light started reaching into corners and alcoves and little recesses and softly and tenderly relieved the darkness from Christs Passion in the Stations of the Cross

The Lord be with you.
And also with you.
Peace be with you.
And also with you.

and the impassioned plea for the forgiveness of mans sins from the Son of Man, and the sweet, bright lives in the windows looked with love upon those Stations and Passion and upon all of those celebrating the Resurrection and exalted them to praise God in the highest

We pray that the risen Christ will
raise us up and renew our lives.
Amen.

and Harry still stared at the same spot, not seeing and not hearing the overwhelming beauty and joy of peace and love that surrounded him, but stayed so completely within himself that all he could feel was the pain and overwhelming despair that he found in the corners and dark recesses, and the huge cesspool that he felt he was, and could not get away from

. . . He went about doing good works
and healing all who were in the
grip of the devil, and God was with
him. . . .

and all that he could feel was an all-pervading sickness that seemed to flow through his body and into his arms and legs and fingers and bones and the sickness was almost visible within and its hideousness and grotesqueness fed itself and the sickness became more and more intolerable and all he could do was stay within himself and become more and more a part of his disease

> *... To him all the prophets testify,*
> *saying that everyone who believes*
> *in him has forgiveness of sins*
> *through his name.—This is the word*
> *of the Lord*
> **Thanks be to God.**

and clutch more tightly to his package and his gut and bend a little more under the weight of his own hopelessness and become more and more appalled at what was about to happen and unable to find the means to yell out, No, and retreat but only able to follow that grinding apprehension in his gut that seemed to sap the very fluid from his spine and the marrow from his bones, leaving his legs so weak he could barely stand to sit,

> *... His mercy endures forever.*
> **This is the day the Lord has made;**
> **let us rejoice and be glad.**

and dragged him unremittingly deeper into that which terrified and appalled him, and the voice of the Cardinal floated through the bright, slanting Easter sunlight and the worshipers knelt and bowed their heads and Harry remained motionless and the organ continued to be felt and the choir sang as the mass continued and the flood of tears sloshed around in Harry and pounded against his eyes as a sea against a cliff

CHRIST HAS BECOME OUR PASCHAL SACRIFICE; LET US FEAST WITH THE UNLEAVENED BREAD OF SINCERITY AND TRUTH, ALLELUIA.

and Harry moved with the others to the rail and got on the end and knelt and waited almost blind from everything that was surging relentlessly through him, and now time started to become alive and he was conscious of the progress of the Cardinal as he came from the other end blessing, praying, putting the Eucharist on the tongues of those kneeling in front of him, and Harry could hear too the organ and choir and his senses became heightened and brittle and the incense stung his nose and he could smell the velvet upon which he was kneeling and the Cardinal came closer, carefully placing the Eucharist on the tongues and blessing in a low almost muttering voice and Harry started to tremble and his vision was blurring as the Cardinal got closer and closer and when he was just a few feet away Harry went almost completely blind and could see only the vaguest of blurs in front of him and then he could feel the Cardinals surplice brush against him as he gave the Host to the man next to him and then Harry could feel him in front of him and as the Eucharist touched his tongue he thrust his hand almost unnoticeably forward and the organ screamed in his head and his whole being screamed with his soul sickness and his head suddenly jerked back and his eyes snapped open as the beloved Cardinal stood erect with his arms outstretched, his shadow forming a large cross, and his eyes staring above him and his mouth open in a silent scream and the chords of the organ thundered through the cathedral and the choir sang the *alleluia* as the sun shone in almost blinding brilliance on the long gold carved handle of the knife sticking out from between the ribs of the Cardinal, after penetrating his body almost to the spine, and the Cardinals blood flowed forth splattering the fallen Hosts and the shimmering gold protruding from his body and Harry rose from his knees and leaned on the railing and looked into the face and mouth of the man of God, the light from the gold handle slashing his eyes, and shouted at him, SPEAK! FOR THE LOVE OF FUCKING KRIST, SPEAK! SAY IT! DO YOU HEAR MEEEEEEEEEE, his voice rolling and echoing through the cathedral of massive stone and light and finding the chords of the great organ and the voice of the choir and blending into music where each was lost in the other, SAY IT, SAY IIIITTTTTTTTTT, and his voice rolled off into the distance as he stared into the voiceless scream, and the bulging eyes of the Cardinal grew ever wider and blood spilled from that silent mouth and Cardinal Leterman slowly fell back onto a crosslike shadow like a crucified Christ and those nearby stood and screamed and Harry leaned further over the railing and stared at the blood bubbling gently from the still open mouth as the eyes of the Cardinal stared straight above him and Harrys legs started buckling from a terrible and terrifying weakness and a hollowness like an insatiable hunger, and the sickness pounded against his head as his screams rose above those of the others and the chords of the organ, SAY IT, GOD FUCKING DAMN IT SAY IT, SAY IT. . . . PLEASE . . . and Harrys voice broke and the last words stumbled from his lips and he collapsed on the railing and was once again on his knees staring at the carved gold handle, almost invisible in the brightness of the sun, and he rolled and stumbled to the side as people stood and screamed and fell over each other trying to see, trying to help, and suddenly the voice of the choir was heard in a loud moan as it discovered what had happened and the organist fell against the keyboard forcing a shatteringly dissonant chord from the massive pipes as people stumbled from their pews and over the railing and screamed in disbelief and terror and for help and the eyes of the resurrected man of God continued to look up and those in the sunlight windows looked down and Harry bounced off and between people to the side until he fell into an alcove and turned and looked up into the eyes of the crucified Christ*AAAAAAAAAAAAAAAAAAAHHH HHHHHHHHHHHHHHHHHHHHH* and was knocked to his knees and crawled away and dragged himself to his feet and was squeezed by the crowd through a door and out into the sudden glare of a cloudless and bright Easter Sunday and continued to bounce off the stone of the cathedral walls and the people until he found himself stretched across the hood of a car, and he righted himself and leaned against the car feeling that terrible sickness pounding inside of him and keeping him doubled over and the horrifying sticky wet weakness in his groin that sent molten lead over his body and he pushed himself away from the car and he stumbled forward faster and faster through the crowd as the bells of Saint Patricks Cathedral rang and rang and rang and tolled and rang through the streets and his head and he tried to ignore that god-awful sticky semen wetness but he couldnt as his pants clung to him and a coldness shook through him and he continued through the streets to a small park and collapsed on a bench and clutched the bench desperately with his hands as everything in and around him whirled and the pain in his head and body were one, and slowly the pounding of his heart slowed and his breathing slowed and he became aware of his surroundings and time once again became time and was once again tangible and painful and he became aware of what he had been staring at, became aware of the little girl pulling up her panties and someone who looked like her grandmother as she bent over to pull down the little girls dress and adjust her new Easter coat, and Harry stared at the exposed flesh until his eyes felt as if they were being burned with a hot iron and he suddenly doubled over grabbing his gut and got up and staggered to a tree and leaned against it and puked and puked and retched as he slowly slid down to his knees and his head hung limply from his neck and he felt that his body would cave in on itself if he did not stop yet he continued to puke and retch and dribble nothing but bitter bile from his mouth and he wanted to scream but he could not even scream silently but could only sob in pitiful muteness as he knelt propped against the tree his head almost hanging in his puke and after an endless time the retching stopped and there seemed to be complete silence in the world except for the sobbing he heard and the terrifying feeling of being lost. . .

he stared at the puke and bile a few inches from his face that was slowly, almost imperceptibly, being absorbed by the earth he was kneeling on. He raised his head slightly. He looked around. There were objects. Familiar objects. People. Some looked. Others ignored. Silence. All silent. Only sobbing . . . sobbing. His breathing slowed. Sounds. Noises. Voices. He slowly got to his feet, leaning heavily against the tree. The shadows were cold. The sun bright beyond them. He looked around. The grandmother and child were there. He could hear them. See them. Only them. He looked. And looked. And trembled. And looked

      NOOOOOOOOOOOOOOOOOOOOOOOOOOOO

and he ran from the park and through the streets from the brightness of the sun into the coldness of shadows and stumbled along the streets until he could no longer get air down his throat and he stopped and leaned against a wall, then continued again from wall to wall, shadow to sun, from warmth to cold through a day that no longer had any time and forced his body forward with the fierce torment of his mind as he felt the sobbing finally burst through and his eyes blurred with tears as he continued down the endless streets to the tip of the island forcing himself with the knowledge that he would be able to finally silence that raging voice within him and whenever he felt as if he would collapse he heard the voice and could feel the faces behind him and he continued until he was finally on a ferry moving through the waters of the harbor and he stood on the bow, the breeze cold and cutting, and stared down at the bright green water as it rolled and foamed away from the side of the ferry and slowly he started to chuckle and then laugh as he realized how simple it would all be and he laughed louder and louder and the few people on the deck and those in the cars looked at him and frowned or smiled and he continued to laugh as he climbed up onto the railing of the ferry, people watching in silence then yelling, and he stretched his arms out to the side like a bird and leaned forward and slowly, slowly, slowly moved forward and down and split his crosslike reflection and shadow as he suddenly hit the cold water and the shock paralyzed him for a moment and then he involuntarily started to move to try and fight his way up to the surface but the weight of his heavy wet clothing and the force of the tide and undertow swept him deeper and deeper into the cold darkness and for the briefest of moments he stopped struggling and hung motionless as the truth of his life was suddenly thrust in front of him and he stared at this truth for a brief and infinite moment then opened his mouth in a scream but no sound came out and his mouth hung open as the last breath of his life floated in small bubbles from the cold darkness to the sun-warmed surface and was imperceptibly and silently carried to the sea.